Baby on Board

LIZ FIELDING

PATRICIA THAYER

RAYE MORGAN

09 AUG 2014

MILLS & BOON

First published in Great Britain 2013
by Mills & Boon, an imprint of Harlequin (UK) Limited,
Eton House, 18-24 Paradise Road, Richmond, Surrey TW9 1SR

BABY ON BOARD © by Harlequin Enterprises II B.V./S.à.r.l 2013

Secret Baby, Surprise Parents, Her Baby Wish and *Keeping Her Baby's Secret* were published in Great Britain by Harlequin (UK) Limited.

Secret Baby, Surprise Parents © Liz Fielding 2009
Her Baby Wish © Patricia Wright 2009
Keeping Her Baby's Secret © Helen Conrad 2009

ISBN: 978 0 263 90547 2
ebook ISBN: 978 1 472 00120 7

05-0313

Printed and bound in Spain
by Blackprint CPI, Barcelona

SECRET BABY, SURPRISE PARENTS

BY
LIZ FIELDING

With many thanks to Carol O'Reilly for her insight into the legal aspects of surrogacy in the U.K.

For more information visit www.surrogacyuk.org.

CHAPTER ONE

GRACE MCALLISTER restlessly paced the entrance to Accident and Emergency, punching yet another number into her cell-phone in a desperate attempt to contact Josh Kingsley.

It would be Sunday evening in Australia and she'd tried his home number first. A woman had picked up.

'Anna Carling.'

'Oh…' The sound of her voice, the knowledge that she was in Josh's apartment answering his phone, for a moment drove everything else from her mind. Then, gathering herself, she said, 'Can I speak to Josh, please?'

'Who's calling?'

'Grace… Grace McAllister. I'm his…his…'

'It's okay, Grace, I know who you are. His brother's wife's sister, right?'

The woman was in his apartment and knew all the details of his personal life….

Grace gripped the phone tighter until it was hurting her fingers. 'Could I speak to him, please?'

'I'm sorry, Josh is away at the moment. I'm his personal assistant. Is there anything I can do to help?'

'Do you know where he is?'

'He's moving about a lot. Hong Kong. Beijing. Can I pass on a message?' she prompted when Grace didn't reply.

'No. Thank you.' This wasn't news she could ask a member

of his staff—no matter how personal—to deliver second-hand. 'I need to speak to him myself. It's urgent.'

Anna didn't waste time asking questions, playing the dragon at the door, but gave her a string of contact numbers. His cellphone. The number of his hotel in Hong Kong in case there was no signal. The private number of the manager of the Hong Kong office, since it was evening there. Even the number of Josh's favourite restaurant.

There was no signal. She left a message asking him to call her, urgently, then called the hotel. He wasn't there and the manager of the Hong Kong office informed her that Josh had flown to mainland China. Apparently Anna had already called the office and primed the manager to expect her call and again, when she wouldn't leave a message, he helpfully gave her the number of Josh's hotel there, and his partner in Beijing.

Beijing? He had a partner in Beijing? That was new since the last time he'd been home. Or maybe not. He hadn't stayed for more than a few hours and no one had been talking about business…

Calling the number she'd been given, she was told that Josh was out of the city for a few days and that the only way to contact him was through his cellphone.

She felt as if she were going around in circles, but at least it helped take her mind off what was happening at the hospital, even if she was dreading the moment she found him.

This time it rang. Once, twice, three times and then she heard him. His voice, so familiar, so strange as he briefly instructed the caller to leave a message.

'Miss McAllister…'

She spun round as a nurse called her name. Then wished she'd taken her time.

She'd been trying so hard not to think about what was happening to Michael. She'd only caught a glimpse of him lying unconscious on the stretcher while the emergency team worked on him before they'd rushed him away to the operating theatre and she'd been told to wait.

One look told her everything she needed to know. Her warm, loving brother-in-law had not survived the accident that had already killed her sister.

'Josh…' She forced his name out through a throat aching with unshed tears. There would be time for tears, but not yet. Not now. 'Josh… You have to come home.'

A day, even an hour ago, the very thought of seeing him would have been enough to send her into the same dizzy spin that had afflicted her as a teenager.

Numbed with the horror of what had happened, she was beyond feeling anything but rage at the unfairness of it.

Rage at the cruelty of fate. With Josh for being so blind. For refusing to understand. For being so angry with them all.

She didn't know what he'd said to Michael.

Remembered little of what he'd said to her, beyond begging her to think again.

All she could remember was his bloodless face when she'd told him that it was too late for second thoughts. That she was already pregnant with her sister's child. She would never forget the way he'd lifted a hand in a helpless gesture, let it fall, before taking a step back and opening the front door, climbing into the car waiting to take him back to the airport.

The nurse, no doubt used to dealing with shocked relatives, put her arm around her. Said something about a cup of tea. Asked if there was someone she could telephone so that she would not be alone.

'I've called Josh,' Grace said, stupidly, as if the woman would understand what that meant. 'He'll come now.' He had to come.

Then, realising she still had the phone clutched tightly to her ear as if she might somehow catch his voice in the ghostly static, she snapped it shut, pushed it into her pocket and allowed herself to be led back inside the hospital.

Josh Kingsley looked up at the majestic sight of Everest, pink in a freezing sunset.

He'd come here looking for something, hoping to recapture a time when he and his brother had planned this trip to Base Camp together. Older, a little wiser, he could see that it had been his big brother's attempt to distract him from his misery at their parents' divorce.

It had never happened. Now he was here alone but for the Sherpa porters, drawn to make this pilgrimage, take a few precious days out of a life so crowded by the demands of business that he was never entirely on his own. To find a way to come to terms with what had happened.

Now, overcome with the sudden need to talk to him, share this perfect moment, make his peace with the only member of his immediate family he cared about, he peeled off his gloves and took out the BlackBerry that he'd switched off three days ago.

Ignoring the continuous beep that signalled he had messages—work could wait, this wouldn't—he scrolled hurriedly through his numbers. Too hurriedly. The slender black miracle of computer technology slipped through fingers rapidly numbing in the thin atmosphere. And, as if he, too, were frozen, he watched it bounce once, then fly out across a vast chasm, not moving until he heard the faint sound of it shattering a thousand feet below.

When he finally looked up, the snow had turned from pink to grey and, as the cold bit deeper, he shivered.

Josh would come, but not yet, not for twenty-four hours at the earliest. Now, numb with shock, incapable of driving, she let the nurse call Toby Makepeace. He was there within minutes, helped her deal with the paperwork before driving her home to Michael and Phoebe's home and their three-month-old baby.

'I hate to leave you,' he said. 'You shouldn't be alone.'

'Elspeth's here,' she said, struggling with the simplest words. 'She stayed with Posie.' Then, knowing more was required, she forced herself to concentrate. 'Thank you, Toby. You've been a real friend.'

'I'm here. If you need anything. Help with arrangements…'

She swallowed, not wanting to think about what lay ahead. 'Josh will be here.' Tomorrow or the next day. 'He'll see to everything.'

'Of course.' He left his hand briefly on her arm, then turned and began to walk away.

Elspeth, a close friend of Michael and Phoebe, had answered Grace's desperate call and stayed with Posie. Now she said nothing, just hugged her and made her a cup of tea and then shut herself in Michael's study, taking on the task of calling everyone to let them know what had happened. She even rang Michael's parents—his mother in Japan, his father in France.

Grace had never met either of them—Michael and Josh had only minimum contact with either parent since their divorce—but Elspeth had at least known them, could break the news without having first to explain who she was. Then she stayed to answer the phone, field the calls that came flooding in.

Calls from everyone but the one person she was waiting to hear from.

Friends arrived with food, stayed to give practical help, making up beds in the spare rooms in the main part of the house while Grace did the same in Josh's basement flat. Even when her world was spinning out of control, she couldn't bear to let anyone else do that.

Then she set about putting her own life on hold, leaving a message on the answering machine in the self-contained flat she occupied on the top floor, before taking her laptop downstairs.

Sitting in the armchair that had been a permanent fixture beside the Aga for as long as she could remember, Posie within reach in her crib, she scrolled through her schedule of classes, calling everyone who had booked a place, writing the cheques and envelopes to return their fees as she went. Anything to stop herself from thinking.

After that she was free to concentrate on Posie. Bathing her, feeding her, changing her, shutting out everything else but the sound of the telephone.

She'd insisted that she tell Josh herself.

'It's night in China,' Elspeth said, after the umpteenth time the phone rang and it wasn't him. 'He's probably asleep with the phone switched off.'

'No. My call didn't go straight to the message service. It rang…'

'Asleep and didn't hear it, then.'

'Maybe I should have told someone in his office—'

'No. They've given you all the numbers they have and if you can't get hold of him, neither can they.'

'But—'

'You're the only person he'll want to hear this from, Grace.'

'Maybe.' Was she making too much of that? What did it matter who gave him the news?

'No question. You're the closest thing he has to family.'

'He has parents.'

Elspeth didn't bother to answer, just said, 'Come and have something to eat. Jane brought a quiche…'

She shook her head. 'I can't face anything.'

'You don't have the luxury of missing meals,' Elspeth said firmly. 'You have to keep strong for Posie.'

'What about you?' Grace asked. Elspeth had lost her best friend. She was suffering, too. 'You've been on the go all day and I haven't seen you eat a thing.'

'I'm fine.'

'No, you're not.' She lay Posie in the crib. 'Sit down. Put your feet up while I boil us both an egg.'

'Do I get toast soldiers?' Elspeth asked, managing a smile.

'Of course. It's my turn to look after you, Elspeth.'

'Only if you promise to take one of those pills the doctor left for you. You haven't slept…'

'I can't,' she said. 'Not until I've spoken to Josh.'

'But then?'

'I promise,' she said. And, because it was the only way to get Elspeth to eat, she forced down an egg, too, even managed a yoghurt.

She had a bath and might have dropped off in the warm water, but Posie was fretful. It was almost as if she sensed that something was out of kilter in her world and Grace put on Phoebe's dressing gown so that she would have the comfort of her mother's scent as she held her against her shoulder, crooning softly to her, walking the long night away—waiting, waiting, waiting for the phone to ring.

Finally, when she knew it was day on the other side of the world, she called again. Again, it was the answering service that picked up. 'Where are you?' she cried out in desperation. 'Call me!' All she got back was a hollow emptiness. 'Michael's dead, Josh,' she said hopelessly. 'Phoebe's dead. Posie needs you.'

She covered her mouth, holding back her own appeal. Refusing to say that she needed him, too.

She'd always needed him, but Josh did not need her and, even *in extremis*, a woman had her pride.

'Did Grace McAllister manage to get hold of you, Josh?'

He'd flown direct to Sydney from Nepal, stopping at his office to pick up urgent messages before going home to catch up on sleep.

'Grace?' He frowned, looking up from the list of messages his PA handed him. 'Grace rang me?'

'Last week. Sunday. I gave her the Hong Kong numbers but I knew you'd be on the move so I gave her your cellphone number, too,' she said. 'She said it was urgent. I hope I did the right thing.'

'Yes, yes,' he said, reassuring her.

Last week? On Sunday he'd been in the mountains, thinking about his brother. Thinking about Grace. There had been a message alert on his phone, but he'd ignored it....

'I dropped the damn thing off a mountain. Can you get me a replacement?' Then, 'Did Grace say why she was calling?'

'Only that it was urgent. It's the middle of the night there now,' she reminded him as he picked up the phone, hit the fast dial for her number.

'It doesn't matter. She wouldn't have called unless it was...' He stopped as the call went immediately to the answering machine.

"This is Grace McAllister. I'm sorry that I can't take your call at the moment. Due to a family bereavement, all classes have been cancelled until further notice. Please check the Web site for further details."

Bereavement?

He felt the blood drain from his face, put out a hand to grasp the desk. Posie...

It had to be Posie. Small babies were so vulnerable. Meningitis, cot death... After so many years of waiting, so much heartache.

'Cancel everything, Anna. Get me on the next available flight to London,' he said, dialling his brother's number.

Someone whose voice sounded familiar, but wasn't Michael, wasn't Phoebe, wasn't Grace, answered the phone.

'It's Josh Kingsley,' he said.

There was a momentary hiatus and then she was there—Grace, her familiar voice saying his name.

'Josh...'

It was all it took to stir up feelings that he'd done his level best to suppress. But this last year he hadn't been able to get her out of his head....

'Josh, I've been trying to get hold of you....'

'I know. I rang your number. Heard your message,' he said, ignoring her question. 'What's happened? Who died?'

He heard her take a long shuddering breath.

'Grace!'

'There was an accident. Michael, Phoebe… They were both killed.'

For a moment he was too stunned to speak. His brother was dead. 'When? How?'

'Last Sunday morning. I've been calling, leaving messages. When you didn't get back to me I thought… I thought…'

'No!' The word was wrenched from him. He knew what he'd thought and why, but it didn't hurt any less to know that he could believe him so heartless.

But then she already believed that.

She had been so happy that she was having a baby for her sister, couldn't understand why he'd been so desperate to stop her. And he hadn't been able to tell her.

'What happened?' he asked.

'The police said that the car skidded on a slick of mud. It went through a fence and then it rolled. It happened early in the morning and no one found them…'

'The baby, Grace,' he pressed urgently. 'Posie…'

'What? No! She wasn't with them. She was here with me. Michael and Phoebe were away for the weekend. It was their wedding anniversary but they left the hotel early. They couldn't wait to get back.…'

Long before she'd stumbled to a halt, he'd clamped his hand over his mouth to hold in the cry of pain.

'Josh?'

'It's okay. I'm okay,' he managed. 'How are you coping?'

'One breath at a time,' she said. 'One minute. One hour…'

He wanted to tell her how sorry he was, but in a situation like this words were meaningless. And in any case she would know exactly how he was feeling. They were faced with the same loss. Or very nearly the same.

Grace wouldn't have to live with his guilt….

Instead, he kept to the practical. He should have been there to deal with this, make the necessary arrangements, but it had been over a week already.

'Who's with you? What arrangements have been made? When is the…' He couldn't bring himself to say the word.

'We buried them on Friday, Josh. Your father insisted on going ahead and, when you didn't call back, no one could reach you…' He heard her swallow, fight down tears, then she furiously said, 'Where were you?'

'Grace…'

He looked up as his PA returned. 'There's a car waiting to take you to the airport. You have to leave now,' she said, handing him a replacement BlackBerry.

'Grace, I'm leaving now for the airport.' Then, 'Keep breathing until I get there.'

Grace let Elspeth take the phone from her as she leaned weakly against the wall.

'Maybe you could get some sleep now,' she said gently, handing her the pills the doctor had left when he'd called after hearing the news. 'You've left plenty of milk in the fridge for Posie. I'll manage if you want to take a rest.'

'I know.' She put the pills in her pocket, knowing she wouldn't take them. She didn't want to go to sleep because when she woke she knew there would be a moment when she'd think it was just another day.

Then she'd remember and have to live through the loss all over again.

But she didn't say any of that. Instead, she hugged her and said, 'Thank you.'

'We're here, Mr Kingsley.'

Josh glanced up at the façade of the tall Georgian town house that Michael had bought when he had married Phoebe

McAllister. It was a proper family home with a basement and an attic and three floors in between. Endless rooms that they'd planned to fill with children.

Instead, they'd got him and Grace. A seventeen-year-old youth whose parents had split up and who, wrapped up in their own concerns with new partners, didn't want a moody cuckoo in the nest. And a fourteen-year-old girl for whom the only alternative was to be taken into the care of the local authority.

Exactly what every newly-wed couple needed.

They'd taken on each other's damaged siblings without a murmur. Had given him his own space in the basement, had decorated a room especially for Grace. Her first ever room of her own.

She'd been such a pathetic little scrap. A skinny rake of a kid, all straight lines when other girls her age had been testing out the power of their emerging attraction on impressionable youths. Only her eyes, a sparkling green and gold mix that could flash or melt with her mood, warned that she had hidden depths.

Like her nose and mouth, they'd been too big for her face. And, until she'd learned to control them, they'd betrayed her every thought.

Eyes like that should carry a health warning.

'Is there anything I can do, Mr Kingsley?'

Josh realised that the chauffeur—a regular who his PA had arranged to pick him up from the airport—was regarding him with concern.

He managed a smile. 'You can tell me what day it is, Jack. And whether it's seven o'clock in the morning or seven o'clock at night.'

'It was Tuesday when I got up this morning. And it's the evening. But I'm sure you knew that.'

'Just testing,' he said, managing a smile.

He'd counted every one of the last twenty-four hours as he'd travelled halfway round the world, coming to terms with the loss of his brother. And of Phoebe, who'd been the nearest thing to a big sister he'd ever had. By turns motherly, bossy supportive. Everything that he'd needed.

Knowing that he would have to live with a world of regret for the hard words he'd said. Words that could never be taken back. For holding on to his righteous anger, a cover for something darker that he could never admit to…,

But the hair shirt would have to wait. Grace needed him The baby would need them both.

He climbed from the car. Grace's brightly painted 'Bauble and Beads' van was parked in its usual place but the space where he expected to see his brother's car was occupied by a small red hatchback that underlined, in the most shocking way, the reality of the situation.

Realising that Jack was waiting until he was inside, he pulled himself together, walked up the steps to the front door as he had done times without number to a house that had always felt as if it were opening its arms to him. Today, though, even in the spring sunshine, with tubs of bright yellow tulips on either side of the front door, it seemed subdued, in mourning.

The last time he'd been here he'd tossed the keys to both the house and his basement flat on his brother's desk—his declaration that he would never return. For the first time since he'd moved in here as a seventeen-year-old, he would have to knock at the door but, as he lifted his hand to the antique knocker, it was flung open.

For a moment he thought it was Grace, watching out for him, racing to fling her arms around him, but it wasn't her. Why would it be? She had Toby Makepeace to fling her arms around, to offer her comfort. At least she had the last time he'd come home on a visit. He hadn't been in evidence on the day he'd turned up without warning, but then discovering his girl-friend was pregnant with someone else's baby must have put a crimp in his ardour.

The woman who opened the door was older, familiar—a friend of Phoebe's. Elizabeth? Eleanor? She put her finger to er lips. 'Grace is in the kitchen but she's just dropped off. Try not to wake her. She hasn't been sleeping and she's exhausted.'

He nodded.

'You must be, too,' she said, putting her hand on his arm. 'It's a terrible homecoming for you. I'm so sorry about Michael. He was a lovely man.' She didn't wait for him to answer, just said, 'I'll go now you're here, but tell Grace to ring me if she needs anything. I'll call in tomorrow.'

'Yes. Thank you…' Elspeth. 'Thank you, Elspeth.'

He watched her until she was in her car, then picked up the bags that Jack had left on the top step, placed them inside and shut the door as quietly as he could. Each movement slow, deliberate, as if he could somehow steady the sudden wild beating of a heart that was loud enough to wake Grace all by itself.

He told himself that he should wait.

Go down to the basement flat, take a shower. But to do that, he'd need the key and the key cupboard was in the kitchen.

For the first time for as long as he could remember, he was frozen in indecision, unable to move. Staring down at the hall table where a pile of post—cards, some addressed to Grace, some to him—waited to be opened. Read.

He frowned. Cards?

He opened one, saw the lilies. *In sympathy…*

He dropped it as if burned, stepped back, dragged his hands over his face, through his hair as he looked down the hall. Then, because there was nothing else to do, he turned and walked slowly towards the kitchen.

He pushed the door very gently. It still squeaked. How many times had he heard Michael promise Phoebe that he'd do something about it?

He'd offered to do it himself, but Phoebe had just smiled. She liked the warning squeak, she'd told him. Liked to have something to complain about once in a while. It wasn't good for a man to believe he was perfect.

He could have told her that Michael didn't believe that. On

the contrary. But that had been a secret between the two of them and, somehow, he'd managed to smile back.

He paused, holding his breath, but there was no sound and he stepped into the room that had always been the hub of the house. Warm, roomy, with a big table for everyone to gather around. An old armchair by the Aga that the fourteen-year-old Grace had taken to like a security blanket, homing in on it when she'd arrived clutching a plastic bag that contained everything she possessed under one arm, a small scruffy terrier under the other.

The pair of them had practically lived in it. And it was the first place she'd taken the puppy he'd given her when old Harry had died a few months later and he'd been afraid her heart was going to break.

The puppy, too, had finally died of old age, but now she had a new love. Posie. The baby she had borne with the purest heart as surrogate for the sister who had given her a home and who was now lying, boneless in sleep, against her shoulder.

Michael, hoping that if Josh saw the baby he would finally understand, forgive him even, had e-mailed him endless photographs of Posie, giving him a running commentary on her progress since the day she'd been born, refusing to be deterred by Josh's lack of response.

There had been no photographs of Grace until the christening and then only in a group consisting of Grace, as godmother, holding Posie, flanked by Michael and Phoebe. A happy picture in which everyone had been smiling and sent, he suspected, with just a touch of defiance. A 'see what you're missing' message.

He hadn't cared about that. He'd only cared about Grace and he'd cropped the picture so that it was only of Grace and Posie. He'd had it enlarged and printed so that he could carry it with him.

Her face had been outwardly serene, but a photograph was just a two-dimensional image. It was without warmth, scent.

You could touch it, but it gave nothing back. But then it had been a very long time since Grace had given anything back to him. Keeping her distance, her eyes always guarded on his visits home.

At least he'd had time to get over his shock that, some time in the last year, she'd cut her beautiful long hair into a short elfin style. He'd come to terms with the fact that her boyish figure had finally filled out in lush womanly curves.

But this scene was not a photograph.

This was an intimate view of motherhood as only a husband, a father would see it and he stood perfectly still, scarcely daring to breathe, wanting to hold the moment, freeze this timeless image in his memory. Then, almost in slow motion, he saw the empty feeding bottle that had dropped into her lap begin a slow slide to the floor.

He moved swiftly to catch it before it hit the tiles and woke her, but when he looked up he realised that his attempt to keep her from being disturbed had failed.

Or maybe not. Her eyes were open and she was looking at him, but she wasn't truly awake. She wasn't seeing him. He froze, holding his breath, willing her to close them again and drift back off to sleep.

She stirred. 'Michael?' she said.

Not quite seeing him, not yet remembering. Still he hoped…

She blinked, focused, frowned.

He saw the exact moment when it all came flooding back, and instinctively reached out to her as he had a year ago. As if he could somehow stop time, go back, save her from a world of pain. 'Grace…'

'Oh, Josh…'

In that unguarded moment, in those two little words, it was all there. All the loss, all the heartache and, sinking to his knees, this time he did not step back, but followed through, gathering her into his arms, holding her close.

For ten years he'd lived with a memory of her in his arms,

the heavy silk of her hair trailing across his skin, her swee
mouth a torment of innocence and knowing eagerness a
she'd taken him to a place that until then he hadn't known h
had wanted to go.

He'd lived with the memory of tearing himself away from
her, fully aware that he'd done the unforgivable, then com
pounded his sin by leaving her asleep in his bed to wake alone

He'd told himself that he'd had no choice.

Grace had needed security, a settled home, a man wh
would put her first while, for as long as he could remembe
he'd had his eyes set on far horizons, on travelling light an
fast. He'd needed total freedom to take risks as he built a
empire of his own.

But nothing he had done, nothing he had achieved, not eve
a hastily conceived and swiftly regretted marriage, had eve
dulled the memory of that one night they'd spent together an
still, in his dreams, his younger self reached out for her.

It had been unbearably worse during the last twelv
months. Sleep had been elusive and when he did manage a
hour he woke with an almost desperate yearning for some
thing precious, something that was lost for ever.

This. This woman clinging to him, this child…

He brushed his lips against her temple and then, his hea
full of the warm, milky scent of baby, he kissed Posie and fo
one perfect moment all the pain, all the agony of the las
twenty-four hours fell away.

Grace floated towards consciousness in slow, confuse
stages. She had no idea where she was, or why there was
weight against her shoulder, pinning her down. Why Michae
was there, watching her. Knowing on some untapped level o
consciousness that it couldn't be him.

Then, as she slowly, unwillingly surfaced, he said he
name. Just that.

'Grace…'

Exactly as he had once, years and years ago, before gath

ering her up in his arms. And she knew that it wasn't Michael, it was Josh. Josh who had his arms around her, was holding her as if he'd never let her go. A rerun of every dream she'd had since he'd walked out of her life, gone away ten years ago without a word, leaving a vast, gaping hole in her world. And she clung to him, needing the comfort of his physical closeness. Just needing him.

She felt the touch of his lips against her hair as he kissed her. The warmth of his mouth, his breath against her temple. And then she was looking up at him and he was kissing her as he had done every night of her life in dreams that gave her no peace.

There was the same shocked surprise that had them drawing back to stare at one another ten years ago, as if suddenly everything made sense, before they had come together with a sudden desperate urgency, his mouth branding her as his own, the heat of their passion fusing them forever as one. A heat that had been followed by ten years of ice....

Now, as then, it was the only thing in the world that she wanted.

It was so long since he'd held her.

Not since he'd left her sleeping. Gone away without a word. No, 'wait for me'. Nothing to give her hope that he'd return for her. Not even a simple goodbye.

He had come back, of course, full of what he'd seen, done, his plans. Always cutting his visits short, impatient to be somewhere else, with someone else.

But she'd never let her guard down again, had never let him see how much he'd hurt her, never let him get that close again. She'd avoided the hugs and kisses so freely bestowed on the prodigal on his increasingly rare visits home, keeping away until all the excitement was over. Making sure she had a date for the celebratory family dinner that had always been a feature of his homecoming—because there had always been some new achievement to celebrate. His own company. His first international contract. His marriage...

Yet now, weakly, she clung to him, drinking in the tender touch of his lips, the never-to-be-forgotten scent of his skin.

Needing him as he'd never needed her. Knowing that even now, in his grief, he would be self-contained, in control, his head somewhere else.

He was holding her now, not because he needed comfort, but because he knew that she did. Just as she had all those years ago.

He'd hold her, kiss her, lie with her even if that was what she wanted. It was how men gave closeness, comfort to women.

That was all it had ever been, even then. When, after years of keeping her feelings to herself, doing a pretty good job of being the teasing friend who criticised his choice in clothes, girls, music, she'd finally broken down the night before he'd gone away—not to university this time, or on some backpacking gap year adventure with his friends—but to the other side of the world to start a new life.

Distraught, unable to express her loss in mere words, she'd thrown herself at him and maybe, facing the risk of the unknown, he'd been feeling a little uncertain, too.

She didn't blame him for taking what she'd so freely offered, so freely given. It was what she had wanted, after all. Had always wanted. Her mistake had been in believing that once he understood that, he'd stay.

He couldn't do it then and he wouldn't now.

He'd comfort her. He'd deal with the legal stuff and then, once everything had been settled, made tidy, the tears dried away, he'd fly off to Sydney or Hong Kong, China or South America. Wherever the life he'd made for himself out there in the big wide world took him. He'd go without a backward glance.

Leave her without a backward glance.

At eighteen she'd been so sure she could change him, that once she'd shown him how much she loved him he would never leave her.

At twenty-eight she knew better and, gathering herself, she pulled back, straightened legs that, curled up beneath her, had gone to sleep so that Josh was forced to move, sit back on his heels.

But, try as she might, she couldn't look away.

It was as if she were seeing him for the first time in years. Maybe she was. Or maybe she was looking at him for the first time in years instead of just glancing at him as if he was someone to be remembered only when he passed through on his way to somewhere else, forgotten again the minute he was out of sight.

She'd perfected that glance over the years.

Now she was really looking at him.

He seemed to have grown, she thought. Not physically. He'd always been a larger-than-life figure. Clever, with a touch of recklessness that lent an edge to everything he did, he'd not only dominated the school sports field but stood head and shoulders above the crowd academically, too.

He'd had those broad shoulders even then, but he'd grown harder over the years and these days he carried himself with the confidence of a man who'd taken on the world and won. And the close-clipped beard that darkened his cheeks—new since his last brief, terrible visit—added an edge of strangeness to a face that had once been as familiar to her as her own.

But this Josh Kingsley *was* a stranger.

She'd known him—or thought she had—and for one shining moment he had been entirely hers. But dawn had come and she'd woken alone, her illusions shattered beyond repair.

Older, wiser, she understood why he'd gone. That it had been the only thing he could do because if he'd stayed ten years ago, he would, sooner or later, have blamed her for his lost dreams. It was so easy for love to turn to hate. And nothing had changed.

He was home now, but once everything was settled, tidied away, he'd go away again because Maybridge was—always had been—too small for Josh Kingsley.

CHAPTER TWO

'GRACE,' he said, repeating her name. Calling her back from her thoughts, her memories. That was all. Just her name. Well, what else could he say? That he was sorry about his last visit? Sorry he'd got it all so wrong?

It was far too late for that and, without warning, she found herself wanting to slap him, yell at him for being such a fool. For staying away when coming home would have made his brother so happy. When it would have meant something.

'Where were you?' she demanded.

Josh shook his head. 'In the mountains. Everest. I was so close that I took a few days to go to a place with no work, no phone…'

He looked so desolate that she wanted to reach out and gather him close. Comfort him. Instead, she turned to the baby at her shoulder, kissed her precious head.

How two brothers could be so different—one gentle, caring, the other so completely cut off from emotional involvement—was a total mystery to her and falling in love with him had been the biggest mistake of her life. But, too young to know better, how could she have done anything else?

He had been her white knight.

Fourteen years old, in a strange town, faced with yet another school—when school had only ever been a place of torment—it could have been, would have been a nightmare if Josh hadn't ridden to her rescue that first terrifying day.

He'd seen her fear and, by the simple action of tossing her a spare crash helmet and taking her into school on the back of his motorbike, he'd turned her life around. He'd made everything all right by giving her instant street cred, an immediate 'in' with the cool girls in her class, who'd all wanted to know Josh Kingsley. And with the cool guys, who'd wanted to be him. At this school there had been no shortage of girls who'd wanted to be her friend.

Not that she'd been stupid enough to believe that she was the attraction.

She'd known it was Josh they all wanted to be near, but that had never bothered her. Why would it when she'd understood exactly how they felt? Not that she had worn her heart on her sleeve. A ride was one thing, but a sixth-form god like Josh Kingsley was never going to stoop to taking a fourth-year girl to a school dance.

She's almost felt sorry for the girls he did date. Each one had thought that her dreams had come true, but she'd known better. He'd shared his dreams with her and she'd always known that he couldn't wait to escape the small-town confines of Maybridge. Discover the life waiting for him beyond the horizon.

Not that it had stopped her from having the same foolish fantasies. Or, ultimately, making the same mistake.

Maybe he read all that in her face—she was too tired to keep her feelings under wraps—because he stood up, took a step back, placed the baby feeder he was holding on the table beside her.

'It was about to fall,' he said. 'I didn't want it to wake you. Elspeth warned me not to disturb you when she let me in.'

Too late for that. Years too late.

'Has she gone?'

He nodded. 'She said to tell you that she'll call in the morning.'

'She's been wonderful. She's stayed here, manned the

phones, organised food for after the funeral. But she's grieving, too. She needs to rest.' Not that Josh looked particularly great. He might have had the luxury of a first-class sleeping berth to take the edge off the long flight to London but there was a greyness about his skin and his eyes were like stones. 'How are you?'

'I'll think about that later.'

'When you're back in Sydney?' she asked, reminding herself that this, like all his visits, was only a break from his real life.

'I'm not going anywhere,' he said. 'Not until everything is settled.'

'Everything?'

'I'm Michael's executor. I have to arrange for probate, settle his estate.'

'A week should do it,' she retaliated, and immediately regretted it. He had to be hurting, whether he was showing it or not. 'I'm sorry.'

'Don't! Don't apologise to me.' He looked up, took another deep breath. 'You and Phoebe were so close. She was like a mother to you.'

'A lot better than the real thing.'

'Yes.' He looked at her, and for a moment she thought he was going to say something she'd find hard to forgive. In the end he just said, 'Have you managed to contact your mother? Let her know what happened?'

She shook her head.

Her mother turned up occasionally, stayed for a week or two before drifting off again, a constant wanderer. Phoebe had bought her a mobile phone, but she had refused to take it and there was never anything as substantial as an address.

'There was a card from somewhere in India a couple of months ago. Whether she's still there…' She shook her head. 'Elspeth rang the consulate and she left messages with everyone who might be in contact with her, but she's even harder to get hold of than you.'

'I'm sorry, Grace. I flew back to Sydney from Nepal so I missed any messages you left at the office.'

'Nepal?' Then she remembered. 'Everest. What on earth were you doing there?'

'Making a pilgrimage.'

And if she felt lost, he looked it.

'I was going to call Michael, tell him I was looking at the sun setting on the mountain, but my hands were so cold that I dropped the phone.' He pushed his hands deep into his pockets as if, even now, he needed to warm them. 'We once planned to take that trip together.'

'Did you? I never knew that.'

He shrugged. 'It was when our parents first split. Before he met Phoebe.'

She frowned. 'She wouldn't have stopped him going.'

'Maybe he couldn't bring himself to leave her, even for a month. She was everything he ever wanted.'

While he'd had nothing, Grace thought. At least her mother did, occasionally, put in an appearance. It was disruptive, unsettling, but it was better than the nothingness that Josh had been left with when his parents had chosen to follow their own desires.

'Michael would have been happy to know that you finally made your dream trip,' she told him.

'Yes, he would. He wanted everyone to be happy. While I suspect all I wanted to do was make him feel bad…'

'No…' Her hand was on his arm before she could even think about it, but he stared at the floor as if unable to meet her gaze. 'Why would he feel bad? You were there. You were thinking of him.' Then, 'Did it match the vision?'

'The mountains were beyond anything I could describe, Grace. They made everything else seem so small, so unimportant. I wanted to tell him that. Tell him…'

'He knows, Josh,' she said, swallowing down the ache in her throat. 'He knows.'

'You think?' Josh forced himself to look up, face her. 'I

should have been here. I can't bear the thought of you having to go through all this on your own….'

'I wasn't on my own. Everyone helped. Toby was wonderful.'

Toby.

Josh felt his guts twist at the name.

Toby Makepeace. Her ideal man. Reliable. Solid. Always here.

'Michael's partners took care of all the arrangements for the funeral. And once your father arrived and took charge—'

'He's here?'

'He flew back straight after the funeral. There was some big debate at the European Parliament that he couldn't miss.'

About to make some comment about his father's priorities, he thought better of it. Who was he to criticise?

'And my mother? Has she raced back to the toy boy in Japan?'

'She's staying with friends in London.'

'Waiting for the will to be read,' he said heavily.

'Josh!' Then, 'She said she'd come back when you got here. I sent her a text.'

'I refer to the answer I gave earlier.' Then he shook his head. His issues with his family were solely his concern. 'I'm sorry. That was uncalled for.' He pushed his parents from his mind and said, 'Thank you for sticking with it, Grace. Not just leaving a message with the Sydney office.'

'I wanted to tell you myself, although if I'd realised how long it would take…'

'It must have felt like a year.'

'A lifetime.' Then, quickly, 'Your staff were terrific, by the way. Will you thank them for me? If I'd thought about it, I'd have anticipated resistance to handing out contact numbers to someone they don't know.'

'Of course they know you,' he said. 'Do you think I don't talk about you all?' Then, almost as if he were embarrassed by this brief outburst, 'Besides, they have an any time, anywhere list.

'And I'm on that?'

'We both know that the only time you'd ever call me would be with news I had to hear.'

Once Grace would have laughed at that.

If only he knew how many times she'd picked up the phone, her hand on the fast dial number, not to speak to him, but simply to hear his voice. How she'd longed to go back to the way it had once been, when they had been friends...teased one another...told one another everything.

Almost everything.

'Grace—'

'I'm going to miss Michael so much,' she said quickly. Taking a step back from the memory of a night that had changed everything. When she'd thrown all that away. 'There wasn't a kinder, sweeter—'

'Don't.' He closed his eyes for a moment, then, gathering himself, he opened them and looked straight at her. 'Don't put him on a pedestal, Grace. Michael wasn't perfect. He had his faults like the rest of us.'

Grace was too angry to answer him. Even now he wouldn't let go of whatever had been driving him...

Instead, she held Posie close as she got to her feet, supporting her head with her hand. Then, when she didn't stir, she laid her in the crib beside her chair.

For a moment her tiny arms and legs waved as if searching for her warmth and her face creased up, as if she was about to cry. Grace laid her hand on her tummy until, reassured by the contact, the baby finally relaxed.

Once she was settled, Grace crossed to the kettle, turned it on, not because she wanted something to drink, but because anything was better than doing nothing.

'Your flat is ready for you,' she said, glancing at him. 'The bed's made up and you'll find the basics in your fridge. It's too late to do anything today and I'm sure you need to catch up on your sleep.'

'I'll hang on for a while. The sooner I slot back into this time zone, the sooner I'll beat the jet lag.'

'Is that right? As someone whose only trip overseas was the Isle of Man, I'll have to take your word for it.'

'The Isle of Man isn't overseas, Grace.'

'Isn't it?' she asked. 'I wouldn't advise walking there.'

That earned her one of those smiles that never failed to light up her insides and, feeling instantly guilty, she looked away.

'There's a casserole in the oven and I'm just about to eat. I'm not sure what meal time you're on but, if you're serious about keeping local hours, you'd be wise to join me.'

He shook his head. 'I'm not hungry.'

'Oddly enough,' she said, 'neither am I, but unlike you I can't indulge in the luxury of missing meals.'

She stopped herself. His body clock must be all over the place and while snapping at him might make her feel better, would certainly help distract her from an almost irresistible urge to throw caution to the winds, fling herself at him and beg him to make it better, it wasn't fair on him.

'Look, why don't you go and take a shower? Maybe have a shave?' she suggested. 'See how you feel then?'

He ran a hand over his chin. 'You don't like the beard?'

'Beard?' Under the pretext of assessing the short dark beard that covered his firm chin, cheeks hollowed with exhaustion, she indulged herself in a long look. Finally shaking her head as if in disbelief, she said, 'Are you telling me that the stubble is deliberate?'

And for a moment, just for a moment, his mouth twitched into a whisper of the smile that had once reduced the hearts of teenage girls to mush. If her heart-racing response was anything to go by, it had much the same effect on mature and otherwise sensible women.

But then she was a long-lost cause.

'I'm sorry, Josh,' she added. 'I just assumed that you'd forgotten to pack your razor.'

'If that were true, you'd have had no doubt about the beard, but I'm still carrying the bag I had with me in China and Nepal so I hope the washing machine is up to the—'

He broke off as a tiny mewl emerged from the crib. A tiny mewl that quickly grew into an insistent wail.

Grace sighed. 'I thought it was too good to be true. She's been so fretful for the last couple of days. Clingy. It's almost as if she knows there's something wrong.'

Josh took a step towards the crib and, very gently, he laid his hand, as she had done, on the baby's tummy.

Posie immediately stopped crying and, eyes wide, stared up at the tall figure standing over her. Then, as if demanding more from her uncle, she reached out a tiny fist and Grace caught her breath as Josh crouched beside the crib and touched her hand with the tip of one finger.

He'd been beyond angry when she'd told him that he was too late to stop the surrogacy, that she was already pregnant with her sister's baby. News that she hadn't even shared with Phoebe, determined not to raise false hopes until the doctor had confirmed it.

She hadn't known how he would react to Posie. As a youth, a young man, he'd been adamant that he would never have children of his own. His marriage to a girl he'd never even mentioned had been so swift, so unexpected that it seemed at the time as if everyone was holding their breath, sure that only the imminent arrival of a baby could have prompted it. But there had been no baby and within a year the marriage had been over.

Now, as he gazed down at this small miracle, she waited, heart in her mouth, for his reaction. For the inevitable question.

How could she do it?

How could she have felt the first tiny movements, watched that first scan, listened to the squishy beat of her heartbeat, cherished the baby growing inside her for nine long months, only to surrender her to her sister and his brother?

Other people had asked.

Not friends, true friends. They had understood. But a re-
porter from the local paper who'd somehow picked up the
story had called her, wanting to know the whys, the hows, the
financial deal she'd signed up to. If the woman had done her
research, she'd have known that anything but expenses was
against the law and Grace hadn't needed or wanted even that.
It was the people who didn't know them who'd seemed most
indignant that she could do such a thing. People who clearly
had no concept of unselfish love.

None of those people had mattered, but she so wanted Josh
to understand. Even though he disapproved of what she'd
done, she needed him to understand, without asking, why
she'd done it.

Don't, she silently begged him. Please don't ask….

'Michael rang me minutes after Posie was born,' he said,
after what felt like an eternity. 'He was almost incoherent with
joy.' For a moment he too seemed to find difficulty in speaking. 'I was in the back of beyond somewhere, the line was terrible but even through the static it came through loud and
clear. His world was complete.' He looked up, looked at her.
'You gave him that, Grace.'

She let out a breath she hadn't been aware she was holding.
He understood.

Then, catching up, 'Michael phoned you?'

'He didn't mention it?'

She shook her head. Why wouldn't he have told her? Had
Phoebe known?

'What did you say to him, Josh?' she demanded.

'I asked him if you were all right and, when he assured me
that you had sailed through the whole thing, I asked him if he
was sure you had no doubts about giving up the baby. Urged
him not to rush you…'

She waited, sure there was something else, but he shook
his head.

'I didn't,' she said. 'He didn't.'

Why had it mattered so much to him? And why wouldn't they have told her that he'd cared enough to ask about her? Had been concerned that she was all right. Hadn't Phoebe known how much it would have meant to her?

Or was that it?

Had her sister suspected what had happened between them all those years ago? Had they been afraid that, in the hormonal rush after Posie's birth, a word from Josh might have been enough to change her mind?

Not wanting to think about that, she crossed to the crib, picked Posie up, cradled her briefly, cherishing the weight of her in her arms, the baby scent of clean hair, warm skin. Then she turned and offered her to Josh.

'Here,' she said. 'Take her. Hold her.' When he didn't move, she looked up to find him staring, not at the baby but at her. 'What?'

He shook his head. 'I thought you'd be married to your Toby by now, Grace. With a home, children of your own. Wasn't that what you always wanted?'

'You know it was.'

She'd wanted what her sister had wanted. A settled home, a good man, children. She also wanted Josh Kingsley and the two were incompatible. No one could have everything they wanted.

Her sister had never borne the children she had yearned for.

And she had never found anyone who could erase her yearning for a man for whom risk was the breath of life, the horizon the only place he wanted to be.

'Unfortunately,' she said, 'life isn't that simple.'

'Maybe men just have it too easy these days. All of the comforts with none of the responsibility.'

'Excuse me?'

'Well, it wasn't for lack of choice, was it? You appeared to be dating someone different every time I came home.'

'Not *every* time, surely?' Her well-schooled, careless tone was, she knew, ruined by a blush.

'You don't remember?'

She remembered.

Given a few days warning of his arrival, it hadn't been difficult to drum up some hungry man from the crafts centre who was glad of a home-cooked meal. Camouflage so that it wouldn't look as if she was living in limbo, just waiting for Josh to come home and sweep her up into his arms, tell her that he'd been a fool. Pick up where they'd left off.

These days, only Toby was left. He'd been brighter than most, quickly cottoning on to what she was doing and apparently happy to play the possessive suitor whenever Josh came home.

Why she'd still been going through the motions after so long she couldn't say. Unless it was because she still wanted it so badly. That it was herself she was fooling rather than him....

Whatever, she could hardly get indignant if he'd been fooled by her deception. Assumed that she'd fallen into bed with every one of them as easily as she'd fallen into his.

'Maybe they could sense the desperation,' she said, burying her hot cheeks in Posie's downy head, before holding her out to Josh. 'Here,' she said, placing the baby in his arms. 'Say hello to Phoebe Grace Kingsley. Better known as Posie.'

Josh held her awkwardly and Posie waved her arms nervously.

'Hold her closer to you,' she said, settling her against Josh's broad chest, taking his arm, moving it, so that it was firmly beneath the baby. 'Like this. So that she feels safe.'

She was desperately anxious for him to bond with this little girl who would never know her real father. For whom Josh, no matter how reluctantly, would have to be the male role model.

'She has a look of Michael, don't you think?' she suggested. 'Around her eyes?'

'Her eyes are blue. Michael has...had brown eyes.'

'All babies have blue eyes, Josh, but it's not the colour.' The tip of her finger brushed the little tuck in Posie's eyelid. 'It's something about the shape. See?'

She looked up to see if Josh was following her and found herself looking at the same familiar feature, deeper, stronger in the man. Remembered the still, perfect moment ten years ago when, after a long, lingering kiss, a promise that all her dreams were about to come true, she'd opened her eyes and that tuck had been the first thing she'd seen.

Josh felt as if he were carrying a parcel of eggs. Just one wrong move and they'd be crushed. Maybe Grace was just as anxious because she'd kept her arm beneath his, laid her long, slender fingers over his hand, as if to steady him.

This was so far from anything he'd imagined himself doing. He'd never wanted children. Had never wanted to be responsible for putting children through the kind of misery he'd endured. The rows. The affairs. The day his father had walked out and his mother had become someone he didn't know.

After a while, as he became more confident, Grace stepped back, leaving him holding this totally unexpected baby, who bore not the slightest resemblance to his brother.

If she looked like anyone, it was Grace, which was strange since she didn't much resemble her sister. He'd always assumed that they were half-sisters, although Michael had said not. The little tuck in the eyelid was familiar though, and he said, 'So long as she hasn't got Michael's nose.'

Grace laughed at that and the sound wrapped itself around his heart, warming him, and he looked up.

'I wish…' he began, then stopped, not entirely sure what he was wishing for.

'Michael never gave up hoping you'd turn up for the christening,' she said. 'He so wanted you to stand as her godfather.'

'He knew why I couldn't be there.'

'Too busy conquering the world?' Then, when he didn't answer, didn't say anything, 'Here, let me take her,' she said, rescuing him. 'I'll change her and put her to bed while you have a shower. Then we'll eat.'

He lifted his head and, glad of a change of subject, said, 'Actually, something does smell good. How long have I got?'

'Oh, half an hour should do it,' she said, not waiting to see whether he took her advice, but heading for the stairs and the nursery.

Josh let the shower pummel him, lowering the temperature gradually until it was cold enough to put the life back into his body, wake up his brain.

Doing his best to forget the moment when he'd come so close to breaking the promise he'd made to his brother. A promise he'd refused to free him from. Would never be able to free him from.

To forget the look on Grace's face as she'd looked up, and for just an instant he could have sworn that she'd seen the truth for herself.

He stared in the mirror. He favoured Michael—no one would have doubted they were brothers—but there were not by any means identical. Still he could have sworn she'd seen something.

He tugged on an old grey bathrobe that had been hanging behind the bathroom door for as long as he could remember, waiting for him whenever he was passing through London and could spare a little time to visit Maybridge, see his family.

He tied the belt and crossed to the alcove that still contained the desk he'd used when he was at school. Where he'd plotted out the future. Where he'd go. What he'd do.

His old computer was long gone, but the corkboard was still there. He reached over and pulled free a picture, curling with age, that Phoebe had taken of Michael and him building a barbecue in the garden years ago, when his brother had been about the same age he was now.

The likeness was striking, but Michael had more of their mother, her brown eyes.

He tossed the photograph on the desk and, turning to the wardrobe, hunted out a pair of jeans that weren't too tight, a sweatshirt that didn't betray his adolescent taste in music.

Then he checked his new BlackBerry for messages, replied to a couple that wouldn't wait. By then it was time to
go back upstairs—to Grace, and to the miracle and disaster
that was Posie.

Grace took her time putting Posie to bed.

She hadn't been so close, so intimate with Josh in years and
she needed to put a little time and space between them. Get
her breathing, her heart rate back under control.

She didn't hurry over changing her, washing her hands and
face, feeding her little arms and legs into a clean sleep suit,
all the time talking to her, tickling her tummy, kissing her toes.
Telling her that she was the most beautiful baby in the world,
just as Phoebe would have done.

Using the sweet little smiles to distract herself from vivid
memories of Josh, naked in the shadowy light from a single
lamp. His grey eyes turning molten as that first kiss had turned
into hot, feverish, desperate need.

He'd been so beautiful. So perfect…

Posie waved a foot at her and she caught it, kissed it, peered
into her eyes. Did all babies really have blue eyes? People said
that, but was it true? Weren't Posie's a little bit grey? Then
she saw the tiny flecks of brown and smiled.

'You're a beautiful, clever girl,' she said, doing up the
poppers, then picking her up and nuzzling her tummy
before putting her in the cot, 'and you're going to be just
like your daddy.'

She carried on talking to her as she wound up the musical
mobile, teasing, laughing and, once she'd set it gently turning,
singing to her, very softly.

Upstairs, Josh stopped at the open door to his brother's
small study. As always, it was immaculately tidy, with only
his address book and an antique silver photograph frame
on the desk.

He picked it up, stared at the picture of Phoebe cradling her new baby daughter. It looked perfect, but it was all wrong. A lie.

Even his perfect brother, who everyone had loved and thought could do no wrong, had one, unexpectedly human, frailty.

He carefully replaced the picture and left the room, closing the door behind him.

Later. He'd go through his papers later. Not that it would take long. He knew that all bills would be paid, life insurance up to date, will filed with the family lawyer.

Then he frowned. Had he changed it since Posie had been born? There hadn't been much time but Michael had never, in the normal way of things, believed in leaving a mess for other people to clear up. But playing fast and loose with life, keeping secrets, even with the best of intentions, had a way of coming back to bite you. And that tended to make things very messy indeed.

Whatever he'd done, it seemed likely that Grace would be the person most affected.

He wondered if she had the least idea how her life was about to change. How, on top of the loss of her closest family, she might also lose the home she loved. The baby who she'd so selflessly surrendered and yet hadn't totally surrendered, knowing that she would always be close to her. That she would still be hers to comfort. To hold.

He wiped those thoughts from his mind, took a breath, pushed open the kitchen door.

'Sorry,' he began. 'I had to make…'

He stopped. Looked around. He could have sworn he'd heard her talking to Posie but the kitchen was empty.

He shrugged, crossed to the cutlery drawer, planning to lay the table. He'd barely opened it when he heard her again. 'Night-night, Rosie Posie…' she said, laughing softly. 'Daddy's gorgeous little girl.'

He spun around, then saw the baby monitor on the dresser. Was it two-way? Could she hear him? No, of course not. But even so he stepped away from the drawer, planning to escape before she came down and found him eavesdropping on her private conversation with her baby.

There was the sound of something being wound up, the gentle tinkling of a lullaby.

'Night-night, sweetheart. Sleep tight…'

His imagination supplied the vivid image of her bending over to kiss this very precious baby.

And then she began to sing and nothing could have torn him away.

CHAPTER THREE

GRACE came to an abrupt halt at the kitchen door. The table was laid. A bottle of red wine had been uncorked. A jug of water beside it on the table. Everything ready for them to eat.

'Oh, Lord,' she said. 'Have you been waiting long?'

'I guessed you were still busy and made a start, that's all,' he said, pulling out a chair. 'Sit down. I'll get the casserole.'

'No, I'll do that…'

'I'm here to help, not add to your burdens, Grace.' He picked up a cloth, took the casserole out of the slow oven and placed it on the heatproof mat. 'Did Posie go off to sleep?' he asked, looking up.

'Like a lamb. Until her next feed.'

'And when is that?'

'Whoa… Enough,' she said as he heaped the meat and vegetables on her plate. Then, answering his question, 'Around ten. There are jacket potatoes in the top oven.' She leapt up to get them, but he reached out and, with a hand on her shoulder, said, 'Stay. I'll get them.'

She froze and he quickly removed his hand. It made no difference. She was certain that when she took off her shirt, she would see the imprint of his fingers burned into her skin.

He turned away, took the potatoes from the oven, placed one on each of their plates.

'No—'

'You have to eat,' he reminded her.

'Yes, but…'

But not this much.

She let it go as, ignoring her, he fetched butter from the fridge, then picked up the bottle of wine, offering it to her. She shook her head and he beat her to the water, filling her glass.

'Michael told me that Posie was sleeping through the night,' he said when, all done, he sat down, picked up a fork.

'She was, but she's started waking up again. Missing her mother.' Then, not wanting to think about that, she said, 'Michael told you?'

'He e-mailed me daily bulletins. Sent photographs.'

Why was she surprised? That was Michael. Josh might have walked away, but they were brothers and he would never let go.

'He wanted you to share his happiness, Josh.'

'It was a little more complicated than that.'

'Your understanding, then,' she said, when he didn't elaborate.

'I understood.'

'You just didn't approve.'

'No.'

'Why? What was your problem?' She hadn't understood it then and didn't now. 'He didn't pressure me. Neither of them did. It was my idea. I wanted to do it.'

For a moment she thought he was going to explain but, after a moment, he shook his head, said, 'When did you have your hair cut?'

Her hair? Well, maybe that was better than a rerun of a pointless argument. Although, if the general male reaction to her cutting her waist-length hair was anything to go by, maybe this was less a change of subject than a change of argument.

'About six months ago,' she said, trying not to sound defensive. Every man she knew seemed to have taken it as a personal affront. She, on the other hand, had found it liberating. 'When did you grow the beard?' she retaliated.

'About six months ago.'

'Oh, right. It's one of those clever/dumb things, then.'

He thought about it, then shook his head. 'No. Sorry. You're going to have to explain that one.'

'Whenever someone does something clever, in another part of the world another person does something stupid to balance it out,' she said, as if everyone knew that. She shook her head and then, unable to help herself, grinned. 'Sorry. It's just a ridiculous advert on the television that drove Phoebe…' She stopped.

'Say it, Grace. Talking about her, about Michael keeps them with us.'

'That drove Phoebe nuts,' she said slowly, testing her sister's name on her tongue. How it felt. It brought tears to her eyes, she discovered, but not bad tears. Thinking about her sister being driven mad by Michael, them both laughing, was a good memory. She blinked back the tears, smiled. 'Michael used to tease her with versions he made up.'

'Like you're teasing me?'

'Oh, I'm not teasing, Josh. I'm telling it the way I see it.'

'Is that right? Well, you're going to have to live with it. But while I'm not prepared to admit that the beard is dumb, I have to agree that your new style is clever. It suits you, Grace.'

'Oh…'

She picked up her fork, took a mouthful of casserole. Touching her hair would have been such a giveaway gesture—

'I really, really hate it,' he added, 'but there's no doubt that it suits you.'

—and much too soon.

'Pretty much like the beard, then,' she said. And, since the food hadn't actually choked her, she took another mouthful.

'Grow your hair again and I'll shave it off.'

It was an update of the arguments they'd used to have about the clothes she'd worn. The girls he'd dated. The music she'd listened to.

'If you hold shares in a razor-blade company, sell them now,' she advised.

Perhaps recognising that step back to a happier time in their relationship, he looked up, smiled.

And it was as if he'd never been gone.

For a moment they allowed the comfortable silence to continue, but finally Josh shifted, said, 'Do you want to tell me about the funeral?'

She sketched a shrug. 'Michael and Phoebe had left instructions…' She swallowed. 'How could they do that? They were much too young to be thinking about things like that.'

'I imagine they did it for one another. So that whoever went first wouldn't be faced with making decisions. What did they want?'

'A simple funeral service in the local church, then a woodland burial with just a tree as a marker for their grave. I imagine that was Phoebe's choice. Your father wasn't impressed, but there was nothing he or your mother could do.'

'One more reason for Michael to lay it all out in words of one syllable.'

'Josh… He was their son,' she said helplessly.

'Not in any way that matters. His mother is living in Japan with someone she isn't married to. His father is in Strasbourg, raising his second family. He hadn't spoken to either of them in years.'

'You're their son, too. Have you spoken to them?'

'We have nothing to talk about.'

She said nothing. What could she say? That they had both been dealt rubbish hands when it came to parents?

In a clear attempt to change the subject, Josh said, 'How are you coping with your business? I heard your answerphone message cancelling your classes for the time being and obviously Posie needs full-time care at the moment, but what are you doing about the craft centre workshop? Private commissions?'

'Beyond asking someone to hang a "closed until further notice" sign on the workshop door?' she asked. 'Not much.'

'Have you actually been out of the house in the last few days? Apart from the funeral?'

She shook her head.

'Go into Maybridge tomorrow. Pick up your post, at least. You need to keep some semblance of normality in your life.'

'Normality?'

How on earth did he expect her to think about something as frivolous as jewellery at a time like this?

'It's all you can do, Grace. It's what Michael and Phoebe would want.'

Of course it was. She didn't need Josh to tell her that. But knowing it and doing it were two entirely different things.

'I'll drop you off there when I go into town tomorrow,' he said. 'I have to talk to Michael's lawyers. I spoke to them from the car on the way from the airport. They're expecting me first thing.'

'Right. Well, I suppose I should go to the workshop. Process what orders I can fill from stock, send notes to people about anything that's going to be delayed, give them the chance to cancel.'

'Maybe you should think about taking someone on to help out for the time being,' he suggested. 'Who takes care of things when you're gallivanting off to the Isle of Man?'

'I wasn't gallivanting. The craft centre received an invitation from a fair being held over a holiday weekend and a group of us went.'

'You're getting very adventurous.' Then, 'A group?'

'I wouldn't have gone on my own, but Mike Armstrong sent some of his smaller pieces of furniture, there was a candlemaker, Toby took some of his toys and one of his rocking horses and there was—'

'So who took care of the shop while you were away?' he asked, cutting her off.

'Abby. She started as one of my students. She's very gifted.'

'Then call her. You can't afford to turn down business.'

'That's the tycoon speaking. I'm sorry, Josh, but the world won't end if Baubles and Beads is closed for a few weeks. I promise you it's never going to trouble the FTSE 100.'

'No? You don't see yourself as a franchise operation with a shop in every shopping mall five years from now?' he asked, with a smile that she remembered from the days when he'd been planning to be the world's youngest billionaire.

Did he make it?

'Er… No.' She liked the way things were. Controllable. Totally hers.

'No surprise there,' he said.

Did he look a touch disappointed in her lack of ambition? He was the one who, when she had made jewellery for college fund-raisers, her friends, had pushed her into taking a Saturday stall at Melchester market. It was Josh who'd printed flyers on his computer, handed them out, called the local press who'd sent out a photographer to take pictures. He'd gone out of his way to prove to her that it wasn't only friends and family who would pay good money for something original, different.

'I'm not into mass production, Josh. People come to me because they know they'll never see anyone else wearing the same pair of earrings. The same necklace.'

'Then you need to find some other way to grow. A static business is a dying business.'

'Possibly, but not now.' Then she groaned.

'What?'

'I promised Geena Wagner that I'd make a wedding tiara for one of her brides. It's almost done. I can bring it home, finish it here.'

'No,' he said, and she looked up, startled by the insistence in his voice. 'I really don't think that's wise.'

'But Posie…'

'You need to keep your work and your home life separate.' Again he had the look of a man with something on his mind.

'Easy to say. Elspeth would take care of her, but Posie needs continuity, Josh. She's already confused. Leaving her with anyone who has an hour to spare just so that I can keep working won't do.'

'I know,' he said. Then, more gently, 'I know.'

'I suppose I could take her with me.' Was that his point? That she was about to become a single mother with a business to run and she needed to think about how she was going to manage that. Answering herself, she said, 'I'd have to install some basic essentials if it's going to be a permanent thing.'

'Like what?'

'You want a list?' she asked, smiling despite everything. 'How long have you got?'

'I'm in no hurry.'

'Do you have the slightest idea how much stuff a baby on the move needs?' It was a rhetorical question and she wasn't expecting an answer. 'Actually, I suppose I could ask Toby to partition off the far end of the workshop so that I could turn it into a little nursery.' Then, irritated at how easily he'd manipulated her into thinking about the future when she didn't want to think about anything, she said, 'Okay, that's my life sorted. Now tell me about yours. About Nepal. China. What are you doing there?'

He began to talk about a major engineering project which should have bored her witless, but just being the centre of his attention, being able to listen to him without pretence was such a rare treat that she didn't actually care what he was saying.

And when he turned the conversation to the jewellery-making workshops she ran, showing a keen interest in what she did, her stories about some of the odder characters who came to them made him laugh.

He told her about places he'd visited, both fabulous and foul. The wonders of the world, natural and man-made. The remote, the exotic, the emptiness of a tropical beach lit only by the stars.

She told him about her recent trip to Brighton for a jewellery convention.

Finally, long after they'd finished eating, Josh stood up. 'It's late, you're tired,' he said, clearing the dishes.

She didn't bother to fight with him over it—he was right, she was finding it hard to stay awake—but instead rinsed plates and cutlery, stacking them in the dishwasher as he cleared the table. She wiped mats as he put away the butter, the wine. Their hands momentarily entangled as they both reached for the cruet and she found herself looking up at him.

'I'll take the pepper. You take the salt,' he said after a moment.

'No,' she said, pulling back. 'It's all yours, Josh. You're right. I'm done and by the time I've had a bath, Posie will be awake again, demanding food.'

'Are you okay up there by yourself now that Elspeth's gone home?' he asked. 'I could just as easily sleep in one of the spare rooms.'

'I'll be fine.'

He lifted a hand, laid his palm against her cheek. 'Sure?' he asked.

She swallowed. 'Really. Besides, if Posie is restless she'll keep you awake.'

'I have to fall asleep first. I'm going to look through some of Michael's things before I go down to the flat.'

'Right, but don't forget you're supposed to be working on UK time.'

He smiled. 'I won't.' Then, before she could move, he leaned close and kissed her cheek. 'Good night, Grace.'

'Um…good night,' she said, backing away until she reached the door, then turning and running up the stairs before she said or did something stupid.

She took a steadying breath before she glanced in at Posie and then, in the safety of the bathroom, she leaned back against the door, her hand to her cheek, still feeling the soft prickle of his close-cropped beard as it brushed against her skin.

Remembering the shock of his kiss as he'd woken her—when she was anything but Sleeping Beauty—knowing how easy it would have been for her to have asked him to stay with her. How easy it would have been to turn into his arms for the comfort they both craved.

Wondering what would it be like to lie beside Josh Kingsley on a white beach in the starlight with only the sound of the ocean shirring through the sand, the chirruping of tree frogs, the scent of frangipani on the wind.

He'd made it sound so magical. Doubtless it had been. And she wondered who had shared that tropical night with him?

He hadn't said and, unable to bear the thought of him with another woman, she hadn't asked.

He'd only once brought someone home. They'd been expecting him, but not the tall, tanned Australian girl he'd married without telling a soul. A girl who was, in every way, her opposite. Outgoing, lively, ready to follow him to the ends of the earth. Or so she'd said. It had lasted a little over a year. Since then he'd never brought anyone home, never even talked about anyone in his life, at least while she was around and although he was, by any standards, a rich and eligible bachelor, he didn't seem to live the kind of lifestyle that brought him into contact with gossip magazines. But just because he didn't date the kind of glamorous women who were pursued by the paparazzi meant absolutely nothing.

Only that he preferred to keep his private life just that. Private.

She ran a bath, added a few drops of lavender oil. But even up to her neck in soothing warm water she discovered that once having thought about it, it was impossible to get the image of Josh, of her, their naked bodies entwined, limbs glistening in the surf, out of her head.

Horrified that she could be thinking about such things at a

ime like this, she sank beneath the water in an attempt to cleanse the thoughts from her mind. Or maybe just to blot out everything. Only to erupt in a panic when she thought she heard Posie crying.

Her ears full of water, she couldn't hear anything, but when she threw a bathrobe around her and checked, she found the baby lying peacefully asleep.

She rubbed her hair dry, then eased herself into bed in the room next to the nursery. Closed her eyes and slept.

Josh replaced the telephone receiver in Michael's study, then opened the door, pausing at the foot of the stairs, listening. Everything was quiet. Grace couldn't have heard the phone— his Chinese partner hunting him down with impatient need to set up a meeting—or she'd surely have come down. Unless she'd fallen asleep in the bath?

The dark hollows beneath her eyes told their own story and, knowing he wouldn't rest until he'd reassured himself, he kicked off his shoes and, as quietly as he could, went upstairs. The bathroom door was unlocked. He opened it a few inches and said, 'Grace?' When there was no response, he glanced inside and saw, with relief, that it was empty. Then, as he turned away, he saw the nursery door was slightly ajar and, unable to help himself, he pushed it open, took a step inside.

He stood for a moment by the cot, looking down at the sleeping infant. Listening to her soft breathing, assailed by a torment of confused emotions as he considered every possible future. For Posie. For Grace.

Grace laughed as, her bottle empty, Posie turned to nuzzle at her breast, searching for more.

'Greedy baby,' she chided softly.

It was just getting light and, miraculously, they had both slept through.

She looked up as the squeak of the door warned her that she was no longer alone.

As Josh padded silently across the kitchen floor on bare feet, unaware that he had company, her first thought was that he didn't look so hot.

Then, as he reached the kettle, switched it on and stood by the window, staring out of the window at a pink and grey dawn while he waited for it to boil, she thought again.

He might have the hollow-eyed look of a man who'd spent the night staring at the ceiling but, in washed thin jogging pants and nothing else, he looked very hot indeed.

'Tea for me,' she said, before that train of thought joined last night's beach fantasy and got completely out of hand. Then, as he spun around, 'If you're offering.'

'Grace... I didn't see you there. Why are you sitting in the dark?'

'I've been feeding Posie,' she said. 'There's more chance that she'll go back to sleep if I leave the light off.' Then, 'Is the kettle playing up again?'

He looked at the kettle, which was clearly working, then at her.

'The one in your flat,' she said. 'Phoebe was going to buy a new one before...' Before the christening. But Josh had been 'too busy' to fly home, so she hadn't bothered.

'What? No,' he said. Then, 'I don't know. It was claustrophobic in the basement. Since I moved last year I've got used to seeing the sky when I wake up.'

'You have to go to sleep before you wake up,' she pointed out.

He shrugged. 'I managed an hour or two. I don't need a lot of sleep.'

'I remember,' she said.

'Do you?'

It was just as well the half-light was pink because she blushed crimson. That wasn't what she'd meant....

'I remember Michael saying that you'd moved to some

abulous new penthouse with views to the end of the world.'
They'd gone out there to visit, just after he'd moved in and
BP. Before pregnancy. 'He said you wanted a closer look at
all those horizons still waiting to be conquered.'

'Is that what you think?'

'I haven't the first idea what you want, Josh.' She shifted
the baby to a more comfortable position, then said, 'So?
What's it like?'

He regarded her for a full ten seconds before he turned
away, dropped a couple of tea bags into two mugs and poured
on boiling water. Then, his back to her, he said, 'It's like
standing on the high board at the swimming pool without a
handrail. You'd hate it.'

That hurt, cut deep, mostly because he was right, but, refusing to let it show, she said, 'I don't have a problem with
views. I just don't have your unstoppable urge to find out what
lies beyond them.'

'Still clinging to the safety net of home, Grace?' he said,
lifting his head to challenge her.

'Still searching for something to cling to, Josh?' she came
back at him.

He was the one who looked away and she realised that
she'd touched an unexpected nerve.

'Will you stay and keep an eye on Posie while I go and take
a shower?' she asked, easing herself to her feet, laying the
sleepy babe in her crib, then fetching the milk jug from the
fridge. 'Milk?' she asked, after fishing out the tea bags.

He didn't answer and, when she looked up, she realised
that he was staring down at the overlarge dressing gown she
was wearing, or rather at the way it was gaping open where
she'd held Posie against her breast as she'd fed her from the
bottle, as Phoebe had, giving the same skin to skin closeness
as breastfeeding.

'This is Phoebe's,' she said, self-consciously pulling it

around her, tightening the belt. 'It's a bit big, but I've been wearing it so that Posie has the comfort of her scent.'

'Until yours and hers become indistinguishable?'

'No! It was just while she was away.' Except, of course, her sister wasn't ever coming back. 'I hadn't thought that far ahead.'

'No,' he said, with a heavy finality that suggested she hadn't thought very much about anything. 'Although I suspect that, unless her table manners improve, all she's going to get is the smell of stale milk or dribble.'

She frowned.

'There's a damp patch,' he said, then, when she looked down. 'No, on the other side…'

'Oh, nappy rash! I'm leaking.'

'Leaking?'

She opened a cupboard, grabbed a sealed pack of sterilised bottles. 'Make yourself comfortable. I may be a while,' she said, heading for the door.

'Wait!' He caught her arm. 'You're feeding Posie with your own milk?'

He sounded shocked. Instantly on the defensive, she said, 'Of course. Why wouldn't I?'

'You have to ask?'

Confused by his reaction, she said, 'Apparently.'

He shook his head. 'You're expressing your own milk, putting it in a bottle and then sitting down and feeding Posie with it. Do I really have to explain what is wrong with that picture?'

'There's not a thing wrong with it. Breast milk is the very best start for a baby. Everyone knows that.'

'In an ideal world,' he replied, 'but I suspect that precious few surrogate mothers stick around to play wet nurse.'

'I'm not!'

'As near as damn it, you are.'

She stared at him, shaken by the fierceness of his reaction. 'You know this isn't a normal surrogacy, Josh.'

'Really?'

How could anyone invest such an ordinary word with such a mixture of irony, disdain, plain old disbelief? Grace didn't bother to respond, defend herself, since clearly he was a long way from finished.

'In what way isn't it normal?' he asked. 'You're not married, so there was nothing to stop Michael's name being put on the birth certificate. I assume that happened?'

'Of course.'

'And presumably you went through all the legal hoops with the court-appointed social worker? Signed all the paperwork so that the Parental Order could be issued, along with a new birth certificate in which Phoebe and Michael were named as Posie's parents?'

'Of course. We were really lucky. It can take up to a year to get everything settled, but there was space in the court calendar and, since the social worker was happy, the paperwork was completed in double quick time.'

'So you are aware that you've surrendered any legal rights you had as Posie's birth mother?'

Grace clutched the plastic container of feeding bottles against her breast, a shield against words that meant nothing and yet still had the power to hurt her.

'You've done your homework,' she said, more than a little unnerved at his thoroughness in checking out the legal formalities. Trying to figure out what, exactly, he was getting at.

'I did, as a matter of fact,' he replied, 'although, since Michael explained everything in his regular progress bulletins, it was more for my own peace of mind than necessity.'

That was Michael, she thought. He would never have given up trying to make Josh see how perfect it all was. Trying to break down whatever his problem had been with this arrangement.

Poor Michael….

'So why are you asking me all this?' she demanded, making an effort to concentrate, trying not to think about what had happened, but how totally happy Michael had been. 'Since you already seem to have chapter and verse.'

'I just wanted to be sure that you fully understand the situation.'

'Of course I understand. And I didn't "surrender" Posie. She was always Phoebe's baby.'

'Truly?'

He slipped his hand inside the gown and laid his hand over the thin silk of her nightgown, fingers spread wide across her waist to encompass her abdomen in a shockingly intimate gesture. Her womb quickened to his touch, her breast responding as if to a lover's touch.

'Even while she was lying here? When you could feel her moving? When it was just the two of you in the night? You didn't have a single doubt?'

It was as if he were reading her mind. Had been there with her in the darkness, the restless baby in her womb keeping her awake, thinking about how different it could have been. How all those years before, she'd longed for the protection he'd used to have failed, knowing that a baby was the one thing that would have brought him back to her.

She'd hated herself for wishing it, knowing how wrong it was to want a baby only to bind him to her. If he'd loved her he would not have left. Or, if he had, would not have been able to stay away.

Knowing that carrying his brother's child for her sister was the nearest she was ever going to get to having Josh's child growing within her womb. But that was for her to know. No one else.

She knew she should move, step back, stop this, but the warmth, strength of his hand against her body held her to him like a magnet.

'Well?' he demanded, pressing her for an answer.

'No,' she mouthed, no sound escaping. Then again, 'No!' No doubts. Not one. 'It isn't unknown for a woman to carry a baby for her sister,' she told him. 'It was once quite normal for a woman to give a childless sister one or even two of her own babies to raise.'

'This isn't the nineteenth century.'

'No. And I've no doubt some of the neighbours believe I actually had sex with Michael in order to conceive but, since you've done your homework, you couldn't possibly think that. Could you?'

'Of course not—'

'Only, for your information, he was at a conference in Copenhagen when all the planets were in alignment but since the clinic already had his contribution in their freezer that wasn't a problem.'

'I know how it's done, Grace.'

'You have been thorough.'

'I didn't need to look that up on the Internet,' he said, his face grim now.

'No? Well, know this. Since I was here, living under the same roof, it made perfect sense to give Posie the very best start possible.'

'Did it? And whose idea was that? The whole breast is best thing.'

'Does it matter?' He didn't answer, just waited for her to tell him what he already believed he knew. And, infuriatingly, she couldn't deny it. 'Phoebe would never have asked.'

'No, I didn't think it was her idea. So how long had you planned to stretch it out, Grace? Six, nine months? Or were you planning to be one of those earth-mother types—?'

'That's enough!' she said, finally managing to step away from his hand. 'This wasn't about me. You told me that Michael was incoherent with joy. Well, I want you to imagine how Phoebe felt. After years of tests, hoping, waiting, longing for a baby of her own. The fertility treatment. All those failed IVF cycles. How do you think she felt when the midwife put Posie in her arms?'

'No one would deny that you did a generous, beautiful thing, Grace.'

'You thought I was wrong then and you still do.'

'No… Not you.'

'Michael, then?' Now she was confused. Who exactly did he blame for what had happened? 'Phoebe?'

'They were desperate. Beyond reason…' He shook his head. 'It no longer matters. All I'm saying is that it might have been better if you'd gone away for a while. Afterwards. Cut the cord, not just physically, but emotionally.'

He was so obviously concerned for her that she couldn't be angry with him.

'Or were you already planning to do this all over again a year from now so that Posie could have a brother or sister?'

She took a step back. He followed her.

'Are you really so terrified of getting out there and making a life for yourself that you were ready to settle for having a second-hand family? One without the risk of making a commitment to a relationship? Leaving the comfort of the nest?'

On the other hand…

'So what if I did,' she retaliated defiantly. 'What possible business is it of yours?'

'It's my business because, unless either of them left specific guardianship instructions,' he said, 'as Michael and Phoebe's executor, I'll be the one playing Solomon with Posie's future.'

She felt the blood drain from her face. 'What are you saying?' And then she knew. 'No. You can't take her from me. You wouldn't. She's mine….'

The words were out before she could stop them.

'I thought we'd just established that she's anything but yours. That you have no rights.'

'No…' It wasn't like that. Okay, so maybe he was right. Maybe she'd never given Posie up in the way that a true surrogate would have done. But she was her aunt. Her godmother. Obviously she was going to be close. Be there for her if ever she needed her. And she needed her now. Then, more fiercely, 'No!' she said again, this time with a touch of desperation. 'You don't want her! You couldn't even be bothered to come home for the christening!'

He bit down hard, clearly fighting an angry retort. Then, very calmly, very quietly, he said, 'Forget me, Grace. Where Posie is concerned, I'm the last person you need worry about.'

Confused, she frowned. 'So what are you saying?'

Before he could answer, the phone began to ring.

Josh, closer, reached out and unhooked the phone from its cradle on the kitchen wall, responding with a curt, 'Kingsley.' He listened impassively for what seemed like forever, then said, 'We'll expect you when we see you.'

'Who was it?' she asked as he hung up, turned back to face her.

'My mother. Michael's mother—'

'Is she coming to see you?'

'—Posie's grandmother,' he said, his face set, his expression grim, 'who will be here some time this morning.'

On the point of objecting to his rudeness, she thought better of it. He clearly had something on his mind.

'Thank you. Now I'll finish what I was saying when the phone rang.' He looked so angry, so fierce. 'When I was telling you that I was the last of your worries.'

'Last? When did you ever come last in anything?' she demanded.

Least of all where she was concerned.

'Last,' he repeated. 'I come a long way down the list of next of kin. The only person who's lower than me on this particular list is you. After my father, my mother, *your* mother even…'

He let the words hang, giving her time to work it out for herself. And, when she did, her heart stopped beating, her legs buckled and there was a crash as the pack she was carrying fell to the floor.

If Josh hadn't reached out and caught her, she'd have followed it but, his arms around her, he supported her, held her close.

'I won't let it happen,' he said fiercely, as she subsided weakly against his naked chest, a rock in a world that was disintegrating around her. Stroked his hand over her hair in a gesture meant to calm her. 'Trust me, Grace. Whatever it takes. You have my promise.'

The temptation to stay in the safety of his arms almost overwhelmed her. To call him on that promise. Leave him to fight her corner. But he wasn't always going to be around to make things right for her. If there was to be a battle, she would fight for her daughter. But she didn't think it would be necessary.

'It's all right, Josh,' she said, lifting her cheek from the steady beating of his heart, the warm silk of his skin. 'They wouldn't want her,' she said, looking up at him. 'They didn't want us.'

'No,' he said, his face grim. 'But then, neither of us had the legacy of a fine house, a couple of generous life insurance policies and whatever Michael's partnership in his architect's practice is worth. Even after the Chancellor has taken his cut in inheritance tax, it's still going to provide a very nice expense account for anyone who can prove their case for bringing up Posie.'

'What?' Then, 'Are you suggesting any of them would take her just for the money?'

'There are other factors. My father has a second family. A young wife. Three little girls who would no doubt welcome a baby sister.'

'But she's *my* baby!' The betraying words flew from her lips and in that instant she knew he'd spoken no more than the truth. She'd given her sister her baby, but she hadn't been able to totally let go.

'My mother would, I'm sure, give up her present precarious existence for this house, a steady income. She would, of course, employ a first-class nanny to take care of Posie. Might even offer you the job.'

Grace shook her head. 'She's mine,' she repeated. 'If it comes to a fight, any court would have to recognise that.'

He shook his head. 'I spent a long time last night researching this on the Internet. You carried a fertilised egg for your sister but, once you've completed the formalities, that's it. In law you're no more to Posie than her aunt. Nothing changes that.'

'No…' That small word held a world of pain, of loss. First her sister and now this. Then, as his words filtered through, she said, 'No. That's not right. You don't understand. I didn't… It wasn't…'

'What?' He was looking down at her, but now his forehead was furrowed in a frown, his grip tighter and, when she didn't answer, he gave her a little shake. 'It wasn't what, Grace?'

She looked up at him. She'd promised Phoebe she'd never tell, but her sister would want her, expect her to do whatever it took to keep her baby.

'It wasn't Phoebe's egg, Josh. It was mine.'

CHAPTER FOUR

'BUT…' Now it was Josh who looked as if he needed something to hold on to. 'They'd been going through IVF,' he protested. 'There were eggs available. Michael told me…'

'Michael…' She swallowed. 'Michael didn't know.'

Grace was propelled back by the shock that came off him in waves. She grabbed for the back of a kitchen chair, then sank down on it as her shaking legs finally refused to support her.

She gestured weakly at the chair beside her. 'Sit down, Josh.' He didn't move and she said, 'Please.'

For a moment she thought he was going to ignore her plea, turn around, walk away, just as he had when she'd told him she was pregnant with her sister's baby. That there was nothing he could do or say to stop her going ahead with the surrogacy.

And so he'd said nothing.

But, after endless seconds, he pulled out the chair beside her and sank down onto it.

'Tell me,' he said. 'Tell me everything.'

Grace looked across at the crib, then back at Josh.

'I couldn't bear to see what they were both going through after the failure of that last cycle, when the consultant called a halt, saying that Phoebe wasn't strong enough to go through any more.'

She reached out, wanting him to understand, but there was

something about the way he was holding himself, something so taut, so close to cracking, that she didn't quite dare cross that line.

'You have to understand how hard it was for them,' she pressed, wanting him to feel their pain. 'It was as if someone had died.'

'I understood,' he said tersely.

'Did you?'

Josh understood only too well.

Maintaining that cheerful, positive front for Phoebe had been tough on his brother. Michael had taken to calling him late at night when Phoebe had been asleep, pouring out his desperation, his sense of failure. There had been one call, when his brother had sounded so desperate that Josh had dropped everything and flown home, seriously concerned that he was on the point of a breakdown. Something Phoebe had been too wrapped up in her own loss to recognise.

Grace pressed him for an answer. 'Did you really, Josh?'

'I understood that it had become an obsession, that it was destroying them both,' he said. 'I wanted Michael to put a stop to it. Let it go. Adopt.'

'That seems such an obvious choice to the outsider,' she said. 'For a woman yearning for a baby of her own…' She let out a long shuddering sigh. 'I loved them both so much, to see them hurting like that was unbearable.'

'So it was you who suggested the surrogacy?'

'Not until I was sure it was a possibility. Like you, I did my research on the Internet, found a Web site run by and for people who'd already been through this. Then I saw my doctor, talked it through with her. Had all the health checks. I didn't want to raise Phoebe's hopes, not until I had the medical all-clear.'

'You should have had counselling. What if you'd found you couldn't give up the baby? It happens.'

'I know.'

'But then you weren't really giving her up, were you?'

She didn't argue. She could see how it must look to him,

but he hadn't been the one lying in the upstairs flat listening to her baby crying in the night, screwing the sheet into knots as she clung to the bed, waiting for Phoebe to call her, ask her to help. A call that she knew would never come.

'When I told them I was ready and willing to have one of Phoebe's fertilised eggs implanted, they both wept.'

'They didn't try to talk you out of it? Either of them?'

Her eyes flashed impatiently. 'Of course they did. Michael said that it was time for them to take the adoption route.'

'But Phoebe was hooked.'

'They weren't that young any more. We all knew that adoption would not have been easy. And I was absolutely certain that it was something I wanted to do.'

'So?'

'Michael had to go to Copenhagen to put in a bid for a new project. He said we'd talk about it again when he got back.' She shrugged. 'While he was gone, Phoebe and I went to see her consultant so that we'd have all the options when he got back. He gave it to us straight. While he was prepared to attempt implanting a fertilised egg, he didn't need to labour the point about how much harder it is to get a result that way.' She was staring at her hands. 'Phoebe had tried and tried, Josh. I'd seen what it did to her. Simple artificial insemination is much easier, much more reliable. By the time Michael came home, it was done.'

Josh rose slowly to his feet.

It was true, then.

Some sound must have escaped him, because Grace said, 'She's still Michael's baby—'

He shook his head and for a moment she faltered, but she quickly rallied and, on her feet, came back at him with a fierce, 'Yes! Posie is still just as much your niece as if Phoebe had given birth to her.'

'No…'

This time the word felt as if it had been torn from the

depths of his soul, as feelings that he'd battling with for a year threatened to overwhelm him.

'Please, Josh,' she said, her hand reaching for his, her voice urgent now, desperate. 'Posie needs you.'

'No!' His bellow, reverberating around the high ceiling, was echoed by a startled cry from the baby.

He was beside her in a stride, lifting her from the crib, holding her out in front of him at arm's length.

'Posie Kingsley is not my niece,' he said. Then, tucking the child protectively against his shoulder, he turned to Grace. 'She's my daughter.'

'What?'

'She's my daughter, our daughter.'

'No,' she said, shaking her head, taking a step back, looking for all the world as if she'd just stepped on the tail of a sleeping tiger. 'Don't…'

If ever her eyes betrayed her feelings, they betrayed them now. Then she turned away, as if she couldn't bear to look at him, walked to where she'd dropped the feeders and bent to pick them up.

'Give her to me,' she said.

'It's the truth,' he said, refusing to surrender Posie when, still not looking at him, she held out her arms to take her. He had to make her look at him. Had to convince her. 'Michael would have done anything and, God forgive me, I conspired in his deception.'

She let her arms drop, turned and walked out of the room.

'You can't hide from this,' he said, following her. 'Or bury your head in the sand. You're going to have to fight to keep your baby.'

She stopped at the foot of the stairs, swung around to face him. 'From you?' she demanded angrily. 'Is that what this is all about?' She gestured at the baby still nestled against his shoulder. 'Control of Michael's baby?'

'My baby. Why else would I have tried to stop the surrogacy? What I did, I did for Michael. To ease his torment. If Phoebe had become pregnant, if she'd had a baby, I could have lived with it. Been glad for them. But to know that you were carrying my child…'

'It was the same, Josh.'

'No, Grace. It was completely different. You were carrying my child. Have you any idea how that made me feel?'

That, at least, gave her pause. The anger died from her eyes, to be replaced by some other emotion. One that was far harder to read.

'How?'

'I can't explain…' It was true. There was no vocabulary for the anguish he'd felt, knowing that a woman he'd loved was carrying his child only to give it away. That she would never—could never—know the truth. He'd felt as if he were stealing something from her. Losing part of himself.

'Why didn't you just tell me, Josh? Instead of going on and on about what a fool I was. How I'd regret it.'

'Michael had made me swear…'

'On what? Your mother's life?' Sarcasm dripped from her tongue and he didn't blame her.

'Not even Phoebe knew,' he said.

'I don't believe you. He wouldn't have deceived her.'

'Just like Phoebe wouldn't have deceived Michael?' he retaliated, and colour streaked across her cheekbones. 'I warned you not to put him on a pedestal.'

'So you did.'

'If it helps, with Phoebe's history I didn't believe there was the slightest chance of her carrying any baby to term.'

'No, Josh, adding cynicism to deception doesn't help one bit.'

'No, I don't suppose it does.' Then, 'If it would have changed anything, despite my promise, I would have told you.'

'But I told you what I hadn't told them. That you were too late. I was already pregnant.'

He nodded.

'Maybe, if we hadn't jumped the gun, if we'd waited until he came home,' Grace said, 'he would have told me.'

'Maybe.' But, as their eyes locked, they both knew that it was never going to happen.

'But...' She shook her head. 'I don't understand. Why? Why would he do it? Why would you?'

'Michael was desperate and I had no choice.'

'They were both desperate, but there was no problem with Michael. It was Phoebe. They both knew that...'

'I know,' he said. 'I know. But while he was holding it together on the surface for Phoebe, he was perilously close to a breakdown. She was going through so much to give them both what they wanted. Michael felt so useless and that somehow morphed into the certainty that it was his fault they couldn't have children. I tried to get him to see a counsellor but he just begged me...' Grace was staring at him and he broke off, unable to continue. 'You're not the only one who owed Michael and Phoebe,' he said angrily. 'They took me into their home, too. I only did what you did, Grace.'

'You think?' She lifted one eyebrow. 'A few minutes in a cubicle with a magazine?'

'If you knew how helpless men feel,' he said. How helpless, how confused he'd felt, knowing that she was carrying a child he'd so unwillingly helped make. 'If I'd had any idea where it would lead, I'd never have gone through with it....'

Grace was in turmoil, couldn't begin to think straight, but one message was coming over loud and clear. That while he had been prepared to assist Phoebe to get pregnant, he'd flown half way around the world in an attempt to stop *her* from having his baby.

'It's okay, Josh. No need to labour it,' she snapped. 'I get the picture. Phoebe could have your baby, but I wasn't good enough.'

'No! That's not right. How could you not be good enough?'

'Then why?'

'Phoebe was just Phoebe. Michael's wife. You...' She'd never seen Josh struggle for words like this.

'What?' she demanded. 'How bad can it be?'

'Not bad. Far from bad, but we were lovers, Grace.'

'Lovers?' She'd never thought of them as lovers. 'Were we lovers?'

'I was the first man who knew you.'

First, last… She didn't want to think about how pathetic that was. 'I still don't understand what your problem was.'

'Don't you?' He looked at Posie for a moment, then back at her. 'My problem was that when Michael told me you were going to have a baby for Phoebe—not his, but my baby—it made me feel the way I did when I left you sleeping after the night we'd spend together, flying away like a thief in the night. I felt as if I was stealing your virginity all over again.'

'You didn't steal my virginity, Josh, I gave it to you with a whole heart, but we were never lovers.'

It struck her now so clearly. All those years she'd clung to something that had been unreal—nothing.

'To be lovers is more than sex. For lovers the whole person is engaged. Not just the body, but the head and heart. My head was missing that night and so was your heart. I don't believe you know how to love.'

She might as well have slapped him. Yesterday she'd wanted to, now…

Now she had to deal with the fact that it was Josh, not Michael who was the father of her baby. That it wasn't simple biology, a surrogacy without emotional involvement or ties, but that, ten years too late, her darkest dream had come true.

She didn't want to slap him, she wanted to hold him. Wanted him to hold her, tell her that it would be all right…

It was never going to happen.

He'd made his feelings plain. He hadn't expected or wanted this child. But then he'd once told her, when she'd found him burning photographs of his father, that he would never have children.

Later, when Michael and Josh had gone to the sports centre

to beat a squash ball to pulp, Phoebe had told her that there had been an announcement in *The Times* that morning, telling the world that his father's new young wife had just given birth to a baby girl.

'I have to deal with this,' she said, clutching the pack of feeders to her.

'You can't run away from this, Grace. Can't hide. Can't curl up in your armchair and make it go away. Posie is our daughter and we're going to have to sit down and decide what's best for her.' He looked down at the dark curls of the baby who was chewing at his shoulder. 'Make decisions that will alter all our lives.'

'She's Phoebe and Michael's daughter,' she replied, a touch desperately. She wasn't ready to talk about anything else right now. She needed time to come to terms with what he'd told her. That she'd had Josh Kingsley's baby. 'It says so on her birth certificate, as you've just taken great pains to remind me.'

'All the more reason…'

'No. You didn't want her, Josh. You never wanted her. You flew from Australia to try and stop her from being conceived.'

'And failed.' He came close to a smile. 'Not that I'm the first man to face that situation. Although I'm probably the first not to at least have had the fun of getting myself there.'

'Sorry, I can't help you with that one, Josh,' Grace said with a desperate flippancy that she was far from feeling. 'You'll just have to dig deep in your memory for consolation.'

'Not that deep,' he replied without hesitation, his eyes glinting dangerously as he lifted a hand to her face, ran his thumb down the side of her cheek. And for a moment all she could think about was how he'd kissed her—not ten years ago, but yesterday, when he'd woken her. Kissed her, kissed his baby. Because he'd always known that Posie was his. And now he knew that she was hers, too.

This was the first time either of them had ever talked about the night they'd spent together and Grace discovered that at twenty-eight years of age she could still blush like the shy fourteen-year-old who'd first come to this house.

Maybe Josh, too, was experiencing whatever similar response men felt when, without warning, they stumbled into emotional quicksand because, for a moment, neither of them spoke.

Then Grace said, 'You're okay, Josh. I don't have a father who cares enough to get out his shotgun and make you do the decent thing.'

'I know all about uncaring fathers, Grace. You're right. Having seen the dark side, fatherhood is not something I ever wanted, but here I am, like it or not.'

And Grace, who hadn't thought beyond the next hour for more than a week, realised that she had better start putting in some serious thinking time about what future she saw for Posie. For herself.

'This changes everything, doesn't it?' she said, sinking onto the stairs.

Josh sat down beside her, put his spare arm around her, pulled her against his chest. 'Everything,' he agreed.

They sat there for long minutes, both of them contemplating the future. Until last week, each had seen the road clear ahead of them. Two separate paths. One a quiet small-town road, the other a challenging climb up a twisting mountain path with the end lost in the clouds. Now their ways merged in a pothole-strewn lane that was shrouded in swirling mists.

It was Posie, waving a hand and grabbing a handful of Josh's hair, who finally brought them back to now, this minute and, as he yelped, Grace lifted her head, smiling despite everything as she rescued him from Posie's tight little grasp.

'Did she pull it out by the roots?' he asked, rubbing at his scalp.

'Not much. Get used to it.'

'Will you help?'

'I'm in it for the duration, Josh.'

And that, she realised, was all that mattered. She was now the only mother Posie would ever have and she just had to get on with it. If Josh wanted to be a father… Well, that was good, but she wasn't holding her breath.

And, with that, the world steadied and, realising that she was still clutching the feeders, she got to her feet. Milk. Shower. Work. Concentrate on one thing at a time. Do what had to be done and the rest would fall into place….

'I'll be as quick as I can,' she said, glancing down at him.

'You're leaving Posie with me?' She saw panic flash across his face. 'What do I do with her?'

She paused, the words *'Be a father'* burning in her brain. Not fair. She wanted him around for Posie, but she wouldn't stoop to blackmail.

He hadn't asked for—or wanted—this.

'Just keep her amused for a while,' she said, forcing herself to walk up the stairs, away from them. She got very nearly halfway before she looked back.

He hadn't moved, but was looking up at her, dark hair still ruffled from bed, ancient jogging pants sagging below his waist, exposing a band of paler skin, feet bare. Posie propped in his elbow, happily sucking at his naked shoulder.

If she had trawled her imagination for a perfect picture of fatherhood, she couldn't have bettered it.

Don't go there, she warned herself. It might only take one little tadpole waking up from deep freeze and eager to explore to make a baby, but being a father required a lifetime of commitment.

Josh thought one night made them lovers. He couldn't even stay married to the same woman for more than a year. He saved his energies for the really important stuff, like dominating his own field of engineering.

'Better still,' she said, a catch in her throat, 'let her amuse you.'

Josh looked at the baby, then back up at her. 'What does she do?'

'Do? She's not a performing seal.' Then, because he was clearly so far out of his depth he was in danger of drowning, she threw him a lifeline. 'She's just learned to roll over. If you put her down on the carpet, she'll show you.'

She didn't wait to see what he did, but ran up the two flights of stairs to her own flat, her brain pounding out the words *Josh's baby* over and over.

She'd been carrying Josh's baby inside her for nine months and not known. Had given birth to Josh's baby and had given her away.

How could she have done that?

How could she have looked at her and not seen? The little eyelid tuck. The grey eyes flecked with amber. A little curl that fell over her right eye.

He was right not to have told her.

To have known and have to give her up, even to her sister, would have been like tearing her heart from her body and, without it, she would never have survived.

Once she finished expressing her milk, Grace took a shower, then sorted through her wardrobe for something suitable for their trip into Maybridge, ignoring her usual bright colours as inappropriate, choosing the navy trouser suit she normally kept for visits to the bank.

She'd suggest walking into town. Apart from avoiding the hassle of parking, it would be good to stretch their legs, get some fresh air. They could cut through the park on the way home, maybe take some crusts. It was way past time that Posie was introduced to the joys of feeding the ducks. Phoebe had always loved doing that.

To the outside world they'd look like any ordinary family, she thought. Mother, father, baby. All they lacked was a dog.

She put her hand over her mouth, squeezed her eyes tight shut. Hung on until the urge to howl passed.

Grace's baby…

The words thumped through Josh's head as he took the stairs down to the basement flat. Last night he'd stood for a long time in the shadows of the nursery, watching his child sleeping, as every shade of emotion raced through him.

Anger, confusion, guilt. Grief at not just the loss of his brother and Phoebe, but of this last year when he'd walled himself up, unable to come to terms with what he'd done, what his brother had done. Feeling somehow cheated, used. Worst of all, having deep buried feelings for Grace stirred up to torment him.

The minute he'd stopped concentrating on something else, his mind would sandbag him with memories of how it had felt to be buried to the hilt in her sweet, hot body, her legs wrapped around him as she'd cried out his name. Creating pictures of her carrying his child, as if the one had led from the other.

He'd never wanted to be a father. No man had ever been more careful to avoid it. Even when he'd gone to that clinic, done what was necessary, he had managed to distance himself from the reality of it. Any baby would be Michael's, not his. And it had worked until he had discovered that it was Grace who'd be carrying his seed, at which point dispassion had deserted him.

Now, lifting his little girl from his shoulder, holding her in front of him, he was faced with more reality than he could handle.

'So, Posie,' he said, 'are you going to amuse me?'

Posie, head wobbling slightly, frowned in concentration as if considering his question, just as her mother had once frowned over her homework.

'Your mother said you can roll. Is that the extent of your repertoire?'

That earned him his first smile.

'What? You think that's a funny word, do you?'

Posie made a grab for his cheek, found the short stubble of his beard and tugged.

'Oh, no, you don't, young lady,' he gasped and, eyes watering, put her down on the carpet, pulled on the sweater he'd discarded the night before, then settled down on the floor beside her.

Posie stuck her fingers in her mouth and flung her legs up in the air.

'Oh, please,' he said. 'Is that any way for a lady to behave?'

Posie blew a bubble.

Grace put the feeding bottles in the fridge, laid the table for breakfast and then, since Josh and Posie had still not appeared, she went looking for them.

They weren't in the living room—the most obvious 'rolling' territory—or anywhere else on the ground floor.

The internal door to the basement flat was still open.

She crossed to it, but hesitated on the threshold. It wasn't that she never went down there. She had always volunteered to prepare it for him when he'd been expected home, whisking through it with vacuum cleaner and duster, checking the bathroom was stocked with everything he might need, the fridge contained the essentials. Smoothing Phoebe's best linen sheets over the mattress, fluffing up the pillows.

She had always avoided going down there when he had actually been in residence.

She'd even weaned herself off going down there once he'd gone, wallowing in the scent of him clinging to sheets, towels.

It had been years since she'd taken a pillowcase he'd slept on to tuck beneath her own pillow. Her own comfort blanket.

As she hovered at the head of the stairs, the rich, deep sound of his laughter drifted upwards and, drawn by this unexpected, wonderfully heart-lifting sound, she took one step, hen another and then she was standing in the small lobby, ooking through the open door into Josh's bedroom.

Unaware of her presence, he was lying face down on the floor, his back to her, playing peekaboo with Posie. Lifting he hem of the sweater he'd thrown on, hiding his face and hen popping out with a, 'Boo.' Posie responded by throwing up her legs and wriggling with pleasure.

Josh laughed. 'Again?'

Posie waved her arms excitedly.

The two of them were locked in their own intimate little bubble, totally focused on each other. It was touching, beau-iful, unutterably sad, and Grace was torn in her emotions, wanting to laugh with Josh and Posie and weep for Michael and Phoebe.

She did neither.

Instead, determined not to disturb father and daughter as hey discovered each other, she clamped her lips together, took a step back, then turned and, as silently as possible, went back upstairs.

CHAPTER FIVE

JOSH couldn't have said whether it was a movement of air, some almost imperceptible sound or something else, but he looked over his shoulder, certain that he'd just missed something.

'I think we'd better go and see if your mummy is ready for us,' he said, scooping up the baby and heading for the stairs, dodging as she grabbed for his beard, catching her hands.

'No, you don't, miss.' She stuck out her bottom lip and he laughed. 'You're going to be a handful.'

His handful...

Then, catching a faint whiff of the faintest scent, he let go of her hands and didn't stop her when she grabbed hold of his ear, distracted by a familiar combination of soap, shampoo, something more that was uniquely Grace, and he knew exactly what had disturbed him.

It was this scent that had always been the first thing to greet him when he'd unlocked the basement door and walked in, usually at some unearthly hour in the morning after a non-stop flight from Sydney.

It was on the sheets when he'd stretched out to sleep, but had instead lain awake, imagining her leaning over to pull them tight, tuck them in, smooth the pillowcases into place.

Leaning over him, her long hair trailing over his skin, the scent of her shampoo—everything about her so familiar and yet completely new.

It had been so real that he had almost fooled himself that this time it would be all right, almost believed that this time she would look at him and the intervening years would be wiped out.

Instead, when he saw her, he'd get a quick, surprised smile as if his arrival was the last thing on her mind and he'd know that she hadn't given him a single thought since the last time he had been home. An impression confirmed when she'd appear at dinner with some decent, straightforward man in tow. A man who'd get the real smile. And he'd be certain that this time she'd found what she was looking for. Not him. Never him.

And he'd tell himself that he'd always known this was how it would be. Tell himself that it was right, that he was glad for her because he was the last man on earth she needed in her life.

Tell himself that he'd imagined the scent.

But he hadn't imagined the scent on his sheets, his pillows. She'd been there time after time in his basement flat, preparing things for his arrival, just as she'd been there a minute ago, watching him with Posie.

As he walked into the kitchen she turned from the stove where, apron wrapped around her, she was laying strips of bacon in a pan as casually as if it were the only thing on her mind.

'I thought you'd be hungry,' she said brightly enough and, if he hadn't known that a minute earlier she'd been down in the basement, he might have been fooled.

'Why didn't you say something?' he challenged. 'When you came downstairs.'

'Peekaboo?' she offered, not looking at him.

'That would have done.'

'You two were having such a good time I didn't want to butt in and spoil your game.'

'Three wouldn't have been a crowd.'

'Peekaboo is a game for two.' She half turned. 'What gave me away?'

'Your scent.'

She frowned. 'I'm not wearing any scent.'

Posie, tired from her games, was falling asleep against his shoulder and he gently lowered her into her crib, held his breath as her eyes flew open, felt something inside him melt as they slowly drifted shut. Awake, playing, she'd been a bundle of energy, but lying asleep he could see just how fragile, how vulnerable she was. Being a parent wasn't just a full-time job, it was a twenty-four/seven responsibility. There was no time off. No putting the job first.

Phoebe hadn't worked since the day she had married Michael. With two tricky teenagers and a large house to run, she hadn't had time. Grace was different. She had her own business, small by his standards, but it had taken years of hard work to build it up from that first market stall and it was her life. Had been her life. Now there was Posie and she couldn't do it on her own. Maybe she wouldn't get that chance.

He'd tried to lay it out in words of one syllable, warn her what might happen, but he knew he could never let anyone take Posie from her mother. His mother could be bought. His father worked in a politically sensitive environment and he wouldn't want his personal life plastered over the tabloids. But that wasn't the end of it. Grace was going to need help, support. And Posie would need a father. Not just a reluctant sperm donation, but someone like Michael.

He felt his chest tighten painfully.

Not him.

He wasn't like Michael. He didn't take in strays. Wasn't a nest-builder. His apartment had been decorated by a professional, looked like a show house rather than a home. He still had worlds to conquer. She needed someone like Toby Makepeace…

He looked up and realised that while he'd been thinking about her, she'd been watching him standing over the baby. She wasn't exactly smiling, but there was a softness about her eyes, her mouth…

He straightened. 'No scent?' he said, stepping back from the abyss yawning at his feet.

'None,' she said, turning away to lift a basket of eggs from a hook.

'I beg to differ,' he said.

'Oh?' She looked over her shoulder at him. 'And just how are you going to prove it, Josh Kingsley?'

He joined her at the Aga. 'Like this,' he said, bending to her hair, the feathery wisps tickling as he breathed in the scent of her shampoo.

'All you'll smell if you stand there is bacon,' she said, twitching away.

'You're using one of those herbal shampoos,' he said.

'Me and the rest of the world.'

'No…' This wasn't something mass-produced. It came from some little specialist shop; it was a national chain now, but it had started in Maybridge and Phoebe had been a fan. 'Rosemary?'

She said something that sounded like, 'Humph.'

As she made a move to escape him, he put his hands on her shoulders and kept her where she was while he lowered his head to lay his cheek against the smooth, fair skin of her neck.

She twitched at the touch of his beard, trembled beneath his hands just as she had when, eighteen years old, she'd come to him. When they'd made love….

'Lemon and myrtle,' she said abruptly. 'From Amaryllis Jones in the craft centre.'

That was it.

The scent on his sheets. The thought acted like an aphrodisiac and he backed off before he embarrassed them both.

'I had the lemon,' he said. 'I'd never have got the myrtle. What is that?'

'A bush. Small white flowers, long stamens, lovely scent. There's one in the garden,' she said, picking up a fish slice and holding it up like an offensive weapon. 'If you'd rather shower first, I can put this on hold.'

A cold shower might be a good idea. But he couldn't quite bring himself to leave her.

He'd dreamed about Grace. Hot, sexy dreams that left him aching with need, but he'd never responded to her physical presence with such an instant hard-on before. Not since the night when, trembling in his arms, she'd kissed him and he'd lost his mind.

But then, since that first night, she'd held him off with all the force of a quarterback scenting a touchdown.

'I'll eat first,' he said, pulling out a chair, sitting down watching her as she fussed with the breakfast, avoiding eye contact, flustered in a way he'd never seen her before. But then she'd always had someone on hand to run interference for her when he'd been home. All those good, steady men. Never the same one twice… 'So,' he said, 'what game can the two of us play with Posie?'

The fish slice slipped from her fingers and clattered on the quarry tiles.

'I thought I might walk into town,' she said, picking it up, rinsing it under the tap, drying it. 'Posie and I could do with some fresh air. You could take my van if you like.' Then when he didn't say anything—since not saying anything was prompting her mouth to run away with her—she pulled a face. 'Maybe not. It doesn't quite fit the tycoon image, does it? Phoebe's car is in the garage.' He saw her eyes dim as she thought about her sister. Tried to imagine what this last week had been like for her. 'Eggs?' she asked. 'One, two?'

'Just one, thanks. I'll walk in with you and Posie, Grace. I seem to have spent the last three days sitting in a plane and I need to stretch my legs.'

Grace, who he'd seen handle the tiniest beads with the precision of a surgeon, missed the edge of the pan and, as the egg shattered against the hotplate, sizzling and burning, she leapt back with a tiny scream.

'Did you burn yourself?'

He was with her before she could answer, taking her hand, turning it over to see what damage she'd done. Leading her to the sink to run it under the cold tap.

She shook her head, not looking at him but back at the stove. 'It's nothing, just a splash. I need to clean up…'

'I'll do it,' he said, leaving her with the utmost reluctance, but knowing that, if he didn't, she'd do it herself. He removed the pan with the bacon from the hotplate and picking up the slice that was having a very hard day, used it to scrape burnt egg off the cooker.

She turned off the tap.

'Grace…'

'It's fine. Nothing. There's so much to do.' She pushed long slender fingers, which could conjure up an original piece of jewellery out of nothing, through her short hair. 'I need to go and make up a bed for your mother. Did you say she's coming this morning? Someone will have to be here to let her in. Maybe I'd better stay. She'll want to see Posie, too. I asked one of my friends to take care of her on the day of the funeral. I thought she'd stay on for a while…'

He saw her stop, think about that and then, as she remembered what he'd said about her being at the back of the queue when it came to Posie's future, turn to him for reassurance.

Thinking that if she hadn't stayed, couldn't spare the time to wait and see her baby granddaughter, there was no possibility that she'd be interested in custody.

He would not give her that. Could not. Not until he knew whether Michael had made a new will. If he had, then he would surely have named Grace as her guardian. If not, it would be open season…

'I have no idea what my mother will do about Posie, Grace. But you can be certain that, whatever it is, it will be for her own benefit rather than as a result of grandmotherly instincts belatedly kicking in.'

He wanted her to understand that she was going to have

to fight to hold on to her baby. His parents, her mother maybe even him.

She stared at him. 'You really do hate her, don't you? Your mother.'

'No,' he said, grabbing the kitchen roll to wipe the surface of the Aga. 'I don't hate her.'

For a long time he'd thought he did but he'd learned, over the years, that relationships were never that simple. He'd come to understand that people were driven by desires, forces beyond their control.

Maybe that was the dominant trait that both he and Michael had inherited—the selfish gene that allowed them to fix on a goal without thought for the havoc created in the wake of achievement.

His father had left them both for a younger woman and, in her misery, his mother had jettisoned him to chase her own second chance of happiness.

Much in the same way that, justifying himself that it was in her best interests, he'd walked away from Grace. Had pursued and married the girl every other man he knew had wanted to bed, without a thought what marriage to him would be like. Alone for weeks on end. Not anger, no sense of betrayal, only relief when she'd found someone to console her…

Then, realising that Grace was still watching him, trying to read his expression, he said, 'If I could have hated her, it wouldn't have hurt so much when she left.' Facing a truth he'd fought since she'd left him with Michael. Sharing it with Grace because she was the one person he knew would understand.

'I tried to hate my mother, too,' she said. 'Hate is so much easier. But the bad stuff is mixed up with all kinds of good memories.'

'What good memories?' he asked. She had never talked about her life with her crazy hippie mother, her life on the road, and he'd never pushed her, even in teasing, instinctively knowing that it was beyond painful. 'What good memories?' he repeated.

Grace thought about it as Josh returned the bacon to the hotplate, cracked an egg into the pan and dropped a couple of slices of bread in the toaster.

'Stringing beads is my first stand-out memory,' she said. 'My mother was making jewellery to sell at a craft fair and, to keep me from bothering her, she gave me a thin piece of leather and a box of big bright beads so that I could make my own necklace.'

She remembered sitting at a table in the old minibus they were living in, sorting through the box of painted wooden beads, totally absorbed by the smooth feel of them, the different sizes, vivid colours. Laying them out in rows until she found a combination of colours and sizes that pleased her. Her delight as each shiny bead slid down the dark leather and the vision in her head became real.

Best of all, she remembered her mother's smile of approval.

'I bet you still have it somewhere,' Josh said, bringing her back to the present.

'No.' She grabbed the toast as it popped up, put it on a plate, reached for a clean slice and flipped the egg over. 'Someone saw me wearing it at the craft fair and asked my mother if she had another one like it.'

'Absolutely not,' he said, smiling at her. 'It was a Grace McAllister original. Your first.'

'Absolutely. My fate was sealed with that first sale.'

'Sale?' His smile faded as he realised what she was saying. 'Are you telling me that your mother sold the necklace you'd made for yourself?' Shocked didn't cover it. 'That's a good memory?'

'Of course. I'd made something someone liked enough to pay for,' she said, glancing up at him. 'That made me feel special. I bet you didn't feel a bigger thrill when you signed your first contract, Josh. And I made myself another one when I got home.'

'She still shouldn't have done it.' He made no attempt to

disguise his disgust. 'If that is as good as it got, I dread to think what the bad stuff was like.'

There were the times they'd been hungry, cold, but she and her mother had cuddled up together—they weren't the bad times. Bad wasn't her mother. It was other people…

'Bad was angry people. Shouting, forcing us to move on in the middle of the night.' She stared at the bacon sizzling in the heavy-bottomed, expensive pan standing on the Aga. The kind of luxury that she took for granted these days. 'Bad is never knowing where you're going to be when you wake up. Another new school where the kids call you filthy names because you live in a camper van parked on the land of someone who wants you gone. Seeing your mother dragged off by the police, arrested, just because she lashed out at someone who'd smashed the windscreen of her home. Running into the woods to hide so that the police wouldn't take you away, put you into care…'

She stopped. Where had all that come from? All those long-buried memories. Things she'd hadn't thought about in a long time. A world she'd left behind on the day Phoebe and Michael had picked her up from Social Services, brought her home. On the day that Josh had tossed her his spare crash helmet and taken her into school on the back of his motorbike.

Memories that she'd almost blotted from her mind. Apart from that apparently everlasting residual fear, the one about waking up and not knowing where she was. The one that still had the power to give her nightmares. That still brought her out in a cold sweat when she had to spend a night away at a craft fair….

Then, having apparently rendered him speechless, she said. 'There's juice in the fridge, Josh. Help yourself.'

'Why didn't you tell me?' he asked, pouring juice into a couple of glasses she'd put on the table, bringing one over to her. 'I knew your mother was a "traveller", that she'd got into a bit of bother with the law. That Phoebe rescued you from care and was granted a Parental Responsibility Order so that your mother couldn't take you back on the road. But not the rest.'

When she didn't answer, he looked up.

'I thought we were friends, Grace.'

Were. Past tense. Because once you'd spent the night naked with a man, utterly exposed, all barriers down, it could never be that simple ever again.

'Are you saying that you told me everything?' she said flippantly. 'I don't think so.'

'Everything that mattered. Do you think I talked to anyone else about my parents the way I talked to you?'

She knew exactly how much his father's desertion had hurt him. What it had done to him when, six months later, his mother had flown off to the other side of the world with someone new.

He'd put on a couldn't-care-less face for the rest of the world but, a few weeks after she'd moved in, when life was suddenly unbelievably wonderful, she'd rushed into the garden with a letter that had arrived for him from Japan. Thrilled by the strangeness of it.

He'd taken it from her, glanced at it and then, without bothering to open it, he'd torn it in two, then torn it again and again before finally discarding it, letting the breeze take the pieces, the savagery of it shocking her into a little scream.

'It was from my mother,' he said, as if that explained everything. Then, 'Sorry. Did you want the stamps?'

The line had been a study in throwaway carelessness, but a shake in his voice had betrayed him, as had a suspicion of brightness in his eyes that she'd recognised only too well. And she'd put her thin arms around him and hugged him while he cried.

This was the first time either of them had ever referred to that moment and their eyes connected as they remembered, relived that moment of anguish when he'd been more completely hers than even at the moment of sexual release.

'So?' he said. 'Why didn't you tell me how it was?'

'Fear.' Faced with the disaster of the last week, the deceit how could she be anything but honest with him?

'Fear?'

Fear that if he knew, he'd look at her the same way those other kids had.

Not that honest…

'I was afraid that if people found out about me, they'd be angry that I was living here. That I'd be forced to leave. And Phoebe, too.'

'But that's ridiculous.'

His response was natural. How could he possibly know how savage people could be when they felt threatened by those who didn't conform to the rules they lived by, who chose to live a different way?

'I know that now. Michael loved Phoebe too much, was too big a man to have buckled under disapproval, peer pressure.'

But she had often wondered what Michael's parents had thought of his wife. While her own mother had been accepted, welcomed on her rare visits, neither of his parents had ever been to this house while Phoebe was alive. And there had been no attempt to reconcile Josh with his parents, something that would normally have been a priority for Michael. He'd never talked about them. Had dismissed without consideration her tentative suggestion that he invite them to Posie's christening. There had to have been more to that than just a messy break-up and divorce.

'Back then,' she said, 'I didn't know, didn't understand how special your brother was.'

'I don't suppose anyone does until it's too late to tell them.' He looked across at Posie, sleeping peacefully in her crib, and said, 'It's going to be up to us, isn't it?'

'Us?' She took a sip of the juice, put the glass down reached up for a plate.

'To make sure that Posie only has good memories.'

'Oh, right. And how exactly do you intend to do that, Josh Are you planning to phone them in from whatever exotic lo cation you're in at the time? Tell her about the great beaches, the palm trees?' Then, 'Or maybe send her postcards? That would certainly give her a head start on a stamp collection…'

She stopped. Swallowed. She'd spoken without thinking but he'd think she'd mentioned the stamps deliberately. 'I'm sorry. I—'

'Maybe I should take her back to Australia with me,' he cut in, stopping her apology in its tracks. 'So that she can experience them for herself. It's a great place for kids to grow up.'

Her grip tightened on the handle of the slice but she refused to be rattled.

'The best place for a child is to be with people who love her enough to put her needs first,' she said, keeping her back to him. 'Who'd look after her in Australia when you're off conquering new worlds?'

'You?'

Now he had her attention and she swung round to face him. 'Excuse me, but are you offering me a job as my own daughter's nanny?'

Maybe it was just as well that the doorbell saved him from answering because this was a conversation going downhill fast.

'Your breakfast is burned,' she said coldly, handing him the slice and, leaving him to take it from the pan or not as he pleased, went to answer the door.

The slender woman standing on the doorstep was swathed in bright silk, jewellery dripping from every possible location. As exotic as any bird of paradise.

'Mum…?'

She didn't reply, just dropped the bag she was carrying, stepped forward and wrapped her arms around her, cloaking her in the faint aroma of some exotic spicy fragrance. For the first time in a very long time Grace did not resist or pull back as soon as she could. Right now she needed her mother in ways she barely understood and they clung together for a long time, not needing to speak.

It was, finally, her mother who drew back first, her gaze fixed on something behind her, and Grace didn't need to turn around to know that Josh had followed her into the hall.

'Hello, Dawn.'

'Josh…' she said, acknowledging him, but her eyes were on the baby he was holding with a possessiveness that made Grace's blood run cold. 'Hello, my sweetheart,' she said, holding out her arms. 'Come to your grandma.'

For a moment Grace thought Josh wasn't going to surrender her, but Posie, attracted by the bright colours, was smiling at this interesting new arrival and, after what felt like the longest hesitation in history, he gave her up.

'I'm going to take that shower, Grace,' he said. 'If you can be ready to leave by half past eight?' Then, 'You do still want to come into town? Dawn can let my mother in if she arrives while we're out.'

She had never wanted to go into town, but she couldn't put it off any longer. And they had unfinished business to discuss that she didn't want anyone else overhearing.

'Will you be all right, Mum? I had a commission for a tiara that has to be delivered by the end of the week.' Then, straightening for a fight she hadn't anticipated but would not duck, 'And you're right about the workshop, Josh. It's my livelihood and I need to make arrangements to keep it ticking over while I think about how I can fit it around Posie's needs.'

That brought something that could almost have been interpreted as a smile to his lips as he recognised the challenge. 'You're not interested in hearing my offer, then?'

'Posie and I are happy here.' And, before he could say any more, 'We'll be ready to leave at half past eight.'

Neither her mother nor Grace spoke until they heard the basement door shut, at which point they let go of the breath they'd been collectively holding.

'That man is so intense,' her mother said. 'Not a bit like his poor brother.'

'No. But they were very close.'

'Were they?' She turned to the infant in her arms and they inspected one another, her mother with a searching look, Posie with her little forehead wrinkled in a frown. 'What offer did Josh Kingsley make you, Grace?'

'He didn't make an offer.' Well, he hadn't. She'd cut him off before he'd said the words. 'It was just a joke.'

'Really? He didn't look as if he was joking. Only I did wonder, if he's been appointed guardian, whether he'll want to take Posie back to Australia with him.'

'He can't do that.'

'Oh?' she said. 'Are you quite sure about that? She's a beautiful child and he seems…attached.'

'He wouldn't. He's never in one place for more than a week and children need stability. Order. He knows that.' They both knew that.

'They are important,' her mother agreed, 'but knowing that they're loved is what really counts.' Then, looking at her granddaughter, 'Phoebe must have been so happy. I'm glad she had these few weeks when her world was complete.'

'Yes…' Grace tried to say more, but there was just a great big lump in her throat.

'And you, Grace? What will make your world complete?'

She shook her head. Some things were never meant to be.

'Come on through to the kitchen. I'll get you something to eat,' she said, anxious to change the subject.

'I'm not hungry, just tired.' Then, 'I'm sorry I didn't get here in time to share the burden, help with the arrangements.'

Grace shook her head. 'They'd left instructions. They chose a woodland burial site. It's very peaceful. I'll take you there when you've recovered. Josh hasn't seen it, either. He only arrived yesterday.'

Her mother nodded. 'I need to make a phone call, let someone know I've arrived. Then perhaps a bath and a nap?'

'Why don't you use my flat? I'm staying down here with

Posie so you'll be quiet up there,' she said, picking up her mother's bag and heading for the stairs. 'Private,' she added, wondering quite how Josh's mother would react when they met.

'Nice idea, but I'm not sure that I could cope with all those stairs.' She pulled a face. 'Years of damp and cold, living in vans, hasn't done my hips any favours.'

Concerned, Grace stopped. 'Are you okay? I could sort you out something on the ground floor for sleeping, but there isn't a shower on this floor.'

'I'm going to need replacement joints sooner rather than later but I can just about cope with one flight. I'd like to make my call before I go up, though. I need to tell a friend that I arrived safely.'

That was such an unexpected thing for her free-as-a-bird mother to say that Grace said, 'A friend?' Then, 'You've met someone?'

'You think I'm too old?'

'No, Mum. I'm just jealous.' Then, 'Help yourself to the phone in Michael's study. I'll put your bag in the front bedroom on the right—it's the one nearest to the stairs. Then I'll get Posie ready for her outing.'

'You're taking her with you?' She sounded disappointed. 'I would have taken care of her.'

'You need a rest and, to be honest, we could both do with some fresh air. I thought we'd come home through the park so that she can feed the ducks. You know how Phoebe loved to do that.'

Her mother laughed. 'Phoebe?'

'Wasn't it Phoebe who once gave all the bread we had to the greedy little beasts?'

'No. She gave the bread to you and you gave it to the ducks.'

'Are you sure?'

'Oh, yes. She was supposed to be looking after you so that I could put together some stuff to sell at a craft market.'

Grace had vivid memories of her mother bent over a table,

working long into the night to put together her intricate necklaces and bracelets. Easy in hindsight to understand how hard it must have been for her, a single mother trying to make enough money to keep her girls fed and clothed as she lived the travelling lifestyle that she'd taken to with the man she'd loved. Had never left, even when he'd disappeared one day. How lonely it must have been.

A scenario that she was now faced with. Not that Posie would ever be hungry or afraid. Not while she had breath in her body.

'Leaving us all without supper was her way of letting me know that she had much more interesting things to do than babysit her little sister.'

'No!' Grace found that hard to believe. 'Phoebe was always so protective. So caring.' So…*good*. Or was that the grown-up Phoebe she was thinking of?

'It was me she had a problem with, Grace. Not you. We both know that I would never have made the shortlist for greatest mother in the world. Something she made very clear when I came to fetch you after my twenty-eight days for vandalism and disturbing the peace.'

'You came for me?' Her mother hadn't just abandoned her, taken the easy option, the get-out-of-jail-free card? 'I never knew.'

Phoebe had never told her. It seemed that her big sister was better at keeping secrets than she'd ever imagined.

'We agreed that it was for the best. You didn't have her rebelliousness, her toughness. You needed to feel safe. I loved you more than words could say and it was like cutting off my right arm to leave you, but I knew you'd be happier with her. That it would be easier for you if you weren't torn by any foolish loyalty to me.' She kissed Posie's downy head and handed her over. 'She would have been such a wonderful mother. But you will be, too. Much better than I ever was.'

There was such a world of need in her eyes that Grace put an arm around her, held her and said, 'You gave me up because you loved me. That's the hardest, finest thing for a mother to do.'

'Oh…' There were tears in her eyes as she pushed her away, saying, 'Go and pretty yourselves up. I've got a call to make.'

CHAPTER SIX

DRESSING POSIE, putting together everything she'd need for the morning, took nearly all the time Grace had so that 'prettying herself up' consisted of little more than pulling a comb through her short hair.

Then she fastened jade button earrings to her lobes and a matching necklace of overlapping disks of the same stone around her throat. Make-up she could live without, but jewellery was her business and she'd never been anywhere since she'd been a toddler without something fancy around her neck or wrist—her 'sparklies'—and she'd feel naked without them.

She settled the necklace into place, trying not to think about Josh, his hands on her shoulders as he'd leaned into her neck to hunt down some elusive scent. The feel of his beard brushing against her skin, sending gooseflesh shivering through her.

The last time they'd been that close, that intimate, they'd been naked. This morning, when she'd felt the warmth of his breath against her ear, been swamped by the scent of a man still warm from his bed, she'd wanted to be naked again.

She slipped on her suit jacket, buttoned it up and, without bothering to check her reflection, fetched Posie from the nursery and went downstairs.

Josh looked up, said nothing, as she hurried into the kitchen ten minutes later than she'd promised. He just looked at her and she was convinced he could see every hot, wicked thought that had been running through her mind, distracting her, slowing her down.

'Ready?' she asked.

Stupid question. He was showered, wearing faded jeans and a soft suede jacket that emphasized the width of his shoulders and brought out the amber flecks in his grey eyes. He had obviously been there for some time since all trace of the breakfast disaster had been removed and he was sitting at the table, looking through the local paper.

He closed it, got up and said, 'Can I do anything?'

'G-get the buggy? It's in the mud room,' she said, opening the fridge, fitting a bottle into its own special little cold box, slipping it into the carrier that contained all Posie's essentials, exactly as she'd seen Phoebe do dozens of times. Keeping her hands behind her back to hide fingers itching to help.

What she wouldn't have given for that yearning now. To see Michael instead of Josh setting up the buggy, take Posie and fasten her into the little pink nest. Put the carrier in the rack beneath it.

'Not bad,' she said. 'For a first effort.'

He didn't answer but took the handle of the buggy, wheeled it into the hall.

The steps weren't exactly easy to navigate, as she knew from experience, and, having opened the door, she made a move to help. Unnecessary. Josh just lifted the buggy, with Posie and all her belongings in it, and carried them down the steps as if it weighed no more than a feather.

A nice trick if you could manage it, she thought and, since possession was nine-tenths of the law, by the time she'd shut the door and reached the footpath he was already walking away from her, forcing her to trot to catch up.

'Slow down,' she said crossly. 'This isn't a race.'

Without taking his hand off the buggy, he lifted his elbow

and, glancing down at her, said, 'Hang on. You can slow me down if I'm speeding.'

He wanted her to put her arm through his? Walk along arm in arm as if they were Michael and Phoebe…?

As if they were a couple. Lovers…

She swallowed, imagining her hand against the soft suede, her fingers resting on the hard sinewy flesh beneath it. She wanted that closeness in a way that was beyond imagining. Wanted it too much to be able to risk it.

'You're all right,' she said.

He didn't argue, simply stopped, took her hand and placed it under his arm. 'Whatever happens, you're not on your own, Grace,' he said, then, without giving her time to resist, to object, he continued, rather more slowly, on his way.

The suede was as soft to the touch as a baby's breath, while beneath it the familiar muscular arm seemed to burn through to her fingers, setting light to the memory of him standing in the kitchen, naked to the waist, in the early light.

As a girl she'd clung to his waist when she'd ridden behind him on his bike, pressed to his back, sheltered from the force of the wind by his body. That had been a secret thrill, one that had given her more of a rush than the speed at which they had been flying along. One that Josh hadn't ever known about.

This was different. This closeness was not some careless thing, just part of being on the back of a motorbike. He'd made a deliberate choice, just as he had on her first day at school when he'd tossed her his spare helmet. As he paused, turned to cross the road, and his sleeve brushed against her cheek it was like the sun coming out. She wanted to lean into it, suck up that protective warmth.

All illusion. This was not his world. In a week, two at the most, he'd be gone, chasing endless horizons. That was fact. He'd be somewhere out of reach and she'd be alone.

And, with that thought, the true finality of what had happened crystallised in her mind. Until now she'd been skimming along, keeping the wheels ticking over, taking care of Posie. Coping with the details. Standing numbly in the church through hymns and eulogies. Even watching her sister and her husband being lowered into the dark earth, it hadn't seemed real.

Each morning, her first reaction was that momentary panic at waking in an unfamiliar room, the remembering that she was in the guest room next to the nursery because her sister was away for the weekend.

Only after that came the sickening moment when she remembered that Phoebe was never coming home again. But then Posie claimed her attention and there was no time for anything but the essentials. Laundry, feeding, bathing her, changing her. She was a full-time job all by herself.

Now, walking with Josh in Michael and Phoebe's place, an icy hand gripped at her stomach, her heart. This wasn't just for a few days. This was her life. There was only her to be responsible, make decisions, make sure that this precious baby…little girl…teenager…had the best life that she could give her.

'Grace?'

Josh stopped as she pulled away, gasping for breath, and, ignoring her as she took her hand off his arm, as she tried to keep him away, he let go of the buggy and, catching her by the shoulders, pulled her against him.

'They're gone, Josh,' she said, looking up, wanting him to see, to understand. 'They're never coming back.'

His only response was to wrap his arms tightly around her, press his cheek, his lips against her hair as if he could somehow keep out the world.

'Hush… It's all right.'

All right…

All right!

'How can anything be all right ever again?' She pulled back, flinging up her arms to push him away. 'It needs more than a hug and words to fix this, Josh. It isn't just us, there's a baby involved, one that you and I made, and we're responsible.' She knew she was making a scene, that people on their way into town were turning to look, but she didn't care. She had to make him see. 'It's not just for this week, or next week, but for *ever*. We're not just spectators in Posie's life, we're her—'

Josh grabbed her by the arm and pulled her, pushed Posie off the street and into the quiet of the park.

'—parents.'

Except it wasn't 'we'. It was her.

Or was it? Josh had said he had gone through Michael's papers last night. What had he found? What had made him warn her that she was bottom of the heap?

'Do you know what guardianship arrangements Michael made for Posie?' Because a man who'd taken time to plan his own funeral to make things easy for whoever was left to pick of pieces in the event of his death wouldn't leave something really important like that to chance. 'Stupid question. Of *course* you know. You're his executor. Even when you weren't talking to him, Michael still told you everything.'

'I can't tell you anything until I've spoken to Michael's lawyers.'

He let go of her arm, leaving a cold empty space, but that was what he always did. Went away. University, gap year, for ever. He leaned forward over the buggy, tenderly tucking the blanket around Posie where she'd kicked it loose in her sleep, then began to move on through the park.

'Can't? Or won't?' she demanded, planting her feet, refusing to take another step until he gave her an answer. 'What is it you're keeping from me?'

He stopped. 'It won't help.'

'I think I'm the best judge of what helps me, Josh.'

He glanced at her. 'You're wrong about Michael telling me everything. He didn't share whatever decision he'd made with me, which suggests there were unresolved issues.'

'I think we can both guess what they were.'

He shrugged. 'Maybe. There was some correspondence with his lawyer regarding the surrogacy and it's clear that Michael and Phoebe intended to draw up new wills once Posie was legally theirs, but as far as I can tell nothing had been signed.'

'So that means…?' She lifted her shoulders.

'I won't know for sure until I've talked to the lawyer. Even a draft setting out their wishes would be something.' He stretched out a hand. 'Come on. The sooner I get there, the sooner we'll both know where we stand.'

He didn't move to take her hand as he had before. This time he waited for her to choose, to meet him halfway. And, ignoring his hand, she tucked her own back under his arm. A gesture of trust.

'Maybe I should come with you.'

'You can trust me, Grace. I'll look after your interests. You'll be better occupied at the craft centre.'

'But…'

'As soon as I'm done, I'll join you. Once we know what we're faced with, we can talk it through. Make decisions.'

It made sense, she supposed. Then, as another thought struck her, 'Will you tell him? About Posie? About…' She swallowed. There was something so intimate about the fact that they'd created a baby together—even though they had been at opposite ends of the earth when it had happened—that she couldn't quite bring herself to say the words. Couldn't bring herself to say *us*.

'About our involvement in Posie's conception?' he filled in for her.

Involvement.

Good word. If you wanted to eradicate any suggestion of intimacy. And why not? There had only been one night of us and while for her it had been the only night, he had been the only one, she had no illusions that he'd spent the last ten years dreaming of her. That dream had been shattered the day he'd turned up with a beautiful young woman and announced they'd stopped over in Bali on their way to England and got married.

'That would be the involvement you just announced to a street full of people?'

Her hand flew to her mouth. 'I didn't!'

'I'm paraphrasing, but "…there's a baby that you and I made…" just about covers it.'

She groaned.

'Relax. Most people just wanted to get away from the mad woman as fast as they could.'

'You're just saying that to make me feel better.'

'No. I swear. At least three people crossed the street.'

'Only three?' She shook her head, but she was smiling.

'That's better. And, to answer your question, I don't think there's anything to be gained by telling him about us and robbing Phoebe and Michael of something they'd longed for with such a passion. It's nobody's business but ours, Grace.'

Ours. Us.

Josh savoured the words, drinking them in like a man who'd been wandering in the desert.

He'd locked himself out of Grace's life a long time ago. He hadn't fully understood why she'd been trapped like a fledgling, too scared to fly the nest that Phoebe and Michael had made for her. He'd accepted that it was somehow mixed up with her childhood, but he'd never pushed her to explain. Maybe he hadn't wanted to, preferring to tell himself that it was for the best, that she'd have slowed him down, instead of being honest with himself. Facing his own demons.

But those two tiny words—*ours, us*—like the infant who'd dropped off to sleep in the buggy, joined them in a unique alliance that set them apart from the rest of the world. They were a family.

He was a father and that was a responsibility he couldn't run away from.

They reached the corner where their ways divided but, instead of parting, they stood, her hand linking them together, and for a moment it seemed that she was as reluctant as him to break the connection.

He was on the point of suggesting that perhaps, after all, she should go with him to talk to Michael's lawyer, when she finally took her arm from his and said, 'I'd better let you go.'

He caught her hand. 'We're in this together, Grace.'

'Are we?'

'I'll do whatever it takes to protect Phoebe and Michael. I owe them that.'

'And Posie?'

'I'll protect her with my life.'

As he would Grace. He couldn't begin to guess how hard this was going to be for her. Desperate with worry about the future of a child who she had never, whether she'd admit it or not, truly given up, when she should be left in peace to grieve for her sister.

'This is all my fault,' she said. 'If I hadn't—'

'Don't!' He'd done everything he could to prevent her from having this baby, prevent himself from becoming a father, but he couldn't bear to hear her put what he'd wished into words. Not now he'd held Posie, seen her smile. 'Please, don't do that to yourself.'

Or to him.

She lifted her stricken face.

'But it's true. I wanted them to go away for the weekend, planned it, gave it to them as my treat because I wanted to have Posie to myself. Just for the weekend. Only for the weekend…'

Oh, dear God. It wasn't colluding with Phoebe that was tormenting her. She was blaming herself for the accident.

'No,' he said. And, when she would have argued, he said it again. 'No. It's always like this when someone dies,' he said. 'The guilt kicks in. You can only think of the things you did wrong. Or didn't do at all,' he added, thinking of his own miserable, selfish response to something that had made his brother so happy. 'They can overwhelm you, take on an importance completely out of proportion to their true meaning.'

She shook her head.

'You have to remember the good things. Remember how happy you made them both.' He squeezed her arm reassuringly, then touched the sleeping baby's head. 'I'll see you both later,' he said, taking a step back, saving the picture of the two of them in his mind before tearing himself away.

Grace unlocked the door to her workshop, kicking aside the mail so that she could get the buggy in, turning on the lights.

She'd expanded from her original tiny workroom, moving into this wonderful airy space when it had become vacant a couple of years ago.

She'd kept the walls and furnishings a stark black and white to accentuate the vivid colours of her jewellery. At one end there was a secure walk-in storage space for the basic tools of her trade and a tiny office. There was her working area, with her drawing board and the workbench where she put together her designs.

The centre of the room offered a display area for photographs of some of the special pieces she'd made, as well as the dramatic spiral stands that Toby had designed and made to display examples of her work.

There was a comfortable seating area for clients who came to discuss special commissions and at the far end was another long workbench where she worked with the students who took her classes.

She didn't waste time going through the mail, but put it to one side to take home with her. Instead, she made the most of the fact that Posie was asleep to download and pack up the Internet orders for beads, findings, the jewellery kits that kept the cash flow ticking over.

After that she called Abby, a stay-at-home mum who'd

taken one of her classes and proved to be one of her most talented students. She was happy to come in for a few hours a day for the next couple of weeks and, while Grace was waiting for her to arrive so that she could walk her through the Web site ordering systems, she took the armature for the tiara she'd designed from the workroom, the tray with the teardrop pearls and each size and colour of semi-precious stone she would use, counted and placed in individual compartments. Then, with the deceptively simple design in front of her, she began to build the sparkling fairy tale confection that a young bride would wear on the most special day of her life.

When, finally, it was finished, she sat back and looked at it, glad she'd come here. Glad she'd done something positive. Something life-affirming.

Posie, who'd been an angel and had slept while she'd worked, finally woke and began to make her presence felt.

'Well, haven't you been a good baby,' she said, as she lifted her bag from the carrier and plugged in her bottle-warmer before changing her.

She was just about to settle on the sofa in the customer area, when there was a tap at the door.

Josh would have just walked in despite the 'closed' sign on the door and, expecting it to be Abby, she called out, 'It's open.' Then, as she realised it was neither, she said, 'Oh, Toby…'

Her disappointment must have been evident because he didn't come beyond the doorway.

'I know you're not open but I saw your light on and I thought I'd come over and see if there was anything you need. If it's a bad time…'

Toby Makepeace restored and made bespoke rocking horses across the cobbled yard of what had once been a huge coaching inn, but had long since been converted into craft workshops and small boutiques. He was easy to get along with and she'd taken him home as her 'date' the last time Josh had come home on a proper visit.

Still trying to prove to him, or maybe just to herself, that he didn't mean anything to her. No, definitely to herself. He hadn't given her a thought a minute after he'd left her sleeping in his bed.

Toby, unlike her other 'dates', had quickly cottoned on to the reason for his presence and had played his part to the hilt. Michael had teased her about him for weeks afterwards, referring to him as her 'lovelorn swain' until Phoebe had finally told him to stop embarrassing her.

Had Phoebe seen, understood more than she had ever let on? She had never said anything, but she'd never pressed her about boyfriends, either. She'd never remarked on the fact, that despite the fact that Grace had always said she was too busy to get involved, she had always managed to have a date when Josh had come home.

It must have been blindingly obvious, now she came to think about it. Bless Phoebe…

Toby had laughed when she had told him and it had somehow cemented a genuine friendship and he had been the first person she'd thought of when she'd needed help at the hospital.

'No,' she said, 'it's never a bad time to see a friend. I don't think I ever thanked you properly for what you did.'

'Don't even think about it,' Toby said, closing the door, coming across and giving her a hug. Leaving his hand on her arm. It was no more than a gesture of comfort from a friend, but it was where Josh's hand had so recently lain. It felt so much like an intrusion that it took all her concentration not to pull away. 'Anything I can do, you know you only have to ask.'

'Actually, I'm just about to feed Posie. If you really want to make yourself useful, you could put on a pot of coffee.'

Posie, growing impatient, began to whimper.

'Poor little angel,' Toby said, touching a finger lightly to her cheek before taking himself off to fill the coffee-maker. 'But at least she's still got her real mummy to take care of her.'

Grace sighed. There really was no point in explaining the

finer points of surrogacy. She supposed most people would think that. She'd thought it herself until Josh had put her straight. She glanced at her watch. It had been more than an hour since they'd gone their separate ways.

What on earth could be taking so long?

Nothing good, she was sure. But there was nothing she could do about it now and she crossed to the sofa, settled herself in the corner against the arm and offered Posie the bottle. She sucked for a moment, then pulled away.

'What's up, sweetpea? I thought you were hungry.' She offered her the bottle again and this time she seemed to settle.

'Do these need posting?' Toby said, distracting her.

'Sorry?'

'These packages,' he said, nodding towards the pile of padded envelopes on her desk as he spooned coffee in the filter. 'I'm going that way at lunch time. I'll drop them in at the post office if you like.'

'Oh, right. Yes. That would be a huge help,' she said, seizing on his offer. 'If you're sure.'

'I wouldn't offer if I didn't mean it.'

'You're a brick. Pass me my bag and I'll give you some money.' Then, 'They all need to be sent "signed for",' she apologised as she handed over the notes.

'No problem,' he said, tucking the money into his back pocket before sitting beside her. 'It'll mean all the more time to chat up that dark-haired girl behind the counter.'

'Sarah?' She smiled. 'Good choice. She's absolutely lovely. So how long has that been going on?'

He shrugged. 'I've been taking my post to her about twice a week since she started there.'

'And that would be what—five, six months?'

'I thought I'd take it slowly.'

'Er… No. That's not slow, Toby. That's pathetic. Why don't you just ask her out?'

'Because, if she said no, sheer embarrassment would mean

I'd have to go all the way into town to the main post office whenever I wanted a stamp.'

Grace clucked like a chicken and he laughed. 'I know, it's pathetic. But the main post office is a mile away.' Then, as Posie spat out the bottle again and began to grizzle, he said, 'What's the matter with her?'

'It's my fault. I usually wear something of Phoebe's when I feed her,' Grace replied. 'For the scent,' she explained. 'But I didn't think to bring anything with me.' She slipped a couple of buttons on her shirt. 'Maybe this will help. Phoebe used to hold her next to her skin.'

'As if she were breastfeeding?'

'What do you know about it?' she asked, laughing.

'I've got sisters,' he said. 'And sisters-in-law. Half a dozen of them. I've lost count of the number of nieces and nephews I have.'

'Right. Well, if I need any advice I'll know where to come,' she said, pushing aside her shirt a little and holding the baby close so that her cheek was against her skin. Drawn by the warmth, Posie immediately turned towards her and, after a moment or two, took the rubber teat of the feeder.

'That's so beautiful,' he said.

'Oh, Toby…'

And when, without warning, her eyes stung with tears that she could do nothing about, he put his arm around her, pulling her against his shoulder so that her tears soaked into his sleeve.

'I'm sorry,' she said. 'This is stupid.' She didn't even know what she was crying about. Phoebe and Michael. Posie. Josh…

Maybe all of them.

'It's okay,' he said. 'Go ahead. Let it out. It'll do you good.'

He still had his arm around her when the door opened and Josh walked in, coming to an abrupt halt at the sight of the three of them.

For a moment no one said anything, then Toby murmured,

just loud enough for him to hear, 'I'm sorry, Grace, I thought I'd locked the door.'

The shock on Josh's face at finding her with Toby's arm around her was very nearly as ridiculous as her own sense of guilt.

She had nothing to feel guilty about.

Toby was a friend—he'd been there when Josh had been communing with his guilt up a mountain.

But Josh was clearly reading something a lot more significant into the situation. And why wouldn't he, when she'd gone to such lengths to convince him that she was involved with the man?

But enough was enough and she pulled free of his arm, rubbing her palm across her wet cheek. 'Haven't you got an urgent date with the post office, Toby?' she reminded him before he completely forgot himself.

'You're going to throw me out before I have a cup of that fabulous coffee I've made for you?' he said, apparently determined to give Josh a reprise of his 'lovelorn swain' act.

'Abby will be here when you get back with the receipts,' she said, cutting him off before he could get going. 'Buy her a cake and I'm sure she'll take the hint. My treat.' Then, 'Buy two,' she said meaningfully.

'Two?'

'A red velvet cupcake is supposed to be irresistible,' she said.

'Got it,' he murmured, finally getting to his feet. Then, as he made a move, she put her hand on his arm, detaining him. 'Thanks for the shoulder.'

'Any time,' he said, covering her hand with his own, kissing her cheek, going for an Oscar. 'Anything.' Then, touching his finger to Posie's cheek. 'Bye, baby. Be good for Grace.'

Then, gathering the packages from her desk, he headed for the door, where Josh was blocking his way.

'Makepeace,' Josh said, his acknowledgement curt to the point of rudeness.

'Kingsley,' he responded mildly. 'I was sorry to hear about your brother. I liked him a lot.' The mildness was deceptive. If he'd actually said, *'Unlike you...'* he couldn't have made himself plainer. 'We missed you at his funeral.'

Josh said nothing, merely stepped aside to let him out, then closed the door after him and slipped the catch.

CHAPTER SEVEN

'I'M EXPECTING someone,' Grace protested.

'Whoever it is will knock,' Josh replied, crossing to the coffee pot. He turned over a couple of cups, opened the fridge. 'There's no milk. Shall I call back your gallant and ask him to bring you a carton?'

Gallant.

It was marginally better than 'lovelorn swain', she supposed. But only marginally.

'Don't bother for me,' she said, and he poured two cups of black coffee and placed them on the low table set in front of the sofa.

'You were a lot longer than I expected,' she said, glancing up at him as Posie spit out the teat, with a finality that suggested that any further attempt to persuade her to take any more would be a waste of time. 'What took you so long?'

'There was a lot to go through, but clearly I needn't have worried that you'd be lonely.'

Feeling trapped on the sofa, Grace got up, lifted the baby to her shoulder and, gently rubbing her back, began to pace.

'I didn't realise you and Toby Makepeace were still a hot item.'

Hot?

Hardly...

'When Toby saw the light, he came over to see if there was anything he could do, Josh. It's what friends do.'

'Yes, I got the "any time, anything" message. Including the shoulder to cry on,' he said, as she turned and came face to face with him. 'You'll forgive my surprise. I had assumed you were, momentarily, unattached.'

He invested 'momentarily' with more than its usual weight, bringing a flush to her wet cheeks, drawing quite unnecessary attention to them.

Josh produced a clean handkerchief and, taking her chin in his hand, he gently blotted first her eyes, then her cheeks, before unbuttoning one of the pockets on her thin silk shirt and tucking it against her breast.

She opened her mouth but no words came and she closed it again. Then jumped as he carefully refastened the buttons she had slipped open for Posie, her entire body trembling as the warmth of his fingers shot like an electric charge to her heart.

'Don't…' was all she could manage. 'Please.'

It was too painful. Too sweet…

He let his hands drop, stepping away from her, and it took all she had not to scream out a desperate, *No*…, because that felt wrong, too.

'In view of the fact that you were carrying a baby for Phoebe,' he continued calmly, as if nothing had happened. As if he hadn't just touched her, switching her on as easily as if he'd flipped a light switch, undoing, in a moment, ten years of keeping all her feelings battened down.

She stared at him, uncomprehending, having entirely lost the thread of what he was saying.

'I don't imagine there are many men who could handle that. Not even Toby Makepeace.'

Toby. The surrogacy…

Got it.

'Actually, you might be surprised. There are surrogates who, having completed their own families, want to help childless couples achieve their own dreams. They're fully supported by their partners.'

She'd done her homework, knew the answers without having to think.

'And is that what your friend Makepeace did? Support you?'

'Friend' was loaded, too.

Okay. Hands up. She was the one who'd gone out of her way to give Josh the impression, over the years, that she had a continuous string of boyfriends. Not that he'd taken much interest on his flying visits.

It was as if, after their one night together, he'd totally wiped her from his mind. As if the minute their relationship had changed from friendship to intimacy she'd become just like any other girl he'd ever dated.

Just like the girls she'd once almost pitied because she'd always known he was going to leave the minute he had his degree in his pocket.

Dispensable.

Which made it doubly surprising that he'd remembered Toby's name. They'd only met once as far as she was aware.

'Well,' she said, 'on the plus side, he didn't arrive in the middle of the night like some avenging angel, demanding that I stop being such a fool. Does that answer your question?' Then, tired of playing games, 'I have no idea how Toby felt about Posie, Josh. I didn't discuss what I was doing with him. It was none of his business.'

'That's pretty much what you said to me a year ago.'

'I didn't know...'

Her mouth dried and, suddenly afraid, she held Posie a little more tightly because it had everything to do with him. Maybe, then, if she hadn't responded with outraged anger, but had taken the time to sit down, listen, he might, despite his sworn promise to Michael, have told her the truth.

'You should have told me.'

'What would that have achieved? You were already pregnant.' Then, 'You're quite sure that Posie is mine?'

'What?' That was so far from what she'd been thinking that Grace took an involuntary step back, stumbling against one of the chairs at the work table.

As Posie let out a startled cry, Josh reached out for her and steadied her, then laid his palm against Posie's head, calming her, giving Grace a chance to catch her breath.

'Is she?' he repeated, so intently that she knew without doubt that he wanted it to be so. That, despite his opposition, despite everything, he desperately wanted this little girl to be his child. For a moment it felt as if the world had truly been made over. But the joy swiftly faded into something closer to fear.

Her mother had warned her. *"He seems attached."*

For ten years she'd been living in a fantasy world in which Josh Kingsley was her hero, the boy she'd fallen in love with. But what did she know about the man he'd become? At home he was just Josh, but in the real world he was a power to be reckoned with. A man who'd built an empire from nothing. Who'd broken her heart when he'd brought home a laughing bride, then on his next visit announced, without apparent emotion, that the marriage had been a mistake. A man who other men treated with respect and, maybe, fear. A man who saw only the prize...

She'd wanted him to bond with Posie and, against all the odds, it seemed that he had. Now, too late, she realised that it was not his mother, or hers, who she'd have to fight to keep her baby. It was him.

'I've only your word for that, Josh,' she said, crossing to the buggy and tucking Posie in, fastening her safely, freeing herself for the fight before turning to face him. 'It never occurred to me to doubt you, but maybe we'd both be easier in our minds if we had a DNA test.'

'What? No...'

Not the answer he'd expected, she noted with a glimmer of satisfaction as he took a step towards her.

Her feet wanted to take another step back, keep a safe distance between them, but her head demanded she hold her ground. One step could be put down to shock. Two looked like retreat and this was a moment for standing her ground.

'Just in case Michael came to his senses,' she continued, as if he hadn't spoken. 'That would let you off the hook, wouldn't it?'

She knew that wasn't what he'd meant, but the alternative was too shocking to deserve acknowledgement.

'You made it very clear that you were simply going through the motions to keep him happy,' she said. 'That an actual baby was the last thing you'd anticipated or wanted, and I can understand why you wanted to put a stop to it…'

She faltered, stopped, hearing what she was saying and realising that it wasn't true. She didn't understand. Worse, she was still pretending, still hiding, protecting herself from hurt. But this was more important than her feelings. More important than his.

Overwhelmed by a heart-pounding rush of anger at his selfishness, she said, 'Actually, no, I can't imagine why you'd be that cruel, but then I do have a heart.'

The raw slash of colour that darkened Josh's cheekbones was a warning that she'd gone too far, but she discovered that she didn't give a damn. He'd just insulted her beyond reason and she wasn't going to stand there and take it.

'Unless,' she continued with a reckless disregard for the consequences, 'you really think that I'd cheat my sister, foist a child conceived out of careless passion rather than a clinical donation on a couple so desperate that they would have done anything, even lied to the person they loved most in the world—'

If she'd hit him the effect couldn't have been more dramatic.

'No!' he said, and it was too late to step back as he surged forward, seized her, his fingers biting into her arms. 'No!'

'No what?' she demanded, meeting his fury head-on and refusing to be intimidated, refusing to back down. She owed it to Posie, owed it to herself, to stand up to him.

'No what?' she repeated, when he just stood there, staring at her as if he'd never seen her before. Well, he hadn't. Not like this. Empowered by motherhood and ready to take on the world.

He took a shuddering breath that seemed to come from deep within his soul and then, never taking his eyes off her, said, 'No. I don't need a DNA test. No. I don't want to be let off the hook. No. I don't believe you'd lie to me…' He broke away, as if he couldn't bear to look at her. 'I'm sorry, but when I saw you with Makepeace, his arm around you, you looked like a family and it just all seemed to make perfect sense…'

He looked so utterly wretched and where a moment before she'd been angry, now she didn't know what to think. She only knew what she felt. Grief. Confusion. Fear at the enormous responsibility for a precious life.

And maybe part of her anger was because she suspected he'd been right when he'd accused her of being too scared to risk a relationship, move on, make a life away from the safety of Phoebe and Michael's home.

Had pining after him been the safe option?

'Josh?'

The muscles in his jaw were working as he clamped down to hold back the tears and in a heartbeat the tables were turned. She could weep, but he was a man. Faced with loss, all he could do was get angry, lash out.

He was grieving, too, and just as he'd reached out to her that moment when she'd woken in the kitchen, now she reached out to him.

'I know,' she said, lifting her hand to his face, feeling the silkiness of the close-cut beard against her palm, the bone that moulded the face she knew as well as her own. Every mark, every tiny dint that life had put into it. The creases that bracketed his mouth when he smiled. The white fan of lines around his eyes where the sun never quite reached. The thin scar on his forehead where he'd fallen as a child. 'It's okay to cry.'

And, laying her cheek against his heart, she wrapped her arms around his chest and held him close.

'You're frightened and that's okay. I understand. I'm frightened, too.'

Josh, crushing her to him, didn't think there was a snowball's chance in hell that she understood one damn thing about what he was feeling. She had never understood and why would she when he'd never told her?

She would never know how he'd felt when he'd come home after that first year, expecting to find her waiting for him, green eyes sparkling, the way she'd always been there. Knowing that he'd let her down.

He'd spent the first week away expecting a call from Michael, hauling him back to face up to what he'd done. When that hadn't happened he'd known that Grace had protected him and that had made him feel even worse.

He'd tried to write, but had been unable to write the words he knew she'd want. But he couldn't stay away for ever and he'd known that she'd be waiting for him, eyes shining with that look he hadn't been able to get out of his head. The look in her eyes when he'd kissed her, undressed her, taken her. It was a 'forever' look. A look that would hook a man, haul him in, nail him down, because a decent man couldn't walk away from a look like that. Not from a girl like Grace.

But she hadn't been home when he had pitched up after twenty-four hours travelling with a ring weighing down his pocket. And when she had eventually turned up, only just in time for dinner, she was not alone, but had brought a boyfriend home with her and those sparkling green eyes had been only for him.

And that had been worse. He'd wanted to grab the guy, beat him to a pulp, then drag Grace down to the basement and make love to her until that look was back in her eyes, but only for him.

And better. Because that selfish gene had been consumed with relief.

Relief, as she'd listened to what he'd been doing with less than half an ear, had won. He could relax, knowing that what had happened between them had meant nothing more than a rite of passage for a girl eager to become a woman.

That she hadn't been sitting around waiting for him to come back and claim her, but had moved on from the jewellery stall and, with Michael's help, had rented a small space at the craft centre, had started her own small jewellery-making business. Had her own tiny van to take her to craft fairs.

Had found someone new, someone closer to home, to share her days and nights with.

That night he'd tossed the ring into the rubbish bin in the tiny basement bathroom, cut short his visit, flown back to his new life. Had found his own substitute for Grace. Lovely blonde, blue-eyed Jessie, who'd had him standing in front of a registrar in the blink of her silky lashes. Jessie, who'd realised her mistake and left him just as quickly. Jessie, now happily married to someone who appreciated her, whose face he could barely remember, while Grace…

She didn't understand but, wrapped like this in her arms, drowning in the warm scent of her, a wisp of hair tickling his chin, he wasn't about to argue with her.

'You're tired. Grieving. In shock,' she said.

No. She hadn't a clue…

'And,' she said, lifting her head to look up at him, her clear green eyes demanding nothing less than the truth, 'I suspect you've got bad news for me.'

'Not bad.' He hadn't thought so, but maybe she'd see it differently. He continued to hold her, meeting her unwavering gaze.

'But not good.'

'Mixed,' he said. 'It was pretty much as I thought. Michael instructed his lawyer to draw up new wills for them both. There were some bequests, but the bulk was left to Posie.'

'That's what I expected,' she said impatiently. 'Tell me the rest.'

'His lawyer had advised naming a guardian for Posie and Michael named me without consulting Phoebe.'

'Because you were her biological father.'

'He didn't tell me about the guardianship, Grace, I swear it. I imagine he thought I'd never know, but it must have seemed to him to be the right thing to do. And maybe he hoped that Phoebe would accept that, as his executor, it made sense.'

'But she didn't.'

'How could she?' He wanted her to know that he understood. 'She apparently blew up in the office, reminding Michael, with every justification, that I had been anything but supportive. That you had given birth to Posie.'

'And?' Then, when he couldn't bring himself to say the words, 'Tell me, Josh!'

'Joint custody was suggested as a compromise, but she just said that with us living on opposite sides of the world that was ridiculous. She didn't stay to argue, but left, leaving Michael to wrap up the meeting.'

'So nothing's been settled? It's all still in the air? Open season on Posie?'

'No…' Then, again, 'No. Michael—because you know how loose ends drove him crazy, how he liked everything to be just so—signed his own will, just a temporary measure until they'd talked it through, before he followed her.'

It took a moment for exactly what that meant to sink in and then she said, 'Oh, dear God.' He caught her as her legs crumpled beneath her, held her, but, before he could reassure her, she said, 'She told him, didn't she? That's why they left the hotel so early.' She looked up at him, her face stricken. 'Why Michael went off the road.'

'No—'

'Yes! He was always so careful, but the police said that he

was driving close to the limit on a winding country road. That he couldn't have seen the mud slick that had run off the fields onto the road until it was too late.'

'You can't know that, Grace!'

'They set out before breakfast and I thought it was just because they were so eager to get home. At least I had the comfort of believing they were happy, excited at coming back to their baby, but if she'd told him…'

'Please, Grace, don't do this to yourself.'

'If he'd told her, Josh.' She shook her head as if to drive the desperate thoughts from her mind. 'What state would they both have been in?'

'Maybe they were relieved. Happy that they didn't have any more secrets. Maybe they just wanted to get home so that they could tell you that.' He thought about the calls he'd ignored on his BlackBerry. Had Michael called him, thinking that if everyone knew the truth, he'd be okay with it? 'Listen to me, Grace,' he said, grasping her by the shoulders, shaking her. 'Look at me.'

She obeyed, raising lashes clumped with the tears she'd shed, eyes stricken with grief that tore at his heart.

'Whatever happened is not your fault. You gave them what they wanted most in the world. We both did what we thought was best.'

'Damned with good intentions.'

She rubbed her hand across her cheek, glancing at it in surprise when it came away dry, then straightened, took a step back and, breaking free, said, 'Well, at least you'll have your daughter to console you.'

'Posie is our daughter, Grace. Yours and mine.'

'You keep saying that, but you'll be the one to make all the decisions about her future. To say where she lives. Who looks after her.'

'Phoebe wanted you to take care of her. I want that, too.'

He saw a flash of hope brighten her eyes. 'Then give me

custody, Josh,' she begged. 'As her guardian you can do that, can't you?'

'Yes,' he said, 'but—'

'You could come and see her whenever you want,' she said. 'She could even come and visit you when she's—'

'I could,' he said, cutting her off before she betrayed exactly how little she thought of his ability to make an emotional commitment. 'But I won't.'

He turned to look at Posie, who was watching the spangle of lights spinning across the ceiling, making excited little sounds as she reached up to catch the colours.

He'd been thinking about her ever since the lawyer had told him that Michael had left her in his care.

He'd been so sure that he was going to be able to hand her over to Grace. Put in flying visits, offer advice, be there for them both when they needed him. But basically keeping his distance.

But Michael had wanted him involved, had wanted his little girl to know her father. And as he'd walked back to Grace's workshop it was Posie's smile as she'd grabbed for his beard, her warm baby smell, the joyful way that she stretched for each new sight, experience that had filled his head and he'd known that.

'I'm the only father that Posie is ever going to have and she deserves more than that from me.' He turned to look at Grace, white-faced at the bluntness of his refusal, her hand to her mouth. 'From us.'

CHAPTER EIGHT

GRACE watched him cross to the buggy and crouch beside Posie, catch her tiny hand, hooking it in one of his long fingers—strong, darkly tanned against her pale pink, almost transparent skin. The baby noises grew more excited as she grasped it tightly, kicking her little feet as she smiled up at him.

'This is something we have to do together,' he said. Then, looking back at her when she didn't respond, 'You know I'm right.'

'Do I?'

'Of course you do. You want what I want.'

Grace stared at him.

'Are you sure about that? You never wanted her, Josh. You never wanted children at all. Remember?'

She did. Remembered, as if it were yesterday, the day he'd heard that his father's new wife had given him a baby daughter and he'd said, '…another kid for him to let down…' That no way, never was he going there….

Easy to dismiss as the angry response of a hurting youth, but he'd never changed.

For a moment their eyes met and she saw he was remembering that moment, too.

'It's easy to say you don't want them, Grace, but Posie isn't some faceless baby. She's real.' Then, with a catch in his throat, 'She's mine….'

Grace swallowed, unable to bear the raw love with which he was looking at Posie.

'I'm so sorry, Josh. You never bargained for this.'

'No? The minute I spilled my seed into a plastic cup it was always a possibility. What I hadn't bargained on was the emotional backlash. I told myself that it was anger that kept me away. I'd signed up for Michael's deal with my eyes open, but he'd changed the rules and I'd been used. That you'd been used, too...' He bent and kissed the tiny fingers. 'I clung to that through nine long months, clung to it when she was born, when I ignored Michael's plea to come and stand as her godfather.'

'You convinced us,' she said, a touch shakily.

'Fooled you. Fooled myself. The truth, Grace, is that I knew that if I saw her, I'd never be able to leave her. Let her go. I'd have fought Michael, Phoebe, even you, to keep her.'

'Are you going to fight me now?'

He took one long look at the baby and then rose to his feet. 'I hope not. I want us to be partners in this, not adversaries.'

'How can we? Phoebe was right. You're in Australia, I'm here. Unless you really do expect me to give up everything I have here, come to Australia and be Posie's nanny.'

'You're her mother, Grace. I wouldn't insult you with anything so crude.'

'I'm sorry.' Then, when he didn't elaborate, 'So? What did you have in mind?'

'I told you. A partnership. As Michael and Phoebe's executor it's my responsibility to interpret their wishes.'

'But...'

'We know what they wanted individually. But if they'd both been in full possession of the facts I know that Michael would have wanted you, that Phoebe would have wanted me to be fully involved in her life.'

Grace frowned, trying to make sense of what he was saying, then, giving up, she said, 'The obvious solution is that I keep Posie. You visit any time you like. Move your headquarters to Maybridge if you want to be a full-time father. The world's a global village these days, so everyone says.' Then, when he didn't answer, 'How much simpler can it get?'

'You think that would be simple?'

She shook her head. 'Of course not, but we've established that we both want the same thing. The rest is just details.'

'Not quite. For a start you're assuming that you'll be able to stay in Michael and Phoebe's house.'

'It's Posie's house,' she reminded him. 'Isn't that what you said?'

'The house is part of Michael's estate. It will have to be valued for probate purposes. I'm not up to date with the property market in this area but I do know that prices have rocketed since Michael bought it fifteen years ago. It's certainly going to be in the seven figure bracket.'

'Over two million. One very like it, a couple of doors down, sold last month.'

'Well, that makes it inevitable. Apart from the fact that it's a very large house for just the two of you, with big running costs that would have to come out of the estate, the likelihood is that it will have to be sold to cover inheritance tax.'

'But it's her home,' Grace repeated, bewildered by this sudden turn of events.

'No, it's your home,' he said, but not unkindly. 'Posie's not four months old, Grace. I don't imagine she's likely to notice where she's living for quite some time, do you? Only who she's living with.'

She swallowed down her protest, knowing that he was right. 'What else?' she asked, knowing that there had to be more.

'I'll set up a Trust with the residue to provide adequate funds to care for Posie, pay for her education, provide all her needs, just as Michael and Phoebe would have done.'

'That's just money. Things. Tell me about the important stuff. About who'll hold her when she cries, who'll take her to ballet lessons, hold her hand on her first day at school. I'll be there, but where will you be?'

'Grace…'

'No! I've heard you say a dozen times that you practically live out of a suitcase. Even if you move your office to Maybridge, you'll never be here.'

'You think I can't change?'

'I think you might mean to,' she said. 'I'm sure you'd try. But how long do you really think changing nappies will be enough? How long before the horizon calls? Can Posie's first step compete with that? Her first word? And what happens when she's sick and you're off somewhere communing with a mountain? You're talking about a partnership, but what's the split? Not fifty-fifty, that's for sure.'

'Is that what you're offering?'

'That's my point, Josh. I can't offer anything. I don't have any rights, remember? You hold all the cards.'

'I could change that.'

'Oh…' The fact that he'd actually been thinking that far ahead took the wind right out of her sails. 'How?'

'Very simply. We'll get married, officially adopt Posie so that we have equal rights as her parents. Fifty-fifty,' he said with a wry smile. 'That is what you wanted?'

Grace felt her heart stop.

Marriage? He was proposing till-death-us-do-part, in-sickness-and-in-health, for-ever-and-ever *marriage*?

Everything that she wanted in one package. Josh, Posie… Except, of course, it wasn't and slowly her heart began to beat again.

'That's a huge commitment just to give me what I want, Josh. As her guardian you could simply put her in my care.'

'I could, but that way neither of us would have any real security.'

She frowned. 'What do you think I'd do, Josh? Run away with her?'

'No, of course not.'

'Then what?' she demanded.

'You might meet someone.'

'Someone?' Then, 'If this is about Toby—'

'No. You told me it's over and I believe you, but it's hardly beyond the bounds of possibility that you'll meet some decent man who'll become part of your life and when that happens, it's inevitable that he'll become the father figure in my daughter's life.'

Then stay with me….

The cry from her heart went unheard, unanswered, as he continued, 'I accept everything you say, Grace. Even if I wanted to, I can't shed my responsibilities just like that. Any change is going to take time and, besides, Posie has had enough disruption in her short life. She needs you.'

Far from delight at getting exactly what she wanted, all she felt was a dull ache at this confirmation that when he said marriage, he did indeed simply mean a partnership, but what choice did she have?

'It's going to take a few weeks to sort things out here, too, Josh. Wind up my business.' Then, trying to make a joke of it, 'Maybe you'd better marry me before you go, just in case I get swept off my feet before we join you in Sydney.'

'Join me?' He looked stunned. 'Would you do even that for Posie?' he said, taking her chin in his hand, lifting her face so that she could not avoid amber and grey eyes that were unexpectedly tender.

Not for Posie. For him….

'Australia is just another island, Josh. It's just bigger than the Isle of Man and you have to cross more sea to reach it….'

A shiver ran through her at the thought, but if that was the only way that Posie could be with her father, the only way Josh could be near his daughter, then, for the two people she loved most in the world, she would do it without another thought.

'No.' Josh's response was abrupt and his hand dropped to

his side. 'I'm not asking you to uproot yourself. Leave everything you know.'

'Only marry you.'

That wiped the tenderness from his eyes.

'Only that,' he said. 'In return for your freedom, I'll buy Michael's house from his estate so that you and Posie can stay there.'

He'd buy the house? Just like that? Without having to even think about it?

'And you? Where will you be, Josh?'

When his baby was crying in the night.

When she was alone…

'At work, like any other father,' he replied. 'As you were quick to remind me, I've got commitments that I can't walk away from, but I'll spend as much time in Maybridge as I can, so keep the bed in the basement flat aired.'

Which answered any questions she had about what kind of marriage he had in mind. Could she live with that? Could he? Living on the other side of the world, did he intend to?

'What happens if I tell you to take your partnership and stick it on the wall?'

'She's my child, too, Grace,' he said, not taking the offence she'd intended. 'I'm prepared to do what's necessary so that you can keep her, but I will be part of her life.'

'In other words, if I don't agree I'll have to fight you for custody.'

'You can try.' He tilted one dark brow. 'Do you think you can afford it?'

'Don't you dare threaten me, Josh Kingsley! Phoebe wanted me to take care of Posie. You know that. Michael's lawyer knows it, too.'

'He knows they were going to talk about it. There's nothing in writing,' he pointed out. 'And the last thing Michael did was sign his will, which suggests that, whatever his wife thought on the subject, he was absolutely clear in his own mind.'

'But he didn't know the truth!'

'Whose fault is that?'

She looked away. Not his. And he was right, she didn't have a case. She'd embarked on a surrogate pregnancy with the sworn intention of giving her baby to her sister. Clear evidence that she had no attachment. And Josh could, if she chose to make a fight of it, make it look as if she was clinging to the baby not just as a free meal ticket, but for the roof over her head.

He wasn't threatening her. He didn't need to. He was simply telling it like it was. And what, after all, was he asking of her? Nothing that she'd hadn't, in her deepest heart, wished for with every fibre of her being. To be his wife.

There was a saying.

Be careful what you wish for.

She managed a careless shrug. 'Well, I suppose a paper marriage is just about one step up from being offered a job as her nanny.'

'You don't have the qualifications to be a nanny, Grace. Marry me and you'll keep your baby, keep your home.'

This was surreal, Grace thought. If they were total strangers, it couldn't be any colder.

Grace had scarcely expected him to go down on one knee, declare undying love, but as a proposal of marriage this lacked just about everything.

'That's it?'

'Would you like me to dress it up with fancy words?'

She shook her head. 'No. It's just a business transaction so we'd better keep it plain and honest.' And, since they were being blunt, she said, 'I imagine you'll want the protection of a pre-nuptial agreement?'

'Imagine again. This isn't a short-term contract. We might be on opposite sides of the world, but we'll be together, partners in Posie's life until she's grown up. Independent. After that... Well, I'd consider half my worldly goods well spent in return for my daughter.'

'I don't want your money. Now or ever,' she managed through a throat apparently stuffed with rocks. 'The only currency worth a damn in this exchange is time and love. Can you spare half of that?'

'Posie will have all I have to give,' he assured her. 'What are you prepared to sacrifice?'

Hope. All her dreams… 'Whatever it takes.'

'Then I have your answer.'

'Yes, I suppose you have,' she said.

And that was it. Two people pledging their life to each other, not with a kiss, not to the soundtrack of champagne corks and cheers but with an awkward silence that neither of them knew how to fill.

'Maybe,' she said with forced brightness when her ears were ringing with the silence, empty and hollow as the years that stretched ahead of them, 'since we're in this for the duration, in a year or two, we could pay another visit to the clinic and make Posie a brother or sister.'

He captured her head, leaning into her and, with his lips inches from her own, his eyes molten lead, his voice crushed gravel, he said, 'Sorry, Grace. If you want me to give you another baby, you're going to have to look me in the eyes while I deliver my fifty per cent.'

Someone tried the door. Then knocked.

She didn't move. Couldn't move as he continued to look down at her, his eyes dark, unreadable, drawing her to him like a magnet until they were standing as close as two people could who weren't actually touching. Until she could feel the heat coming from him, warming her through the thin silk of her shirt, through the navy linen trousers. Until her breasts yearned for his touch and her mouth was so hot that in desperation she touched her lower lip with her tongue.

Closer…

'Grace? It's me…' Abby called, tapping again.

It was Josh who spun away from her, crossed to the door and unlocked it.

'Grace,' Abby said, reaching out for her. 'I'm so sorry….'

They hugged wordlessly for a moment, then Grace turned to introduce Josh.

'Abby, I'd like you to meet Josh Kingsley, Michael's brother,' she said. 'Josh, Abby is a genius with enamel.'

'Hello, Abby. Thanks for stepping in to help Grace.'

'No problem. I'm glad to do it. I'm really sorry to hear about your brother.' Then, glancing at her, Abby said, 'You never said he had a beard.'

'It's a temporary aberration,' she said rapidly, before he could wonder just what she had said about him—she couldn't remember saying *that* much, but when you were working together… 'Josh, this is going to be boring. Why don't you take Posie home?'

Josh didn't want to go anywhere. He wanted to stay right here and stare at the gleam of her lower lip where her tongue had touched it. Wanted to rub his thumb over it, lick it, taste her just as he did in his dreams….

'Your mother will probably have arrived by now.'

Not much of an incentive, even if she had trusted him with Posie.

'I'll wait,' he said. Then, before she could object, 'You wouldn't want to disappoint the ducks, would you?'

She looked up and for a moment their eyes closed the distance between them.

Then, without another word, she turned to Abby.

He wandered around her workshop. It was his first visit and he was impressed by the drama, the simplicity of the design, the uniqueness of the display shelves. There was nothing to detract from the jewellery—each piece was individually lit within its own compartment—which alone provided the colour, the richness. Drew the eye.

He touched a collar of gemstones, closing his eyes as he imagined Grace wearing it. Imagined fastening it around her neck… He glanced across at her, head to head with Abby as they went through something on her computer.

As if feeling his eyes on her, she looked up, a slight frown puckering the smooth space between lovely arched brows. Then as Abby asked her something, she turned back to the computer.

'You never said he had a beard.'

She'd talked about him to her friends?

He rubbed his hand over his chin. A temporary aberration was it? Maybe…

Posie whimpered. 'What's up, angel?' he said, bending over the buggy. He was rewarded with a smile and an excited wiggle. Did she know him? So soon?

Oh, no. The wiggle had an entirely different cause.

'Grace, Posie needs changing.'

'You'll find everything you need in her bag,' she said, not turning round, but concentrating on the screen. 'Wipes, clean nappy, plastic bag to seal up the used nappy.'

'But—'

'The washroom is behind my office.' Then she did turn round, one exquisitely arched brow challenging him to put all those big sentiments he'd been throwing around, all his protestations about wanting to be a father, to practical use. 'Put a couple of towels on my desk.'

He had two choices. Throw himself on her mercy or get on with it. He kicked the brake off the buggy and wheeled Posie into Grace's office, closing the door firmly behind him. He did not need an audience for this.

Then he looked down at Posie.

'It's my first time, kid,' he said. 'Be gentle with me….'

Grace had been holding her breath. As Josh shut the door of her office, she let it go and Abby said, 'Bless.' Then, 'Has he ever changed a nappy before?'

'I shouldn't think so.'

She raised her eyebrows. 'You're that mad about the beard?'

Josh, feeling much as he'd done when he'd secured his first contract—exhausted but triumphant—put Posie to his shoulder and continued his exploration of Grace's workshop. Flipped through sketches for a new design.

Then he saw a fairy-tale confection sitting on a stand.

'Ready?' Grace asked, reaching for Posie, apparently finished with her briefing.

'This is pretty,' he said, picking it up, turning it so that it caught the light. She didn't answer and he turned to look at her. 'Do you get much call for tiaras?'

'Only from brides.'

It was much too late to wish he'd looked the other way, kept his mouth shut. Impossible to just put it down and walk away. 'What stones did you use?' he asked, sticking with practicality.

'Pearls, obviously. Pink jade and quartz to match the embroidery on the bride's dress. Swarovski crystals.'

'Lucky bride,' he said, replacing it carefully on the bench. 'You've come a long way since your first bead necklace.'

'There's more than one way to travel, Josh,' she said, tucking Posie into the buggy. 'Give me a call if you need anything, Abby. Help yourself to the drawing board if you want to work on your own designs.'

'How good is she?' Josh asked as they headed for the park, eager to get the *'bride'* word out of his head.

'She's got real flair. I was going to offer her an exhibition later in the year—nearer Christmas when everyone is looking for something special….'

'Was?'

'I'm not in any position to make promises at the moment. I've got to put Posie first. I need to be able to see a way ahead.'

'You seem to work well together. You obviously trust her.

Is she serious about making a career in jewellery design, or is it a pin-money hobby?'

'She came along to a class after her marriage broke up. Therapy, she said. She obviously doesn't need to work, probably doesn't need the pin money, but you do reach a point at which making jewellery to give away is no longer enough. I think she's passed that.'

'She sounds as if she'd make you an ideal partner.'

Grace stopped, staring at him. 'Partner?'

'You'd halve the workload and costs, double the stock,' he pointed out. 'It's worth thinking about.'

'I can see why you're a tycoon, skimming the stratosphere, while I'm still bumping along on the cobbles.'

'Hardly that. You've obviously managed to maximise all your skills and you have a wonderful selling space,' he said, taking her arm as they crossed the road and entered the park. Then, as he was assailed by the scent of frying onions, he realised just how long it had been since breakfast, 'Mustard or ketchup?'

'What?' Spotting the hot-dog van, she said, 'Oh, no…'

He tutted. 'It's lunch time and you're the one who can't afford to miss meals.'

'It's half past eleven.' Then, with a grin like a naughty schoolgirl, she said, 'Ketchup. No onions. And chips if they've got them.'

'I'll catch you up,' he said, surrendering the buggy.

It was the half-term holiday and the nearest benches were all occupied by mothers watching small children and she wandered alongside the path, following the lake until she was out of sight of Josh. It didn't matter. He'd find her, she thought, trying to remember the last time they'd eaten hot dogs from the park van.

He must have been at university, home for the holidays… Her musings were brought to an abrupt halt by the sight of a small boy teetering dangerously on the edge of the lake as he strained to reach a football that was getting further away from him with every lunge.

Letting go of the buggy, she grabbed the back of his sweater just as gravity won.

'What on earth do you think you're doing?' she said as she hauled him back from, at best, a very cold bath, at worst…

'I can't go home without the ball or my dad'll kill me.'

'Now, is that really likely?' she asked, trying not to think how very much she wanted to shake him herself.

'If he doesn't kill me, my brother will. It's his ball.' Then, looking up at her with big brown eyes, 'You're bigger than me. You could probably reach it.'

They both studied the ball as, driven by a light breeze, it drifted slowly, but inexorably, towards the centre of the lake.

'No one could reach it.'

'You could break a branch off one of those bushes, miss,' the boy suggested helpfully. She wasn't, for a minute, taken in by the 'miss', but even if she had been prepared to indulge in such vandalism, it wouldn't have helped. The ball was too far out for anything but direct action.

She looked around. There was no sign of Josh, but with the children off school there was probably a queue.

She looked again at the ball. While she didn't, for a moment, believe that either his brother or his father would kill him, she did know that, as soon as she turned her back, he'd try to get it himself and, without pausing to consider the wisdom of such a move, she parked Posie by the bench, kicked off her shoes, rolled up her trousers as far as they'd go. Then, with a stern, 'Watch the baby!' she waded in.

A gang of loutish ducks who'd gathered in anticipation of a free lunch flapped away in a flurry of outrage at the invasion, driving the ball even further into the centre of the lake.

'No crusts for you,' she muttered, sucking in her breath sharply at the coldness of the water and doing her best not to think about the slimy stuff oozing over her feet as she took a

step towards the centre of the lake. Or how slippery it was
How easy it would be to lose her footing. Instead, she grabbed
a low overhanging branch for safety and she eased herself
closer to the ball.

Josh, cardboard tray holding cartons of tea, hot dogs, Grace's
chips came to an abrupt halt as he saw Posie, parked on the
path with a small boy clutching the handle of the buggy. Saw
her shoes. Then, as he saw Grace wading out into the lake
his heart turned over.

'What on earth are you doing, Grace?' he thundered.

Josh. *Now* he turned up, Grace thought, wishing she had kept
her shoes on as she felt something hard beneath her toes and
belatedly thought of all the things that got thrown into the lake

'Going for a paddle,' she tossed back, without turning
round to see if his face matched his voice, afraid that if she
made any sudden moves, she'd slip. 'Why don't you roll up
your trousers and come on in? The water's lovely.'

'Say that again without your teeth chattering and I might
just believe you.'

'Wimp,' she countered, keeping her eye on the ball
which her own movement was driving further towards the
centre of the lake.

She didn't need Josh Kingsley to tell her—from the dry
vantage point of the footpath—that this was probably the
worst move she'd made in a very long time. Too late now, she
thought, gritting her teeth as the water edged above her knees
and soaked into her trousers.

Then she ran out of branch.

It was much too late to wish she'd stuck to looking helpless
on dry land. Instead, she made a sideways tack, taking the long
way round to come at the ball from behind.

It was only as she turned to face the path that she realised
just how far out she was.

She had no one to blame but herself, she reminded herself

s she scooped up the ball, tucked it under her arm and waded back, grabbing for the safety of the branch.

There was a crack like a pistol shot as it broke off and, before he could save herself, she was sitting up to her armpits in water.

The shock of it drove the breath from her body and, unable to move, unable to speak, unable to think, she just sat there clutching the ball to her chest.

CHAPTER NINE

JOSH abandoned the tray and plunged into the water, grabbed Grace by the arms and hauled her upright. He wasn't sure which of them was shaking the most as he said, 'I'm sorry was so long. I had to wait for the chips.'

'That's good. That means they're fresh,' she said. 'Hot.' Then, 'Did you remember—'

'Salt and vinegar,' he said, and suddenly he was grinning as he said it. Laughing.

He'd remembered. He remembered everything about her.

Her legs buckling beneath her as she'd climbed off his motorbike the first time she'd ridden pillion.

The happy way she'd danced at her first school disco. Phoebe had asked him to keep an eye on her, something he hadn't been exactly happy about—he'd had bigger plans than babysitting a fourteen-year-old—but she'd been having such a good time that it had made him almost envious.

He remembered the way she'd flung her thin arms around him, her tears soaking into his shirt, when he'd bought her a puppy. The way she'd rolled her eyes at his choice of girls, music, clothes. Her quietness. The way she'd listened to him when he'd told her his dreams…

Remembered her face as he'd left her asleep in the tangled sheets.

She was always there. When he thought of home, it was

always Grace who filled his mind. Always Grace who was the '…ever fixed mark…'

'I remembered,' he said, and her lovely mouth tilted up at the corners, a snort of laughter escaped her because it was beyond ridiculous that two sensible adults would be standing up to their thighs in a muddy lake, talking about chips. 'So, are you done with paddling for the day? Only they'll be getting cold.'

'C-cold?' That made her laugh again so that she was in danger of dropping the ball. He took it from her, turned and tossed the ball to the boy. 'There you go. And keep away from the water in future,' he called after him as he grabbed it and ran.

'H-he d-didn't even say th-thank you,' she said, and that seemed to make her laugh even more.

'No doubt he thought he was in trouble,' he said, picking some waterweed from her shoulder, before taking her hands and helping her back up onto the path. He took off his jacket and wrapped it around her shoulders.

'It'll be ruined,' she protested.

'Then it will be a match for the trousers and the shoes. Here, drink this,' he said, handing her a carton of tea. And they sat dripping on the bench, drinking scalding tea, eating hot dogs.

'Aren't you going to eat the chips?' he asked, taking one. 'They're very good.'

She groaned. 'I shouldn't have vinegar,' she said, looking at them with hungry longing. 'Because of the milk.'

'Right.'

Then, as he took another one, 'I don't suppose one would hurt…'

'Better?' he asked a couple of minutes later as she wiped her fingers on a paper napkin.

'Brilliant,' she said, unpeeling herself from the bench and tossing the rubbish in a litter bin, while he fished out the bag from under the buggy and hurled a handful of crusts far into the lake, sending the birds spinning and flapping to reach it. 'Greedy little beggars. They've no manners.'

'That's what I love about them,' Grace said, watching him, hair blown by the breeze, shirt clinging to shoulders broad enough to prop up her entire world. Muddy trousers, wet shoes where he'd come to her rescue. 'They go for what they want. No pretence. No hang-ups.'

Then, because she didn't want to think about what she couldn't have, she told him about the time Phoebe had used up all the bread, not just to keep her amused, but to annoy her mother.

'Are you telling me that perfect Phoebe was once a terrible teenager?' The idea seemed to amuse him.

'Apparently.' And she smiled, too. 'Once she slipped away when we were packing up to move. She took the bus into town and didn't come back until dark, forcing everyone to stay another night.'

'I'll bet that made her popular.'

'Most of the kids loved the freedom, but Phoebe just wanted to have a proper home. After that, Mum called someone she'd known at school, got her a pocket-money job as a home help with bed and board and a part-time business course at the local college. She never looked back.'

'And you? Was that what you wanted?'

'I didn't know what I wanted.' In hindsight, though, she could see why her mother had decided to leave her with Phoebe once she'd been released from custody. She must have known it was only a matter of time. 'Thanks for jogging my memory,' she said, when she realised he was waiting for more. 'Perfection would have been an impossible ideal to live up to.'

'You think?' He took her hands. 'I don't believe you have a thing to worry about on that score, Grace,' he said, his grip tightening, his gaze suddenly more intense. 'You were born a giver. Ducks. Kids with lost balls. A sister desperate for a baby. You're always there.' Then, rubbing his thumbs over the backs of her fingers, 'And, speaking of giving, you'll need a ring. Do you want to design it yourself? Or will you allow me to choose something for you?'

'There's no need for that,' she said. A ring was a symbol, a token of deep and abiding love. Then, because that sounded ungrateful, 'It seems…inappropriate to make a big thing of this.'

'Because it's so soon?'

Josh had known from the moment the facts had been laid out in the lawyer's office what he had to do. Maybe he'd known it from the beginning. He'd told himself that it was no more than a piece of paper that gave Grace back her baby. It wasn't as if he'd planned to repeat the mistake of marrying a woman who'd want more than he could give.

Then, coming around the corner, seeing her wading out into the lake, imagining glass, rusty cans, imagining her slipping and getting tangled up in weeds or rubbish while he was stranded on the path, hands full, unable to move, it had hit him, like running full tilt into the Rock of Gibraltar.

That he didn't want a paper marriage—he wanted Grace. Had always wanted Grace.

Now, hearing the hesitation in her voice, he wanted to wrap his arms around her, kiss away her doubts, put that laughter back into her eyes. Somehow reassure her that if she'd give him the chance, he would strive to make her happy. Give her all the children she wanted, with love, passion, the two of them becoming one in that precious moment of conception.

Instead, he did the very opposite, because to say those things would be selfish beyond belief. In two weeks, three at the most, he'd be on the other side of the world and she'd be on her own, picking up the pieces, making a life for their little girl, while he came and went as he always had, pleasing himself.

The one selfless thing he could do was give her Posie. A home that would be hers for ever. Security.

She deserved that. They owed it to her—Michael, Phoebe and, above all, him.

'People will understand,' he said.

Grace, her hands clasped in his, understood just one thing. Josh didn't have to do this. He was, incredibly, doing it for her. That he was everything she'd ever wanted and now they had a common purpose that would bind them together more tightly than fleeting passion.

'How soon?' she asked.

'I'd like to settle everything before I leave.'

Grace remembered the way he'd made lists on a lined pad—an organisational skill he'd learned from Michael. He'd numbered each item, ticking it off as each task was accomplished so that he could forget it, move on.

And she had, of course, copied her hero.

It was a good system. It kept you focused on what was important. But the idea of being an item on a list, something to be ticked off, was so mortifying that she said, shivering, 'Leave it to me. I'll contact the registrar when we get home and check what we need to do.'

'Let's worry about that later. You need to get home and out of those wet things.

They went in the back way through the mud room. Grace hung up Josh's jacket so that the lining could dry while Josh eased off his wet shoes, peeled off his socks, tossed them in the sink while she struggled with the buttons of her own jacket.

'Here, let me do that,' he said, bending to tackle them, so that she was staring at his thick, dark, wind-tousled hair.

He peeled it away from her shirt, draped it over the draining board, then, while she was still struggling to catch her breath, slipped the button at her waist. The zip, always dodgy, peeled back under the added weight of water and the lot fell in a crumpled heap at her feet.

'I can manage,' she said, kicking free of her trousers, slapping his hand away as he set to work on her shirt, clearly believing her incapable of undressing herself.

'Sure?' he said.

'P-positive…' Even if she had to rip it off. 'If you leave your trousers, I'll put them through the wash….'

Her mouth dried as, taking her at her word, he slipped the buckle on his belt, undid the button at his deliciously narrow waist and slid down the zip.

Later. She'd meant later, she thought as she groped for the door handle, backing into the kitchen. She was almost sure she'd meant later, she told herself as she turned and found herself face to face with her mother, who was at the table preparing vegetables. Josh's mother, who was watching her.

While Grace stood there, too embarrassed to speak, Josh eased her aside so that he could push Posie into the kitchen, then, looking round, said, 'This is probably a good moment to tell you all that Grace and I are getting married as soon as we can make arrangements.'

Josh's mother reacted first.

'Married? Well, congratulations, Grace. And at least no one will put the obvious construct on the unseemly haste since you've already had the baby.' Then, while Grace was still cringing with embarrassment, she turned to Josh. 'I suppose you'll be giving her my grandmother's engagement ring, too?'

About to step in and read his mother the riot act, he saw the compassion in Grace's eyes and realised that she had seen what he, on the defensive, protecting himself and Grace from her barbs, had missed. How, looking beyond the plastic surgery, the perfectly applied make-up, the exquisite black designer suit, his mother was a fragile, desperately unhappy woman who'd just buried her oldest son—a son she'd lost years before.

'Would you look after Posie for me, Mrs Kingsley,' Grace added, 'while I go and take a shower?'

And he saw how like Phoebe she was.

Her gentleness. Goodness.

She would never look back with regret on an unkindness. Cling to hostility, as both he and Michael had done. And he knew at that moment that he wouldn't want to die with that leaden weight in his heart.

He wheeled the buggy closer to his mother, touched her shoulder and said, 'I'll take your bag upstairs, while you and Dawn get to know your granddaughter.'

His reward was a smile from Grace. It was a moment of revelation. Truth.

'Mum?' Grace prompted, obviously wanting to get any unpleasantness out of the way in one fell swoop. 'Have you anything to say?'

'Only… What happened to your clothes?'

'What are you looking for?'

Grace looked up as her mother stood at the study door. 'My birth certificate. I know it's here somewhere because I had to get a copy when I needed a passport for a school trip to France.'

'I didn't know you'd been to France. You've never mentioned it.'

'No…' She'd spent the week before the trip in a state of rising panic. On the surface she'd been just as excited as all the other kids in her class, but deep down she'd known with a cast iron certainty that when she got back everything would have shifted. That it wouldn't be Phoebe, but some stranger from Social Services waiting for her… 'I was sick the morning we were due to leave and couldn't go,' she said.

'That's a pity.'

'It happens…' Then, looking back at the drawer, she saw her name typed on a neat tab and lifted the surprisingly thick folder from its sling, put it on the desk and opened it. 'Good grief.'

'What is it?'

'My entire life, apparently.'

At least everything that related to her life since she'd come into Michael's house. Correspondence with Social Services, the Parental Responsibility Order they'd applied for when she had come to live with them. All those horrible Grace-tries-so-hard-but…end of term school reports.

She'd known a lot of stuff—far more about some things than the other kids—but not in an organised, exam passing way. But she'd shone in art and that had got her a place at the local tech.

And then, at the back, tucked away in plastic wallets, she found her medical card, passport and, finally, her birth certificate.

She took it out, unfolded it on the desk and looked at this public record of who she was. Wondered what a stranger would make of it. Josh, even.

Date and place of birth: 28 July 1980, Duckett's Farm, Little Hinton.

Actually, in a van illegally parked in a field at Duckett's Farm. She'd been told the tale a hundred times. How Grace Duckett, ignoring her husband's fury at having a dozen New Age 'travellers' pull over and set up camp on one of his fields when her mother had gone into labour, had been so generous, so kind that, instead of being called Aurora, a twist on her mother's name, she'd been called Grace after the farmer's wife. As a little girl she'd longed for the exotic Aurora. These days she was deeply grateful to Grace Duckett.

Name: Grace Louise.

She turned to her mother. 'Who was Louise?'

'One of the women in our group. A herbalist. She helped me with your birth.'

'I don't remember her.'

'You wouldn't. She met someone at a music festival and settled down with him in a semi somewhere near Basingstoke.'

'Oh. Right.' She turned back to the document.

Father: Steven Billington, wood-carver.
Mother: Dawn McAllister.

'Did you ever hear from him?' she asked. 'My father? Ever try to find him? For maintenance?'

Her mother shook her head. 'What would have been the point? He'd found someone else, they had a baby and he never did have any money. It hurt, but that's how life is, Grace.' She smiled. 'I loved him enough to let him go.'

As she'd let Phoebe go. And her.

'I can't let Posie go,' she said. 'I've lost so much....'

'I'll stay as long as you need me,' her mother promised. 'Once you're married...'

'It's just a piece of paper,' she said, not even bothering to pretend to her mother.

'For Josh, maybe.' Her mother touched her shoulder. 'You always did light up around him, Grace.'

What could she say? Denying it wouldn't change anything. Or convince her mother.

'It seems indecent to be even thinking of a wedding so soon after burying Michael and Phoebe. Almost like dancing on their graves.'

'The human spirit needs to affirm life at these dark moments, Grace. To celebrate new beginnings. Rebirth.'

'We weren't planning on a celebration. A ten minute in-and-out job at the register office rather than a fertility ceremony,' she replied. Then wished she'd kept her mouth shut. 'Josh has to get back to Australia as quickly as possible. He's just got some big new contract in China.'

'You're not going with him?'

'He'll be all over the place and I've got commitments here. The house. My business...'

'I'll keep the fertility dance on hold for the time being, then.'

'That's probably wise,' Grace replied. 'At least until you've had your hips fixed.'

Her mother laughed out loud at that, then said, 'So? What are you going to wear?'

'Wear? I hadn't thought about it.'

She didn't want to think about it. About the design for a tiny sparkly tiara that she'd drawn years ago and never made. About walking down the aisle in the dream dress on the dream day when she married her dream man.

'It's not important.' And, firmly changing the subject, she said, 'Were you looking for me for something special?'

'Oh, yes.' Her mother opened the book she was holding and handed it to her. 'I've been looking for some way to commemorate Phoebe and Michael. I know a man who carves words into slate stepping stones and I thought maybe a quotation from this one. Elizabeth Barrett Browning...'

Grace recognised it instantly. Had learned it by heart years ago at the height of her teenage infatuation with Josh. She had no need to read it, but closed her eyes and said the words out loud. '"How do I love thee? Let me count the ways..."'

But when she came to the final line, it was Josh who completed the poem.

'"—and, if God choose, I shall but love thee better after death."'

Her eyes flew open and he was there, standing right in front of her, and she swayed towards him.

'Steady,' he said, catching her. 'Standing with your eyes closed can do crazy things to the balance.'

'I'm fine,' she said. She wasn't. But she would be.

'Right.' And after a moment he let go of her. Then, taking the book from her hand, he turned to Dawn. 'That last line. It's perfect.'

'I thought so.'

'You do understand, Dawn? Why we're getting married so quickly.'

'You're giving Posie a family,' she said. 'That's a noble thing, which is entirely different from being solemn about it.' She lifted her hand to his cheek. 'You're allowed to be happy, too.'

'Mum...' Grace warned, afraid she was going to start on her

earth mother, circle of life, fertility thing again. 'I called the registrar, Josh. We need some paperwork. Birth certificates…'

'And?'

'Your decree absolute.'

He nodded. 'I've got them both at home. I'll get Anna to courier them overnight.'

Anna, the personal assistant.

She slammed the door on that thought and said, 'Right. Good. So all we have to do is call in at the register office, present the necessary documents and give sixteen clear days notice of our intention to marry.'

'Sixteen days? I thought maybe a week…'

'Is that going to be too long? Once we've given notice, we have a year in which to go through with it. If it's not convenient, we could wait…'

Josh put down the book and took out his new BlackBerry. 'It's going to be tight. Let's see. It's the twenty-seventh tomorrow…' he checked the diary '…which makes the first available day the twelfth of June. I have to be in Beijing on the fifteenth… It's just do-able. I was coming to London next week for meetings. I've managed to bring them forward.'

'Not too much of an inconvenience then,' she said.

'No…' He made a note, then slipped it back into his pocket.

When he looked up he realised that both Grace and her mother were staring at him.

'I think I'll go and see what Laura is doing,' Dawn said, picking up her book and heading for the door.

Josh didn't take his eyes off Grace.

'I've just been incredibly insensitive, haven't I?'

He'd watched a variety of expressions chase across her face since she'd opened her eyes when he'd finished her poem.

She'd hadn't been this easy to read since she was a girl, he realised. All those years ago, he'd watched her putting on a brave face for Phoebe, but it had been obvious to him that she was scared out of her wits at the prospect of facing a new school. He knew she was right to be scared. Knew how bad it could be for anyone arriving in the middle of the school year when friendship groups had been established.

And she had 'outsider' written all over her.

She was a quick study, though. Maybe it was living in the wild, but she'd been swift to adapt, learning the most acceptable labels to have on her clothes, the right way to fix her hair. And that most vital survival technique—how to keep her feelings under wraps.

Right now there was too much going on. Too many feelings to hide. He'd just had a glimpse of one more loss she was being forced to bear, this time by him.

He wished he could blame his complete boorishness on the fact that he'd retreated to the basement to deal with things that could not be put off. He'd had to reorganise meetings, arrange for busy colleagues to stand in for him, reassure his Chinese partner that he was going to be there to hold his hand at the next round of meetings with the bureaucrats, but it wasn't that.

It was the glow that had lit her up as she'd recited that poem listing every way in which a woman could love a man, knowing that he could have had that if he'd cared about anyone but himself.

'You don't have to answer that,' he said. 'I already know the answer.'

Grace sighed. 'It's all right, Josh. You don't have to pretend with me. We both know that you're only doing this so that I can keep Posie. I'm truly grateful.'

Pretend?

Grateful…

'Dammit, Grace, you don't have to be grateful.'

He turned away, raking his hands through his hair, locking his fingers behind his head to keep them from reaching out to touch her lovely face. From telling her what she truly meant to him. Telling wouldn't do it. He was going to have to show her….

'I'm the one who's grateful and I'll say now what I should

have said earlier.' Then, because some things had to be said face to face, he dropped his hands, turned to look at her. 'You're the mother of my child and I'll do my best, whatever it takes, to make you happy.' And in a gesture that he'd have sworn was completely alien to him but now seemed as natural as breathing, he laid his hand on his heart. 'You have my word.'

She looked up at him, her heart in her eyes. 'Anything?'

It was what, when he'd challenged her, forced her to face reality, he'd demanded of her. He could offer no less.

'Anything,' he affirmed with all the conviction he could muster. Then, rather more gently, 'Tell me, Grace.'

'Well, it's just that I was wondering if we could hold the actual wedding ceremony somewhere other than the register office.' This was so far from what he'd been expecting that he was left floundering for something to say. 'It's where I had to go to register Michael and Phoebe's deaths…'

She faltered, clearly unable to find the words to express what that had done to her.

She didn't have to.

She shouldn't have had to ask. He should have thought, at least discussed it with her.

'I'm sorry, Josh. You've got more than enough on your plate without me being a pathetic wimp about something so unimportant—'

'Don't!' He caught her to him, held her close. 'It's important to you and that makes it important to me. I should have talked this through with you instead of just assuming that because it's the simplest solution it's the right one.'

'But it is. Simple is good. Just…'

'Just not that simple.' He leaned back a little so that he could look at her. So that she could see that he meant what he said. 'It's not a problem. We can have the ceremony wherever you like.'

'Thank you.' Her smile was exactly like the one she'd given him when he'd tossed her his spare crash helmet. Thrown her a lifeline… 'I'm sure we could find somewhere with a licence that isn't all white doves and string quartets,' she added and, with her this close, looking up at him as if he were her white knight, he felt a surge of hope that this could, truly, be more than a paper marriage.

More than hope.

An almost unbearable need to kiss her, show her that if only she would take her courage in both hands, trust him…

Trust. It kept coming back to that. He had asked her to trust him and she had, despite the fact that he'd not walked, but had run from her after that night when she'd given him everything.

He'd told himself that it had been the right thing for her, but it been his own fear, the prospect of his vaunting ambitions being hampered by a girl who needed more than he could ever give that had sent him out into the cold dawn.

Rebuilding the trust that he'd shattered so selfishly would have to be earned with bone-deep commitment. Kisses would have to wait.

'What exactly have you got against doves, Grace?'

'Well,' she began, quite seriously, 'for a start they're not ducks…' Then she shook her head and without warning that smile hit him again. 'You know what I mean.'

'Yes, I know,' he managed. 'Simple.'

'I thought that's what you wanted, too. Especially as you'll be flying off to China the minute the ink's dry on the certificate.'

Josh hadn't thought about what might happen after the event. Now he did. Did she expect them to say their vows and go their separate ways? That he'd have his bag packed and the taxi waiting to take him to the airport? The idea so appalled him that he said, 'Perhaps not the *very* minute. I thought I'd wait until the following morning. Just for appearance's sake,' he added when she started nervously. 'We both know that the wedding is no more than a formality but there's no reason to share that fact with the rest of the world. In fact, I think your mother might have a point.'

'She might?' she squeaked. 'And what point would that be?'

'That there's a fine distinction between a quiet wedding and something that is, to all intents and purposes, invisible.'

Invisible meant the marriage would pass unnoticed. He suddenly discovered that he wanted the entire world to take note. Having always steered well clear of the gossip column lifestyle, right now he'd actively welcome the prospect of a ten-page spread in *Celebrity*.

'We will need two witnesses. And convention suggests I should have a best man. Maybe,' he said, 'Posie would like to be your bridesmaid?'

'My bridesmaid? That would be the person who's supposed to lead me astray on my hen night, help me with my make-up, carry my train and catch the bouquet?'

'You could have one of those, too. Posie is going to need a little help.'

'I don't think so.'

'Don't be a spoilsport. She'd love being dressed up in pink frills.'

'Oh, please,' she said, trying not to laugh, but a giveaway dimple appeared in her cheek. How could he have forgotten that dimple?

'You think pink is too much of a cliché?'

'You don't want to know what I think.'

'You do know that she'll hold it against you. When she's older. Feel deprived. Just ask her...' Then, 'Where is she?'

'Asleep,' Grace said firmly, the dimple back under control. 'I put her upstairs after lunch so that she wouldn't be disturbed.' Right on cue, there was a gurgle from the baby monitor sitting on the desk. 'Was asleep,' she said. 'I have to go.'

He caught her hand. 'Leave the wedding arrangements to me, Grace. I'll organise everything.'

'I thought you had to be in London all next week for meetings?'

'All you'll have to think about is what you're going to wear,' he said. 'I promise.'

'No problem. I'll have that navy-blue trouser suit cleaned. It'll be perfect.'

CHAPTER TEN

FOR a moment Josh actually believed her. Then Grace laughed and said, 'I'm going to give Posie a bath before teatime. You can be in charge of the plastic ducks if you promise not to say another word about her being a bridesmaid.'

'You asking me to help?'

'You've already proved yourself in the nappy department. Bathing is next on the agenda. If you can spare the time?'

'Yes... Thank you.'

'Save your thanks until afterwards.'

'How hard can it be?' he said with a flippancy that earned him another smile. One that suggested he'd just said something very foolish. That was okay. Making a fool of himself would be a small price to pay for raising one of her precious smiles.

Actually, it wasn't that difficult. Between them, Grace and Posie made short work of cutting him down to size.

'You undress her while I run the bath,' Grace said.

Easier said than done. He was still wrestling with a minute vest when Grace came looking for him.

'The water's going cold while you two are playing,' she said, leaning against the door, apparently enjoying the spectacle of him reduced to a wreck by an infant.

'I'm not playing,' he protested. Playing he could do. 'It's Posie.' Then, 'No. It's me.' His hands were too big and Posie was so small, her skin so delicate. 'She's so tiny.'

'Oh, please. She's a great big hulk,' Grace said, picking her up with the confidence of practice. Kissing her, then gently tugging the little vest over her head, pausing for a quick peekaboo, before pulling it free, then kissing her again. 'You should have seen her when she was first born,' she said, then looked away, clearly afraid that she'd said something hurtful.

'I wish I had been, too, Grace.' Been there at the birth to hold her hand, do whatever it was that useless men did while the women they loved suffered to give them sons, daughters. Except that would never have happened. He'd have been the outsider, excluded, while Phoebe and Michael supported her through the birth.

She put a hand on his arm, rubbed it gently in a gesture of comfort. 'The first time Phoebe let me bath Posie I was certain I was going to drop her.'

And in that one brief phrase—'Phoebe let me'—she told him that she knew. Understood.

'It's just a question of holding gently but firmly,' she went on as if she'd said nothing of importance. 'Come on. You'll soon learn.'

The small baby bath was on a low stand and Grace sat on a stool with Posie on her lap. She gently washed her face and only then did she lower the baby into the water. Posie immediately went rigid with excitement, then drew back her little legs and kicked.

Water erupted over the end of the bath, where he was poised with a bright yellow plastic duck, hitting him full in the chest.

Posie screamed with pleasure and, while he was looking down at the damage, she did it again, this time showering his head.

He was kneeling in water, was soaked to the skin and his hair was dripping down his back. It was the second time that day he'd been soaked. The second time that they had been laughing together.

Half an hour later he left a smiling, composed Posie, dressed in a tiny white T-shirt and soft blue overalls, in complete command of the nursery while he retreated, dripping, to the basement. Dripping but wrapped in the warmth of the towel Grace had taken from the heated rail and draped around his neck.

'You'll soon get the hang of it,' she said, and he felt like the victor at some ancient games who'd just been garlanded with laurels. 'Next time you'll be ready for her.'

Personally, he didn't care how wet he got if he could be shoulder to shoulder with Grace as, together, they'd bathed their baby.

The undercurrent of tension that had seemed to stretch to breaking point since he'd been home had completely evaporated in the splashing, the laughter, the play of Posie's bath time.

'Ready for her? You mean, you knew that this was going to happen?' He indicated his sodden T-shirt and trousers.

'Why do you think I chose the end that doesn't kick?'

'Oh, I see.' He bent to tickle Posie, who was sitting like a little princess in the crook of her mother's arm, to kiss her downy head. 'I think your mummy set me up.'

'It's a rite of passage,' Grace said, still laughing, as he straightened. Then, as he looked down at her, the laughter died away and in that instant it was as if the last ten years had never happened. They were both still young, untouched, with all their dreams intact.

He was twenty-one, about to embark on the greatest adventure of his life so far, skirting around unsettling feelings for this girl he'd watched out for ever since she'd arrived in his life. A girl who'd come downstairs to bring him a pair of cufflinks she'd made for him, to say goodbye. Except they hadn't been able to say goodbye. Instead, her huge green eyes had provoked an explosive, straight-to-hell physical response that neither of them had had the will or desire to resist.

Her green eyes had that same look now and the effect was, if anything, more devastating. But older, just a touch wiser, he recognised it for what it was. Need, fear of change, of losing someone you care for—only this time it was not him she was afraid of losing, but Posie. And he stepped back, turned away before he embarrassed them both.

Dawn met him as he crossed the hall. 'I was going to ask you how you got on, but I can see,' she said, laughing. 'You're having a very wet day.'

'I'm not complaining,' he said, pulling the towel from around his neck and rubbing at his hair.

'Seize every moment, Josh. They grow up far too quickly.' Then, 'Your mother was talking about ringing an agency to engage a nanny.'

'A wedding planner would be more use right now.' Then, 'No, forget I said that. Grace wants simple.'

'I thought you had simple,' she said.

'Simple,' he said, 'but more complicated.' Then, hearing Grace at the top of the stairs, 'Let's go into the sitting room,' he said. 'Can I get you a drink?'

'I don't,' she reminded him. 'But you go ahead.'

He poured himself a Scotch, sat on the leather footstool that wouldn't suffer from his damp clothes.

'Grace isn't happy with the idea of having the ceremony at the register office,' he said. 'It has too many negative associations. And, since we've decided to invite a few more people, we're going to need somewhere that can provide lunch.' Actually, that was his idea, but she hadn't out-and-out vetoed it. 'Any thoughts?'

'To be honest, Josh, very few of the people I know actually bother with the paperwork. I didn't myself.'

Her sigh was, he thought, unconscious.

'Do you regret that?'

'Maybe. Not that it would have made any difference. Once a man's eyes begin to wander there isn't enough paper and ink in the world to keep him from following them. I wish he'd made an effort to keep in touch with the girls.'

'It must have been hard for you.'

He found it difficult to imagine this slender woman taking on a bunch of thugs who'd been hell-bent on destroying her home. But that must have been easy compared with giving up her precious girls so that they'd have a more settled life than the one she'd chosen for herself.

'I managed. Mostly.' She smiled. 'It's different for the two of you, of course. You're marrying to give Posie a family.'

'I thought it would make adoption simpler, especially in view of the fact that we live in different hemispheres.'

'Maybe that's the problem you need to address,' she said, giving him a very straight look.

'We both have commitments, Dawn,' he said, staring into the glass he was holding as if that somehow held the answer. 'Maybe later…'

'So what's the rush to get married?' She tilted her head to one side, looking for all the world like a small, brightly plumaged bird. 'What are you afraid of, Josh?'

'Of losing her.' The words slipped out. He hadn't intended to say them, but there it was. Plain and honest.

'Posie? Or Grace?'

'Both of them.' He glanced up. 'You do know that she's Posie's natural mother?'

'Not just the shell, but the egg, too? How generous. I'm so proud of her.'

'You raised an amazing daughter, but one who, right now, has no legal rights as far as Posie is concerned. Michael named me as Posie's guardian in his will.'

'And why would he do that?'

'Because Posie is my biological daughter, too, Dawn. Michael had problems of his own…'

'I see.'

'Do you? I'm doing what I can to give Grace a legal right to her own child.'

'While protecting your own?'

'You think that's selfish?'

'I think it's a very natural instinct,' she said, which didn't answer his question. Or maybe it did. Maybe instinct, the urge to survive was, at heart, selfishness. 'But thank you for telling me. It explains a great deal.' She tilted her head again. 'Although not, perhaps, everything.'

'Everything is, for the moment, beyond me, Dawn. I'm adrift. I can't cry. I feel guilty when I forget for a moment…' He looked up. 'Guilty for not being here. If it wasn't for Grace and Posie…'

'Love is the most powerful emotion there is, Josh.'

Love?

'It gives us the strength to hold on long after reason suggests that all is lost. The courage to let go when it feels as if you're tearing your heart out.'

'I let go once. I convinced myself that it was the right decision but I've come to realise that it was a mistake.'

Was he making a mistake now? Still being ruled by that selfish gene?

'How do you know?' he asked. 'How can you tell?'

'Ask yourself who will gain most from the choice you make. Who will be hurt. Whose happiness you truly care about.'

'It's that easy?' he said with a wry smile.

'I didn't say it was easy. Being honest with yourself is the hardest thing in the world. But if you truly love someone, you'll have the courage to face the truth.' Then, 'But you wanted me to help you find somewhere for the wedding. Why don't you go and get into some dry clothes while I take a look at the local paper? That might give me some ideas.'

'You won't mention any of this to Grace? I told her that all she'd have to do was turn up and say "I do",' he said, getting up, then moving to help her as she struggled to get off the sofa.

'Wretched hip,' she muttered.

'How bad is it?'

'A bit like Melchester Castle. A crumbling ruin.' Then, waving away his concern, 'Did you know that they hold weddings there?'

'In the ruin?'

She gave him a look that he recognised. Grace didn't look much like her mother, but that cool, please concentrate, I'm being serious, look was familiar from a hundred teasing exchanges.

How he'd missed that.

Missed her.

'I know they hold those big glossy affairs in the manor house that was built much later,' he said hurriedly.

'They also have a folly—a mini Greek temple affair—that overlooks the lake. I believe they hold less formal weddings there. I'll make some enquiries.' Then, 'And, to answer your question, no, I won't mention this to Grace. She's just about holding herself together for Posie. Anything that feels like a celebration is beyond her.'

'I can understand that. At least she was here…'

'That was not your fault, Josh. You'll honour Michael and Phoebe's memory far more by bringing up his daughter than by standing in church, singing hymns.' Then, patting his hand, 'It's hard when you're young. Everything is so sharply defined. Right, wrong. Black, white. Pleasure, pain. As you get older you realise that life is mostly a greyish muddle and the best you can do is embrace each moment, learn each lesson and move on.'

'Easier said than done.'

'You can't change anything that's happened. Regret is futile. Only the future matters.'

'I wish there was more time but I don't know when I'll get back and I don't want to leave Grace in limbo. I want her to feel safe.'

'Don't worry. Between us we'll make it as painless as possible. Give her a wedding that at the moment she can't allow herself to believe she has a right to enjoy.'

'Thank you. I'll arrange a credit card for you, Dawn. Do whatever you think best. Invite whoever you think she'd want to be there. Just—'

'Keep it simple.'

'Actually, I was going to ask you to make sure my mother doesn't get carried away.'

'Don't worry, I won't let her sell the exclusive to *Celebrity*.'

He managed a smile.

He'd never given Dawn much thought in the past but now he thought he was going to like her rather a lot. Then, remembering Grace's very specific reservations, 'And absolutely no string quartets or doves.'

Josh had been dreaming. It was the same dream that had haunted him for years. Grace, sensuous, silky, fragrant and forever—tormentingly—out of reach.

He'd come awake with a start and for a moment he just lay there, almost awake, not sure where he was.

Then his memory kicked in and the past week came rushing back like a news bulletin that he couldn't switch off. The loss of his brother, the discovery that Posie was not only his daughter, but Grace's, too.

The first small steps towards reconciliation with his mother. He wouldn't let one more night pass without making his peace with his father.

Now he had to face something bigger. His marriage to Grace. The fact that in two weeks she would make a vow that tied her to him. That she would be coming to him, not as a bride should in a once-in-a-lifetime gown, a delicate tiara sparkling like raindrops in her elfin hair as she walked towards him down the flower-decked aisle of the local church, but in a ten-minute ceremony in some mock Greek temple.

Not with her heart in her hands, but to be tied to him by a paper marriage because there was no other way she could keep her baby.

His in name, but still forever out of reach.

He threw back the sheet, sat on the side of the bed, his face in his hands.

As he'd walked back from the lawyer's office, everything had seemed so simple. He and Grace would get married, they would bring Posie up together. She had, after all, said she'd do anything and he'd hoped, believed that their baby would bring them together.

And then he'd walked into her workshop and she'd been wrapped around the guy she'd brought to dinner the last time he'd been home.

Funny, attentive, too good-looking by half, he'd known then that Toby Makepeace was the man who was going to take Grace from him once and for all.

He'd told himself, as he'd flown away, his heart like lead in his chest, that all he wanted was for her to be happy. Had waited, expecting every phone call, every e-mail from Michael to tell him that they were engaged.

Instead, he'd got a phone call from Michael telling him that Grace was going to act as a surrogate mother for Phoebe. The unspoken subtext a silent reminder that he had sworn to keep his role in that pregnancy a secret.

In his desperation, knowing that she was carrying his child, he'd clung to the one small crumb of comfort in the whole business—that if she'd loved Toby Makepeace, it would have been his baby she would have wanted. Taking reassurance from the fact that when she had Mr Perfect at her feet, Grace had still been looking for something more and there was still hope that one day she'd look up and see him, waiting for her, to let go of the side of the pool, cast off, swim out of her depth to join him...

He'd never truly understood her fear. Only now began to have a glimmer of why, after a childhood spent being dragged around by her hippie mother, Grace had clung to this house as her rock, her refuge.

He, on the other hand, had begun life with certainty only to have it ripped out from under him. He didn't cling, didn't believe in roots put down by other people, but instead had

spent every day since his parents deserted him plotting his
escape, eager to travel the globe, build his own world. One
that no one could ever take from him.

He'd thought he had that. Had everything.

He got up, pulled on tracksuit bottoms, a T-shirt, needing
air. But, as he came up from the basement and heard Posie's
thin wail float down the stairs, he knew that he'd been fooling
himself. That the universe was nothing beside the power of a
love you would gladly die for and he took the stairs to the nursery two at a time.

The only light spilled in through the doorway, gleaming off
the thin silky wrap that floated above her bare feet, giving a
glimpse of ankle as Grace turned to look at him. He quickly
looked up but her face was in the shadows, all dark hollows
around her eyes, in her cheeks that told of nights without sleep.

'Josh… I'm sorry if we disturbed you.'

'No. I was awake. How long have you been up?'

She shook her head. 'I don't know. Half an hour, maybe
longer. I thought she was hungry….'

She was trying to coax the baby with a bottle but Posie,
fractious, turned away, refusing to take it and all he could
think was that he must do something.

Be a father.

'What can I do?'

Grace shook her head. 'I don't know. I was just about to
go and wake my mother.'

'You're that worried?' He moved closer.

'She had two of us. She's got to know more than me.'

'Let me take her for a while.'

She surrendered Posie without an argument and he laid the
infant against his shoulder where she clung to him, snuffling and
nuzzling into his neck like a tiny puppy, for a moment quiet. Then
she pulled away and resumed her miserable little grizzle.

Grace hadn't moved. 'Do you think she might be sick?
Maybe we should call the doctor?'

We.

Such a small word to mean so much.

He felt Posie's cheeks. 'She's not hot,' he said. 'I think she' just like the rest of us. Feeling the strain. In need of comfort.

'Who isn't?' she snapped, then, as he put his arm around her, she collapsed against his other shoulder and for a moment with both arms full—even if both shoulders were getting wet—his world seemed complete. 'I don't know what to do!

He rubbed his hand against her back, feeling the warmth of her skin through the thin silk. Silk?

'Where's Phoebe's robe?' he asked. Grace was a couple o sizes smaller than her sister, even with the fuller curves tha motherhood had given her, and this soft, silky robe tied loosely about her luscious body was out of an entirely different wardrobe.

'In the wash.'

Guilt welled up in Grace. If she'd been more careful….

'You did warn me,' she said, pulling free of the comfort o his arm. Comfort she didn't deserve. Then, palming away tears that were clinging to her lashes, 'I'm sorry. I'm trying so hard to hold it together, but I hadn't realised what it was like. Being a mother, totally responsible for a precious life has nothing to do with whose egg made the baby, or even giving birth. This is what's real….'

'I know, Grace. I'm here.'

'You're here now,' she said. 'But what about next month? Next year…?'

It wasn't fair, she knew that, but she'd been struggling to settle Posie for what seemed like forever and was at her wits' end.

'I used to lie awake upstairs, listening to Posie cry in the night, and I actually envied my sister,' she confessed. 'I wanted to be the one to go to Posie, pick her up, comfort her.'

'That's perfectly natural, Grace.'

'No. You were right. I should have gone away.' She looked up at him. 'I saw the fear in Phoebe's eyes. Every time I picked her up. That's why I did everything I could to get the paperwork through so quickly.' She sighed. 'Be careful what you wish for, Josh.'

'You did not wish for this.'

'No.' She hadn't wished for this. 'I had no idea how alone new parents must feel. How frightened. She's so little, Josh. So vulnerable…'

'Hush…' For a moment she wasn't sure whether he was talking to the baby or to her. 'Try to relax—'

'Relax!' She shook her head. The baby was picking up her tension, they both knew it. 'I'm sorry. Shouting at you won't help.'

'Maybe we all need a good shout,' he said. 'But not right at this moment.' He lifted the baby from his shoulder, held her for a moment, kissed her head, then laid her in the crook of his arm and, taking the feeder from her, offered it to Posie.

She turned her head away.

'She won't take this, Grace.' Then, 'Maybe you should try feeding her yourself.'

'No…' She swallowed. 'No, Josh, I couldn't.'

Even as she said it, Posie started to grizzle again and, without saying another word, Josh took her hand and led her from the nursery and into her own bedroom.

'She wouldn't…'

'Just try,' he said.

'For Posie?' If it was for Posie, she could do it.

'For Posie. And for you, Grace.'

He pulled at the knot tying her robe and the silk slithered from her shoulders, leaving her standing in a thin nightgown that clung to her breasts, her legs, and she felt naked, exposed, in a way she hadn't on the night they'd made love and she let slip a little cry. Anguish. Heartache. Longing…

'Will you trust me?' he asked.

She looked up at him. With his tousled hair, the dark stubble of his chin, he didn't look like any baby guru, but yes, she would trust him with her life. He had been—was still—her hero. Her white knight. And she sat on the edge of the bed, eased herself back against the pillows.

'Ready?'

As soon as he'd laid the baby in her arms she began to cry and Grace instantly tensed again.

'Forget Posie,' he said, sitting on the edge of the bed, turning to her. 'Just relax. Let your shoulders drop.'

But she was shaking. Afraid. 'What if I can't do it?'

'You can.' And he laid his warm hands on her shoulders and began to gently knead the tension from knotted muscles, soothing, relaxing her so that her breathing became easier and the shivering stopped.

'Trust me,' he said, briefly laying his hand against her cheek, before letting it slide down her neck, slip beneath the thin strap of her nightgown.

She tried to speak, to protest, but the only sound that emerged was a tiny squeak from the back of her throat. The truth was that she couldn't have done or said a word to stop him. Didn't want to stop him….

Josh held his breath, knowing that they were both on the precipice of something special. Keeping his eyes fixed firmly on her face. She was wearing something soft, silky with narrow straps and he slipped one over her shoulder, let his hand slide down over the full, soft mound of her breast where once her nipple had hardened eagerly for him, as if begging for his touch.

But this was not a girl's breast. Not the small, high breast that tormented his dreams. It was full, womanly, filled his hand as he lifted it, bent to kiss it.

'Please…'

'Anything,' he said, his eyes never leaving hers, 'you said you would do anything.' And, seized by some atavistic need to make his own mark, he touched his tongue to her nipple.

It leapt in response and, feeling like some great hunter bringing home food for his tribe, he offered it to his baby.

Grace gasped as Posie's eager mouth found her nipple, fastened on. Groaned as she began to suckle and Josh, not knowing whether it was pain or joy that sent the tears cascading down her cheeks, took her face between his hands, brushing them away with his thumbs.

'This is for Posie, Grace,' he said, kissing each of her cheeks, tasting the salt on his lips. 'For your baby. Our baby.' And he silently swore to cherish them both for the rest of his life.

Grace, feeling closer to being a mother than she had since the cord had been cut, looked down at her baby who, eyes closed in ecstasy, fed with serene contentment.

'Well?' Josh asked.

'Very well...' She palmed away the stupid tears and smiled. 'How did you know?'

'Just call me Mr Spock,' he said.

'I think you mean *Dr* Spock,' she said, catching her lower lip to stop herself from laughing. And then she knew he'd done it deliberately, just as he had when she was still a kid and he was halfway to being a man. He'd always known what to do. When her dog had died, it was Josh who'd dug a grave for him at the bottom of the garden. Who'd carved his name into a piece of wood and hammered it into the ground. 'Thank you, Josh. I don't know what I'd have done without you.'

He touched her cheek. 'You'd have figured it out.' Then, 'Can I go and make you something to drink? Something milky to help you sleep?'

'I'll be fine now. But you must be exhausted,' she said, shuffling up to make more room beside her. 'Put your feet up.'

'I don't need much sleep,' he said, but he settled down beside her. 'I got up for some air. I'm used to being outside.'

'In your penthouse? On top of a skyscraper?' she teased.

'It has a deck.'

'Oh.'

'And a pool.'

'For goldfish?'

'For swimming.'

'Ouch.'

'No. You're right. It's wasted on me. I'm never there,' he said. He was never anywhere….

Posie stopped suckling, looked sleepily up at her. 'Had enough, baby?' she asked.

Her mouth began to work and Grace turned her round, jumped as she latched on to her other breast.

'Does that hurt?'

Her laugh was slightly shaky. 'Not hurt, but it does take your breath away for a moment or two. She's very strong.'

'I'm sure your mother would have something to say on the subject of the life force.'

Grace smiled. 'My mother has a lot to say about almost everything.'

Whereas Josh…

'I suppose you let friends use it when you're not there. The pool?' she said.

He glanced at her. 'Why would you think that?'

'Isn't that what people do?'

'Not if they've got an atom of sense,' he assured her. 'Besides, most of my friends have pools of their own.'

'In that case, maybe you should do something about your security because someone was there when I tried to get you on the phone.'

He frowned.

'Anna Carling?' she prompted. 'Your personal assistant?'

'Anna? Oh, right.'

Wrong, wrong, wrong!

'She wasn't actually in my apartment. My number is diverted to hers when I'm away.' Then, looking at her, 'Has that been bothering you?'

'No,' she said, much too quickly.

'She's a married woman, Grace.'

'Really?' And since when did that make any difference…?

'Married, with three grown-up kids and at least two grandchildren.'

'She didn't sound that old.'

'Grace?' When she wouldn't look at him, he leaned forward. 'You didn't think…'

'Stop it.'

'Of course you did.'

He was grinning while she was blushing like a girl. It wasn't as if she had any right to feel jealous, but when had that ever stopped her? She might have pitied the girls who Josh had dated way back when, but that hadn't stopped her hating every minute of every night he had been out with each one of them.

'You've never talked much about your life in Australia, Josh. Where you live. Your friends. Only about your work.'

'It's been my all-consuming passion,' he said.

'You've really never found anyone?'

'I found a lot of someones. They all suffered from the same problem.' He leaned across and kissed the frown from her forehead. 'They weren't you,' he said, yawning, settling lower into the bed. He muttered something else, then turned towards her, so that the entire length of his body, relaxed and fluid, seemed to mould itself to hers. His face against her naked breast, Posie's toes against his chin.

'Josh?' She stared down at him. His eyes were closed, but he couldn't be asleep. Not just like that. 'What did you say?'

No response. Jet lag had finally caught up with him and it would be cruel to disturb him. Instead, she turned to Posie. Her little girl was asleep, too, and she eased herself from beside Josh, put her back in her cot. Stood over her for a while before going back to bed.

Josh was dreaming again. It was the same dream that had haunted him for years. Grace, sensuous, silky, fragrant and forever—tormentingly—out of reach.

He turned, trying to escape the image, but it only made things worse. The scent so familiar, but warmer, closer. And the silky body so real beneath his hand that he could feel the slow beat of her pulse.

He opened his eyes and discovered that dreams really did come true. He was lying beside his sleeping love, his arm draped over her waist, her lips temptingly within kissing distance.

He resisted that temptation, knowing that once he kissed her she'd wake up, and this was a moment he never wanted to end. Then Posie woke and Grace opened her eyes.

Grace woke to the sound of Posie shouting joyfully from the nursery to let her know that it was time to get up. She lay for a moment, relishing the pleasure of a warm bed, the fact that she'd slept soundly, that the only weight pinning her down was Josh's hand on her hip.

Josh's hand.

And then she remembered.

What Josh had done. How, last night, when she'd been in despair, Josh had been there. Had made her truly a mother....

Had fallen asleep beside her.

She opened her eyes to look at him, only to find that he was watching her. That he hadn't just fallen asleep, but that he had stayed with her.

'Thank you,' she said.

He didn't answer, just gave her the sweetest kiss. A close-your-eyes-and-feel-the-tingle-in-your-toes kind of kiss. A first-kiss kind of kiss that was making her body do giddy little loop-the-loops.

And she knew that was where they had gone wrong. They hadn't started at the beginning but had gone for no-holds-barred, straight-to-hell passion. From here to eternity in one night. No words, all action.

He eased away to look at her. 'This is nice. Maybe we can do it again very soon?'

Now. Her body was screaming now and he was close

enough for her to be aware that he was heading the same way. But she wasn't making the same mistake again and, lifting her hand to his lips, she said, 'We need to talk, Josh. I have a thousand things to tell you.'

Or maybe only one....

'Now?'

Posie was shouting for attention and then her mother called up the stairs to let Josh know that his driver had arrived to take him to London. Even so, she knew that if she'd said yes, now, he would have stayed right where he was. But then there would be no conversation.

'It will keep,' she said. And then she returned his kiss with a sweet, soft touch of her lips to his. A promise that she would be waiting. Always.

CHAPTER ELEVEN

'YOU'RE getting married, Grace. I know you want a quiet, simple wedding and we all respect that, but you do have to have a new dress and the wedding is the day after tomorrow.'

'That's plenty of time to buy a dress.'

Grace saw her mother and Laura Kingsley exchange meaningful looks. Whoever would have thought those two would become bosom buddies? Arranging a wedding made strange bedfellows.

The thought made her smile.

'We had a look in that boutique in the craft centre the other day,' Laura said casually.

'The one next to the aromatherapy place. I needed some lavender oil,' her mother added, as if to establish the fact that they hadn't actually been *looking* for a dress.

'Yes?'

'Gorgeous clothes,' Laura said. 'I fell in love with a jacket. I think I might go back and get it today.' Then, 'They had a beautiful dress in your size.'

'Really? I didn't know they did large sizes…'

'Layers of different fabrics cut asymmetrically,' her mother continued, ignoring her attempt to distract them, force them into reassuring her that she wasn't fat.

'Simple but very stylish,' Laura added.

They made a great double act.

'Stylish sounds good,' she said, playing along. 'What colour?'

'It was cream.'

'Cream? Outsize and frumpy, then.'

'Did you have any particular colour in mind?' Laura asked, and she just knew that the pair of them had been through every shop in Maybridge and, whatever she said, they'd have an answer.

'I always thought that if I ever got married, I'd wear one of Geena Wagner's designs,' she said absently. 'She has a small showroom in a department store in Melchester, but her workroom is in the craft centre. She commissions me to make the tiaras to match her gowns. Have you seen her work, Laura?' Josh's mother was a fashion plate and probably knew every hot designer who could stitch a seam. 'She uses appliqué, embroidery and beading to stunning effect. One of her dresses was featured in a spread in *Celebrity* last year,' she added. 'With one of my tiaras.'

'Yes…' Laura cleared her throat. 'I believe I saw it. Quite lovely. But I think you've left it a little late to go for a hand-made designer dress.'

'She's a friend. And I wasn't thinking of anything elaborate. A simple ankle-length column dress with one of those little jackets that just covers the shoulders and arms?'

'Even so. These things take months…' Then, 'If you don't like cream—and I admit it can be very draining—what about peach? We did see something in peach, didn't we, Dawn?'

'Not white, you think?' Grace interjected, all innocence.

'Grace…' Her mother's eyes narrowed as she belatedly twigged to the fact that they were being teased.

'Sorry. I couldn't resist.'

Laura was looking from one to the other. 'Am I missing something?'

'I called Geena last week, Laura. When I went to check that Abby was still managing without me.' Which she was. Brilliantly.

It was the day she'd woken in Josh's arms and she'd known that they weren't just going to have a wedding, but a marriage.

They still had to talk, but she'd known, deep in her heart, that after that night, after what he'd done for her, it would never be just a marriage on paper. And she wanted, when she stood beside him and said the words that would make them man and wife, to show him that it really meant something to her. Wanted it to be a day that neither of them would ever forget.

'I'm going for a fitting today. In fact,' she said, making a point of looking at her watch, 'if you can be ready in twenty minutes, you can come with me.'

There was a moment of stunned silence and then a frantic scramble as the pair of them rushed to change. Well, Laura rushed. Her mother was slower, but just as determined.

She was still grinning to herself when the phone rang and she picked it up, knowing it would be Josh. He'd phoned her morning, noon and night while he'd been in London. He was later today.

'You're late this morning. Did you oversleep?' she asked, without preamble.

'I had an early meeting and didn't want to call you before six.'

'Good decision. How are you?'

'Busy. Lonely without my little girl. How is she?'

'Thriving. Sleeping through without any problems now.'

'Good. And the grannies?'

'I'm not asking and they're not telling, but your credit card—or maybe it's Laura—appears to have totally corrupted my mother.'

'I'm delighted to hear it. Sufficiently to give up her principles about jumping the queue and allowing me to pay for her hip replacement, do you think?'

'Oh, Josh…'

'I have to go, Grace. I'll call you later.'

'Later,' she repeated, but was talking to the dialling tone.

Josh smiled as he shut off his cellphone, pushing open the door to the kind of jewellery store that had been beyond his wildest dreams when he'd bought that first ring for Grace.

Something unusual, antique, he thought. Emeralds to match her eyes....

He'd just handed over his credit card when his phone rang.

Still haunted by the thought that he might have missed a call from Michael, missing Grace's call, he moved away from the desk to check the caller.

It was his Chinese partner calling from Beijing. He let the call go to voicemail while he punched in his pin code. He wasn't due back in Maybridge until tomorrow, but he planned to surprise Grace, take her out, ask her to marry him. Be his wife.

'Congratulations, sir. I hope you'll be very happy,' the jeweller said as he handed him the ring.

His smile lasted until he was in the back of his limousine, when he listened to the frantic voicemail, the you-have-to-be-here-tomorrow bureaucratic foul-up that he couldn't ignore. It was his responsibility and his alone. He'd signed a contract. There were billions of dollars, thousands of jobs at stake.

He could call Grace, explain, put off the wedding until he could get back. She'd understand. But what would it be next time? How long would it be before he could get back to see Posie again? Months. She'd have grown, changed, forgotten him. And that was how it would be through all the years. He wouldn't be a father, or a husband in anything but name. He'd be the stranger who turned up once in a blue moon, when it fitted in with his plans.

And he thought about what Dawn had told him to ask him—

self. Who gained, who would be hurt by the choices he made? But it was the latter that was important. Whose happiness you truly cared about.

He didn't, he discovered, have to agonise over that one. He knew.

It was late, long after Josh would normally have phoned, when a courier arrived with a package addressed to Grace and she knew—just knew—that whatever it contained she didn't want to know.

She shut herself in the study and opened the envelope. The letter inside was handwritten, brief and to the point:

Grace,

By the time you receive this I will be on my way to Beijing. It seems that you were right all along. I was fitting in our wedding, not because I was making time for it, but because it fitted in with my own schedule, just as I would fit Posie into my life.

I asked your mother how you knew what was the right to decision to make. She told me that if I was honest with myself it would be clear. It's time to be honest and admit that my life is not one that lends itself to either marriage or fatherhood. Posie is your child in every conceivable way and it is right and proper that you should have full care of her.

Enclosed with this letter you will find a copy of my instructions to Michael's lawyer that he should apply to the courts for a Parental Responsibility Order on your behalf. If you wish, later, to formally adopt Posie, I will make no objection.

I will, of course, stand by my agreement to buy the house once Probate is granted. Arrangements have also been made for the estate to pay a maintenance allowance

for Posie and you as her carer, as well as any other necessary expenses.

I have no idea when I will return to Sydney, but if you
need any further help in the future please contact Anna
Carling. She has been instructed to treat any request
from you as if it were my own.

Yours, Josh

'Why?' She waved the letter at her mother. 'Why is he
doing this? What did you say to him?'

Her mother said nothing.

Laura looked as if she might say something but, when
Grace turned on her, she shook her head. Then, 'He was
marrying you to keep Posie? Why would he do that?'

'Because she is his daughter, Laura. Our daughter. My
egg, his sperm…'

'Oh.' Then, 'But…' She shook her head. 'I don't understand any of it.'

'I think I do,' her mother said. 'It's a sacrifice move.'

'Sacrifice?'

'He's giving her up, surrendering her to you.'

'What?'

'We talked about it. About love. The choices you make.
Holding on. Letting go. Whether you loved enough to let go
even when it felt like tearing your heart out of your body.'
Then, 'I think he just did that, Grace. Tore out his heart and
gave it to you.'

Grace said something completely out of character. 'He's
giving up his daughter just because he had to fly off to Beijing
and sort out some emergency and miss a ten minute ceremony
in a *folly*? What kind of idiot is he?'

'I'm sorry. It never occurred to me… I thought…'

She shook her head. 'No, Mum, this isn't your fault. It's
mine. I kept telling him he wasn't committed, that he'd never

be here for Posie, when I should have been telling him that I love him.' She got up, walked to the phone. Picked it up. 'Clinging to my safe little nest instead of telling him that wherever he was I wanted to be, too.'

'Who are you calling?'

She stared at the phone. 'Good point. Who do you call when you want to book an airline ticket?'

'The Internet?'

'Right.'

'Where are you going?' Laura asked.

'Where do you think? Bei-flipping-jing.'

'Why don't you let me do that?' her mother said, taking the phone from her and replacing it. 'While you go and pack.'

'Two seats,' she said, backing out of the room. 'Or what-ever they have for babies. On the first available flight.'

Her mother, flipping through the telephone directory, stopped. 'You can't take Posie.'

'I have to. I'm breastfeeding…'

'But you haven't got a passport for her.'

For a moment the world seemed to stand still. Then she said, 'Phoebe had. They were going to France this summer…'

Josh swiped the key to his suite and walked in, desperate for a shower, a drink, sleep.

It was finally sorted. Something or nothing that would have been fixed in ten minutes in Australia had required delicate diplomacy, tact, face-saving manoeuvres, when one phrase in a contract had been incorrectly translated.

He opened the mini-bar, took out a Scotch, put it back and took out a bottle of water instead.

His body was in enough trouble without adding alcohol to the mix.

He tossed his jacket on the sofa, loosened his tie, opened the bedroom door and stopped. When he'd left it, this room ad contained nothing except the carry-on grip he used when travelling.

Now there was a bright pink holdall, a box of disposable nappies, a very familiar buggy and a cot had been set up at he foot of the bed. The cot contained a sleeping Posie and in he bed Grace lay, fully dressed, flat on her back with her arms hrown out.

Grace?

It couldn't be. The longing, the need, the unbelievable oneliness were inducing hallucinations.

He closed his eyes. Opened them again. She was still there out, needing to convince himself that she was real, he put out a hand and very gently, so as not to wake her, touched her cheek. Then kissed her just as gently.

No illusion, but warm, real flesh.

Grace, who never went anywhere, who had made herself sick rather than go on a school trip to France, had flown half-way round the world to… What? He'd given her everything she wanted.

He turned to Posie. She was lying exactly like her mother. Flat on her back, arms flung wide.

He didn't think he could bear it.

He wanted to hold them both, tell them how much he'd missed them, how much he loved them. But he'd made his decision and, leaving them to sleep, he shut himself in the bathroom, showered as quietly as he could, half expecting that when he opened the door, they would have disap-peared.

He was half right. Posie was still asleep, but the bed was empty and he walked through to the living room where Grace was signing the bill for room service.

'I tried not to wake you,' he said.

'Kissing a girl when you've got a beard is not something

you can do without repercussions, Josh,' she said, as sh
poured two cups of tea. Helped herself to a sandwich.

'You're not giving me much of an incentive to shave it off
Grace. I thought you'd be asleep for hours. Why are yo
here?'

'You have to ask? You bailed out on our talk, Josh. Th
one we were going to have about the future, about us. An
you bailed out on our wedding, too. Okay. It happens. Yo
walked out on me after the most incredible, most perfec
night of my life and I should have been ready for you to cu
and run again.'

Perfect?

'If it had just been me,' Grace went on, 'I could hav
lived with it. I've lived without the man I love for ten year
so the rest of my life would be a breeze. But I'm here to tel
you that I don't believe you'd run out on your daughter
Joshua Kingsley.'

'Ten years?' He shook his head. That didn't make sense
The fact that she was here didn't make sense. 'I did what
thought was for the best, Grace,' he said.

'I'm here to tell you that you're wrong. And that I'm reall
tired of you leaving before the credits have rolled. Before
can tell you that I love you. That I've always loved you. You'r
an impossible act to follow, Josh Kingsley.'

There. She'd said it. It was over. And, right on cue, Posi
woke up and began to chatter to herself.

'Your daughter is awake, Josh,' she said, getting up an
walking back into the bedroom. 'I've left a couple o
feeders of breast milk in the fridge to keep you going unti
you can buy some formula and there are enough nappies t
keep you going for a day or two. Anna is interviewing
nannies.' She picked up the pink holdall and began to wal
to the door.

'Grace?'

She didn't stop. Didn't turn round.

'Where are you going?'

'Home,' she said, not missing a stride. 'I've done what I came for. I've brought you your daughter.'

'No!'

She reached the door.

'Please, Grace.'

Opened it.

'I love you.'

She let out the breath she'd been holding but still didn't turn round.

'I've always loved you. I came back that first year with a ring in my pocket.'

'No…' That couldn't be true. He'd scarcely looked at her. 'No,' she said, turning to face him. 'You never called. Never wrote. Not even a postcard.'

'I meant to, but I didn't know what to say. Sorry? Thank you? There was only one thing you'd want to hear and I couldn't write it.'

Plain and honest… She was certainly getting what she'd asked for.

'So why the ring?'

'I couldn't face you without it and then, having screwed myself to the sticking point, admitted that I wanted you, I discovered that you'd found someone else.'

'And you just accepted that? Didn't bother to put up a fight? Josh Kingsley, who always got what he went after?'

'I was…relieved.'

'Off the hook, you mean. That wasn't love, Josh. That was guilt. And you were married to Jessie within a year. Still, when you've got a ring…'

'I didn't give Jessie your ring. I threw it in the bin, then I realised that Phoebe would find it, so I took it out again. I still have it.'

She shook her head, not wanting to believe it.

'It's in my apartment in Sydney. At the back of my sock drawer.'

'No…'

It was a cry from the heart for everything she'd lost and in a second he was there beside her, his arms around her, but she had to tell him. Now. This minute, before her heart shattered

'There was never anyone else, Josh. There has never been anyone else. They were all just camouflage. You'd left me and I didn't want you to know how much that had hurt me. One word. If you'd just said one word…'

'I was afraid. I thought you'd slow me down.'

She looked up at him. 'You were right.'

'Was I? Truly? If I'd had an ounce of your strength, purpose, if I'd had the courage to tell you that I loved you, you would have braved anything to come with me.'

She shook her head, but he caught her chin, forced her to look at him.

'It's true. How did you do it now, Grace? Where did you find the strength to fly into the unknown?'

'Love,' she said. 'Your love, your sacrifice gave me wings.'

'And now you're prepared to do the same?'

'Actually, Josh, I was banking on the fact that having done it yourself, you'd finally get the message.'

'Tell me anyway.'

'"…whither thou goest, I will go; and where thou lodgest I will lodge…" We're a family, Josh. It doesn't matter where we are, so long as we're together.'

Josh felt as if his heart were bursting. He'd given everything and in return he'd gained the world.

'There's just one more question,' he said. 'Will you marry me? Not a paper marriage, but a making babies, till-death-us-do part, forever and a day marriage. In a wedding with flowers and bridesmaids and doves and string quartets. I'll even shave off the beard.'

'No,' she said. Then, while his heart was still recovering from the shock, 'No doves, no string quartets and I'll take a rain check on the beard until I've road-tested it.' Then, when he just grinned, 'That's a hint, Josh. We've got ten years to catch up on.'

From the Maybridge Gazette:

DUCKS ADD DELIGHT
AND DRAMA TO WEDDING

Local businesswoman Grace McAllister and Maybridge-born tycoon Joshua Kingsley were married today in a charmingly simple ceremony in the folly at Melchester Castle.

The bride wore a Geena Wagner gown in ivory silk with a matching high-collared bolero that had been appliquéd and embroidered in shades of green and turquoise. Her matching tiara was designed and made by the bride's business partner, Abby Green.

The couple's niece, Posie Kingsley, and the groom's half-sisters, Lucy, Alice and Maude Kingsley were bridesmaids.

The ceremony was followed by a country picnic for family and friends beside the lake where the guests were entertained by a traditional fiddler, folk singers and morris dancing. A dozen white ducks, decked out in emerald bows, added rural charm to the scene, but during the afternoon they escaped their handler and made for the lake. So far all attempts to capture them have failed.

The couple, who have now left on an extended honeymoon that reportedly includes India, the United States and Japan, have homes in Maybridge and Sydney, Australia.

* * * * *

HER BABY WISH

BY
PATRICIA THAYER

Originally born and raised in Muncie, Indiana, **Patricia Thayer** was the second of eight children. She attended Ball State University, and soon afterwards headed west. Over the years she's made frequent visits back to the Midwest, trying to keep up with her family's numerous weddings and births, but Patricia has called Orange County, California, home for many years. She not only enjoys the warm climate, but also the company and support of other published authors in the local writers' organisation. For the past eighteen years she has had the unwavering support and encouragement of her critique group. It's a sisterhood like no other.

When not working on a story, you might find her travelling the United States and Europe, taking in the scenery and doing story research while thoroughly enjoying herself, accompanied by Steve, her husband for over thirty-six years. Together they have three grown sons and three grandsons. As she calls them, her own true-life heroes. On rare days off from writing you might catch her at Disneyland, spoiling those grandkids rotten! She also volunteers for the Grandparent Autism Network.

Patricia has written for over twenty years and has authored over thirty books. She has been nominated for both the National Readers' Choice Award and the prestigious RITA®. Her book *Nothing Short of a Miracle* won a *Romantic Times* Reviewer's Choice award. She has been a guest reader at elementary schools and lectured aspiring authors. A long-time member of Romance Writers of America, she has served as President and held many other board positions for her local chapter in Orange County. She's a firm believer in giving back.

Check her website at www.patriciathayer.com for upcoming books.

To all the couples
who know the struggles and pain of infertility.
I pray you all will be blessed some day.
And a special congratulation to Michelle and Rod.

CHAPTER ONE

"I NEED you to come back home."

Trace McKane's grip tightened on the pitchfork as he spread fresh straw around Black Thunder's stall. He'd waited two long months to hear his wife say those words. The only problem was she didn't exactly sound sincere, and too many harsh words had passed between them to repair the damage so casually.

"I can't see how that's going to change anything." He continued to cover the floor as if Kira's presence hadn't affected him at all. But it had. He'd give up the family's Colorado ranch to have things back like they were before their problems started. And from the look of things lately, that might not be too far from the truth.

"Trace, please, just hear me out," she said.

He stopped his chores and finally looked at her. "Why, Kira? Haven't we said enough?" He straightened and tipped his hat back off his forehead. This was the first time he'd chanced a close up look at his wife since he'd moved out. She'd kept her distance, and so had he.

She placed her hands on her hips. "Oh, you made

your feelings perfectly clear. Things got rough so you walked out, without even trying to work things out."

"We were getting nowhere."

Kira Hyatt McKane was a natural beauty with curly wheat-blond hair that hung to her shoulders. She had an oval face, with a scattering of freckles across a straight nose and full, pouty lips. Her large brown eyes locked with his, causing his pulse to shoot into overdrive.

He wasn't going to take the bait and fight with her. "It's better I moved into the bunkhouse," he told her. He hated that they couldn't make their marriage work.

Yeah, he'd been running away. He'd spent a lot of time moving the herd to a higher pasture for the approaching summer. Many of those nights he'd slept under the stars, anything to keep from facing his lonely bunk. To keep from thinking about how he couldn't—no matter how much he loved Kira—make his marriage work.

"We both needed a breather."

God knew he'd missed her. The torture went on as his gaze moved over her navy T-shirt and the faded jeans that hugged her curves. Shapely hips and legs that he'd touched and caressed so often that he knew where every freckle was hidden. He also knew exactly where to touch to bring her pleasure.

He glanced away. Don't go there. That was past history. Their future together was bleak. He never thought he was a greedy man. He'd only wanted a traditional marriage; a wife to come home to and children to carry on the legacy of the ranch.

That had been when the trouble started, when their

marriage began to crumble and he couldn't do anything to stop it.

"Spring is a busy time," he told her. Especially this year since he had that payment due to his half brother, Jarrett. And it didn't look like there was much chance he could come up with the money.

Kira shook her head. "I know, Trace." She sighed. "And turning away from our problems doesn't help."

He cursed. "Yes, Kira, we have problems, but face it, lately we've been unable to come to terms with things. And I'm tired of beating my head against a wall." When he saw tears form in her eyes, he wanted to kick himself.

"I never meant for it to be this way."

He shrugged. The last thing he wanted was to argue. In the months before their separation that was all they'd done. Then they'd stopped talking altogether. What broke his heart was knowing he hadn't been able to give her what she needed.

"I just wanted us to be a real family," she added in a whispered voice.

"You had a funny way of showing it." He'd needed her to stand by him, and help him with his struggles with the ranch, but she was obsessed with her own problems.

Her eyes filled with tears. "There might have been a solution to help us both."

How many times had they tried? Even counseling, with some stranger listening to every way he'd failed his wife. He'd done about everything he could think of to make their marriage work. "How? More counseling?"

Kira shook her head. "I never should have asked you to go to counseling. I'm the one who's got the problem," she said, her voice husky with emotion. "I'm the one who needs to deal with things."

"As long as you feel that way, then you don't need me around."

Kira stepped closer and began to speak, but stopped. With a swallow, she tried again. "But, Trace, I do need you. I need you to stay with me another six months so I can have a baby, then you can have your divorce."

Trace glared at her. "What the hell?"

So finally she'd gotten his attention.

The first moment she'd seen Trace McKane, Kira knew for sure that he was the perfect man for her. That hadn't changed. Tall and lean, the handsome cowboy had gained his muscular build from years of working the McKane's Cattle Ranch. He had brown hair that always hung too long, brushing his shirt collar. His green-gray eyes were deep-set and when he looked at her she felt he could see into her soul. At first that had intrigued her, now it frightened her. The past months apart told her she didn't want to face a future without Trace. He was the one person she'd allowed to get close when she'd come to Winchester Ridge, Colorado, to take a guidance counselor job at the high school.

But there were some secrets she could never share…with anyone.

Now it was too late to do anything to save their marriage. "We received a letter today," she said, pulling the folded envelope out of her pocket. "It's from the adoption agency." Her voice trembled. "We've passed another screening for a baby."

Trace's eyes narrowed, then he threw his head back and laughed. "It's a joke, right?"

She didn't expect this reaction. "No."

"So for months we've been giving everyone the impression that we're the perfect couple and acceptable parents. Then we break up and we get the okay."

Kira squared her shoulders and looked him in the eye.

"No one knows you moved out, and I don't want anyone to. Not yet. Not until we receive a baby."

He froze, his jaw clenched. "If you want the divorce so bad, then adopt as a single parent." He tossed the pitchfork against the railing and marched out of the stall.

Kira hurried after him. "Trace, wait. Just hear me out." His fast pace had her nearly running to keep up. "We'll both get what we want. I'll have a baby, and you'll be free to marry someone who can give you what you want…children."

He stopped abruptly. "You have everything figured out, don't you?"

She shrugged, trying to hide her pain, wishing he'd say he'd stay with her and together they'd raise the baby. "No, but I know you want your own children. I can't give you that."

His eyes flashed his pain. "Yeah, I wanted a child— with you. But it didn't happen, and I wasn't enough for you." Without waiting for another word, he started out of the barn, leaving her in shock.

"It wouldn't be enough for you, Trace," Rushing after him, she caught up to him again on the small porch of the bunkhouse. "I loved you and our life together." She meant it. Her life on the ranch with Trace had been perfect. For a while. Then her dream had slowly unraveled. It seemed as if God were punishing her for her past. She didn't want Trace to be punished because of her. That's the reason she had to put an end to this.

She forced away the thought. "Trace, I have a chance for a child…maybe my only chance. You can remarry and have a dozen children. So if you could be happier without me, I'm willing to let you go."

Trace closed his eyes and gripped the wooden post. He didn't know if he could handle this again. Their marriage had gone through so much turmoil while they'd tried several procedures to be able to conceive a baby. Toward the end, he couldn't take the look on her face every time they failed, until finally, the pressure drove her from him. He might have been the one who'd moved out of the house, but emotionally Kira had left him long before that.

Now, after long weeks of separation, he'd become reconciled to losing her. Then her sudden appearance today made him ache with want and need. But she was here only because of her need for a child, and to end their marriage.

"Do you honestly think we can pull this off? The last words we spoke to each other weren't exactly loving."

"The pressure is off now," she said. "We just have to go through the motions of being a couple. I've accepted that I may never conceive a baby, but I can still have a child." She held out the letter. "The agency says we've met their requirements and we can move on to the next step."

How could he forget the classes, the long interviews, the background checks. They'd even been fingerprinted. He glanced from the paper in her hand to the hopeful look on her face. He felt the familiar tug in his chest.

"They'll send someone out for a home study. To visit with us and see our home."

"So what do you want me to do? Play the loving husband?"

She rested her hand on his arm, her dark eyes pleading. "Would that be so hard?"

Damn, she didn't play fair and he had trouble denying her anything. "I don't think we can pull it off, Kira. Not where we are right now."

She paused. "It's only for about six months. That's how long it takes for the adoption to be final." She looked sad. "Is it that hard to pretend you love me?"

The next evening, seated at the kitchen table at the house, Kira tried to finish the end-of-the-year paperwork, but her mind kept wandering back to Trace.

"What else is new?" she grumbled as she got up and went to the coffeemaker. After refilling her mug, she walked to the window and stared out at the breathtaking view of the Roan Plateau. She'd come to love this place. So different from the busy streets of Denver.

Five years ago she'd come to Winchester Ridge to start a new life. With her new college degree in hand, she'd come to interview for a teaching position at the high school. She'd gotten the job and needed a place to live.

The town's real estate broker, Jarrett McKane, had shown her an apartment, then taken her to lunch. At the local café, they'd run into his younger brother, Trace.

It had been an instant attraction. After that she'd accepted a few more dates from Jarrett in the hope of running into Trace.

Finally two weeks later, the rugged rancher showed up at school and asked her out. It seemed like forever before he kissed her, but it had been well worth the wait. She closed her eyes, remembering his slow hands skimming over her, softly caressing her skin.

Trace's kisses were lethal. She remembered each touch of his lips against her heated flesh. How hungry he'd made her, stirring her desire. Suddenly warmth ran down her spine settling low in her stomach. Her eyes shot open as she groaned in frustration.

"Oh God," she whispered as she sank against the counter, her body aching. Never in her life had anyone made her feel the way Trace McKane had. After her parents' automobile accident and death, she'd been alone for a lot of years. She'd thought she'd finally found a home, a place where she could belong.

Yesterday, she'd wanted to beg Trace to come home, but her own pain and hurt prevented it. She knew the past few months she'd been horrible to live with. But how could any man understand the anguish she'd gone through, not just with the pain of her disease, but knowing she hadn't been able to conceive a baby?

She glanced back through the window, seeing the light in the bunkhouse. "Oh, Trace, would you have loved me if you knew the truth about me?"

The past flooded back. She tried to push it away, but it always hovered close enough to force her to remember, taking the brightness away from any happiness she tried to grasp. Maybe the guilt had been what drove her, caused her to keep pushing Trace away.

The familiar sadness blanketed her. With each passing month her fertility problems had loomed ever darker. With the endometriosis, her chances diminished daily until the day would come when she'd probably need more surgery to relieve her of the recurring scar tissue.

But with the passing of time, her dreams seemed to be fading anyway, along with her marriage.

The sound of the back door opening caught Kira's attention. Living this far out in the country, she knew it could only be Jonah Calhoun, the ranch foreman. Or Trace. Her heart raced as she waited, and her hopes were rewarded when her husband walked into the kitchen.

She tried to breathe but it was difficult. Trace McKane still affected her in the same way he had when she'd first met him. It was obvious he had just showered and put on a fresh shirt and jeans. Hope spread through her as she realized he might have done it for her.

"Hi," she managed. "Would you like a cup of coffee?"

He nodded. "I could use one." He walked to the counter and took the steaming mug she offered. Then Kira picked up her cup and started for the table.

"I thought caffeine was bad for your condition," he said.

She was touched that he remembered. "I usually don't drink it, but tonight I have work to finish. I need all the help I can get to stay alert."

"I guess school is getting out soon. So it looks like it's going to be a busy time for both of us." He drank from his cup, then studied her. She felt the heat of his silver gaze spread over her, warming her. She hated they were talking so politely, when she desperately wanted him to take her into his arms and tell her he wanted to move back permanently to be her husband and father to her baby.

He glanced away. "Cal wants to know if you're still planning the senior roundup to be here this year."

She nodded. "I hope to. The kids have been talking about it for weeks. That is, if it's okay with you?"

He shrugged. "Not a problem. Cal just wants a head count so we'll know how many hands we need to hire."

Trace leaned against the counter, trying to relax. Impossible. Since his dad's death three years ago, he'd had to run the cattle operation mostly on his own.

"Do you have a date set for the roundup?" she asked.

"In two weeks."

She nodded. "That's perfect. Graduation will be over, so we don't have to worry about interrupting study time."

Trace hated the silence lingering between them. What he hated most of all was feeling like a stranger in his own house, a stranger to his wife.

"Have you given any thought to what we talked about?" she finally asked him.

"It's kind of hard not to." He shifted his weight trying to ease the tightness in his chest. "You tell a man you want to adopt a child, and in the same breath give him his walking papers."

"I'm sorry, Trace. I never wanted it to turn out this way. But in the end it might be best for both of us."

He heard the tears in her voice. "Is it really that easy, Kira? Well, it's not for me. If I agree I also sign papers for this child. I'm responsible for him or her, too."

"Trace, I know I'm asking a lot."

"No, you don't," he interrupted her. "You're asking me to move back into the house and take responsibility for a child, then just to walk away."

She wanted more, so much more from him. But she couldn't ask for another chance. "I don't expect to have things be like they once were. Yes, we have to live in the same house, but if we're lucky enough to get a baby, I'll handle all the child's needs. I won't ask for any help."

He was silent for a long time. "And after the six months, I sign away all rights to the child."

He made it sound so calculating. She managed a nod.

He cursed and turned away.

"Please, Trace, I'm afraid if we tell the agency we're not together now, then later, I'll have to start from the beginning as a single parent."

He drove his fingers through his hair. "I'm not sure I can do this, Kira."

She bit down on her lower lip. "Please, I want this opportunity, Trace. It might be my last chance."

Trace fought to control his anger. It had always been about a baby. What about them? Why couldn't she offer to work out their problems? Instead of wanting to push him aside when he wasn't needed any more.

"Trace, I don't magically expect us to return to our roles of husband and wife. I'll move into the guest room and you can have your bedroom back."

This was all so crazy. Trace wasn't sure if he could resist Kira, living under the same roof. If he moved back into the house now, it'd be damn difficult to resist going to her bed.

He placed his coffee mug in the sink, then went to her, bracing his hands on either side of her. He stared into those honey-brown eyes, knowing there were secrets hidden in their depths. Secrets she wouldn't share with anyone, not even with him. "You talk about this situation like it's a business transaction. I have my doubts about us being able to pull this off."

She swallowed hard, but didn't speak.

His attention went to her mouth, tempting him like no woman ever had. His heart raced and his gut tightened. He ached to taste her, to stir up those feelings that made him crazy with need. It had been so long.

"Trace." Her voice was a throaty whisper as her hand came up to his face. "Can't we try?"

Her sultry voice swept over him like a caress. He closed his eyes, picturing her in their bed, willing and wanton, welcoming his kisses, his touches as he moved over her heated body.

"Damn you, Kira." His mouth closed over hers in a hungry kiss. She wrapped her arms around his neck as he jerked her against his body already hard with desire. Her mouth opened on a sigh, and he dove inside to taste her. He moved against her, hungry for the contact. It wasn't enough, he needed all of her.

But Kira couldn't give it to him. Would they ever be able to be what the other needed?

He broke off the kiss and stepped back. "I've got to go." He headed to the door only to have her call to him.

He didn't turn around, knowing he'd weaken to her request. "Kira, I need more time."

"Please, Trace." She hesitated. "Just keep up the pretense that we're married until you decide what to do."

In his heart Trace would always be married to Kira. He'd loved her since the moment he laid eyes on her. That hadn't changed. But could he hang around and watch their marriage die a slow agonizing death?

He faced her. "So you expect me live in limbo until the adoption goes through?" The words stuck in his throat.

She blinked, looking surprised. "No. I'm asking if you would give it six months until they give us permanent custody. After that I won't try to hold you, or make you responsible for the child. I'll move into town and not ask anything more of you. As soon as I get another counseling job, I'll move away."

Damn, there it was. She couldn't say it any plainer. The chant rang repeatedly in his head. *She only wants a child.* "You're asking a lot, Kira."

"I know," was all she said in her defense.

"What do I get out of this deal? What are you willing to give me?"

She blinked at his question, but soon recovered. Her arms tightened around his neck. "What do you want, Trace? If it was me, all you had to do any time was walk through that door. I've been here the whole time, wanting you."

His body stirred at the feel of her length pressed against him. The easy way would be to give them what they both wanted. He wasn't sure he could, knowing in the end he could lose everything anyway. Everything. Not only would he give up Kira, but a child.

"Like I said, I'll have to think about it." He removed her hands, and walked out before he changed his mind. Before he did something crazy like agreeing to her request.

CHAPTER TWO

OF ALL mornings to oversleep.

Kira pulled her leather satchel from the back seat, slammed the car door and rushed off across the parking lot toward the large brick building, Winchester Ridge High School. And the nine o'clock meeting.

After Trace had left the house, she hadn't been able to finish her work until well after midnight. Then she lay awake a long time, reliving her husband's visit, their kiss.

Trace's familiar taste. The way he held her, reminding her how well their bodies meshed together. She delighted in the fact she could still make his control slip, just as hers had. She had to stop herself from trying to convince him to stay and make love to her.

Oh God, it had been a long time since Trace had touched her.

"Mrs. McKane, are you all right?"

Kira shook away the fantasy and glanced at her student, Jody Campbell. "Oh, Jody. Yes, I'm fine. Just a lot of things on my mind." She picked up her pace toward the counselors' office, realizing the student was staying right with her. "What are you doing out of class?"

"Mr. Douglas let me leave early because I needed to see you." The pretty girl hesitated. "It's about volunteer time at the retirement home. All the kids voted it as our class project, but some don't have enough hours to come to the senior roundup."

"Give me the list and I'll talk to them," Kira said as she stopped at the counseling department's door and took the paper.

Seeing Jody reminded her that she'd gotten a notice from her English teacher. The promising student's work had been suffering the past month. Kira hated that her own personal distractions had caused her to neglect one of the best students in the senior class.

"Why don't you come back at three o'clock? We should talk."

Jody hesitated again. "I work at four so I need to catch the three-thirty bus."

She couldn't let this slip any longer, not with finals next week. "Well, I could give you a lift if you like and we can have a quick chat."

Her once-enthusiastic student kept her eyes cast down. "Okay."

Kira signed Jody's pass and sent her off to class just as the bell rang. She walked inside the guidance office and into the first glass cubicle. She hated being distracted from her work. And these last few weeks, it had been especially difficult for her to keep focused on a job she was crazy about. She loved doing extra things to stay involved with the teenagers.

Kira was the sponsor for this year's senior class, including all activities. Doing service hours and giving back to the community was an important part of their curriculum. It helped to develop their social skills, and it looked good on their college applications. She rewarded those students with senior roundup at McKane Ranch.

Winchester Ridge was a small ranching town, but the teenagers loved to spend the day helping with the roundup and branding. Followed by a barbecue and barn dance that closed out their senior year with wonderful memories.

Kira sank into her desk chair. Not all kids were that lucky. Suddenly the last fifteen years faded away as her thoughts went back to her own high school days. Shy and naive, she'd been passed around to so many different foster homes it had been difficult to make friends. So when someone gave her attention, she'd been eager for it, and easy to be taken advantage of. Those lonely years had been a big motivator for her career choice.

At the sound of the knock on her door, Kira looked up to see her fellow counselor and friend, Michelle Turner, peer in.

"Michele," she greeted. "Are you coming for the meeting?"

"It's been postponed until one o'clock," her friend said as she walked inside the small enclosure and closed the door. "Kira, are you all right?"

She gave her friend a bright smile. "I'm fine."

The young teacher sat down in the only other chair. "No, you're not."

Kira shook her head. Michele had been the one person she'd confided in about her inability to conceive. The fellow teacher had been her first friend when she'd come to the western Colorado town. "No, really. We've gotten word from the adoption agency."

Michele's pretty blue eyes lit up. "Oh, that's great news." She frowned. "Why so sad?"

Kira shrugged. "Hormones, probably. And Trace. He's a little hesitant about the idea."

Michele leaned forward. "You two have been through a lot over this and now that you're so close to having a baby, he's probably a little scared."

And he wants his own child, Kira added silently. "It's more." She looked her friend in the eye, knowing she'd never betray her confidence. "It hasn't been easy living with me this last year."

"You've gone through a lot, trying to have a baby."

Kira released a shuttering breath. "Trace moved out to the bunkhouse two months ago."

"Oh, Kira." Michele shook her head. "Isn't that just like a man? When they can't deal with things, they up and leave. Well, I know Trace loves you."

And Kira wasn't so sure of that anymore. "I might have pushed him too far this time. We both said things that can't be taken back." She recalled the hurtful words she'd thrown at him. And yesterday she mentioned the "D" word. It was all or nothing now.

"Then march out to that bunkhouse and convince him to come back home."

"I'm not sure that will work."

"How do you know if you don't try? So go and

seduce your husband." Michele glanced at her watch. "I've got to get back. Can we do lunch later in the week?"

"Sure. Are you going to help chaperone at the roundup?"

Michele grinned. "I wouldn't miss it. Is your good-looking brother-in-law going to be there?"

Kira was surprised by her friend's interest in Jarrett. "I'm not sure."

Michelle waved off the question then hugged her. "I'll see you later." She walked out.

Kira leaned back in her chair. Could she get Trace to come back home, and get him to change his mind about the divorce? Could they work together to repair their mess of a marriage?

She thought back to the last time Trace had wanted to be close to her. In the weeks before he'd moved out, her once-loving husband hadn't wanted to touch her, or even be in the same house with her. And she couldn't blame him. The sad part was she'd driven him out. Out of his own home.

Trace loved the McKane Ranch, one of the oldest in the area. He was a cattleman like his father and grand-father before him. There had been times when she was a little jealous of his dedication, maybe if he'd talk about the operation with her it would help. Even when he'd bought out part of his brother's land, she hadn't been asked anything about it until it came time to sign the loan papers. She just wanted to feel like a part of his dreams.

Kira felt her chest tighten with the familiar ache. The

same feeling she'd had when she'd lost her parents in the accident and her grandmother wouldn't take her into her home. *Rejection.* When she had to go into foster care, then from home to home. *Rejection.* When she fell in love with the first boy who gave her the time of day, he'd abandoned her, too. *Rejection.* Now, her marriage…

Kira sat up straighter. Why was she thinking so much about the past? She'd worked so hard to put those years behind her. A glance at the calendar gave her the answer. It was approaching the seventh of June. Fifteen years had passed and it still hurt like a fresh wound.

No! This baby was going to change things. She was going to have her family, even if it was only part of one.

"Kira…"

She turned around to see Trace at the door. He was dressed in his usual jeans and Western shirt, his cowboy hat in his hand. With her heart pounding, she stood.

"Trace." He never came to her school. "Is something wrong?"

"Do you have some time to talk?"

"Sure." She stepped aside. "Come in."

He glanced around the busy office. "I'd rather go somewhere else. Can you leave for a while?"

She checked her watch. "I'm free for the next hour."

"Let's go for some coffee."

"Sure." Kira grabbed her purse, stepped out into the hall and together they walked out of the building. When Trace placed his hand against the small of her back, she shivered.

"Are you okay?" he asked.

"Yes," she lied. "I'm fine. I just need some coffee."

He gave her a sideways glance. "You should switch to decaf."

She studied his profile. Trace McKane had always been serious by nature. He didn't smile easily, but when he did he was irresistible.

They were quiet as he helped her to his truck, then drove past all the recently built, chain restaurants to the older section of Winchester Ridge to Bonnie's Diner. Still a favorite with the locals.

They took a booth by the picture window. The red vinyl seats were worn and cracked, repaired by tape over the years. The place was clean and the food good. Right now, there weren't any customers, only the sound of a country ballad coming from the old fifties-style jukebox.

Trace signaled the waitress for two coffees and sat down across from Kira. He wondered if he should have waited until she got home to talk with her.

After what happened between them last night, he should be staying away from her, completely. But here he was, sitting across from her. Just looking at her had him working to breathe normally. Nothing had changed. Kira Hyatt had gotten to him from the moment he laid eyes on her, right here in this diner. It had been the only time he'd ever won out against his older sibling. For once Jarrett hadn't gotten the girl. Younger brother, Trace had.

But Trace had nothing now. Not a wife. Not a marriage. It helped to remember the bad times. That kept him from storming back into the house they'd shared for five years. To a life he'd thought was perfect, but reality hit and he'd learned nothing was perfect.

That it hit home again as he recalled that Kira only wanted a six-month marriage.

The waitress placed their mugs on the table. The older woman, Alice Burns, gave them a warm smile. She'd worked here for as long as he could remember. "Well, how are Mr. and Mrs. McKane doin' today?"

"Just fine, Alice," Trace answered.

"How's your granddaughter?" Kira asked.

The fifty-something woman grinned. "Best not get me started on little Emily. But she's gonna have to share me soon because Carol's pregnant again. A boy this time."

Kira's smile froze. "That's wonderful. Congratulations."

Alice eyed the couple. "You two should think about having a few yourselves." Before they could answer, the waitress walked away.

Trace watched Kira fight her emotions as she took a drink.

"Alice didn't know, Kira," Trace said.

"I know that." Kira wrapped a strand of golden-blond hair behind her ear, leaving the wispy bangs along her forehead. "Why did you need to see me?"

Okay this was all business. "A woman from the adoption agency called after you left."

Her brown eyes widened. "So soon. What did she say?"

"I didn't get to talk to her. Just a message on the machine. It just said that she'd call back again."

"Darn, I wonder if she'll call the office." She glanced at him. "Did she leave a number where I could reach her?"

It hurt when she used the word "I" and not "we". He pulled the paper from his pocket and slid it across the table. "I don't think you should call her just yet."

She looked hurt. "But I have to."

"What are you going to tell her, Kira?"

She blinked at him. "We're just talking to her, Trace. I don't want to delay the process, it takes a long time. We're probably just going to be put on a waiting list."

"I still have to pretend we're married."

"You are married—to me." She lost her attitude. "But as I told you the baby will be my responsibility."

So she hadn't changed her mind. He was to do nothing concerning the child. "We aren't even living under the same roof."

"I never asked you to move out in the first place."

"You know why I did, Kira. We were headed for disaster." He'd hated leaving, and if she'd asked him to stay just once, he would have in a heartbeat. Now, it was too late.

She sighed. "Please, just listen to what Mrs. Fletcher has to say, that's all I ask."

"Okay, I'll talk with the woman. See what she has to say."

"Really?" Tears flooded her eyes. "Oh, Trace, thank you."

He raised a hand. "Don't thank me, yet. I'll agree to another home visit. Afterward we'll see where we go from there. I can't commit to anything more."

She nodded. "Does that mean you're moving back to the house?"

Before Trace could come up with an answer they were interrupted.

"Well, look who's wandered in off the range."

They both glanced up to see Jarrett McKane standing at their table. He was tall, athletic and good-looking. He knew it, too. Jarrett knew a lot of things, all you had to do was ask him.

Trace straightened. He didn't want his half brother here. Not now. "Hello, Jarrett."

"Trace." His brother turned to Kira. "Hello, pretty sister-in-law."

Kira smiled. "Hi, Jarrett."

Grabbing a chair, he turned it around and straddled it. He glanced between the two of them. "You two look serious. There wouldn't be trouble in paradise, would there? Kira, you just let me know if this guy isn't treating you right and I'll knock some sense into him."

Kira shifted in her seat as she continued to smile at her brother-in-law. "Everything is fine, Jarrett, but thanks for asking."

At their first meeting when Kira arrived in town, Jarrett had laid on his easy chair but it hadn't taken her long to realize that Jarrett McKane was out for himself. He was attentive to his women though, but that was another problem, there were a lot of women.

Both brothers were handsome, but Jarrett had been the school sports hero and a college graduate. Meanwhile Trace had stayed and worked on the ranch with his father, going to college locally.

"Anytime." He looked at Trace. "I need to talk to you about our arrangement. Could you come to my office?"

"Later. Kira and I are talking right now."

"Seems like you could do that at home. Hell, you sleep in the same bed." There was a wicked look in Jarrett's eyes. "That's right. It's branding time so you sleep out with your calves." He winked at Kira. "Makes for a lonely wife left at home."

"And sometimes I sleep out with the calves, too," Kira said, worried things might come to blows.

The brothers had never been close. Jarrett had been six years old when his mother died, and his father, John, remarried Claire, and a year later she had given birth to Trace. The distance had grown when their parents retired and moved to a warmer climate in Arizona. Now, both parents had passed away.

"My brother's a lucky man to have you. Although I tried my best, he won you fair and square." He winked at Kira. "But it's still a long way to go before the score is even, bro."

Later that afternoon, Trace rode toward the barn. After returning from town, he'd saddled up Thunder and went out to check the herd. He'd wasted the morning already when he needed to finish things before the roundup.

He rotated his tired shoulders, felt his eyes burn, a sure sign that lack of sleep had taken a toll on him. And confronting his brother hadn't exactly made his day. He'd wanted to spend more time with Kira, but they hadn't managed that, either. So far, they'd talked very little of what was most important to him: their marriage.

Trace climbed off his horse and walked him into the

barn. The immaculately clean structure had been the result of too much time on his hands. Since moving to the bunkhouse, he'd tried to stay busy, and his already organized barn had gotten a complete sweep, with every piece of tack on the property being cleaned or polished.

It had been his sleep time that suffered. Even his fatigue hadn't helped him on those long nights. He walked his stallion into the stall, removed the saddle and carried it to the tack room. On his way out, he ran into his foreman, Cal.

"Hey, Trace. What's up?"

"You tell me, Cal," he said. "How many men have you got for the roundup?"

The forty-one-year-old foreman, Jonah Calhoun, took off his hat and scratched his gray-streaked brown hair. A single man, he'd worked for the McKane Ranch for years, and was also Trace's friend. "Besides our two part-time hands, another half a dozen like you asked. I also ran into Joel and Hal Lewis at the feed store. They're willing to come and help out, too, as long as we can give them a hand next month."

Trace nodded. "Can do. I'll give them a call."

Together, they walked back to Thunder's stall. Trace removed the horse's bridle and blanket, then took the brush and began grooming him.

Cal snapped his fingers. "Oh, I forgot, your brother stopped by earlier, looking for you."

Trace didn't like Jarrett dogging him. "He found me at the diner."

Cal frowned. "I thought you went to see Kira."

Trace nodded. "We went for coffee."

The foreman smiled. "Good idea, take her to the place where you two met."

"I just wanted to talk to her. Alone."

The smile grew bigger. "Get anything settled?" Then he raised his hand. "Sorry, Trace, that's none of my business. I'm just glad you two got together."

Trace continued to stroke the animal. "We were talking until Jarrett showed up."

The foreman's eyes narrowed. "He seemed bent on seeing you. What's he up to?"

Cal knew as well as Trace that Jarrett never did anything unless it benefited him. "He probably wants to know when that last payment I owe him is coming."

The foreman frowned. He knew the conditions of the loan. "Are you late?"

Trace shook his head. "No, but I'm not sure I can make the full amount on the final payment." He could lose it all.

"Would your brother give you more time? I mean, with the market the way it is."

"I doubt it. When has he ever done me a favor?"

Five years ago, Jarrett couldn't wait to sell off most of his share of the ranch, and offered Trace the first opportunity to buy it. Trace hadn't hesitated, but things had been tight this past year, and the payment was due to Jarrett in thirty days.

"I might have to sell the breeding bulls."

"No way. You need another year or two to build the herd. There's some serious money in those guys. Rocky will sire some good stock."

Trace put down the brush. "But I can get ready cash

for them. Joel Lewis is interested. And I can't lose everything now." His thoughts turned to Kira. He could lose more than the ranch.

"You know Lewis is mostly talk. Look, Trace, I have some money saved I could loan you."

Trace was touched by the offer. "Thanks, Cal, I'm grateful for the offer, but it's not a good idea to borrow from friends."

"Maybe I want to invest if Jarrett is threatening you. Not a full partnership, but just a percentage of the place." Kind light-blue eyes studied Trace. "Well, maybe you can talk it over with Kira before you nix the idea."

Trace walked out of the stall. "She's never shown much interest in the running of the ranch."

"Maybe she would this time."

Trace pushed his hat back and sighed. He didn't want to add to their troubles. "She has enough on her mind."

Cal nodded. "If you say so. Well, I guess I better go put away the feed that was delivered."

Trace stopped him. "Has Kira said something to you?"

"No. She just always asks about things, and seems genuinely interested when I tell her." The foreman shrugged. "But I can't tell you how to talk to your wife, Trace."

He hadn't been talking to Kira at all until she'd come to see him yesterday. And she wasn't going to be his wife much longer. "Hell, I've been living in the bunkhouse for the past two months. I haven't been doing such a great job of it myself."

"And you don't need a lecture from me. But I think if there are problems with the missus, living out here and keeping things from her isn't the best way for fixin' things between you."

Cal was probably the only one who knew about their problems. "The adoption agency notified us. Kira wants me to move back to the house and pretend we're a happy couple."

A smile appeared on his friend's face. "You don't look very happy about it."

"All she wants is six months. After the adoption becomes final she's going to leave."

Cal raised an eyebrow then he said, "I know it's been rough. Kira's gone through a lot and she wants a baby."

"So do I. And how can I just walk away from a child?"

"Who says you have to? You can still be the kid's father, Kira's husband. Who's to say you can't get an extension on the six months?"

So much had already passed between them, so much hurt. He didn't know if they could go back to how it was before. "I don't know if I can."

"If you're not ready, then take it slow."

Trace never had been one who shared things, but Cal was as close as they came. He valued his opinion, and advice. "She wants me to stay in the house but not in the same room."

His friend smiled slowly. "Hey, it's a start."

"Trace?"

At the sound of Kira's voice, he turned to find her standing in the barn entrance, holding a bag of groceries.

"Kira." He walked toward her and took the sack from her. "Is there a problem?" Great, is that all he could come up with?

She glanced away shyly. "I had an easy afternoon at school and decided to cook supper." She looked at Cal and smiled. "Hello, Jonah."

"Kira, it's nice to see you."

"It's nice to see you, too. I hope you're ready for about thirty teenagers coming out."

"Are we ever ready?"

Kira laughed. "I guess not, but it's fun."

Trace found he was jealous of their easy banter. "Is there a reason you came to see me?"

Kira looked at him. "I wanted to ask if you'd come to supper." She turned back to Cal. "You're welcome, too, Jonah."

The foreman blushed. "Thank you for the invitation, Kira, but it's my bowling night." He tipped his hat. "I should finish up my chores." He leaned toward his friend and whispered, "Slow and easy." Cal turned and walked out.

"What did he say?" Kira asked.

He shrugged. "Just something I need to remember."

An hour later when Trace stepped inside the house, the scent of apples and cinnamon teased his nose. Ordinarily he didn't take time to look around; he'd grown up in this house, but today he was mindful of it all.

A wide staircase led to a second floor where there were four large bedrooms. The living room was painted gray-green to offset the dark woodwork and floors. An overstuffed green sofa faced the used-brick fireplace.

That was when he noticed them, Kira's touches. An easy chair she'd bought for him right after they were married, saying he needed a place to relax. The large coffee table where the photo album of his childhood rested. More family pictures hung on the brightly painted walls. His family, not hers. He remembered her saying she lost her parents' pictures while moving around in foster care. He'd never thought much about her being alone in her life. She'd always seemed so outgoing and everyone liked her.

Trace moved quickly down the hall through the dining room, which was a sunny-gold color trimmed in oak wainscoting. The scent of lemon oil rose from the long, drop-leaf oak table and eight high-back chairs that had also belonged to his parents. He entered the kitchen, the one room that he and Kira had changed. And it had needed it. Everything had been out-of-date, from the appliances to the cupboards. Just a few months after their small wedding, the room had been gutted and everything was replaced.

A bowl of red apples sat on the round maple table. Everything looked the same, but it wasn't. He wanted desperately to push time back to when everything was perfect in his marriage.

He found Kira at the counter, taking pieces of chicken from the skillet. She glanced over her shoulder and smiled. "Hi."

He had trouble finding the words. "Hi. Am I too early?"

"No. Just in time."

His gaze combed over her. He was starved for her. Denying himself the pleasure she could give him had been punishing. Today she had on one of her prim schoolteacher blouses, his favorite, a rose-pink one that brought out the color of her skin.

He swallowed back the dryness in his throat. "How did school go today?"

"Fine," she said. "Everyone is complaining about finals."

He leaned against the counter. He'd missed talking with her. "I remember that age, it seemed to take an eternity to get to the end of school."

She smiled and started setting out the food. "The seniors are anxious to graduate, and get me out of their hair."

He knew that wasn't true. They all loved her. The girls considered her a friend, and the boys were half in love with her. She was young, barely thirty-one, and attractive. They all gravitated to her. "And a lot are going to be heartbroken at saying goodbye to you."

"What does that mean?"

"You've always given your students a lot of attention."

"And that's a bad thing?"

"No, it just means you're dedicated, and very good at what you do. Not to mention pretty."

Kira couldn't believe she was blushing at her husband's compliment. Trace had told her she was attractive before, but not for a long time. He hadn't talked to her at all.

"Thank you," she said.

He shrugged. "I'm not saying anything that isn't true."

"It's still nice to hear," she said. They looked at each other for a long time. Kira tried not to react, but it was impossible. Trace McKane was a handsome man. She'd thought that the first time she'd seen him. She'd been in town less than twenty-four hours before falling hopelessly in love. Something she'd never thought would happen, but the quiet rancher somehow convinced her to trust again. His slow hands and eager mouth coaxed her into giving herself to him, and they married within two months. From that first night of loving to now, she'd never regretted that decision.

She turned and opened the refrigerator to get the milk. The cool air felt good against her heated face. She couldn't believe how nervous she was acting. He was her husband, for God's sake. No, Trace hadn't been her husband for weeks. And sadly that wasn't going to change.

CHAPTER THREE

AN HOUR later, Kira sat at the kitchen table and watched as Trace finished the last of his meal.

He leaned back in the chair. "That was delicious, Kira."

She let out a breath, not realizing she'd been holding it. "I'm glad you liked it."

He gave a half smile. "Can't deny I've always loved your fried chicken."

And she loved his praise. "I shouldn't fix it. It isn't exactly healthy, especially the gravy."

"Once in a while won't hurt me."

It definitely hadn't hurt his waistline, she thought, visualizing the six-pack abs hidden under his shirt. She nodded and started to get up. "Coffee?"

He touched her hand to stop her and she felt a sudden jolt. "I'll get it," he said.

Kira relented, but her hungry gaze followed Trace to the coffeemaker. He stood nearly six-feet-two-inches tall, and since she was nearly five-nine, she loved his height. Her attention moved over a Western shirt that outlined his broad shoulders and narrow waist. She loved that long, lean look, especially when he wore Wrangler jeans.

And nothing else.

Heat suddenly swarmed her body just as Trace turned around. He gave her a curious look, but remained silent as he walked back to the table. He set down the mugs and she noticed his hands. Memories flooded her head, as she recalled his firm, but gentle touches, how he stroked her, bringing her pleasure.

He took a seat across from her. "I'm glad to see you've taken my advice and are on the decaf."

She sat up straighter. "I realized I need more sleep."

"We could all use a little more of that." His gaze locked with hers. "Though I doubt I can blame my problem on the caffeine."

Kira swallowed hard. She wanted to explore his comment further, but couldn't. They had another topic that needed attention. "I called Mrs. Fletcher at the agency," she said in a rush.

Trace didn't look surprised. "I figured you would." He set down his mug. "What did she have to say?"

"She wants to come for another home visit the first of next week."

Trace took a sip of coffee, then asked, "What did you tell her?"

"That I'd check with you, but Monday seemed okay for us." Kira held her breath, waiting, praying that Trace would agree to this.

"What are we going to say to her when she gets here?"

She hesitated, feeling her heart pounding. "That we want a baby."

Trace met Kira's anxious gaze. He could see how much she wanted this. There had been a lot of disappointment in the past two years for both of them. She'd gone through so much, both physically and emotionally, trying to get pregnant.

His own excitement began to build. A family with Kira. Was it still possible?

He wanted to make their marriage work, but her need for a child had become an obsession, leaving no room for them. By the time he moved out, she seemed relieved he was gone. Once she got her child would she turn her attention back to them? Either way he couldn't deny her.

"I'll be around Monday."

Those big brown eyes widened. "Really? Oh, Trace."

She jumped out of her chair, threw her arms around his neck and hugged him. Trace reached for her, gripping her by the waist so they both wouldn't topple over.

Kira ended up on his lap and when she pulled back there were tears in her eyes. "Thank you," she whispered.

He couldn't resist, and brushed away a tear off her cheek. Seeing her rich brown eyes staring back at his caused his blood to stir. It always had, but he couldn't let it happen, not after all the pain they'd caused each other.

He stood her on her feet. He got up, too, then backed away but ran into the counter. "You don't have to thank me. We'd always planned on children. I haven't agree to everything."

She refused to look away. "Under the circumstances…and reasons you've agreed to do this, I still thank you."

The hard ache in his body told him he was crazy to be this close to Kira. "Like you said it's a long waiting list." He drew a breath and inhaled that soft, womanly scent that was only her.

"Well, you've made me very happy." She leaned forward and placed a tender kiss on his mouth. He sucked in a breath as another jolt of desire shot through him. "And I promise I'll give you what you want."

"That'd be a first time in a long time," he murmured, trying to guard against his weakness for her.

"You know what I mean," she added. "You're doing this for me, I promise when it's over, I won't contest anything."

What had happened to them? At one time, he'd wanted to give her everything. They'd planned a lifetime together. Now, she wanted nothing from him, especially not his love.

"I should go," he told her, not wanting the conversation to go sour if they brought up any more of the past hurt. "I need to go check on that bad section of fence. I don't want Rocky to wander off," he rambled on. He stole another look at her and his pulse accelerated, weighing down each step he took.

"We still have things to talk about," Kira called to him. "Maybe after I'm home from school tomorrow."

Trace nodded, then headed for the back door, praying she wouldn't stop him. He worked to remember the misery they'd caused each other during their last months together. He hurried out into the cool night, and it felt good against his heated skin, but even jumping into a pool of ice water wouldn't cool off his need for Kira. He doubted anything would, ever. That still didn't give him any hope that they were meant to be together.

The next morning, Kira had renewed hope that things were going to work out. She knew she needed to take things slow with Trace. He never rushed into anything.

She walked into her office to find Jody waiting for her. When Kira had driven the girl to her job yesterday, there wasn't much time to talk about anything except plans for the senior roundup. That was why Kira had set up this morning's meeting.

Jody stood. "Hello, Mrs. McKane."

"Good morning, Jody." Kira unlocked her office, went inside and set her things on her desk. After putting her purse in the bottom drawer, she motioned to Jody to take a seat, then she did the same.

"Okay, Jody, there are no distractions now." She worked up a smile. "It's just you and me." She took the file from her in-box and opened it. "I've talked with your teachers, Mr. Franklin and Miss Meehan, who informed me your grades have dropped considerably as of late. Jody, is there something going on, has something happened?"

The young girl looked pale, almost sickly. Her blond hair was long, but it looked unkempt today. She wasn't wearing any makeup, not even lip gloss. So different from the impeccably groomed girl Kira had known. Jody looked tired, no exhausted. Then it started adding up, the bad grades, and the sudden breakup with her boyfriend. Could Jody be pregnant?

Kira's heart sank as she worked hard not to look down at the girl's waistline. "I know I'm your guidance counselor, but I hope after our four years together, I'm your friend, too."

The student glanced away and shrugged. "I know you've helped me so much." She hesitated. "It's just…it's hard to talk about."

Jody Campbell lived with her single mother, and money was always tight. With Jody's high grade point average, Kira had been working tirelessly to help her get scholarships and financial aid for college.

"Jody, two months ago you were excited about going away to college. Has something changed that?"

She drew an unsteady breath and nodded. "Ben and I broke up." Tears filled her eyes. "He signed up to go into the Army."

"I'm sorry, Jody." Ben Kerrigan was another senior. The two had been dating for the past few months. She could see the girl's heartbreak. "When does he have to leave?"

A tear rolled down the girl's cheek. "The end of June. He said he won't have time for me, and doesn't even want to write me, or anything. He said it's better this way." The girl broke down and sobbed.

Kira reached for Jody and hugged her close. "I'm so sorry."

She knew too well how much teenage romance hurt. And in some cases you never lost the scars. Her thoughts went back nearly sixteen years earlier to her first love, Mike Purcell. Mike had broken more than her heart—he'd nearly destroyed her when he hadn't stood by her. That painful time still lingered in her memory. She had never shared it with anyone, not even Trace.

She blinked away her own tears and pulled back. "Jody. Listen to me. If you need me, for anything, I'm here."

The girl nodded, taking the tissue from Kira. "It's too late," she whispered.

"No, it's not. Unless you're changing your mind about college?"

The girl glanced away. "It would be hard for my mom if I go away. She depends on me."

Mrs. Campbell had depended on her daughter, and wasn't eager to see her go off to college. "Yes, but having a degree would make it so you could make more money. And what of your dream to be a nurse?"

"Maybe some dreams never come true."

Kira took the girl's hand and felt her tremble. "I know it seems hard right now, but you can do it. You are so talented."

She didn't look convinced.

"Okay, I won't push for now. Just don't blow off your finals."

"It's too late, I can't catch up."

"No, it's not too late. I've talked with both teachers. They'll give you makeup work, and if you do well on the final, you'll be okay. So you've got three days."

"But, I can't—"

"You can, because I'm going to help you," Kira insisted. "I want you back here after lunch."

Jody looked surprised. "Why? Why are you doing this?"

"Because I care about you, Jody. Right now you need to know that someone has faith in you. Someone cares."

Something Kira never had, until Trace. She just hadn't realized it soon enough. Now it was too late.

Trace paced the main room of the four room bunk-house, but stopped to glance out the window. Kira was well-past due being home and there was a storm brewing. A big one. He checked his watch—it was after five o'clock.

"Why don't you just call her?" Cal said.

It was silly to act as if he didn't know who the foreman meant. "She's probably busy with graduation stuff. It's just she never pays attention to the weather."

"Then warn her." The wind picked up and lightning flashed in the dark sky.

Trace pulled out his phone and punched in Kira's number. When she didn't answer, he cursed his stubborn, independent wife and headed outside. The rain began falling in big drops and just as he reached his truck, her Jeep Cherokee pulled up next to the house. Anger mixed with relief as he ran toward her. Seeing her frightened look, he remained silent. He took her by the arm, rushed her up the steps and through the back door.

"Where the hell have you been?" he demanded as he forced the door shut against the strong wind.

Inside the mudroom, she put her briefcase down on

the washing machine, then wiped the rain from her face. "I was helping a student, Jody Campbell, then I took her home."

"There's a severe storm warning. Didn't you hear it?"

"Not until I got into the car." She glanced out the window. "It's bad, isn't it?"

Another flash of lightning and the electricity went out. "I guess that answers your question."

He went to the pantry and pulled out the flashlight and a box of candles. No matter how brave Kira acted, he knew she hated storms. He hurried back into the kitchen and shined the light toward her. "You okay?"

"Ask me after this storm passes."

"I don't think there's any chance of that for a while. There's a series of them across the area. It could go on all night." He called Cal on his cell. "How are things down there?"

"I'm heading over to the barn to check the horses. If there's any problems, I'll let you know."

He turned back to see Kira, lighting the half-used candles. The threatening clouds make it darker than normal at this time of day. They had a generator, but he didn't feel it was necessary right now.

The rain pelted against the roof, and Kira jumped at another flash of lightning, followed by the booming sound of thunder. "I should buy some new ones."

"Do you want to start up the generator?"

Kira sat down in the kitchen chair. "Not unless we have to go down to the basement."

Trace glanced out the window, but couldn't see

anything with the blowing rain. "I'll check the forecast." He walked into the den they'd used as an office, and she followed. He had a battery-powered radio and flipped it on to the local weather channel.

"No tornados sighted in the area, so far. But the warnings won't be lifted for the area until after midnight."

She sighed. "I was afraid of that."

Even in the shadows, he could see her hand pressed against her stomach. Something he'd seen her doing many times during their marriage. It helped ease the cramps that came with her monthly period. It also gave them the sad news that once again they'd failed, failed to conceive a child.

He released a breath. There had been far too many of those times. And it had only gotten worse after the fertility treatments. In the end he could hardly bear to continue to try for a baby, or watch her heartbreak when the same result had been repeated with no pregnancy.

Trace swallowed his own pain. "Come on, I'll fix you a cup of tea." He waited for her to stand, then led her back into the kitchen. He turned on the gas stove, then went to the cupboard and took out a mug and tea bags.

Waiting for the water to heat, Trace leaned against the counter and studied Kira. She was dressed for summer, in her bright blue T-shirt and a long, flowered skirt, covered mostly by a bulky sweater.

It wouldn't be sexy to anyone else, but he knew what lay underneath. Long smooth legs, and a cute bottom and curves that drove a man wild.

She looked up at him, and her sweater opened. He didn't stop his open examination of her breasts. Her nipples quickly hardened under the thin material. He felt his own body respond and he looked up at her dark eyes. He didn't have to ask her if she wanted him, he could see it in her heated gaze. God, she was easy to read. It was one of the many things he loved about her. She didn't play games when it came to sex. If she wanted him, she let him know. And she was definitely letting him know now.

Suddenly the teapot whistled and he shook away any thoughts about carrying this any further. He removed the kettle, poured the water into the cup and placed it in front of her.

"You hungry?"

She shook her head. "My stomach is a little unsettled."

Seeing the stress in her face, he asked, "Cramps?"

She nodded as if embarrassed.

"You should be in bed."

The rain pelted against the windows. "I'm not going upstairs in this storm."

"Did you at least take your medication?" He knew she hated to resort to the painkillers, but sometimes she didn't have a choice.

She didn't respond.

"Where is it?"

"The bathroom, upstairs."

Trace grabbed the flashlight and headed out toward the stairs. He went into the room they'd shared for the past five years. He felt like the intruder now. Lightning suddenly illuminated the space, showing the neatly made bed. Kira never would go off and forget to make it. Something he knew she'd learned early on in foster care.

He liked it messy. He liked her messy after making love in the early mornings. When the sun wasn't up just yet, and all was fresh and new, the problems were pushed aside and they were lost only in each other. He shook away the thought as a crash of thunder rumbled through the house.

He went into the medicine cabinet and grabbed her pills, then went to the closet and took out a pair of sweatpants and a sweatshirt, along with a pair of tennis shoes. He hurried back downstairs and handed her the bundle. "I thought you might be more comfortable in these."

She looked surprised and pleased. "Thank you."

He went to the sink and got her a glass of water. On his return she was already removing her skirt. He went to the refrigerator, making himself busy, trying to think about food, and not his wife stripping off her clothes.

She stopped and took the medicine with a drink of water.

"Lie down and try to relax."

He walked back to the refrigerator and took out some bread, lettuce and sliced ham. Then he grabbed a plate from the cupboard and prepared the tray, wishing that a pill could make the problems between them disappear.

Ever since the moment he'd fallen in love with Kira, he'd known there was something she'd kept back. A tiny part of her that she'd never shared with him. He figured it had something to do with her parents' death and her years in foster care.

Her one living relative was a grandmother, Beth

Hyatt, but as far as he knew, Kira hadn't been in touch with her since their marriage. Whenever he asked about her family, Kira clammed up, only saying her parents had died when she was young.

Sometimes her eyes showed such sadness and no matter how much he'd reassured her, he couldn't make it go away. Could a child do what he never could?

Trace walked to the sofa and found Kira lying on her side, her legs pulled up, indicating she was still in pain.

He placed the tray on the coffee table and sat down at one end. Without a word, he placed Kira's head on his lap. He reached under her sweatshirt and touched her warm skin. He began a slow, circular motion over her back and down her spine. In the past, this helped relax her and ease her suffering.

Kira shifted a little and released a soft moan. He continued to stroke her skin, feeling his own need surfacing, but he didn't have to touch Kira to want her. He could stand across a room and she'd just have to glance at him and he wanted her. Hell, he'd been sleeping in the bunkhouse these past weeks and it hadn't changed anything.

She groaned again, then started to roll over.

"Stay still," he said.

"I can't. My stomach hurts." She managed to turn over on her back. Without hesitation, he placed his hand on her abdomen and continued the gentle motion.

"Is this helping any?"

"Oh, yeah," she murmured. "You can stop in about an hour."

It killed him to see her in pain. With the progressive

disease, her periods seemed to have gotten more and more painful. And no one could do much to help her.

"I expected you to be asleep before this." He ached to stretch out beside her, to hold her close.

She smiled sleepily. "The pills are doing a good job. Just don't tell my students I'm a druggie."

"Your secret is safe with me."

For a few moments, it seemed like old times. But it wasn't and he had better remember that. Playful words didn't make a marriage work.

But he sure as hell would like to know what did.

Kira was in heaven. She didn't know if it was the pain medication or the fact that Trace was there holding her. She liked this dream. She fought the drugging sleep because she didn't want to wake up and find him gone again.

She felt him get up, then before she could protest, he lifted her into his arms. "Trace?" She couldn't even open her eyes.

"Shh, darlin', the worst of the storm is over and I'm taking you up to bed."

She smiled and curled in closer to his warmth. "Oh, I like the sound of that." But suddenly she felt the soft mattress as he laid her down and pulled away.

"Don't go," she whispered as she reached for him. "Please, Trace, don't leave me."

She felt his weight on the mattress, then his reassuring words. "I won't, Kira. I'm here."

With his comforting words, she let herself drift off

to sleep. She felt his kiss against her hair. For the first time in weeks she allowed herself to think that maybe everything would be all right.

Kira's comfort was gone by morning when she woke up and found herself alone. There was no sign of Trace, or that he'd been there during the night. Even though she wanted to stay in bed, she got up, into the shower, then dressed for work.

Downstairs, she found coffee already made and poured herself a cup. She went to the window and glanced at the sunny morning and a deserted bunkhouse. Trace's truck was gone, too.

Disappointed, she knew he and Cal were probably out checking the herd. She wondered if there was any damage to the outer buildings. Would Trace even tell her if there were? He'd always been pretty closemouthed about the running of the ranch.

She'd shown more interest in the first couple of years after they were married. Once they'd started concentrating on a baby, she'd stopped horseback riding.

Looking back, she realized how much she'd pulled away from him with her self-absorbed guilt about not being able to conceive a baby. Trace had only been loving and supportive, never saying anything about the cost of medical procedures their insurance didn't pay for. That had been thousand of dollars.

That only added to her guilt. And when Trace suggested they take a break from trying, she blew up. Didn't talk to him for a week, then they fought some more, saying things that hurt. Things they couldn't take back. She drove him away, first emotionally, then finally, physically he packed his clothes up and moved to the bunkhouse.

Kira went to the sink and poured her coffee out. Not her proudest moment. She loved Trace more than anything, but she had to push and push to see if once again someone she loved left her. And he had.

Kira brushed a tear from her cheek.

Trace didn't have a clue about what was going on inside her. But it wasn't his fault. In the past, she'd only let him see what she wanted him to see.

She'd been unfair to him, but most importantly right now, she hadn't been honest, either. That had to change if they were going to survive. He deserved to know the truth. But, after all this time, could she take the chance that he might not forgive her?

Did it even matter? In six months, she'd lose Trace forever.

CHAPTER FOUR

BY NOON the next day, the heat was pounding against Trace's back. It was nearly unbearable to work, but he kept going. They had to get the storm-damaged roof replaced on the feed barn.

"Man, you'd think the rain would cool things off," Cal said, as he took off his hat and wiped his forehead on his sleeve.

Trace moved another shingle into place, knowing he had no extra money to replace it. "We're in for more rain tonight. So we better get this done, or we'll lose all the hay and feed."

"It was one heck of a storm, but at least they got the electricity back on this morning." Cal reached for a nail and hammer. "I bet Kira was frightened. I wasn't surprised when you didn't come back to the bunkhouse last night."

Trace continued to work. "She wasn't feeling well. Once she took some medication, she finally fell asleep. I guess I did, too."

"Looks like I'll be losing a roommate soon."

"It doesn't look like that to me," Trace argued. "Nothing is settled."

Cal grinned. "If you say so."

"Damn, straight, I say so." Trace pounded in a nail for emphasis. "Can you get more work done and do less talking?"

"Sure, boss." Cal glanced toward the road. "But I doubt you will." He nodded to the black, luxury sedan. "Seems Jarrett has found you again."

Trace turned around to see his brother climb out of the car. This was not what he needed today. "I better go get this over with."

Trace made his way down the ladder and caught up with his brother at the corral gate. Jarrett was dressed in tailored navy slacks, a fitted white dress shirt and Italian loafers that probably cost more than Trace's entire wardrobe.

"Hey, I thought I told you to come by the office."

"I've been busy," Trace said. That was the only excuse he was giving him.

"We're all busy, but this is business. Didn't want to say anything the other day with Kira there but the loan payment is due."

"Not until the end of June," Trace corrected. "Don't worry you'll get your money." He started to walk away, but Jarrett stopped him.

"Hey, I'm not here to hound you. I'm here to make you an offer."

Trace frowned. His brother never did anything unless it benefited him. "Not interested."

"Come on, Trace. You haven't even given me a chance."

"Okay, what is it?"

"How about I buy back that southwest section of land? Then your loan will be paid in full."

Trace remained silent for a moment, knowing without a doubt his brother was up to something. "Are you going to develop that section?"

Jarrett shrugged. "Eventually, when the market recovers. Westchester Ridge is growing with new businesses and housing will be needed." He glanced toward the mountains. "There's a lot of pretty scenery around here."

"And I plan to keep it that way. We've talked about this, Jarrett, I'm not crazy about running cattle up to a tract of homes." He started to walk away.

"What if I put in writing that I won't develop that section of land for ten years? Would you be willing to listen then?"

"What is it with you? When Dad and Mom died you couldn't wait to unload your share of the ranch. I bought you out, now you want some back." He shook his head. "What are you up to?"

Jarrett's gaze darted away. "I'm not at liberty to talk about it now."

"Well, then I'm not talking, either."

"I guess I'll just wait until you lose it all," his brother called to him.

"I haven't lost anything. You'll get your money."

"Sure you can afford it?" He cocked an eyebrow. "Adoption can get pretty expensive."

Trace's chest tightened. Of course Jarrett would have been contacted by the agency. "I'm handling it. Now, I need to get back to work." He marched off, refusing to argue any longer with his brother.

Mostly Trace hated that he didn't have all the money. He was going to have to come up with some other way to pay off the loan. Worse, how was he going to be able to give Kira what she wanted, too?

After getting Mrs. Fletcher's phone call that morning, Kira finished her appointments at school and hurried home. The counselor had asked if she could move up the interview time for today instead of Monday. Kira would have liked the rest of the week to prepare, but she couldn't say no.

Except she couldn't get ahold of Trace. She'd been calling him for hours, but kept getting his voice mail. It was nearly one o'clock when Kira pulled into the driveway. She rushed into the house and put on a pot of coffee, then straightened up the kitchen. She called down to the bunkhouse and left a message for Trace. Then tried his cell phone again, before noticing it on the table. He must have left it last night.

A shiver went through her as she recalled the feel of his arms around her. The way she felt pressed against his strong body during the storm. Kira wanted that again. If only she could convince Trace to come back home, and back into their marriage.

Kira's thoughts turned to the possibility of a baby. Is that what Mrs. Fletcher would tell them today? There was also the intense scrutiny for an adoption. They could dig up a lot of things from her past. They knew about her time in foster care. All those years she hadn't shared with Trace.

He deserved to know the truth.

There was a knock on the back door. Kira took a calming breath, put on a smile and opened the door to find a middle-aged woman with a big smile and warm blue eyes.

"Kira McKane?" she began, "I'm Lucy Fletcher from Places in the Heart Agency."

"Welcome, Mrs. Fletcher. Please, come in."

Kira stepped back and allowed the woman to walk inside the big farm kitchen.

"Oh, this is lovely." She glanced around the newly remodeled room. There were maple cabinets and natural stone countertops and the walls were painted a spring green.

"Thank you. My husband and I remodeled right after we were married. I just wish I could spend more time at home." Kira directed her to the round table. And they sat down.

Mrs. Fletcher opened her briefcase and took out a file. "I know you've worked with Jessica Long for the past several months, but I'm taking over some of her cases while she's recovering from surgery. I hope that's not a problem."

"Not at all."

"Good. When opportunities arise, there's no time to wait." She glanced over the paper. "You're a high school guidance counselor. So are you planning to stay home if you have a child?"

Kira hesitated. She wanted to, if they could afford it.

"There's no wrong answer, Kira. It's hard these days to make it without two incomes."

"I'd like to stay home, of course, but adoption is expensive."

Mrs. Fletcher nodded. "It's true you have to help absorb the expenses of the biological mother. One good thing about working in the school system, you have holidays and the summers off." She glanced around. "Is your husband going to be here today?"

"I hope so. I just realized that he left his cell phone here on the table this morning. And after the storm he needed to check for damage. He usually comes in for lunch."

"Good, I'm anxious to meet him." She smiled. "Why don't you show me your lovely home?"

"Sure." Kira took a breath and stood. "Would you like to see the nursery?"

"Eventually. Maybe we can start downstairs."

Kira relaxed some as they made their way through the rooms until the tour finally ended upstairs in the master bedroom. The walls were painted a soft blue, to offset the large, dark furniture.

She had made the bed this morning, but she couldn't help but recall last night with Trace. How he held her so tenderly. She quickly shook away the memory.

"The antique furniture belonged to my husband's grandparents. I discovered it in the attic after we were married. I don't think Trace was crazy about bringing it down."

"It's beautiful."

The next room across the hall was the nursery. Kira hesitated, then opened the door. It had been a while since she'd come in here. The walls were a buttery-yellow, with an old rocker she'd sanded and painted white. And there was a hand-carved cradle that had been in Trace's family for generations.

"Oh, this is lovely." Mrs. Fletcher walked to the row of windows that overlooked the pasture. "I see you are prepared." She went to the cradle. "Is this another treasure from the attic?"

Kira nodded. "I know we'll need a proper baby bed, but it's hard to get too excited, yet. I don't want to be disappointed."

"I hope that isn't the case, too." Mrs. Fletcher gave her a soft smile. "You and your husband have been very cooperative, releasing all your records to us." She glanced down at her notes. "We've just received your medical file states that you have advanced endometriosis. No miscarriages, but a live birth."

Kira hesitated, then knew she couldn't risk a lie and cause her to lose this chance. "Yes."

Mrs. Fetcher blinked in surprise. "You have a child?"

Kira's heart drummed against her chest, she paused, then rushed on to tell the social worker what she'd never told anyone. "Yes, I had a child fifteen years ago. I…I gave him up for adoption."

"I see." Lucy Fletcher studied her, then said, "I appreciate you telling me, Kira."

"Do you think this will hurt our chances for a baby?"

"Of course not." The woman touched her hand. "I believe you did what was best for everyone, especially the child."

Just then Kira glanced up and caught sight of her freshly showered husband standing in the doorway. Panic froze her, seeing the intense look from him.

Mrs. Fletcher turned around. "Oh, you must be Trace. I'll Lucy Fletcher from Places in the Heart. I've looked forward to meeting you."

Trace accepted her hand and shook it. "It's nice to meet you, too. Sorry, I'm late, I needed to shower off the mud."

"We did get quite the storm last night, didn't we."

"And I needed to do some repairs first thing this morning."

Kira couldn't help but wonder how much of the conversation Trace had overheard. "I explained to Mrs. Fletcher you forgot to take your cell phone with you. So I couldn't get hold of you."

Mrs. Fletcher stepped in. "I've enjoyed spending time talking with your wife while she showed me around your beautiful home."

"Kira has done most of the decorating." Trace stood beside her, but he didn't touch her.

"Well, if you have a few minutes, Trace, I'd like to talk with you both."

"Let's go downstairs," Kira suggested, praying there wouldn't be any more talk about her past. She led them into the dining room, then went to get the coffee.

In the kitchen, Kira willed herself to stop shaking. If Trace overheard she'd deal with it. If he hadn't she needed to tell him. Everything. With a calming breath, she returned to the dining room table with coffee and cookies. She sat down next to Trace. He continued to answer questions she knew he'd been asked before by the other counselor.

Finally Lucy Fletcher sat back and eyed the two of

them. "Would you both be available again on Monday afternoon?"

Kira immediately nodded. "Of course."

Trace hesitated. "You have more questions?"

Mrs. Fletcher shook her head. "I'm in agreement with Jessie Long that you two would make wonderful parents. It's a birthmother who wants to speak with you."

"Birthmother?" Kira said, barely capable of breathing.

"Yes. I gave her your file and she's asked for a home visit." Mrs. Fletcher smiled. "She has chosen you two as possible parents for her baby."

Heart pounding, Kira glanced at Trace, unable to read his thoughts. She turned back to Mrs. Fletcher. "She wants to meet us?"

"You said you don't have a problem with an open adoption. Have you changed your mind?"

"No! It's just I didn't expect it would happen so fast."

"Sometimes that's how it works. So is Monday afternoon okay?"

Kira didn't know how to answer, but Trace took it out of her hands. "Monday will be fine."

Mrs. Fletcher stood. "Good. We'll see you here then."

Kira walked the woman out and stood on the porch until she got in her car and drove off. Hugging herself, she tried to control her trembling as a hundred thoughts raced through her head. A baby. Were they really going to get a baby?

Her excitement died knowing she had to face Trace.

Had he heard their conversation? And how was she going to try to explain why she'd kept her past a secret? What if Mrs. Fletcher brought it up again? She turned to go back into the house, praying Trace still cared for her enough to listen to her reasons.

Inside, she found Trace carrying the cups to the sink. He didn't look at her. Instead he busied himself with the cleanup.

She couldn't let him shut her out again. "Do you have time to talk before you go back to work?"

He grabbed the towel and wiped his hands off, then looked at her. "Don't you think it's a little late for that now?"

Trace had gotten Kira's voice message on the bunkhouse phone. Filthy, he'd jumped into the shower and dressed before he'd headed to the house to meet with Mrs. Fletcher. He'd known how important this was to Kira, and to him, too. He was willing to go through another round of invasive questions. Anything to help Kira. So she could have the child she'd always dreamed of.

He heard Kira's voice from the nursery, but by the time he went into the room, she'd stopped talking. She'd looked surprised to see him there. But wasn't he supposed to play a part in this?

"What do you mean there's nothing to talk about?" Kira asked.

"It seems already settled and Monday we're going to be talking to a woman about raising her child. It's what you want, Kira."

She looked hurt. "You agreed for her to come here. Please tell me now if you've changed your mind."

Trace's mind was reeling. He didn't realize it would be this hard. He'd be lying if he said he didn't want a child with Kira, but like this? He began to think about the next six months, living in the same house. Just walking by her and inhaling her heavenly scent. He would never feel her warmth, her softness against him. When he raised his head, those big brown eyes stared up at him, mesmerizing him.

All the things he would lose forever. This short time was all they had together. Was this the only way he could be a part of her life?

"It's happening so fast," he said.

"Isn't it better this way?" she asked.

Trace studied Kira. He could see the strain on her face, knew how anxious she was. She wanted a baby, even at the cost of their marriage.

He walked toward her. "This is life changing, Kira. You're taking on a lot by yourself, trying to raise a baby."

"I don't have a choice."

"There's always a choice." He stared down at her. He wanted her. If only to taste her mouth, bury himself into her body. But that would be a temporary fix for their problems.

He sighed. He had some thinking to do.

"I've got to get back to work." He practically ran out, more frightened than he'd ever been in his life that he could lose everything. And he wasn't talking about the ranch.

* * *

Later that afternoon, Kira stood in the Winchester Ridge High School auditorium, trying to concentrate on the graduation rehearsal that was going on. But it wasn't working. Between her lack of sleep, and the earlier visit from Mrs. Fletcher, her head was all over the place.

Especially Trace's disappearance. She'd planned to try to talk to him some more, but he conveniently couldn't be found. Worse, her plan had backfired. She'd hoped for some enthusiasm about the possibility of getting a baby, instead Trace was off brooding.

The last thing she wanted was to end their marriage. She loved Trace. When the letter arrived from the agency, she'd hoped her husband wanted to work on saving it, too.

Now with the graduation ceremony tomorrow, she had no choice but to be at school. Then she had to get through the class roundup Saturday before the seniors would go off for the summer. After that she would have Trace alone. They couldn't go on avoiding each other. She knew she'd pushed him away over the past year with her mood swings, her needy attitude. That wasn't going to happen again.

She sighed. In the beginning of their marriage it was simple. He'd loved her, and she'd loved him. Then with her difficulties to conceive a baby, things had turned sour. Instead of turning to each other, they'd turned away. So how could she ask him to just forget everything and convince him to be her husband again? So instead she offered him a divorce with no strings. She just prayed he wouldn't take it.

Tears burned behind her eyes. What she wanted more

than anything else was the chance to make another go of their marriage. Maybe if she'd been honest with him from the start things would be different, but she couldn't even tell him about the child she'd given away. The child who claimed a big piece of her heart.

Hearing her name called brought her back to the present. Kira looked up in time to see the last of the students march across the stage as the principal handed them a substitute diploma. Then they all returned to their seats, the recessional march played and the students filed out. Kira followed them. Once outside she gathered the group for last minute instructions.

"Another thing, class," she began, then looked up feeling her throat tighten. She'd known most of these kids since they were freshmen. Now, some were going off to college, some to the military and others into the work force. She only prayed that she'd given them enough help to survive. More than she ever got at their age.

"This is the last time I'm going to be able to say that." She looked up at Jason Rush, Steve Matthews and Michael Begay. All of them were well over six feet tall. "It's been a delight to have you all this past year," she said, fighting the emotions. "I'd like to continue our friendships, so please…please, when you celebrate be smart. Please don't drink and drive."

She reached up and tapped Steve on the side of the head playfully. "I worked too hard for any of you to end up as roadkill on the highway."

The group released a groan.

"No, I don't want to hear any excuses. I just want your promise."

There were disgruntled murmurs of response, then the group dispersed. All except Jody Campbell. She seemed to be hanging back. Maybe she wanted to talk again. Kira walked toward the young woman.

"Do you need a ride home, Jody?"

"I can walk," the girl said as she hugged her slim body. She looked too thin in her baggy jeans and T-shirt.

Kira glanced up at the threatening clouds as the wind began to pick up. "Come on, Jody. If I don't give you a ride you'll get drenched."

The girl reluctantly followed Kira to the car. Once they were inside the Jeep Cherokee, the sky opened up. Hearing the rain pelt the top of the car, Kira decided to wait out the downpour. She looked across the seat at her sullen passenger.

"You know, Jody, I'm proud of you. You managed to ace your finals and save some of your grade-point average."

"I lost out on first honors, though." She shrugged. "Oh, well, I'm not going to college anyway."

Kira hated it when any of her students gave up. "Jody, there are other ways to go to school than going away. You can attend community college."

Jody brushed her blond hair from her shoulders and stared out the rain streaked window. "I told you my mom can't afford for me to go to college."

"You could apply for a student loan," Kira suggested. "I'll help you fill out the paperwork."

Jody turned to her. Tears clouded her eyes. "I don't

want your help." She began to sob. "You're wasting your time on me."

"Don't say that, Jody, you're worth every bit of my time."

The girl glanced away. "It doesn't matter anymore, nothing matters." She started to climb out, but Kira reached for her.

"It matters, Jody. Please, don't be so hard on yourself. I promise I won't talk about college. Just tell me you're coming to the roundup."

"I have to work that day."

"That's a shame since you've worked so hard on organizing the party. You've got to come, Jody."

The girl hesitated.

"I promise it'll be the last thing I'll ever ask of you. Come on, you need to celebrate."

"I'll try," the girl said, then jumped out of the car, and ran off in the rain.

Kira didn't go after her. She knew from her own experience that she couldn't make Jody confide in her if she didn't want to. But Kira was going to be darn sure that she was there for her. And she had a strange feeling the girl was going to need her.

Trace was angry with himself for riding Thunder so hard. And what had it accomplished? Nothing. He climbed down and immediately removed the saddle and blanket, then began walking the lathered horse around to cool him down.

"Sorry, fella. You're the one who had to put up with my bad mood today."

Twenty minutes later, Trace led him into the barn and stall, then started brushing him.

"Did the ride help your mood?"

Trace looked over the stall gate to see Cal.

"Probably not." He stopped brushing. "I've got a lot on my mind. You have a problem with that?"

He shook his head. "You're the boss. I'll just stay out of your way." Cal started to leave, then stopped. "Is the senior roundup still on? Are the kids still coming?"

"As far as I know it is, but maybe you should ask Kira."

Cal looked past him toward the doorway and smiled. "I think I will. Hi, Kira, we were just talking about you."

Trace glanced over his shoulder and saw her. She was dressed in jeans and a red and blue print blouse. Her hair was pulled back, showing off the delicate line of her jaw, the softness of her skin.

"Hi, Jonas." She nodded. "Trace."

He didn't have much to say back. "Cal wants to know about the roundup."

"That's why I'm here." She directed her attention to Trace. "I need to double-check on things."

"As long as I have bodies to bring in the herd, you can do whatever you want." The last thing Trace wanted to do was pretend that everything was perfect between them all day, but why disappoint the kids.

"You sure?" she asked. "With the day of activities, the music and dancing afterward? It's a long day."

"Why would it be any different than in the past four years?" Senior roundup had been Trace's idea after they'd first gotten married.

"Because it is different this year," she told him.

"I've got things to take care of," Cal said and disappeared from the barn.

"That's separate," he said, continuing to brush Thunder. "The roundup has nothing to do with us."

"Trace, it all has everything to do with us." She came to the railing. "I guess we can put off the personal stuff until the roundup is over. But we can't ignore the fact that there is a counselor and birthmother coming Monday."

He closed his eyes a second and took a breath. "Surely we can get through a day together. Call it practice for our interview to see if we qualify as the perfect parents."

When he opened the gate and stepped out, she touched his arm to stop him. "I know the past few months have been hard, but is it that difficult to act as if you care about me? My feelings for you haven't changed, Trace, I love you." She rose up on her toes. Her hand slid up his chest, burning a path of need that threatened to destroy his resolve.

With a groan, Trace captured her mouth in an eager kiss, hating his weakness for her. Yet, it didn't stop his wanting her, needing her. He drew her against his body, hoping to ease some of the ache. It didn't. He released her with a jerk, his breathing labored. Seeing the desire in her rich brown eyes, he had to glance away.

"You can't deny you still care about me," she argued.

"A few heated kisses doesn't make a marriage, Kira." His gaze moved over her pretty face, unable to ignore the hurt his words caused her. He cupped her face. "I couldn't give you what you wanted then, Kira. I'm not sure I can now."

So why in the hell did he want to try so badly?

CHAPTER FIVE

I COULDN'T give you what you wanted, and I'm not sure I can now.

Trace's words still echoed in her head as Kira walked out to the back porch at dawn on Saturday. Over the last forty-eight hours she tried to stay hopeful. Hopeful that he would say yes to staying with her during the adoption process. It was a perfect opportunity to work on their marriage. That was if he still wanted to be a part of her life, and their baby's life.

All those answers had to be put off until the roundup was over. Once alone Sunday night, they could discuss things and make a decision before the biological mother's visit on Monday.

Trace had stayed away from the house as he prepared for the roundup. And even though she'd had the graduation to help supervise, Kira still found time to think about the future.

Would it include Trace, and a baby?

Now she just had to get through this day, the senior roundup. Kira stepped off the back porch and walked toward the rows of tables that had been set up the night before by the graduates' parents, grateful their kids would have a safe place to celebrate. To protect the guests and the food from the hot sun, several canopies shaded the area. A big banner hung across the barn that read, Winchester Ridge High School Senior Roundup, Class Of 2009.

Kira smiled. She loved doing the party. Both Trace and she had enjoyed it the past. And as far as she could tell, he was okay with it this year, too.

Some of the senior boys had showed up ready to ride in the roundup. They were gathering in the corral with their mounts. Then she saw Trace lead Thunder out of the barn and head to the group. She watched him give directions to the men, then grabbed hold of the saddle horn and easily swung onto his mount.

Panic rose in Kira when she realized that he was ready to leave without saying goodbye. Then he looked in her direction, giving her a sliver of hope that he wanted her to send him off like she had in the past. Trace shouted something to Cal, then walked his horse in the opposite direction, toward her.

Kira caught up to him about halfway. "You're leaving already?"

He nodded and watched the group of men walking their horses through the gate toward the range. "I want to have the herd back by ten. Barring any problems, we should be."

Nodding, she stepped closer to stroke Thunder, but the animal was anxious to take off, too. "The rest of the kids should be here by then to help with the branding."

He tugged on the reins to get the stallion back under

control. "I'll send one of the hands back ahead of us." He hesitated. "Just to make sure none of the kids get in the way. I don't want anyone to get hurt."

"We have some of the dads assigned to help out."

She couldn't take her eyes off Trace, and the way he handled the horse. In jeans and a chambray shirt, he wore his usual belt with the large buckle with the McK brand. It had belonged to his grandfather.

"Be careful," she said, placing her hand on his knee. If the contact bothered him, he didn't let on. Darn. "And tell the men there'll be plenty of good food waiting for them."

He cocked an eyebrow. "Will there be some of your potato salad?"

The request surprised her. "I might be persuaded to whip up a batch." She already had it made and chilling in the refrigerator.

She'd been encouraged after he'd kissed her last night, knowing he was fighting his feelings toward her. She wasn't going to make it easy for him, either. She stared at him, catching his incredible gray eyes.

"Be careful today."

"I'm not foolish, especially with green kids to look out for."

Her fingers flexed against his knee. "Just make sure you look out for you, too."

Trace started to speak, but someone whistled to him. He glanced at the riders off in the distance. "I've got to go."

"Stay safe." She stepped back as he tugged his hat lower, kicked Thunder's sides and they shot off. She trembled as she watched until he disappeared over the horizon.

"Now, I'd say that man wants to stay married."

Kira gasped as she swung around. She found her friend smiling at her. "Michele. I didn't expect you so soon."

Her fellow counselor smiled. "You weren't exactly paying attention. So I take it things are okay with you two?"

Kira released a breath. "It isn't that simple." She knew she had to tell Trace everything. "There's a lot we need to deal with."

Her friend frowned. "Maybe you should skip the talking and go straight to…other things."

That had never been the problem. "I can't rush Trace." Kira had never lived in one place long enough to make any close friends. Not before Michele.

"Well, if it were me, I'd hang onto that cowboy any way I could." Michele looked around. "Um, do you think Jarrett is going to show up today?"

Kira frowned, surprised at her friend's question. "Why would Jarrett come today? He's never helped out before, well, not since I've been here."

"I ran into him at the diner yesterday." Michele shrugged. "I told him about today, and he said he might drop by."

Kira studied her. Michele was interested in her brother-in-law? "Well, if he does it's because he wants something."

Michele grinned. "Yeah, and I'm hoping it's me. You're not the only one who wants a good-looking McKane man."

* * *

Three hours later, Trace was riding drag behind the herd. Thanks to the recent rain, there wasn't much dust kicked up. Just the steady sound of mamas calling to their calves.

He relaxed in the saddle, letting Thunder do the work as he glanced at the incredible scenery. North was the Roan Plateau and thick rows of tall pines of the White River National Forest. He had grown up in this area, hunted and fished here all his life. He never wanted to live anywhere else. He wanted to continue on the family tradition, to raise a family here on McKane land and hand it down to his kids.

Sadness took him by surprise. Now his marriage was possibly coming to an end. What was he supposed to do, just walk away and find someone else? Trouble was, there wasn't anyone else for him. He'd known that the second he'd laid eyes on Kira Hyatt. He fell in love. Now, she wanted to end it all.

Suddenly a few calves ran by and caught up with their mamas, then Cal rode up beside him.

"Did you get them all?"

The foreman nodded. "Yeah. Jerry's hanging back to make sure."

Trace glanced over nearly three hundred heads. "That's about a hundred and fifty calves to brand. It looks like we'll be busy today. If we get them separated fast, break for lunch, then we can work four teams on the branding irons and castrating. We should finish up by afternoon."

Cal grinned. "That's if those senior boys are willing to work. Remember there will be teenage girls hanging on the fence watching them."

"Then you'll have to keep them in line."

Trace could still remember Kira's first roundup, and how distracted she'd made him. It was long before there had been a senior roundup. They had only been dating a few weeks. He shifted in the saddle, recalling that had been the first night he'd made love to her. He released a long breath. That seemed like another lifetime ago.

"Sure, boss," Cal said. "Are there any other miracles you want today?"

Trace remained quiet, but there was one. All he'd ever wanted was Kira, but it might take a miracle to save their marriage.

"They're coming," one of the kids yelled.

Kira climbed up on the stock pen fence, and excitement raced through her as she looked for Trace. It was hard not to be swept up in it. She could imagine a hundred years ago the ranchers' wives doing the same thing, cheering for their men as they brought in the herd.

About a dozen teenage girls were all decked out in their best Western clothes. Kira smiled. Some things never change. It was all about the boy getting the girl. She glanced down at her own dark denim jeans, and new teal Western-style blouse. Since she wasn't planning to do any branding, she could dress up, too.

Would Trace care, or would he be too busy with his work? In the past, he'd always noticed her. Maybe he didn't say a lot, but he couldn't hide his reaction.

When Cal rode in, he assigned jobs to the boys who were to help separate the calves from the cows. Mooing sounds filled the air as the first of the herd arrived.

Things got busy as riders did their jobs to corral the herd.

Trace arrived and was busy shouting orders when suddenly a calf bolted away. He shot off after the wayward bovine. Kira was mesmerized watching the two, man and horse working in unison, cutting off the animal and forcing him back.

"Well, that was impressive," Michele said.

"Thunder is a great cutting horse."

"The cowboy isn't bad, either."

Kira finally smiled. "No, he's not." She glanced past her friend to see Jody arrive.

She started toward the girl who was dressed in faded jeans and a white blouse. She didn't have any fancy boots, just athletic shoes. The girl reminded Kira so much of herself at that age.

"Jody, I'm so glad you could make it."

"I can't stay too late. My mom can't pick me up."

"Then I'll take you home," Kira offered. "You're not missing all the fun."

"But I didn't bring anything to wear to the dance tonight."

Kira smiled. "I have something you can wear," she whispered. "I'm sure we can find something you like."

Jody looked surprised. "Really?"

Kira nodded as another classmate, Laura Carson, came up to them. "Please stay, Jody. This is our last time the class will be together."

Jody glanced around, sadness etched on her face. "But Ben's here."

"So what?" Laura said. "He's a jerk anyway. We'll hang out together."

"How about I put you two in charge of the food tables?"

The two friends exchanged smiles. "Okay."

"Then let's get the other girls together and haul the food out. The guys will finish soon and be hungry."

Jody and Laura gathered up some classmates and they headed off to the kitchen.

"Oh, to be that young and carefree again," Michele said.

Kira nodded, but realized she hadn't felt carefree since the day her parents died and she was left alone.

Trace had been busy most of the day, and so had Kira. Their paths had only crossed once when he'd gotten in line for the noon meal. She served him a plate of fried chicken, a big helping of potato salad and a smile.

He liked the smile the best.

Now, one hundred and forty-one calves had been branded, and eighty-seven castrated into steers which he'd once planned to run in a summer herd. But with the loan payment coming due, he needed to sell them off now, along with some of his heifers. If he got enough money, he could hang on to his breeding bulls a while longer. They were a big part of their future and keeping the ranch going.

A dark sedan car pulled into the driveway, catching Trace's attention. The tall, athletic, Jarrett McKane climbed out and walked toward him with that cocky attitude that demanded people's attention. And he got it.

Trace was surprised, but more suspicious of his brother's casual appearance in faded jeans and a dark Western shirt. What reason would Jarrett have to show up at the roundup?

Trace's thoughts turned to his older brother's business proposition. It would be easy to hand back the land, but he knew Jarrett had never felt the same way he did about the ranch. If someone wanted it, for the right price, his brother would sell. Somebody had to want that section of land—and badly—for Jarrett to work so hard to get it back.

"Hey, bro, I hear you could use some help," Jarrett said.

"I'd say you were a little late. We finished the branding a while ago. But if you really want to help out, Cal can use your help separating the yearlings." He raised an eyebrow. "That is, if you still remember how to ride a horse."

His brother's eyes narrowed. "As I recall, I've beaten you in a few rodeos."

Jarrett had beaten him in a lot of things. "Then prove it."

"I will, but first, I need to say hello to a few people."

Trace took hold of his arm. "I won't have you wheeling and dealing at Kira's school function."

"You're pretty protective of the little mother-to-be."

Trace stiffened as he glanced around. "I'd appreciate it if you'd keep that to yourself. Nothing is definite yet."

Jarrett relented. "Sure."

"I mean it, Jarrett."

"Okay. Okay." He pulled away and walked off, but

slowed his gait when Michele Turner came toward him. Then together the two went toward the branding pens.

"Trace."

He turned around to see Kira. He put on a smile. "How's it going?"

"Good, so far. We're just about to start the contests. Are you able to help with the cutting competition? Mark Petersen is going to handle steer wrestling, and Cal will do the roping."

Trace shook his head. "Where do these kids get so much energy?" They started walking toward the branding pen. "I could use a nap."

She smiled. "I wouldn't mind one, either."

His gaze locked with hers. "You think they'd notice if we disappeared?"

Kira swallowed hard, and turned away. "Yeah, I think so."

Trace's body tensed. He tried not to remember those past lazy afternoons when they'd go up to the bedroom and make love for hours. Where had those carefree days gone?

"I better get going," he murmured, then turned and walked away. He quickened his steps. He didn't need to be thinking about Kira right now, especially since they hadn't been intimate in months.

He groaned and kept walking. Today was about the kids. He needed to keep his desire for Kira out of it.

A nearly impossible task.

Kira stood at the corral fence along with the other kids and parents, watching Trace work Thunder. She'd always been in awe of her husband's skill with horses. He looked so at ease on the powerful stallion, but there was no doubt who was in charge. Trace.

She glanced down at his gloved hands. She knew that along with that power came gentleness. A shiver raced through her, recalling the nights he'd stroked her, caressed her body, bringing her endless pleasure.

"He's pretty good."

Kira fought a blush as she turned to find Jarrett next to her at the railing. "Yes, he is."

A mischievous grin appeared on his face. "That's because I taught him everything he knows."

Cheers broke out from the crowd. "Really?" She hadn't known her brother-in-law as a young man. And just barely got to know him better over the past few years because Trace and he weren't close. A few holidays here and there when their folks were alive. "Since I've never seen you on a horse, I can't judge."

"And you're loyal to your husband."

"Always."

"Lucky guy."

She'd known Jarrett was attracted to her when she first came to town. But the minute she saw Trace, she couldn't think of anyone else. "Okay, what do you want, Jarrett?"

"Can't I give my sister-in-law a compliment?" He looked toward the corral. "I know things have been rough for you both lately." He glanced around, then lowered his voice. "Well, what I mean is the adoption."

Of course Trace's brother would be interviewed by the agency. She stepped down from the railing and Jarrett followed her away from the other people. "We're still in the beginning stages. I'd appreciate it if you kept it quiet for now."

"Of course." He paused. "I never realized that things…I mean I know you two wanted kids, but I never dreamed it was like this."

She managed a smile and touched his arm. "It's okay, Jarrett. I've accepted it," she lied, not wanting to go over this now, or with him.

He nodded. "Well, if there's anything I can do. There's a doctor I knew in college. He's made a name for himself in the fertility field."

It was nice that he wanted to help, but they'd already been to two specialists. "Thank you, Jarrett. We've been to doctors, and it hasn't helped." She blinked back tears. "Hopefully adoption will give us the family we want." She told him about the appointment on Monday.

"That's great news." He hugged her. "Is there anything I can do to help? I know it's expensive."

Kira started to answer, when she heard, "We can handle it."

They both turned to see Trace.

She stepped back from Jarrett, seeing the look on her husband's face. Jealousy? "Trace. I thought you were working with the kids."

He moved up beside her and stood close. "Cal and some of the other hands are handling the competition." He looked at her, but his gray eyes were unreadable. "Thought you might need some help."

She managed to pull her gaze away from his. "I've just been waiting for the DJ to set up for the dance. Jody Campbell organized everything, she's assigned all the kids with a job." She glanced around the area. "Maybe I should go find her. If you men will excuse me."

Trace watched Kira walk off. He wanted to go after her, and he would, just as soon as he figured out why his brother was here.

"Okay, what's going on, Jarrett?"

"I told you, I just came by to help out. You should have called me about the roundup."

"I've called you for help over the years. You've always been busy. Why is the ranch suddenly important to you?"

"Just because I don't want to run the place doesn't mean I don't care about the ranch."

"Then prove it. Don't call in my loan in thirty days. Give me more time."

Jarrett hesitated. "If you really don't have the money, do you think you can keep the ranch going?"

"Yes, the ranch is making money. I just have other expenses." He hated telling his brother the details. "Like you said, adopting a baby is expensive. If I need to, I'll sell off my breeding bulls."

Jarrett looked distracted, and Trace caught Michele walking toward them. "Come by my office next week, we'll talk." Jarrett rushed off before Trace could say anything.

Trace had wanted to look up to his older brother, but years of watching him take from people and receive all the benefits of the favored son had changed that.

The one time Trace came in first had been with Kira, when she'd chosen him over his brother. Now, he could lose her, too. If that happened, it didn't matter if he kept the ranch, or not.

CHAPTER SIX

THE afternoon was in full swing as Trace kept busy sharing his expertise with the kids. He had Jake Petersen on Thunder, instructing him on the art of cutting.

Kira noticed that the teenage girls were watching intently. Most of the females were eyeing the boys, but a few of the mothers had their attention square on her husband.

Had Trace noticed it, too? Did he notice the other women? Desire other women? A woman who could give him a child?

Suddenly cheers broke out in the arena as Jake completed his task. The boy pumped his fist in the air in celebration. Kira smiled, refusing to let anything interfere with this great day. It was for the kids. Next, Ben Kerrigan climbed on the horse and began his turn. Although he wasn't as successful, the crowd cheered him on. All except for Jody.

Kira noticed the teenage girl stayed back from the group, but when Ben got down from his ride, she was waiting for him at the corral gate. After talking a moment, Ben shook his head and stormed off.

Not good. Kira threw up a prayer, hoping it was nothing more serious than a silly fight, that she'd been wrong about a possible pregnancy. Something she knew about firsthand and could change your life, forever.

Kira heard her name called and turned around and saw Trace walking in her direction. "Want to try a turn at cutting?"

"You're kidding. You want me to make a fool of myself in front of the kids?"

"You're a good rider, Kira. I doubt you could ever look foolish." He tugged on her arm. "Come on, I dare you."

Just then a chant started amongst the kids. "Mrs. McKane. Mrs. McKane." That and Trace's sexy grin, she couldn't resist. The kids began to cheer as Trace led her to the horse. "Just remember it's been a long time since I've been on a horse."

"It's okay, Kira. I'll be close by," he assured her.

"Promise?" That had been something they used to say to each other.

He nodded. "Promise."

Kira tore her gaze away to concentrate on her task. She placed her foot in the stirrup and found Trace's hands on her waist, boosting her up. Once in the saddle, she pulled her cowboy hat down on her head to shield her eyes from the bright sunlight, then looked at her husband. "Refresh me on what to do."

"First of all, relax." He reached up and placed her hands on the horn, letting the reins go slack. "Let Thunder do the work."

"Yes, sir."

With a wink, he strolled to the side of the corral and

called out instructions. When one of the boys released a young steer, the cutting horse took off, twisting and turning, trying to maneuver the cow back toward the fence. Kira kept her legs pressed firmly against the horse and her hands on the saddle horn. It took a while but she relaxed as Thunder did his job, then the bell rang to signal time was up.

The kids broke into cheers as Trace came out to help her off. "You were great," he said, then surprised her with a quick kiss on the lips. The crowd roared with approval. A sudden heat rose to her face as Kira made her way back to the fence. *Don't make anything out of his attention,* she told herself. *It's only for show.*

Two classmates, Amy and Marcy, rushed to her. "Oh, Mrs. McKane, that was so cool," Amy gushed. "And Mr. McKane is so good-looking." Then the girls ran off giggling, quickly distracted by another boy riding Thunder.

Back to work. Kira turned her attention to the barn and the truck unloading the audio equipment for the dance in a few hours. At the patio area she saw the volunteer fathers starting up the barbecues for the hamburgers. She checked her watch to see that everything was on schedule.

"Mrs. McKane."

Kira turned around to see Jody and Laura hurrying toward her.

"Jody, Laura, are you having fun?"

They answered with smiles. "Oh, yes," Laura said. "We're going to eat soon. By then the DJ will be ready to start the music. Some of the girls want to change their clothes. I've put the Girls Only sign on the bunkhouse door."

Kira thought about the room that Trace had been staying in and wondered if he'd locked it. "Do you know what rooms to use?"

"Mr. McKane gave us permission to use three rooms and a bathroom. He said he locked the rooms we can't use. And Cal will make sure the boys stay away."

"Good. Laura, would you ask your mother to help supervise?"

"Sure. Come on, Jody."

Kira placed a hand on Jody. "I need her to help me with something first." Kira wanted Jody to stay for the evening, and if that meant finding her something to wear, then that's what she'd do. "She'll meet up with you later."

At the girl's nod, Kira took Jody to the house.

"You don't have to do this, Mrs. McKane."

"I know. But I want you to stay and enjoy the party. You're a graduate, this is supposed to be a wonderful time for you. Enjoy it."

They passed several mothers in the kitchen, setting out the leftovers for supper. With a promise to be back soon to help out, she took Jody through the house and up the stairs.

"Your house is so beautiful, Mrs. McKane."

"Thank you. It's my husband's family home." The first home she'd had in a very long time, since her parents' death. She wondered how much longer she would call it home.

Kira walked down the hall into the master bedroom,

but when she turned around she'd lost her companion. Then she saw Jody across the hall in the nursery.

"Jody."

The girl jumped. "I'm sorry." She pointed to the cradle. "Are you going to have a baby?"

"Sadly, no." Kira forced a smile. "Trace and I would love to have a child, but so far, it hasn't happened."

"Oh. Sorry, I didn't mean to be nosy."

"It's okay." Kira nodded and together they walked into the master bedroom. She went to the closet and began the search. She pulled out a couple of gauzy skirts and a peasant blouse. Kira glanced at Jody. "What size are you, about a four?"

The girl hesitated, then nodded.

Kira stopped. "Don't worry, Jody. I've never worn these clothes to school. No one will know that they aren't yours. Besides, don't girls borrow clothes from friends?"

She nodded. "But you're my guidance counselor."

Kira smiled. "Not anymore."

Jody finally smiled, too. "I guess not."

"Okay, I think this multicolored skirt will work. It has kind of a Western look." She went to the dresser and took out a bright-pink, cotton top and a wide belt. Then she went to the closet again and found a denim jacket. "It'll get cool tonight." She glanced at the girl's white canvas shoes. "I think your shoes will work with the outfit, but if not, I have boots."

The teenager eyed the clothes draped on the bed. "These are so beautiful. What if something happens to them?"

"They're only clothes, Jody." Kira headed out. "When you leave, go out the front door and no one will see you. Now, you better get dressed. I'm depending on you to help supervise the party."

"Thank you, Mrs. McKane."

"You're welcome." Kira shut the door and was surprised to see Trace waiting for her in the hall. "Trace. Is there a problem?"

"No, but since the girls have taken over the bunkhouse, I was going to shower and change here. Then I heard you in there with Jody."

He was coming to their bedroom to change. "Can you wait a few minutes?"

"I could shower in the guest bath, but my good jeans and boots are in the closet," he suggested.

"You go and I'll bring you your clothes." She nudged him toward the bathroom.

He hesitated. "Have I told you what a great job you're doing today?" He jerked a nod toward their bedroom. "And getting Jody something to wear was awfully nice of you."

She shrugged. "She doesn't have the money to dress like the other kids." Kira glanced away. "I know what it's like to be different. To feel left out."

He only nodded, then went to the bath, and closed the door. Soon, she heard the sound of the water running in the shower.

The bedroom door opened and Jody stepped out. "Oh, Jody, you look so cute," Kira told her.

"You think so?"

"Yes, just let me put a little makeup on you," She

guided her into the bathroom. Ten minutes later, she'd fixed her hair and added color to the girl's cheeks. Pleased with her work, Kira sent Jody off to her friends.

Trace felt foolish sneaking down the hall in his own house, practically naked. And he wasn't about to put on his dirty clothes. Not hearing a sound, he peered into the bedroom. His heart shot off pounding when he found Kira standing in front of the full-length mirror. She had on a bright pink and green sundress, and a matching sweater. Her hair was pulled back from her pretty face, hoop earrings hung from each delicate lobe.

She turned and suddenly gasped when she saw him. "Trace. Oh, I'm sorry, I forgot your clothes."

"It's okay. Is the coast clear?" He glanced around, then stepped inside, closing the door behind him.

He couldn't help but notice how her gaze roamed over him. It was so intense it felt like a caress. His breath grew labored, his body definitely aware. "I need to shave. Are you finished in the bath."

"Oh, yes, of course."

In the past, he'd play this little game and they'd end up in bed. Now, they both seemed awkward, unable to speak. He walked across the room into the bathroom they'd once shared. It smelled of Kira, her shampoo, her body spray.

He drew a breath like a suffocated man.

She came to the doorway. "I should get back to the party."

He opened the cabinet and was surprised to find all his things still there. He took out his shaving cream. "It should only take me ten minutes and I'll be down." He found he liked her standing there, watching. It was like so many times they'd shared and taken for granted. He caught her reflection in the mirror as he applied the cream to his jaw. She still hadn't left.

"You did a nice thing for Jody."

She shrugged. "It's important she feel good about herself."

He took a swipe across his jaw with the razor. "I'd say you helped her with that tonight."

"Kids can be cruel."

Trace knew that Kira was talking about herself. Although she never talked much about her life in foster care, he knew it had been a bad time. He'd never gone without in his childhood, not for the basic things anyway. So he couldn't share that experience with her.

He paused. "I never want you to feel that way, Kira. Ever again."

She swallowed. "Oh, Trace, I don't. You've always made me feel special. You've given me a great home and life here."

Then why did he feel like he'd let her down?

Two hours later, the barbecue was finished and the music had started just outside the barn on a portable dance floor that had been set up for the nighttime festivities.

Several kids were already dancing, including Jody. She looked adorable. For the next hour, the music switched back and forth between country and rock. When the country came on a lot of the parents made their way to the floor, showing up the kids with their two-stepping.

Cal and some of the ranch hands hung around playing chaperones, making sure the teenagers didn't go off by themselves. There had been strict rules for tonight's party, but that didn't mean some weren't going to try to break them.

She glanced around to see Trace talking with some of the fathers. So far he'd kept his distance since their meeting in the bathroom. Her breathing grew labored, recalling his near-naked body. All at once Trace looked her way. Their gazes locked momentarily, then someone called to her.

"Mrs. McKane."

Kira turned around to see Laura Carson hurrying toward her. "Have you seen Jody?"

"No, I thought she was with you."

The girl's eyes narrowed. "She was until Ben started bugging her. I left them alone because I was hoping they would talk and work things out." She pointed toward a group of trees. "The last time I saw them, they were over there, talking. Later, I saw Ben back with his friends but I can't find Jody anywhere."

"Did you ask Ben?"

She nodded. "He said he didn't know or care where she was."

Well, he was going to care. "Don't panic yet, I'll go look for her."

Kira was worried this would happen. She searched the area and ended up near Ben Kerrigan. She motioned for him to come to her.

"What's up, Mrs. M?"

"I'm concerned about Jody. I can't seem to find her. Would you know where she is?"

He shrugged. His gaze refused to meet hers. "Maybe she left."

"No, I was going to take her home later. I heard you two talked earlier. Was she upset about something?"

He glanced around nervously. "Maybe. We broke up a few weeks ago. She wants to get back together. I told her no way."

"Is that all you told her?"

He didn't say anything.

"At least tell me what direction she went."

"I don't know, maybe that way." He pointed past the corral.

Kira didn't say anything. She took off, knowing there was an upset girl out there, alone. Panic raced through her. She knew what that felt like.

Stopping to grab a flashlight from the barn, Kira headed through the empty corral toward the grove of trees. If Jody wasn't there she'd go back for help, but the last thing the girl needed was an audience for her humiliation.

She approached the trees and heard something. The soft sound of crying. Kira pointed the light toward the ground and kept walking. On a downed tree log, she found Jody. Her legs were drawn up and her head was on her knees, sobbing.

"Jody," Kira whispered as she approached.

The girl suddenly straightened and looked at her. "Who is it?"

"It's me, Kira McKane." She walked to her. "Are you okay?"

"Yeah, I'm fine." She stood and moved away. "Please, just leave me alone."

"I can't, Jody. And you're not okay. Let me help you."

She shook her head. "No! No one can help me. Everybody will hate me when they find out…" She started to walk away.

"No, Jody, they won't. I won't, I promise. I want to help, no matter what it is." Kira hesitated, trying to choose just the right words. "Let me help you."

"Why?"

"I understand what you're going through."

"No, you don't. Nobody does. And Ben doesn't care. He said he never cared about me. And now, he'll hate me."

"That's not true. He's just scared. So are you."

"What do you know about it?"

Kira took a breath and released it, catching movement by a tree. She tensed even more when she recognized the familiar silhouette. Trace. He stepped out so she could see his face in the moonlight. Luckily Jody couldn't.

"I know what it's like to feel alone," She continued to talk. "You think you have nowhere to turn, no one to trust enough to tell them you're pregnant."

She gasped. "How did you find out?"

This wasn't how she wanted Trace to learn about her past. Tears filled her eyes, praying he would understand. "Because I've been there, Jody. I was fifteen. And pregnant."

* * *

Trace froze, fighting to draw air into his lungs as he stared at his wife. Kira? Kira had a baby? In five years of marriage, she'd never told him.

"You're just saying that," Jody countered.

He tried to make out Kira's face in the moonlight. He heard the pain in her voice as her arms hugged herself.

"No, Jody, I'm not," she went on to say as she went to the girl. "And I felt exactly like you do right now. Alone. Like there's nowhere or no one to turn to. But there is, Jody."

The girl began to sob again. "No. My mother can't handle this. I…I let her down. Oh, what am I going to do?"

She took the girl's hands. "Jody, listen to me. You're not alone. There's help out there, and a lot of options for you."

Jody was quiet for a long time, then asked, "What happened to your baby?"

There was a long pause. "I gave him up." Kira's voice was raw with emotion. "I had no family to help me, and I was too young to keep him."

Jody looked up and started to speak—that was when she spotted him in the shadows. "Oh, Mr. McKane." She stumbled to stand.

Kira turned around, too. "Trace."

"Sorry to interrupt." He stepped further into the lit area. "I just wanted to make sure you were all right."

Kira went to him. "We're fine."

"That's good. Then I'll leave."

"No, we'll go back with you." She squeezed Jody's

hand. "We'll talk more later. We'll deal with this together, Jody."

The girl nodded. "Thank you."

This time Kira had no doubt that Trace overheard her admission. Maybe it was better it happened this way. She wouldn't have to figure out a way to explain why she gave away her son. The guilt she'd felt every day since. And no matter what kind of absolution she got from him, it wouldn't make up for the loss she'd felt every day for almost fifteen years.

The night had finally come to an end as Trace watched the last of the graduates and their parents drive off.

Everyone had been exhausted from the day's events, but the roundup was completed successfully and the students had a great time at the party, not realizing what had gone on behind the scenes.

Trace looked at the house. He needed to talk to Kira. With everything going on at the party, there hadn't been time. He fought the anger building inside him. Though could anyone blame him? She'd kept a secret from him, a big secret.

He released a breath and walked up the back steps to the house. No matter how it ended up, it was time she told him everything about her past.

After sending Jake Peterson's dad off with the last of the tables and chairs, he walked into the kitchen and found Kira wiping off the counter. There wasn't much evidence left of the party. She finally turned around and met his gaze. "Oh, Trace. Is everyone gone?"

He nodded. "Yeah, it's just you and me. What about

Jody?" The last he'd seen of the girl had been after they'd brought her back. She sneaked her upstairs until the party ended.

"Laura's parents took her home. I'm going by tomorrow to help her explain things to her mother."

Trace nodded, but he was barely holding it together. Why were they discussing mundane things when their marriage was hanging by a thread? And it was weakening quickly with the weight of the secret she'd kept from him. Just another thing she couldn't share with him

"Were you ever going to tell me, Kira?" When she started to speak, he raised his hand. "And no more excuses, you owe me the truth. In two days we have another visit from the adoption agency, and a birth mother."

She hesitated, then said, "I know you won't believe me, but I was planning to tell you tomorrow."

"Is that what you were talking about with Mrs. Fletcher when I walked in the nursery that day?"

She nodded. "She was going over my medical records, asking about miscarriages and live births. I didn't want to lie."

That did it for Trace. "But it's okay to lie to your husband."

"I didn't exactly lie, Trace."

"No, you just omitted something very important in your past."

"It was a painful past. I never shared that time with anyone. Can't you understand I wanted to forget, to start over," she pleaded. "I wanted a life with you."

He cursed and looked away.

Kira felt the familiar rejection shoot through her body, nearly crippling her. But somehow she found the strength not to let it show.

"Okay, Trace," she began. "What do you want to know? How I could give up my own baby? How could I let a boy talk me into sex at barely fifteen?" She glared at him. "Don't you know all foster kids are wild? We'll do anything." More tears flooded her eyes, blinding her. "I was no better than trash."

"Stop it," he ordered.

"Oh, but you want to hear the truth, don't you? Do you have any idea what it feels like to be an outcast, to have no friends?" She paced along the island counter, glad it was separating them. "It wasn't so bad in grade school, but by the time I was in high school, kids wanted nothing to do with me. Then Michael came along and gave me a little attention, and I grabbed it. Gullible me, I believed him when he said he loved me." A laugh escaped as she swiped at the tears on her cheeks. "Oh God, it had been so long since I'd heard those words. Then when I told him I was pregnant, he acted as if he didn't know me.

"I was devastated," she said in a hoarse whisper. "Worse, the father of my baby was my foster family's nephew. I was packed up so fast and shoved out the door, I didn't know what was happening."

"Where did you go?"

"Girls like me go into a group home. There were several of us who were pregnant. I stayed there until I delivered my baby. My little boy. But I couldn't keep him."

She tried to hold it together, but failed, covering her

eyes she began to sob. Then she felt Trace's arms around her, holding her.

"I'm sorry, Trace. I know I should have told you. But I was afraid that you wouldn't want me either."

"Shh, Kira. Don't talk."

Trace couldn't stand to hear any more of her pain. What she had to go through alone. He was hurt by her lack of trust, but he understood why she'd kept the secret.

Why she desperately wanted another baby.

Kira lifted her head, pain etched on her face. "It's better now that it's out in the open. I was wrong to push you for a baby, Trace. I'm sorry for everything." She turned and hurried out of the room.

He was left dazed. She truly thought that he would leave her because of her past. Why not, everyone else had in her life. He wanted to go to her, but knew if he did he had to make the commitment he was staying, if not as her husband, at least as the father to a baby. He knew he wanted to be both he just didn't know how to make it happen.

A chill rushed through him at the thought of never having Kira in his life. He wouldn't have much of a life without her. The past few months had proven that. He made his way through the house, and when he reached the stairs, took them two at a time and nearly ran down the hall to their bedroom. The door was open and he looked inside to find Kira on the bed.

His chest tightened painfully. "Kira," he breathed.

She wiped her eyes and sat up. "Do you need some clothes?"

"No. I don't need any clothes. I came to see you."

Her blond hair was mussed, her brown eyes were searching for any encouragement from him.

His eyes watered and his throat tightened. "I wish I could have been there for you." He thought about the agony she must have gone through trying to fill that void in her life. "I understand why you want a baby so desperately." She had no family, except for a grandmother who hadn't wanted her and a child she hadn't been able to keep.

A son Kira had never been able to see grow up.

He came further into the room. Now, he understood so many things. And he loved her more for her strength to survive the cards life had dealt her.

"So you're going to leave me, too."

He swallowed. "It would be easier to forget to breathe. Do you have any idea how many nights I've lain awake in that damn bunk, thinking about you? Thinking about the talking, the sharing, and about how we used to turn to each other in the night and how sweet it was to hold you in my arms. How loving you was heaven. How badly I wanted you."

Kira sucked in a breath, eager to hear every word, praying she wasn't dreaming.

He reached the bed, his gray gaze locked with hers, his voice husky with emotion as he continued, "It's been hell."

Kira's eyes searched his. "For me, too. I know I turned away from you and that hurt you."

He placed his finger against her lips. "No more talking, Kira. Not now." He leaned forward and brushed a kiss over her mouth. She froze as his lips slowly moved over hers, drawing feelings out that she hadn't acknowledged in so long.

She wanted Trace, and she knew he still wanted her. He broke off the kiss and studied her. "I want you, Kira. Don't push me away, not tonight."

"Oh, Trace, I won't." She wrapped her arms around his neck and kissed him, letting him know her desire. It wasn't long before they had stripped off their clothes.

Under the covers, Trace pulled her against his body and his hands moved over her. Soon he made her forget everything.

At least for a little while, everything was perfect between them.

CHAPTER SEVEN

AT DAWN the next morning, Kira opened her eyes to see the familiar surroundings of the master bedroom. And to the once familiar feel of Trace's body as she lay pressed against him. She shifted her gaze to his face relaxed in sleep.

She stared up at the ceiling and recalled every precious moment they'd shared. The few hours they'd stolen together. It had been like their first year of marriage before her obsession for a baby. Before Trace learned of her past. And it didn't solve anything.

Her eyes filled. After last night it was going to be harder to stay away from Trace, but she had to. If she wanted to survive giving him up, she had to find a way.

Trace stirred and instinctively drew Kira tighter against him. She forced herself not to react. She fell back into a doze waking again only when, she felt him move away and get out of bed. Slipping on his jeans, he pulled his T-shirt over his head as he walked out of the room.

Kira opened her eyes as her husband walked out of the bedroom, relieved that they skipped the-morning-after-talk. He'd probably gone off to do chores. She collapsed back on the pillow, trying not to think about their perfect night together. No matter how good they'd been together, it still hadn't changed anything. They had problems. And in the end, she still couldn't give Trace a biological child.

Trace stood in the kitchen trying to hold onto his common sense. A perfect night in bed with his wife didn't mean their marriage was back on track, but it was the closest they'd been in months. And he wanted this to be a new beginning for them. Although words weren't spoken, he knew she still loved him. He felt the same way.

He poured some coffee. But he couldn't help but have hope, hope that they could make it work between them.

He went to the refrigerator and took out the orange juice. After filling two glasses, he carried them to the table. There were two place settings already set out for their breakfast.

Kira walked into the room, wearing a floral satin robe. He immediately paused, registering she didn't have a damn thing on underneath. Great. Had she suddenly run out of clothes? He sucked in a long breath and released it.

"I thought we could use some coffee and a little sustenance," he informed her.

Kira went to the table and picked up a mug. She brushed her blond curls back from her face and took a sip. The fabric clung to every curve of her luscious body.

"Thank you," she told him.

He also savored the hot brew, letting the caffeine kick-start him. Then he watched as she sipped from her mug, her big brown eyes locked on him. He could feel the tension.

"You want a sweet roll?"

"Maybe later," she said. "I think we should talk?"

He turned a chair around and straddled it. He didn't have much choice. "Okay, tell me what's on your mind?"

Kira joined him, sitting down across from him. "What happened last night wasn't planned." She held up her hand. "And I want you to know that I don't expect anything from you."

He tensed. "So we just used each other for comfort."

Her eyes widened. "Stop putting words into my mouth. A lot happened yesterday, and I turned to you because I trust you…and I care about you."

"And I care about you. Dammit, Kira. Do you think I can just turn off feelings after all these years."

"Right now, we're both too vulnerable to jump back into this." Kira knew she had to protect herself. "I think we should back up a little while."

"You mean for six months, until you get a baby."

She tried not to flinch. "I want to use the six months to see how we get along."

"And then you walk away."

She sighed. "No, so we can both rebuild our lives. I thought you agreed to this?"

"I agreed to meeting with the counselor. We're well past that."

"Okay, here's your chance. Tomorrow, we're possibly going to meet a birth mother who may choose us." She took a breath and released it. "That's hard to comprehend."

He remained silent and let her talk.

"I know it's happening quickly, Trace, but we need to make a decision." She set down her mug and looked at him. "I know you were blindsided yesterday when you learned about my baby, but it's something I can't change. So now, we have to decide if we move ahead."

He could hear the trembling in her voice. He wasn't too steady, either. He'd made a lot of mistakes in the past.

"There's nothing to forgive, Kira." He wished he could have been there for her. "And I know how much adopting a baby means to you."

Kira tried not to get too excited over Trace's words. "So you want to go along with it for…six months? To see how things work out."

She watched his eyes flare. "Your idea isn't foolproof, Kira. What happens if we don't get picked tomorrow?"

She'd be heartbroken. "I have to stay positive. I didn't want you to feel trapped, either."

"Trapped into what? We agreed to adopt a long time ago."

"We need to act as if we have a real marriage for the full time, Trace." She blinked back tears. "I don't want a man who walks out if things get tough."

"Isn't that what you're going to do, eventually?"

She ignored his sarcasm. "So are you moving back home?"

He paused. "I can't just jump back into it as if we never had problems."

"I know. That's why I'll be moving into the guest room."

"Like hell!"

She suddenly got hopeful.

"I'll sleep there."

She worked hard to hide her hurt. "If it's what you want?"

"Hell, no, it's not what I want." He shot up and marched to the window. "This isn't easy for me, Kira. And last night with you didn't help. I hate to fail. But if we're lucky enough to get a baby and that's no sure thing," he warned before shrugging. "Who knows, we might just get along."

Barely containing her excitement, Kira boldly walked over to Trace, raised herself up on her bare toes and brushed her mouth across his. Hearing his groan, she deepened the kiss and he quickly joined in. By the time she pulled back she could see the desire in his eyes. "That was to officially welcome you home." She turned and strolled off. Her husband needed something to think about on those lonely nights in the guest room.

A few hours later, heading into town, Trace was still wondering if he'd done the right thing by moving back into the house. Kira had gone to see Jody, and he needed to talk to his brother.

Since it was Sunday, Jarrett was at home. Trace drove

to the custom-built home on the land that his brother had kept when he sold him the half of the ranch their parents had left him.

The two-story, modern structure sat on a hill with rolling green lawn in front, and the back overlooked a picturesque view of the mountain range. Trees lined most of the property, adding privacy to the large deck and hot tub.

Trace made his way along the blue stone walk and rang the bell. His brother quickly answered, dressed in jeans and a blue collared shirt.

"Hey, Trace, you made it. Come in."

"I said I'd be here." Trace stepped into the slate tiled entry, then into a huge great room with a stone fireplace that took up most of one wall. Oversize brown leather furniture made up a cozy seating area around the hearth. He followed his brother across the hardwood floors to the dining room, off a kitchen with black cabinets and marble countertops.

"Nice place."

Jarrett frowned. "You haven't been here before?"

"No. I guess my invitation got lost in the mail."

His brother ignored the comment. "You and Kira are always welcome anytime."

"I'll pass that along to my wife." He didn't care if he was added to Jarrett's social list or not. "Okay. So what do you want to talk to me about?"

"I have everything laid out here."

Trace turned and looked at the table. "What are you talking about?"

"The property deal."

He had contracts drawn up? "I never said I would sell, just that I'd talk to you."

Jarrett studied him. "Come on, bro, you know you can't come up with the payment."

Was his brother just waiting for him to fail? "You know nothing, *bro*. I have the money."

His brother motioned for Trace to take a seat, then he sat across from him. "We both know that the adoption costs could run to a sizable amount."

Trace didn't want to talk to Jarrett about this. "I'll take care of it."

"What if you can't? You could lose the ranch and the baby."

And Kira, he thought. "Okay, what's your plan?"

"Simple." Jarrett slid a paper across the table. "I want to buy back the section of the land that borders my property."

Trace didn't believe this was out of the kindness of his brother's heart. "We talked about this before, Jarrett. I don't want that land developed with homes."

"And I won't, not for ten years."

That made Trace suspicious, too. His brother didn't do anything that didn't benefit himself. Yet, did Trace have any other options? The past few years, they'd had a lot of expensive medical procedures for Kira, costs that the insurance hadn't covered, combined with two lean years of cattle profits. The money he'd held back for emergencies was nearly gone.

He glanced down at the property agreement. The balloon payment was due the end of June. Three weeks. He looked at his brother. Something told him not to trust him. There had been too many times his older brother had used him.

"Can you give me a week to think about it?" Trace asked.

Jarrett hesitated, then nodded. "That's about all I can give you."

Why was that important if his brother wasn't going to do anything with the land? He needed to think about this.

Jarrett nodded. "Also, I wanted to give you this card for Kira."

Trace took it. "Dr. Thomas Faulkner, Fertility Specialist."

"We knew each other in college and kept in touch. I told Kira about him."

Why the hell was Jarrett discussing anything with his wife?

"I thought she'd mention it to you."

Trace thought they'd exhausted every avenue on fertility. Besides, they were ending their marriage. He suddenly thought about the parting kiss she'd given him earlier. Between last night and this morning, it didn't feel like things were ending to him. "Did she say she wanted to get in touch with this doctor?"

Jarrett shrugged. "I don't think you should give up, Trace. That's another reason you should sell me back the land."

Trace didn't want to listen anymore. "I need to go. I'm meeting Kira for lunch," he lied.

Jarrett watched Trace. "Okay, but think it over…this is a good deal for you."

Trace knew from experience that wasn't true. His brother was up to something, and he was going to find out what it was.

Two hours later, Kira tried to hold on to the afterglow as she drove into town. Not just from Trace making love to her last night, but because he was moving back into the house, and agreed to the adoption. Okay, it was only to the guest room, and he wouldn't be around to be a daddy to her baby, but it was a start. A big one. Although he seemed angry about her dismissing their love making, at least they were talking again.

Kira sobered as she turned down Elm Street toward Jody's house. It wasn't the best neighborhood, bringing back memories of her own childhood. When she was a little girl, she remembered her parents had lived paycheck to paycheck, so when they'd died, there wasn't any extra money to help raise their only child. Just the little that her grandmother got, but the ailing woman decided not to take her granddaughter in.

Kira pushed away the bad memories and parked at the curb of the small rental house. The lawn needed to be mowed, and the house could use a fresh coat of paint. It amazed her that Jody could deal with all this and still make the grades in school. Kira was going to do everything she could to help her now.

She climbed out and went up the walk. Soon, the door opened and Jody greeted her. The teenager looked tired and worried.

"Hi, Mrs. McKane."

"Hello, Jody." She hugged the girl. "How are you feeling today?"

"Better now that you're here." Jody nodded toward the door. "My mom just got up. It's her day off so she sleeps in."

Kira knew she was making excuses for Marge Campbell. She'd bet that it was Jody who took care of things around the house, along with going to school and working a part-time job.

"We're going to deal with this together, Jody."

Tears flooded Jody's eyes.

Kira hugged her again.

"Jody, who are you talking to?" Mrs. Campbell came to the door. "Oh, Mrs. McKane. What brings you here today?" Dressed in an old chenille robe, the forty-plus woman pushed back her wild, bleached-blond hair. Years of hard living showed in her lined face.

"Hello, Mrs. Campbell. Sorry to bother you, but Jody and I want to talk with you."

Marge Campbell glanced back and forth between the two, then slowly opened the squeaky screen door. Inside, the living room was furnished with a faded print sofa and two mismatched chairs. Although the ashtrays had been emptied the place still reeked of cigarette smoke.

Jody directed her to the sofa. Once they were all seated, Kira exchanged a glance with Jody.

"If this is about Jody going away to college," the mother began, "it just isn't possible. I need my daughter here to help out."

"No, Mom. It's not about college. I'm pregnant," the girl blurted out.

"What?" Marge gasped. "You promised you wouldn't do anything. That you'd stay away from those boys." She jumped up from her seat. "Now, what are we going to do raising some kid's brat? I warned you this would happen." She wheeled around on her daughter. "Who did this to you?"

Kira stood. "Mrs. Campbell, please can't we sit down and talk calmly about what to do?"

"She's going to get rid of it that's what she's going to do. I'm not going to be saddled with another kid. I've been through that once. Never again."

Kira could see the hurt on Jody's face. "Your daughter isn't saddling you with anything. This is her decision to make. She can get financial help if she decides to keep the child."

"Well, she's not bringing the baby here. So she can just get out right now."

After his visit to Jarrett's place, Trace returned to the ranch, packed up his things from the bunkhouse and carried them up to the house.

Things were far from perfect, but he would deal with it. He only had to stay out of his wife's bed. Sure. He couldn't even stop himself remembering how willing she'd been in his arms last night. In the dark they didn't need words, just their bodies to express their need for one another. He'd never shared that level of intimacy with anyone but Kira. How could he live without her now?

That was the reason he was going to use this time to try to make things work. He might go crazy wanting his wife, but he had to think beyond his own needs; there could be a baby added to the mix. Maybe if he'd worked harder, instead of moving out, he'd have a wife, a lover. He couldn't leave her now, especially with the possibility of a baby. Not without a fight, anyway.

He'd finished putting his shaving kit in the bathroom when he heard the back door open. She was home. Good. Cal could handle the chores today, and he could spend the day with his wife. Just maybe he could convince her to change some of the rules. He hurried down the steps and went into the kitchen to greet her. He quickly stopped when he saw she wasn't alone, Jody Campbell was with her.

Kira saw him. "Oh, hi, Trace."

"Kira. Hi, Jody."

She shyly looked away. "Hello, Mr. McKane."

He turned back to a nervous Kira.

"Jody is going to be staying with us for a few days. Her mother was upset about the…news. So I brought her home to discuss options."

So they weren't going to be alone. Hiding his disappointment, he turned to his houseguest. "Welcome, Jody. You stay as long as you need."

"Thank you, Mr. McKane."

Kira turned to their guest. "Why don't you go upstairs and rest? The guest room is the door just past the nursery. We'll bring your suitcase up later."

The girl nodded and left the kitchen. Once alone, Kira released a breath and turned to her husband. "I guess I should have called, but Jody was literally out on the street." She frowned. "You sure you don't mind her staying here?"

He shook his head. "A few days won't be bad."

Kira grimaced, hoping Trace would understand. "It might be longer. Her mother didn't take the news of the baby well. I want to make sure Jody has some kind of support."

"What about the baby's father? Shouldn't he be here for her?"

"Jody said she tried to tell him, but he wouldn't listen."

"Maybe he'll listen to me," Trace said. "He's got to take responsibility."

"Ben leaves for the Army in a few weeks. He's not a bad guy, but he's a kid, and Jody will be eighteen next month." She shook her head. "Neither one of them are ready for this. I'm sorry, but when her mother threw her out, I just couldn't let Jody go through this alone."

He stepped closer, taking her hand. "She's lucky to have you, Kira. I just had some plans for us today. I thought we could go riding."

"You wanted to take me riding?"

"You sound surprised. I thought we should practice getting along—since Mrs. Fletcher will be watching us."

Kira was thrilled Trace wanted to spend time with her. It had been so long since they'd done anything carefree. "Could I get a rain check?"

He nodded. "Seems we have another problem. I just moved my things into the guestroom." He raised an eyebrow. "Have any idea where I put them now?"

* * *

When Kira woke the next morning, smiling, she stretched her arms out. She reached across the big bed but Trace wasn't there. Not that she should expect him to be. Although he'd come to their room to give the appearance all was normal, after Jody retired for the night, he had gone to the bunkhouse. Since Trace was up before the sun, their houseguest wouldn't even suspect he wasn't sleeping next to his wife.

That hadn't stopped Kira from missing him. She better get used to it, though, because his absence was going to be a permanent feature soon enough. Trace was only playing the part of attentive husband.

Kira got up and headed for the shower to help her focus on her day. This afternoon Mrs. Fletcher was coming with a special visitor. And it could mean they'd have a baby by summer's end. Kira tried to hold in her excitement, but couldn't as she began singing in the shower.

Thirty minutes later, she went downstairs and found Jody doing the dishes.

"Good morning, Jody," she greeted her. "I hope you slept okay."

"Good morning, Mrs. McKane. I slept fine. The bedroom you let me use is so pretty."

"It is pretty, isn't it?" Kira smiled and went to the coffeepot and poured a cup. "I especially love the old iron bed. I found it in the attic." She sipped from her mug. "I'm sure glad that my husband's family didn't throw anything out."

"Your house is beautiful. I hope you don't mind, I

dusted the living room. I can fix you breakfast if you want."

"Jody, I didn't bring you here expecting you to work."

"I just want to help out."

"I know you do," Kira said. "But I think it's more important that you see a doctor. Have you been to one?"

"I went to the clinic on Main Street just to confirm my pregnancy."

"How far along are you?"

"Fourteen weeks."

Kira sat down at the table and motioned Jody to do the same. "Have you thought about what you want to do?"

Jody shook her head. "Only that I can't end this pregnancy."

"What I told you, Jody, about me giving my baby up. It was the right decision for me, and the best for my baby. That doesn't mean it's what's right for you."

"I know that." Jody's gaze met hers. "I'm never going to tell anyone about what you told me."

"It's okay, Jody," Kira assured her. "I'm not ashamed of what I did. My baby was given a life I never could have offered. Two parents for one thing."

The girl looked thoughtful. "I don't know what I want to do."

"Well, we'll go to the doctor first. I'll set up an appointment for tomorrow. What time are you working today?"

Jody gasped. "I have the dinner shift."

There was no way Kira was going to miss Mrs. Fletcher. "I have an appointment here this afternoon, so you can take my car."

"I can't drive your car."

"Why not? You have a driver's license don't you? I trust you."

Tears filled the girl's eyes. "You've been so nice to me. I don't know what I'd do…if you hadn't took me in."

Kira hated to see the girl's lack of confidence, but she understood it. "You're easy to be nice to, Jody. Don't let anyone tell you anything different. And I'm going to stand by you for as long as you need me."

She knew too well what it was like to be alone, and pregnant. Maybe she could make a difference in Jody's life.

"They're here," Kira gasped.

Trace went to the kitchen window in time to see two women get out of the car. He recognized Mrs. Fletcher, but his attention went to the young girl with her. She was tall and slender, her stomach protruding with the late stage of pregnancy.

"Do I look okay?" Kira turned to look at Trace, brushing at her blue print sundress. Her wheat-colored hair was pulled away from her pretty face.

"You look perfect," he said truthfully. "Please, Kira, take a breath. She's going to like you. Remember, though, this is an interview. We might not even find out anything today."

He needed to stay calm, too. Mainly because he didn't want Kira disappointed if things didn't work out.

Her hand rested on his arm. "What about you, Trace? Are you sure this is what you want?"

He wanted whatever Kira wanted and a baby would be nice. "Yes, Kira, this is what I want. Now, we better go answer the door before they leave."

Together they walked to the back door and opened it as the two women came up the steps. "Hello, Mrs. Fletcher," Kira called.

The counselor smiled. "Trace, Kira, it's nice to see you again." She stopped on the porch to make the introductions. "This is Darcy Heaton. Darcy, this is Trace and Kira McKane."

"It's so nice to meet you, Darcy," Kira said and took her hand. The greeting was repeated by Trace to the girl in her late teens or early twenties.

"Hello," the girl said shyly. "You have a beautiful place here. I always wanted to live in the country."

"I could show you around if you want," Trace said. "We just finished the roundup this past weekend, and this morning shipped off the steers to the feedlot. But we have several horses."

Darcy's eyes lit up. "I love horses."

"Then let's go to the barn and I'll introduce you to Thunder."

Trace walked off with the young mother-to-be, followed by Mrs. Fletcher and Kira. Once inside the barn, he took Darcy along with him to see each animal. Thunder was willing to show off a little. Cal arrived with his mount, and Darcy was intrigued even more. They explained about the ranch operation, then Kira suggested they come into the house.

For the next hour, Kira found it easy to talk to Darcy as she and Trace showed her around the house. They sat down and had iced tea and cake while Darcy asked questions about the ranch. Then finally they ended up in the baby nursery. After a few moments Kira noticed that Trace and Mrs. Fletcher had wandered off, leaving her alone with the girl.

"This is a pretty room," Darcy said as she touched the cradle. "I like the yellow."

"Since I don't know the sex of the baby, I think it's a safe bet. But it's a good color to add pink or blue to."

Darcy nodded, eyeing the walls. "Do you want a boy or a girl?"

Kira couldn't help but wonder if this was a test. "Honestly, Darcy, it doesn't matter to us. We've tried everything for the last few years. We just want a baby to love."

Darcy nodded, then suddenly she looked sad. "I want to keep my baby, but I can't. My boyfriend, Wade, was in college." She hesitated. "He was so happy when he got the news about the baby. We were going to be married, but then, he was killed three months ago in a car accident coming to see me."

"Oh, Darcy." Kira fought to keep from going to her. "I'm so sorry."

A tear found its way down Darcy's cheek. "I can't raise my baby by myself. I have no family and it's important to me to know my baby will be loved and in a good home."

Kira felt a little shaky. "Your baby will be loved here. This home has seen several generations of McKanes. If you decide to let us raise your baby, he or she will be a McKane, too."

Darcy looked thoughtful. "I never had much of a home growing up, so it's important my little girl does."

Kira's heart tripped. "Your baby is a girl?"

"Is that all right?"

Tears filled Kira's eyes this time. "A little girl is perfect."

Just then Trace and Mrs. Fletcher walked into the room. He went to his wife's side. "Is everything okay?"

She nodded. "Darcy's baby is a girl."

Darcy went to Mrs. Fletcher. "I've decided."

The counselor sobered. "Are you sure, Darcy?"

"I'm sure." The pregnant girl placed her hand protectively on her stomach. "Trace and Kira, I want you to be the parents of my baby."

CHAPTER EIGHT

IN LESS than five weeks they were going to be parents.

The next evening, Trace glanced at Kira across the truck's bench seat as they rode into town. She hadn't stopped smiling since the announcement from Darcy. He wanted this for her, but it was all happening a little fast.

Just a few hours ago they'd all sat down at the kitchen table, Mrs. Fletcher laid out what Darcy would need. Top of the list was paying for the birth mother's medical bills. When the counselor gave him the approximate amount it nearly staggered him. Where was he going to get that kind of money? Thoughts of his brother's offer came to mind, but he quickly pushed them aside and turned his attention back to Kira.

Last week they were barely talking, now they were going to be parents. He let out a breath. No matter what she said about doing this on her own, he couldn't just walk away from her or this child. Somehow he had to figure out a way to keep her.

"Trace?" Kira's voice interrupted his thoughts. "Are you having second thoughts?"

"No, just a little overwhelmed."

He looked at his wife who was all dressed up for their night of celebration in town. Jody's idea and treat. Kira looked beautiful dressed in a silky blouse that outlined her full breasts, and a flowing skirt that hit the middle of her shapely calves. Even her feet looked sexy in a pair of high heeled sandals. She was distracting as hell. How was he supposed to live with her for the next six months, and not touch her, or kiss her?

"If it's the money, I planned to use the savings in the teachers' credit union."

Trace knew Kira had the account since before they'd married. He'd insisted it was hers. "I think you should hang onto it for now. I'll talk to Jarrett. He wants the southern section back. He'll pay well for it."

Kira turned toward her husband. "No, Trace. You wanted to keep that land, if just so he wouldn't develop it. Besides, I'm the one who asked you to do this."

He worked to control his anger. "We both wanted this adoption, Kira."

Tears welled in Kira's eyes. "Oh, Trace. You don't owe me this."

He pulled into the restaurant parking lot and shut off the engine. "Look, Kira, you already refuse to take anything from me, I sure as hell can at least help with this." And he was going to do a lot more whether she liked it or not. There was a child involved now.

Kira sat there staring out the windshield. She had hoped they could work this out, but Trace hadn't said much during the discussion with Lucy Fletcher. He hadn't expressed to her that he really wanted to be a family. Okay, she'd pushed him into this. And she hadn't a choice but to offer him a six-month deal.

If they couldn't make their marriage work, there would be a child involved then. At least this way, Trace could move on and have a family of his own.

She turned to him. "Thank you, Trace, for today. I promise I won't ask anything else from you."

"Ah, Kira." He reached for her and drew her against him. "You can ask me for anything."

She closed her eyes, reveling in their closeness, letting herself dream. The same dream she'd carried around since childhood. To have someone love her enough to always be there. She'd thought it was Trace, but in the end he would leave her like everyone else.

"We're going to make this work, Kira," he whispered in the darkness as he drew her closer. "You're going to have a baby."

Her heart gave a jolt as she raised her head. The truck was dark enough she couldn't see his eyes, but she felt them on her. "I wish I could be what you needed, too, Trace. I wish—"

Suddenly her words were cut off when he cupped her face and his mouth came down on hers. She only moaned as his lips coaxed hers until she gave in and opened so he could deepen the kiss.

He finally pulled back, his breathing labored and her hand felt the pounding of his heart. "Don't ever say that, Kira. You're everything a man could want."

"I couldn't give you a child," she managed to whisper.

He started to speak, but headlights from another car drew them apart. "We better go in," he said.

Trace climbed out of the truck and took the time to cool off as he walked around to the passenger side and helped her out. Their eyes locked in the dim parking lot. The mountain air hadn't helped—he wanted to kiss her again, then turn around and take her back home. Show her how much she meant to him.

Instead he escorted her toward the restaurant. Once inside the high-end steak house, Kira excused herself to go to the ladies' room.

"I'll check on our reservation," Trace said and went to the desk to speak to the young girl. "McKane."

"Oh, Mr. McKane. Your table should be ready shortly, Mr. Rhodes from EnRockies is waiting in the bar."

Trace quickly realized the girl's mistake; it wasn't the first time he'd been mistaken for his brother. Jarrett must be having a business meeting. "There must be a mistake. My wife and I have a reservation tonight. We're Jody Campbell's guests."

The young girl look flustered. "Oh, you're the other Mr. McKane."

Great. Now, he had the distinction of being the *other* brother. "I'm Trace McKane," he said as Kira returned to his side.

"Yes, here it is." The hostess smiled, embarrassed. "Your table is ready now, Mr. McKane." She called for a waiter, and he escorted them to a circular booth. Kira slid into the seat, and Trace was close behind her. After ordering cocktails, they were left alone.

Kira looked at him. "Is everything okay?"

He nodded. "Just a mix-up with the reservations. Seems Jarrett is here for a meeting."

"Wonder who Jarrett's wining and dining tonight."

Trace wondered, too. "Have you ever heard of a company called EnRockies?"

She frowned. "That's the name of the energy company drilling for natural gas in the area."

"Why would Jarrett be having a meeting with them?"

Kira shrugged. "Probably trying to lease them office space in town."

"Maybe." But an odd feeling gnawed at Trace. If the real estate business was so bad why would his brother want the land back? Something wasn't right.

"I can't believe he's looking to buy part of the ranch back."

"I don't want you to worry about it, Kira."

"How can I not? You could possibly lose part of the ranch."

"McKane Ranch is a big place. Dad meant for it to be divided between Jarrett and me, anyway."

Kira didn't look convinced. "That's great if he wanted to ranch, but we both know he'll develop the land if the price is right." Sighing, she leaned back. "I'm sorry, I shouldn't have said that. I don't know your brother that well."

"He's my *half* brother. And don't be sorry, Kira. It's true. I'm surprised Jarrett has stayed in Winchester Ridge. Of course he's made a good living being the hometown hero." A title he was all too familiar with having grown up in his older brother's shadow, the best quarterback to ever play at Winchester Ridge High School. "Who wouldn't trust him?"

Kira couldn't believe Trace could still be jealous of

Jarrett. "He's a little too smooth for my tastes." She looked down at her husband's hands. His palm was rough from hard work, but could be so gentle, remembering his touch against her skin. "I prefer the rugged type," she continued, unable to stop herself. "A certain cowboy got my attention from the first day I arrived in town."

Trace's intense gaze locked with hers. "I guess I owe my brother for taking you to lunch." He leaned in closer to her. "That day I walked into the diner and saw you, you took my breath away." His voice turned husky. I don't have all the smooth words and moves, Kira. I'm just an ordinary guy who works hard to make a living."

It had always amazed her that he never knew the effect he had on people, on women. "Nothing about you is ordinary, Trace McKane."

He looked embarrassed.

She nodded. "I've made a lot of mistakes, Trace. You deserved to know about my past."

Her keeping that secret had hurt him, but he understood why she found it difficult to open up about it. He also knew how hard her life had been. The toughest part was knowing she had a child out there that she couldn't see. The only child she would ever give birth to. "I hated that you couldn't come to me."

The waiter dropped off their drinks, and asked for their order. Kira decided on the salmon, and Trace a steak. The waiter picked up their menus and left them alone.

Kira lowered her voice. "I know I should have trusted you, Trace. But at the time, I was made to feel ashamed about what happened, and the only way I could put it behind me was to bury it. I never planned on meeting you. When we started dating everything was so perfect. I was afraid I would lose you if you learned I gave up my baby."

Trace shook his head. "Like I said, Kira, that wouldn't have happened."

Kira still couldn't believe it—they were finally talking. Maybe if they'd managed it sooner, he'd be moving back into their bedroom, and not the guest-room.

She suddenly heard someone say her name.

Kira looked up to see Jody arrive at the table. "I'm glad you made it." The girl smiled, dressed in her uniform. A white Western blouse and black jeans.

"You didn't need to do this, Jody," she said.

"I know, but I wanted to thank you for letting me stay with you."

"You should be saving your money."

"I am. And I make good tips here. So order what you want—we get a discount on the food." She glanced over her shoulder, then back at them. "I better get back to my tables. Have fun." She hurried off.

"She looks so much better now."

Trace stared after Jody. "You've given her hope."

Kira turned her velvet-brown eyes to him. "So you don't mind her staying with us?"

"She's not around much to be a bother." Although he'd like to have more privacy with Kira. "Besides, she needs us."

She smiled. "Thank you."

He hated her acting like a stranger. "Hell, Kira, it's

your home, too. It has been since the day I carried you over the threshold nearly five years ago."

She glanced away. "Things are different now."

He hated this time frame she'd concocted. "I don't want to be different, Kira. I can't walk away from the child, or from you. And I'll be damned if I'm letting you. Not if there's a baby involved."

The rest of their meal was eaten in silence as was their drive home. Kira wanted to talk about what Trace had said, but he'd clammed up.

Men.

They pulled up at the back door and she climbed out of the truck, not waiting for him. Well, she wasn't about to let him make a statement like that and refuse to explain.

They walked into the kitchen. "If you've changed your mind about the adoption, Trace McKane, you better tell me now."

"What makes you think that?"

"Maybe because you said you weren't going to walk away if there's a baby involved."

He glared at her. "That's true. You seem to think that I can sign papers, then turn around and walk out the door."

"No, *I'm* walking out the door," she corrected. "The baby is the only thing I'm taking." She never let herself feel the ranch belonged to her. "This is your place, your land."

"Dammit, Kira. That's what I mean. Why can't you believe me? I don't want you or the baby to leave."

Her breath stopped as she replayed his words. But before she could speak the sound of a car distracted her.

Soon Jody walked into the dimly lit kitchen. "Hi. You guys home long?" She smiled.

"No, not long," Kira said. "Thank you again for dinner."

"Yeah, thanks, Jody. Now, we all need sleep," Trace said as he locked the back door, then came back and took Kira's arm, leading her through the house to the stairs. Jody followed.

Kira's heart raced as they made their way down the hall and Trace opened the master bedroom door. "Good night, Jody," he called to her.

"Good night," the girl called as she went to her room.

Once Jody was out of sight, Trace pulled Kira across the threshold and closed the door behind them. He pushed her back against the raised wood panels. The room was dark, but she could feel his rapid breathing on her face.

"Let me turn on a light," she said, wanting to move away.

"No, Kira. It's better like this." He sighed. "I have something to say to you."

She shut her eyes tightly and began to pray. "Please don't say you're not going through with the adoption."

"No, I wouldn't do that. It's just not going to be your way. I want to negotiate a new deal. I want to be a father to this baby girl…and I want to be a husband to you." There was a long pause. "With no time limit."

Kira's chest tightened. "What if it doesn't work?"

"Then it won't be because we didn't try hard enough." He leaned forward and brushed his lips across hers.

She gasped. "Our track record isn't good, Trace."

She slipped her arms around his neck, knowing she couldn't let him go.

"At least we'd have tried," He kissed the side of her neck as his arms wrapped around her waist. "And I want to try with you, Kira. And for this baby."

His mouth found hers in the dark as if a magnet drew them together. The kiss grew intense along with their need, a need that hadn't diminished in their long months apart.

"Oh, Trace," she breathed as he broke off the kiss. She tried to come up with more resistance, but she was weak.

"Trust me, Kira." He tugged on her arm and together they walked to the bed. Slowly he began taking off her clothes, but she soon grew impatient and helped the process along, then did the same for him.

As she lay down on the mattress Trace leaned over her, his hands working their magic on her body, stealing her breath away, along with any doubts.

"We'll make this work, Kira."

Hope sprang inside Kira. Was this really going to happen? Was she finally getting her wish? A family.

A blissful three days and nights had passed, and Kira woke every morning, smiling. Trace had been a wonderful, attentive, considerate lover since the night they…re-negotiated their marriage. Of course they had to steal their time together around their houseguest. But that was good practice for when their own child was here.

She walked into the kitchen to find Jody at the stove, cooking bacon. She glanced at the clock to see it was only seven o'clock. She told Jody repeatedly she didn't need to fix breakfast, but the girl kept doing it anyway.

"Jody, you should sleep in since you worked late last night."

The girl turned around. "Oh, Mrs. McKane. It's okay, I usually get up early."

Kira went to the coffeepot and poured a cup. "But you need your sleep, too."

The teenager's coloring had looked better this past week. "I'll rest later. I want to help out." The girl studied her for a while. "I don't want you to worry that I'll still be around when your baby comes. Cal is helping me figure some things out."

Jonas had been helping her? "Have you heard from your mother?"

Jody shook her head. "I don't expect to."

It was sad that her mother couldn't be there for her. But the baby's father needed to take responsibility, too. "Jody, have you told Ben you're pregnant?"

The girl took the bacon out of the skillet. "No. I tried at the party, and I've called, but he won't talk to me."

"He needs to know about the baby."

Jody turned around, tears in her eyes. "That's what Jonas says. But Ben will hate me."

Kira understood that feeling; she'd been there herself. "Ben has no cause to hate you. He helped make this baby."

"And he needs to take responsibility."

They both turned to see Trace and Cal standing at the doorway. They walked in and Trace came to Kira and kissed her, then turned to Jody. "If Ben won't listen to you, I think I should talk to him."

The girl blinked in surprise. "You don't have to do that, Mr. McKane."

"Someone has to. It's time for him to man up," Cal spoke up. "When does he go off to the Army?"

"In a few weeks."

"Then there's time," Trace said. "We'll drive you into town today." He rubbed his hands together. "Now, how about some breakfast? I'm starved."

"Me, too," Cal added.

Jody beamed. "I just need to cook the eggs. Is scrambled okay?"

The two men nodded. "That's our very favorite," Cal answered.

The teenager went to work, Cal went to get coffee, and Trace sat down at the table. He winked at Kira as she joined him.

She smiled in return. "Thank you for standing up for Jody. I don't think many people have."

"I'm just practicing for when we have our daughter."

It had been getting easier for Kira to believe. That she and Trace were going to be parents. A child together. "So you don't mind that the baby's a girl?"

"Mind having two beautiful women in my life? I don't think so."

She gripped his hand. Things were getting better every day. "I think we're pretty lucky, too."

After chores Trace and Kira drove Jody into town to see Ben. He glanced in the rearview mirror of the SUV and saw the nervous teenager in the back seat. A strange protectiveness came over him.

"Jody, it's going to be all right. Ben just may surprise you."

Jody nodded. "I think he suspects already. I think that's why he's been avoiding me."

Trace looked at Kira, then turned onto Ben's street. After finding the right house, he parked in front. "Well, that's going to end now."

"Do you want us to go with you?" Kira asked.

Jody shook her head. "No. I need to tell him by myself." She climbed out of the car and walked to the door.

"Are you sure we should let her go on her own?" Trace said, watching Jody.

"I think she wants to hear what he has to say." Kira sighed. "I hope she doesn't have any delusions that they're going to get married and raise this baby."

Trace glanced at Kira. "This has to bring back bad memories for you."

She shrugged. "Teenage girls at that age want love."

"And teenage boys are only after sex."

Kira kept her gaze on the house as she swallowed. "In the end everyone gets hurt."

Just then Jody came running out the front door. She climbed into the back seat and wiped at the tears streaming down her face. "Please, just go."

"What happened?"

"Ben doesn't want anything to do with the baby. He said it wasn't even his, and just to get rid of it." She sobbed. "It is his, Mrs. McKane. I loved Ben. There's never been anyone else."

Trace fought his anger as he climbed out of the car and marched up to the house. He rang the bell, but got no answer. So he began pounding until finally Ben came to the door.

The teenager stood eye to eye with Trace in height, but was about twenty pounds lighter. He looked shocked and a little frightened to see who was on the porch. "Mr. McKane."

"That's right, Ben. Let's see how you handle what I have to say."

His gaze went to the car, then back at Trace. "If it's about Jody—"

"You're damn right it's about Jody. And your child. The girl didn't get pregnant on her own. She came to ask you to help, and you humiliated her by saying the baby wasn't yours."

"Well, how would I know, she could have been with someone else."

"Do you honestly believe Jody would lie to you?"

The boy glanced away as he shook his head. "No. But I can't have a kid. I'm going into the Army."

"What about Jody? She applied to college. Instead she's going to be raising a baby."

The boy didn't say anything.

"As least think about what Jody is going through. Help her decide what to do. If she does decide to keep it, are you going to be a part of the baby's life? I guess what I'm trying to say is act like a man. If you're man enough to join the Army, you should be man enough to accept your responsibilities." He turned, stormed off the porch and back to the car, knowing he'd taken on the job of Jody's protector for the long haul.

All he could think about was no one had been there for Kira.

Two days later, Trace rode out to the land that was soon—if he couldn't find any money—going to be Jarrett's. He pulled up on the rein, and just sat back in the saddle. He'd always loved this area covered in rows of birch trees. It was prime property that Jarrett had initially wanted for himself. But at the time, his brother had wanted the money for another project and the home he wanted to build. That had been when they'd struck the deal.

Trace had agreed to a five-year plan to pay Jarrett for the property. The land he'd thought to use for raising a herd of free-range beef. He needed a few years to prepare the grazing land, and to put up fencing to keep the cattle in the allotted area. There would be a lot of up-front expenses, but in the long run the payoff would be worth it.

Ranchers these days had to have numerous business ventures to keep afloat. He'd thought about following his neighbors and opening some land to hunters, maybe building some cabins to rent. That, too, took capital. And he didn't have any right now.

So maybe what he had to do now was make sure that the McKane Ranch would be around for future generations. That meant selling this prime section back to his brother.

There were other priorities now. Kira, and the baby

that would arrive in just weeks. Oh, boy. He sucked in a long breath. Getting used to the idea took some doing.

A girl. Would she like to ranch? Maybe not. It was a hard life. But who was to say they couldn't adopt more children? Whoa! Slow down, man. She wasn't even born yet.

His thoughts turned to Kira. They'd come a long way in the last few weeks. He'd been welcomed back into their marriage bed. More importantly, he'd managed to convince her he wanted to be a part of her and the baby's future.

He smiled, thinking about Kira back at the house already adding pink paint to the walls in the nursery. And maybe he should help her.

Trace pulled on Thunder's reins to turn and started back to the house when through the trees he spotted a vehicle. He rode toward the property line that separated his and Jarrett's land and saw what looked like a survey crew marking off areas.

They stopped when he rode up. "Excuse me, is there something I can help you with?"

"Hello, Mr. McKane, I presume. Trace McKane?"

"That's me."

The man walked closer. "It's nice to finally meet you, Mr. McKane. I'm Frank Rhodes and this is John Thompson. We're from EnRockies and we're doing a survey."

There was that name again. What was Jarrett up to? It was still his property. "You do know that this is my land. I never agreed to any survey."

Frank Rhodes frowned as he exchanged a glance

with John Thompson. "Mr. McKane, I was assured that you'd already okayed us having access to this section."

"By who? I hold the deed to this land." At least he did until he couldn't make the balloon payment.

"Jarrett McKane. He said he'd talked to you."

Trace felt the anger building. "About what?"

"About leasing the mineral rights under your land."

"What the hell?"

Rhodes hurried on to say, "It's directional drilling, Mr. McKane. There won't be a drilling tower on your land at all. EnRockies has always followed the strict guidelines of the Bureau of Land Management to protect the environment. If there are any more concerns, I assure you we will answer any questions."

"I have one big one. My brother. He never told me about any lease." Trace thought back to Jarrett's eagerness to buy back this land. That wasn't going to happen now. "Do you think you could come by the house in a few hours? I'd like to discuss this at length."

"We would be happy to. I'll give Jarrett a call, too. I want to get this settled."

Thunder shifted away. "Believe me, it's going to be settled once and for all."

CHAPTER NINE

Two hours later, Kira stood in the nursery and eyed her handiwork. The light pink vertical stripes below the white wainscoting looked great. This was definitely a little girl's room.

She also had her eye on a white Daisy Garden crib she'd spotted in the shops. The bedding had pink and yellow colors with a floral design. It was an extravagant purchase, but Trace was fine with her using the money in the credit union, so she didn't mind borrowing a little from it.

Excitement raced through her. She was going to be a mother. All these years of dreaming, praying for a baby and now it was going to happen.

As much as she wanted the experience again of a baby growing inside her, she was already in love with this little baby. She planned to do everything possible to bond with this child, to welcome Jenna Margaret into the McKane family.

The door slammed downstairs, bringing Kira out of her reverie. So Trace had come home to help her with the painting. She smiled and headed down to the kitchen, thinking how nice it would be to have her husband around once again. She reached the kitchen, but no Trace. She tracked him down in the office, bent over the desk going through files.

"Trace, is something wrong?"

He didn't even look up at her. "There's plenty wrong. I found a survey crew in the south section. The land I was going to sell back to Jarrett."

"Who was doing the survey?"

"EnRockies," he said, then filled her in on the rest of the story.

"No, Jarrett wouldn't do that to you." She'd always believed there was good in her bother-in-law.

"You're defending him?"

"I'm not, but why would he do this behind your back?"

"Money. It's not enough he's leasing them his own land, he wants more. Mine." He slammed a drawer. "Forget that, he has no regard for my feelings about drilling on McKane land."

Kira had only known what she'd heard in town, from students who had parents employed by this company. There seemed to be more positive than negative about EnRockies.

"I think you should listen to what they have to say."

Trace stared at Kira. She didn't understand, this was a bond he'd shared with his dad. Their love of the land. "Dad trusted us to protect the ranch. And by the looks of it with Jarrett, I'm going to have to do it on my own."

"Trace, I want to help you, too. All I ask is that you calm down and find out more information."

How could he stay calm when he could lose everything? "Why? It's not going to change my mind, Kira." He frowned. "And since when have you cared about the ranch? You've been wrapped up in other things."

His words hurt her. "I've always cared, you just chose to exclude me."

An hour later, Mr. Rhodes arrived at the house. Kira came into the room and introduced herself. She refused to be shut out of the meeting. If they were going to make their marriage work, she needed to be a part of everything, and that included the ranch operation. She listened to the lease offer and bit back a gasp when Mr. Rhodes quoted the amount of money that would be paid out monthly.

She tried to read the map of the area, telling them where they had drilling towers located. How the Bureau of Land Management and the state of Colorado had approved the project.

"Like I stated earlier, Mr. McKane," Rhodes began, "there won't be any tower on your property."

"But close," Trace challenged. "Close enough to the Roan Plateau."

"It's no secret you and your brother's properties are prime locations, but the drilling can be done by one tower, which Jarrett has already agreed to place on his property."

Kira watched her husband struggle to remain calm. So she came up with a question. "How long is your company's lease for, Mr. Rhodes?"

"It varies, Mrs. McKane, but when we leave, the

land is left just like it was before we began drilling. We plan to do everything possible to protect the environment and that includes the wildlife. So that means we have to proceed slowly and cautiously in selecting locations around the plateau's base."

Suddenly there was a knock on the back door and Jarrett walked into the kitchen. He glanced around the table. "Looks like you started without me."

"You got that wrong, brother. You started a long time ago and left me out altogether."

Mr. Rhodes stood. "I'll leave you all to hash this over. We'll talk again. Here's my card. You can reach me anytime." He nodded to Kira. "Mrs. McKane."

Kira let their guest walk out on his own. She wasn't about to leave the brothers alone.

Trace spoke first. "Were you ever going to tell me?"

"Why? You'd just reject the idea."

"So instead you tried to take away my land and go ahead when you know how Dad would have felt about this?"

"The ranch will still be here, Trace. Besides, Dad gave us the ranch."

"But you never wanted to work it."

"Is it so hard to believe that I don't want to work eighteen hour days and never know if you'll make enough to live on?"

Kira was steamed by her brother-in-law's arrogance. She wouldn't blame Trace if he threw Jarrett out of the house.

"I do just fine," Trace argued. "Making money isn't all that makes a person happy."

"That may be all right for you. I want a better life and the lease will guarantee that."

"It also doesn't mean I have to go along with it."

"Fine. But you're going to lose the land anyway. Word is you don't have the money to pay off the loan, Trace. That means it comes back to me. I'd say I win either way." He grinned. "Once again I'll come out on top, little brother."

Kira could only watch the scene unfold like a bad movie. She wanted to help her husband, but knew he wouldn't appreciate it. Trace had to handle this his own way.

"I have other ways to get my hands on the money."

Jarrett smiled. "It's just a matter of time before you can't keep up the ranch. You'll be borrowing until there's nothing left."

"Get out of my house, Jarrett. And don't come back."

Jarrett looked at Kira. "Call if you need anything."

She couldn't believe the nerve of the man. "You'd be the last person I'd call." She moved closer to her husband. Jarrett finally turned and left.

"I'm sorry, Trace."

Trace stiffened when Kira touched him. He pulled away and walked to the back door. "I need to get out of here."

"Trace, wait," she called to him. "Let me help."

He glared at her. "You can't, Kira. I'm about to lose everything."

Kira felt a pain deep in her chest, making it hard to breathe. He said "I" not "We." Like so many times before when it came to the ranch, she'd been excluded from his life.

* * *

Trace couldn't think clearly so he stalked out to the barn. A long, hard ride on Thunder was safer than getting behind the wheel of his truck.

Inside, he went into the tack room where he found Cal. With a nod, he grabbed a bridle and his saddle.

"I'm going for a ride." He walked out into the barn.

Cal followed him. "What's going on, Trace?"

"Nothing, I just need to get away."

"I saw the EnRockies' truck and Jarrett's car. I take it the meeting didn't go well."

Trace lifted the saddle onto the stall railing, opened the gate and went inside. "Yeah. My brother's trying to pull a fast one." He went on to explain the situation to his foreman.

"I have to admit, the man doesn't let anyone get in his way. What are you going to do about it?"

He slipped the bridal on Thunder. "No way is Jarrett getting the land back."

"Good. So you're talking a deal with EnRockies?"

Trace blew out a long breath. "It goes against everything Dad wanted."

Cal hung his arms over the railing and watched Trace saddle the horse. "Your daddy isn't here. He didn't have the problems you're facing, either. If you want to run a cattle operation, plus stop Jarrett, you'll need capital."

Trace looked at his friend. He'd earmarked most of his savings for the adoption. "What do you expect me to do?"

Cal raised a hand. "You have options, Trace. You can borrow the money from me. Or you can sell off your breeding bulls, or look over EnRockies' proposal. It might not be that bad."

Trace began running some of the things Rhodes had said through his head. "They want to do directional drilling onto my land." He tightened the cinch and dropped the stirrup in place. "The drilling tower and roads go on Jarrett's side of the property. I can't stop that."

"I think a lot of the reason this bothers you so much is because your brother's involved. Right there it seems shady." Cal was quiet for a moment, then said, "What does Kira think?"

Trace shrugged. "It doesn't involve her."

"It sure as hell does. She's your wife."

He didn't want a lecture. "I know that." He led his horse out of the stall. It was all a mess.

Cal went after him. "Come on, Trace, don't get all stubborn about this and close up."

Trace turned and glared at his friend.

The foreman backed off. "Okay, one thing at a time. At least ride over to Joe Lewis's place. They drilled on his ranch last year. It seems to me it would be nice to have extra money coming in every month to ease your worries, even help start up those projects you've always wanted."

Kira had suggested the same thing. Trace stopped outside the corral. "What, are you moonlighting for the energy company?"

"No, I'm just a friend who doesn't want you to lose everything. I know what this place means to you, but even if you lose it all, don't lose Kira. You two love each other."

* * *

Three hours later, Trace still wasn't back and Kira wasn't sure what to do. Kira was both angry and worried. How dare Trace just walk out. What did she expect? He'd done it before.

She marched into the office. This had always been Trace's domain, but no more. She began to go through the financial files and found the ranch account. It had a pretty hefty balance after the selling of the calves. Yet, she also knew that the land payment was coming due. She went to the accounts payable and scanning the pages discovered the last payment was due to Jarrett at the end of June.

Kira gasped, seeing the considerable amount. This would pretty much wipe them out. How would they survive if she wasn't going back to work in the fall? And there were the adoption costs and Darcy's medical bills.

"What are you doing?"

Kira jumped and looked toward the doorway to see Trace. Why did she feel so guilty? "Since you wouldn't share the facts with me, I was seeing how much we owe Jarrett." She stood. "I had no idea it was so much."

He walked to the desk. "The payments over the years were reasonable, but the balloon is due."

"You should have told me, Trace."

His gaze held hers. "I was handling it."

Kira felt the tightness in her chest as he continued to push her away.

"Besides, we haven't exactly been on speaking terms in the past few months."

Another dig that hit hard. "There's money in the credit union. You can use that."

Trace shook his head stubbornly. "At this point it wouldn't do any good. That's your money anyway."

"No, it's ours."

There was a long silence, then Kira spoke up, "Trace, maybe we should sit down and talk with Mr. Rhodes. You didn't get the chance to listen to the stipulations about the mineral lease."

Trace didn't hide his tension. "This is a cattle ranch, Kira. It has been for three generations."

She started to speak, but he stopped her. "I need to handle this."

Trace's dismissal hurt her. If she hadn't known before, she knew now, he didn't want her to be a part of his life.

Over the next few days, Kira wasn't encouraged about her relationship with her husband. Trace spent his evenings in the office. He hadn't even made an effort to come to bed until late. Their magical nights together, their promises of a future together seemed like a fleeting memory.

She had hoped that their bedroom would be a place where they reached out for each other, to share things, to work on renewing their commitment to each other.

But Trace had turned away from her.

Breakfast time hadn't been much better. Even Jody was uncomfortable around them. So when the teenager needed a ride to work, Kira offered eagerly to get out of the house.

Kira drove the car up to the highway toward town.

"Mrs. McKane…" Jody began.

"It's time you called me Kira."

The girl smiled. "Kira. Ben asked me to marry him."

This was a shock to Kira. "Oh, my. So you two have been talking, a lot." There had been nights she'd heard Jody crying. She'd comforted her, but knew she had to work through things herself. "Have you decided on what to do?"

"Not marry Ben for one thing. We're too young." Her voice lowered. "And he doesn't love me. Besides, Ben wouldn't be around. He'd be in the Army, and I'd be here alone."

"So you've decided to raise the baby yourself?"

The girl sighed. "I don't know yet. But I know I need a place to live."

"You're welcome to stay with us for as long as you like." Crazy since Kira was beginning to wonder where her home would be, but she would take Jody with her.

The girl shook her head. "No, that's not fair to you or Mr. McKane. So Cal is helping me find a place. My boss at the steak house has been wonderful. He says I can stay on as long as I'm able to work."

"That's good. It's still going to be hard, though. So please stay at the ranch, at least until the baby is born."

"I'm hoping not too long. Cal's got an idea where I can live cheap. The place will need some repairs, but he's offered to do them."

Seemed Cal had taken Jody under his wing.

"I can help paint and Cal said there's some furniture there," the girl said excitedly. "And I can get my bed from my mom's house. I paid for it anyway."

Kira glanced away from the road to Jody. "Sounds like you've thought about this."

"You and Mr. McKane have been wonderful to let me

stay with you, but I can't anymore. I should be paying you rent. And I still need to get a car, but I have some money saved. Because I'm a single mom, I can get some help with my medical bills. And Ben's going to help out."

Kira smiled. Jody had always been an organized student. This shouldn't surprise her. She drove into the restaurant parking lot. "What about your mother?"

"I'll be eighteen soon, so I don't have to ask her anything. Besides, she's moving away." The girl lowered her head. "Seems I've embarrassed her."

Kira parked the car. "If you were my daughter, I'd be so proud of you. You have a lot to handle for someone so young."

"You were young, too, Kira, when you had your baby," Jody said and hesitated. "Do you think you made the right decision? I mean giving your baby up?"

Kira still felt the emptiness; she always would. "I'll always feel the loss. But yes, I gave him a chance at a better life, better than I could give him. It wasn't easy, but it was the only way for me."

Jody smiled. "I'm glad you're getting a baby now."

"So am I."

"Thanks for bringing me to work. I'm going to spend the night with Laura, and she'll bring me back to the ranch tomorrow."

"Good. I'm glad you're hanging out with your friends. Have fun and I'll see you tomorrow."

Jody grabbed her overnight bag and got out of the car. Kira watched her go inside, then she pulled out of the parking lot. She headed across town to the teacher's credit union. Her stubborn husband refused her help, so she was taking matters into her own hands.

An hour later, she'd finished filling out the loan application and was told she'd get an answer in a few days. With renewed resolve, she headed back to the ranch. She knew Trace would probably be upset, but she couldn't let his pride take everything from him.

When she pulled into the driveway she was surprised to find Mrs. Fletcher waiting for her. She climbed out of the car and walked over to the counselor.

The sad smile on Lucy Fletcher's face caused Kira alarm. "Hello, Kira."

"Mrs. Fletcher. Is something wrong?" Oh God, please, no. Her anxiety grew. "Is Darcy okay?"

"Darcy is fine and so is the baby." She glanced around. "Is your husband here?"

"I'm not sure. Do you need to speak to him?"

Mrs. Fletcher hesitated. "Could we go inside?"

Okay, this wasn't good. They walked up the steps together and went into the kitchen. "Please, tell me why you came all this way."

"I have some news." She sighed. "Darcy got a call from her boyfriend's mother. It seems that she never knew about Darcy until she went through her son's things." A long pause. "She's offered to help Darcy raise the baby."

Kira's heart stopped as she sank into a kitchen chair. "Is she serious?"

"Yes, I checked it out." Mrs. Fletcher sat, too. "When Marion Clark learned about the baby she contacted Darcy and begged her to come live with her. Darcy agreed. Together they're going to raise the baby. With her son's death, Marion wants a part of him."

A tear found its way down Kira's cheek. She hated this, but deep down she understood. If there had been someone to support her, she would have kept her son, too. "I'm glad Darcy has someone to help her."

"I'm so sorry, Kira." Mrs. Fletcher took hold of her hands. "Darcy was adamant about finding a home for her child. She wanted you and Trace to raise her baby." She paused. "There was always a chance the mother could change her mind."

"I know." She was numb.

"I assure you, you and your husband are back on the list."

Another list. Her time had run out on her having a family with Trace. Kira stood. She couldn't talk anymore. "Thank you for everything, Mrs. Fetcher."

"You're welcome, Kira. I'll be in touch." She walked to the door. "Goodbye."

Kira didn't speak, she just walked upstairs to the nursery. She ran her fingers along the new crib and the dresser that had arrived just yesterday. She looked at the wall where the name JENNA was spelled out in large ceramic letters.

There was no baby girl.

She'd never felt so alone. So lost.

CHAPTER TEN

TRACE had taken Kira's advice and that afternoon drove over to see his neighbor, Joel Lewis. Together, they saddled two mounts and rode out to the EnRockies' drilling tower. The energy company had built an access road across the Lewis's pasture, but that was the most noticeable change. The high tower was partly hidden by the tall pines.

"It's not bad," Joel said as he leaned forward against the saddle horn. "I mean I had concerns at first, but in this day and age, farmers and ranchers need all the help they can get." The longtime neighbor looked at him. "I'm sure my daddy and yours would have raised a stink, but it's a different world now."

Trace couldn't help but think of all the money he owed, and how much easier it would be to have some extra income. "So you're okay with this arrangement?"

He nodded. "The extra money comes in handy when you have two college-aged kids, or when the wife needs a new car. We even took a vacation last year and started a retirement fund."

Trace thought about his parents and their struggles

running the cattle operation. He looked ahead to his own future. Would it be with Kira and the baby?

The sound of Joel's voice broke into his thoughts. "You've got it easy with your lease offer," he began. "It's Jarrett's property that's going to house the tower and handle the truck route. They're only going to do directional drilling onto your property. What's to think about?"

Trace sighed. "I guess I was just wondering what my dad would do."

Joel nodded. "It's your place now and you're the one fighting to keep it." He glanced around. "Where else could we live and enjoy this incredible backyard? Besides, I wouldn't survive in the city, nor would have wanted to raise my sons there. Have a couple of your own kids, Trace, and you'll change your mind quick."

It suddenly hit Trace. He had to think about his responsibilities to Kira, and the child. No matter what the original arrangement, he was definitely committed to the roles of husband and father.

This energy lease could help secure their financial future so he could continue to ranch. And so much more. Kira wouldn't have to work. He thought back to the past few days and his avoiding her. He needed to let her know how much he wanted her to be a part of his life, to include her in this decision.

Suddenly he couldn't wait to get home to talk to her about this.

"Thanks, Joel. You've helped a lot."

"Good. And if need be, I'll take Rocky off your hands."

They turned their horses back toward the barn. "Afraid

not, Joel, that bull is going to be too busy, but I'd be happy to sell you one of his calves."

"Sounds like you're in the ranching business for a long time."

"What can I say? It's in my blood." He thought about the baby coming soon. "I plan to stay here to see another generation take over." And he was going to do everything he could to convince Kira to stay by his side for a lifetime.

Thirty minutes later, he pulled his truck up beside the barn and headed toward the house to talk with Kira. If they were going to make their marriage work, he needed to listen to her. He'd made it to the back porch when he heard Cal saluting him.

The foreman caught up to him. "I was wondering if you have any plans for the old foreman's cottage?"

Trace frowned as he looked past the new bunkhouse to the small house that had been abandoned for years. "It's just storage for my parents' stuff." He looked at his friend. "Why, did you want to move into it?"

Cal shook his head. "No, Jody needs a place to live."

Trace hadn't figured their houseguest was staying much longer. "Isn't she going home to her mother?"

Cal shook his head. "Her mother's leaving town. Jody hasn't any other place to go."

"She's leaving her daughter?"

"Jody will be eighteen next week. Her mother doesn't want to be saddled with a teenager with a kid. She's moving on with her new boyfriend."

Trace couldn't help but think of Kira at that age.

There hadn't been anyone for her, either. "The cottage must be in bad shape."

"Not so bad. There's some water damage in the bathroom, but I can fix that. And a good cleaning would help a lot."

"I don't want Jody living out there until it's fixed up," Trace said. "And I'm sure there's plenty of furniture in the attic to furnish the place."

"Thanks," Cal said. "Now, the biggest job will be to convince her to stay."

"I'm sure Kira can manage that." Trace started backing away. "Speaking of Kira, is she in the house?"

Cal nodded. "She came back about an hour ago. That Mrs. Fletcher was here, too. She didn't stay long, though."

Trace tried to remember if the counselor was scheduled to come by. Had he missed a visit? If so, why hadn't Kira called him? He hurried into the house.

"Kira," he called. The only sound was the refrigerator clicking on.

He walked through the house to the staircase. Taking the steps two at a time, he felt his pulse drumming in his ears as he reached the second floor, then down the hall. She wasn't in the bedroom, then he heard a noise in the nursery. He pushed open the door and found Kira on the floor. With a screwdriver in hand, she was taking apart the crib he'd put together just a day before.

His heart beat erratically as he moved to his wife's side. "Kira, what's going on?"

Refusing to look at him, she continued her task. "We're not getting the baby."

His throat threatened to close up. No baby. "Why?"

She gave a shaky sigh and closed her eyes. "Darcy changed her mind." A tear rolled down Kira's cheek. "She wants to keep her baby."

It felt as if a huge weight landed on his chest, making it hard to breathe. No. He was just getting used to the idea of becoming a father.

"Oh, Kira." He reached for her but she avoided his touch.

"Don't." Kira climbed to her feet and moved away. "Don't tell me it's going to be okay because we both know it's not. It's never going to be okay, Trace. Not ever again." She swiped at the flood of tears.

Trace stood and went after her, but she continued to back away, his heart clutched in pain. Losing the baby was hard, but losing Kira was harder. Suddenly he felt his world being ripped apart.

"God, Kira, I know this hurts. We were warned this could happen." The words were so feeble. "We're still on the list. We can still have a baby."

"Another list!" she cried. "Then what? We wait some more and maybe have another baby jerked away again?"

Kira shook her head. She couldn't keep doing this to herself. Every time she began to hope, it was ripped away. And Trace. This had been their last chance.

"No, I'm not doing it anymore. I can't, Trace."

"Okay, we stop for now."

"No, I've stopped for good." Kira raised her gaze to his. There was pain in his beautiful gray eyes. It hurt her to know she couldn't be what he needed. It was time to stop it. "Your dream doesn't have to end, Trace. You can still have children."

He frowned. "What are you trying to say?"

She couldn't lose her nerve now. It was killing her to send him away, but better now than later when they ended up hating each other. She had to do what was best for Trace and the legacy he wanted to leave.

She straightened and wiped away her tears. "You can have the family you want, just not with me."

"I don't want a family unless it's with you."

She shook her head. "I can't keep doing this." She glanced away from his confused look. "And I can't keep putting you through this, either."

"You're not putting me through anything I don't want to do. I agreed to the adoption."

She straightened, fighting tears. "Well, I'm through." She stared at him. "Our original deal was for six months. We didn't get a baby, so you're off the hook."

"Off the hook?" He looked as if she'd struck him. "That's all you think of our marriage? That I came back because of the baby?"

She managed a nod, praying to stay strong. This was for the best.

Trace turned and walked out.

It was over.

With no desire to sleep, Trace took out his frustration by working through the night. By morning he had worked up a good anger as he continued his labor, mucking out stalls, repairing fence. He headed over to the foreman's cottage to see what needed to be done.

Anything to keep him from thinking. Thinking about what he was about to lose. Everything.

He heard the sound of pounding in the foreman's cottage and wandered over to find Cal busy at work on repairs.

Trace maneuvered through the boxes stacked in the small living room to find his foreman in the kitchen putting down new subflooring. He was surprised how much Cal had gotten done since yesterday.

"You're not wasting any time."

"Jody needs a place." Cal stood and pushed his hat back. "Since you've pulled an all-nighter, I take it things aren't good between you and Kira."

"We're not going to get the baby," Trace said.

He frowned. "So you left?"

"Sometimes we're not given a choice."

"And you're just going to give up?"

He hated to keep beating his head against the wall. "She's not fighting for me, either."

Cal sighed. "Marriage isn't a contest, Trace. It's hard work. Kira is hurting. She probably said things she didn't really mean."

"What are you, a marriage counselor?"

"No, but I've been there, dammit. I messed up big time. I walked away without fighting. It cost me my wife and my daughter."

"You have a daughter?" Trace asked.

"She's not mine anymore. I gave her up and I let my ex-wife's new husband adopt her. She'd be about Jody's age."

Trace watched Cal swallow hard.

"I regret it every day. Hell, Trace, I'd crawl back if I could have my family again, but I was too damn bullheaded to see anything beyond my pride."

Suddenly Cal glanced toward the doorway and saw Jody standing there in her jeans and T-shirt.

The teenager smiled shyly. "I'm sorry to bother you." She looked at Trace. "There was a phone call and I heard the voice on the recorder. It sounded important, and Kira isn't around. Here's the man's name and number." She handed him a piece of paper, then looked back at Cal. "I hate to ask, but do you think you could take me to work?"

"Sure. What time?"

"In two hours."

He nodded. "Just come and get me when you're ready."

After Jody left, Trace looked at the note paper to see the name of Greg Carlson from the Teacher's Credit Union. Trace pulled out his phone and punched in the number.

It rang twice then was answered, "This is Greg Carlson."

"Hello, Mr. Carlson, this is Trace McKane. You left me a message."

"Yes, Mr. McKane. We wanted to let you and Mrs. McKane know that your loan has been approved. Since this is a joint loan, I need you to come in and sign some papers before we cut a check for Jarrett McKane."

Trace wasn't sure how to react. Kira had applied for a loan? To pay Jarrett? "Could you just put a hold on the paperwork until I talk to my wife?"

There was a pause. "That's not a problem. We can hold it for forty-eight hours."

"Thank you, Mr. Carlson." He flipped his phone closed. "Dammit, why did she do that?"

"Do what?" Cal asked.

"Kira got a loan to pay off Jarrett."

Cal raised an eyebrow and folded his arms over his chest. "Okay, now, tell me she doesn't care about the ranch. And you."

CHAPTER ELEVEN

THE next morning, Trace went to his brother's office downtown. There weren't any pleasantries or announcements as he bypassed the blond secretary and walked through the door. He found Jarrett on the phone.

The young woman ran after him. "Sir, you can't go in there."

His brother hung up the phone and stood. "It's okay, Sarah. I've been expecting him."

The blonde backed out and shut the door. "Well, it's about time you showed up," Jarrett said.

"I wanted the satisfaction of telling you, you're not taking my land. I was just with Frank Rhodes and signed a contract with EnRockies. You'll have your check for the land in plenty of time before the due date."

Jarrett shrugged. "You can't blame a guy for trying."

"Why, Jarrett? Do you hate me so much that you want to destroy me?"

"Hell, I don't hate you. I saw an opportunity and took it." Then his shoulders sagged as he leaned a hip on the desk. "The real estate market is a mess. I had to do something to save my business."

"If you'd let me know about EnRockies' offer from the first, maybe we could have worked together."

In his younger years, Trace had always looked up to his big brother. He was popular and a talented athlete in school. Trace had been shy and uncomfortable around girls. But Jarrett never had time for him. As adults, it had become a competition.

"Honestly, I didn't think you'd go for it."

"But you never asked. We're supposed to be family, Jarrett."

His brother didn't say anything as he studied him. "Did Kira talk you into signing on for this deal?"

The question hit a nerve. He'd never gotten the chance to talk to her. "She's with me on this. We're adamant about keeping the land. EnRockies' lease seems to be the best way to assure it. Now that section of land is mine free and clear."

Jarrett smiled. "You're married, bro, nothing is completely all yours, and since you're having a kid, you're going to need all the extra money you can get."

Sadness shook Trace. That dream was long gone. "There isn't going to be a baby."

His brother's smile faded. "Sorry to hear that. What happened?"

Trace found he was angry. "The biological mother is going to keep it." *And Kira doesn't have any need for me any longer,* he added silently.

"Okay. What's your next move?"

Trace didn't want to share his private business. "I don't have any." He suddenly felt defeated. "Kira's pretty upset."

"Which is understandable," Jarrett told him. "But there are other options out there."

It was strange talking to his brother about this. "Not when this baby was the main reason we've been together. Now that's gone."

Jarrett shook his head. "Nothing is gone until you let Kira leave. Come on, Trace, I know you're brighter than that." He smiled. "You managed to steal her away from me."

"Hell, I can't make her stay."

"Then give her a good reason not to leave," he began as he folded his arms over his chest. "Have you told her how much you love her, and that you can't live without her?"

Trace straightened. "What is this, Romance 101? I've tried."

"Seems to me a woman who goes out on a limb to get help so her husband can keep his ranch isn't a woman who doesn't care."

"Have you been talking to Kira?"

"No, but the credit union called about the balance on the loan. Like I said, a woman doesn't risk her future if she's leaving."

"That was before we lost the baby."

"So she just turns off her feelings for you?" He shook his head. "I don't think so."

Trace felt sad. "What about the baby? I can't fix that."

"No one expects you to, but hold on to her until you get another shot at it. You're going to have the financial means to pursue other avenues, too." He walked around the desk, sorted through his Rolodex and pulled out a business card. "When you're ready, give this fertility specialist a call."

Trace shook his head. "No, Jarrett. I can't handle this again."

Jarrett paused with a frown. "You can't handle it? What about Kira? Think what she's going through right now. And she doesn't have any family to turn to."

Trace started to speak, but knew it was true. Even he'd walked out on Kira. It had been her who'd come to him, begging him to move back to give her a chance at a baby. To give them a chance.

Even after he learned about the child she'd given up years ago, he felt hurt she hadn't shared it with him earlier. A revelation hit him. All along, he'd been the one who never gave her a reason to trust him. Maybe she felt she couldn't count on him to stand by her. And when she needed him the most, he'd run out on her. Again.

He glanced at his brother. "I need to get home."

Jarrett smiled. "Give Kira my love."

Trace headed for the door, praying it wasn't too late to do just that.

"You're not leaving town, or Trace," Michelle said.

That same morning, Kira paced her friend's apartment. "It's the only way. People won't understand why we broke up and I can't answer all the questions. It's the only chance for Trace to start over." She brushed a tear off her cheek. "He can find someone. Someone who can give him a family."

"What about you?" Michelle asked. "You deserve a

life, too, Kira. A man who loves you. And don't try to say that man isn't Trace."

She recalled yesterday when she was so upset about losing the baby. He'd left her. "He walked out."

"Maybe because you didn't give him a chance."

Kira swung around to deny it and suddenly a wave of dizziness hit her. She reached for the back of the chair to steady herself.

Michelle rushed to her side. "You okay?"

Kira sank into the chair feeling a wave of nausea. "It's probably because I haven't eaten today."

"Great. Like you can stand to lose any more weight." Her friend walked into the small kitchen and took out some yogurt. "Eat."

Kira caught the aroma of the fruit flavor and her stomach roiled in rebellion. She barely made it across the room and into the bathroom before she lost what little food was in her.

With a groan, Kira leaned against the counter. Michelle handed her a cool washcloth. "Could this be more than lack of food?"

"Stomach flu. I haven't felt good for a few days."

Michelle gave her some mouthwash, then helped her to the sofa. "How many days?"

"Two or three, I guess."

"What are your other symptoms?"

"I haven't had any energy. Upset stomach, but a lot has been going on…with the baby and all."

Michelle's eyes widened. "And Trace has been staying in the guestroom since moving back?"

Kira felt herself blush. "Mostly."

"Okay, you better give me some more symptoms."

It suddenly dawned on Kira what she was asking. "No, it's not that, could never be that. The doctor said it would be close to a miracle."

"I'm Catholic. We believe in miracles. My mother and I have had you on our novena list for the past year." She shrugged. "So why not? Are your breasts tender? When was your last period?"

Kira refused to answer, because she refused to hope. "It's too crazy to think about."

"It's not crazy."

She shook her head. She couldn't even hope.

"There's only one way to find out." Michelle grabbed her purse off the entry table. "I'm going to the drugstore." Before she could stop her, her friend was gone out the door.

Kira didn't want to take a pregnancy test. She'd taken dozens over the past few years and they'd all come back negative. She didn't need that today.

Ten minutes later there was a knock on the door. Thinking Michelle forgot her key, Kira got up and opened the door to find Trace.

"What are you doing here?"

Trace hadn't expected Kira to greet him with open arms, but he'd hoped for a warmer greeting. "I've been trying to find you." He walked in. "We need to talk."

"We've said everything, Trace. I'll be out of the house in a few days."

"I don't want you to move out. I want us to stay together."

She walked across the room. "For how long, Trace?"

Tears flooded her eyes. "Until the next time I try to get involved in your life?"

"Can't we go back to the house and talk this out?"

She shook her head, fighting tears. "No, it's better this way. I'll come back another day when you're not around and move the rest of my things. And I don't want any part of the ranch. It was never mine."

"Yes, it is. The ranch is yours, too. You're my wife, Kira. I was wrong not to include you in all decisions concerning the operation."

He could only watch as she fought her emotions. "No, I don't want any part of the McKane Ranch. So just please go, Trace." She pointed toward the door and, as if by magic, it opened and Michelle walked in.

"I got you the last test at the drugstore." Kira's friend pulled a box from the bag. She froze when she glanced up to see they weren't alone. "Oh, Trace."

"Michelle." His gaze went to the box. He'd seen the same pregnancy test in their bathroom cabinet back when they'd been trying for a baby. He swallowed the sudden dryness in his throat as he glanced at Kira. Pregnant? Could she be pregnant?

"It's the stomach flu," she assured him unconvincingly.

"But you don't know for sure."

She didn't answer.

He went to her and took her by the arm. "We're going home." As they headed for the door, he grabbed the pregnancy test from Michelle.

"Good luck," she called to them.

Trace knew if he was going to have a chance to repair

things between them, it was going to take a lot more than luck. He had to convince Kira that he wasn't going to give up on them. No matter what the test said.

CHAPTER TWELVE

THIRTY minutes later they arrived back at the ranch. Silently Trace led Kira through the house and upstairs to their bedroom, and into the connecting bath. Before she could argue, he set the test on the sink, then walked out, shutting the door behind him.

Kira relented and after the deed was done, she came out ready to give Trace a piece of her mind. "I don't appreciate you railroading me into doing this. The test will only show what we both already know." Her voice softened. "That I'm not pregnant…once again."

He got off the bed, but didn't apologize. "How long for the results?"

"Five minutes."

Kira released a breath and watched as he paced the room they'd shared over their five-year marriage. The memory of the night he'd learned her secret flashed into her head. The one night they'd made love and the times after that. Could they have made a baby? Could those nights in Trace's arms have created a miracle? She shook away the thought, refusing to let herself hope.

She straightened. "You go look, I can't go through the disappointment again."

He studied her. "It could be different this time."

"I don't want you to get your hopes up."

"Why not? After your last procedure six months ago, the doctor said removing the scar tissue could possibly help you conceive."

She sank against the dresser, trying to ignore the glimmer of hope. "Please, Trace, don't. I can't take seeing your disappointment again."

He walked to her. "Is that what you think? That I brought you back here just to find out if there is a baby?"

She was unable to look him in the eye.

"I brought you here because I wanted us to talk in private. So I could apologize to you."

"Why?"

"For walking out on you, especially yesterday." He paced as if agitated. "You needed me, Kira, and I felt helpless to do or say the right thing. When you pushed me away I was hurt. And maybe you won't believe this but I wanted the baby, too."

He sighed. "I wanted her for us. All I thought about was that little girl, how she was going to be the start to our family...the next generation." He forced a laugh. "I was looking forward to teaching her to ride, to rope and herd cows." When he glanced back at Kira, there were tears in his eyes, too. "How selfish is that?"

"Oh, Trace, that's not selfish. We all have dreams for our children."

He nodded. "Of course, she might have wanted to be

a ballerina," he went on. "But none of that mattered, only that this baby would be ours."

"I'm sorry, Trace," she breathed. "At the beginning I pushed you into this adoption. Neither one of us was close to being ready for a family."

"That was my fault, too, Kira," he admitted. "I excluded you. You had a full-time job. I didn't think you wanted to be involved with the ranch, too."

She knew how hard it was for him to admit that. "I only wanted to share your life, Trace. Your love for the ranch."

"I wanted to share your past, too," he answered, his hurt surfacing. "No matter how bad it was for you. I wanted to share your pain." He went to her, gripping her arms. "I was never angry that you had a child. God, Kira, you were so young. What you did was so unselfish. You gave your son the best chance at life. No matter what it cost you. I guess my problem was I wished you could have shared it with me."

"I was wrong not to trust you. But I thought if you knew my secret, I would lose you."

He reached for her and cupped her face in his hands. "God, Kira. You could never lose me." He kissed her hard and long, and when he broke away, they were both breathless.

He moved back a fraction, but she could feel his breath on her face. "From the moment I laid eyes on you, I couldn't think of anything else. You had me spooked as a green colt. You have no idea how many times I drove to the school to see you, then stopped short of going inside. I'd turn around, drive back to the ranch and convince myself that someone as beautiful as you wouldn't want to go out with me."

His admission thrilled her. "It took you thirteen days to ask me out, Trace McKane. Thirteen long days."

He blinked at her statement, then he sobered and said, "I'm not good at saying all the fancy words, Kira. But you need to know that you're my life. You're all I ever wanted. The only woman I've ever loved."

With her heart racing, she couldn't speak.

"I was wrong to exclude you from ranch business," he went on. "My mother didn't get involved, so I took it for granted you weren't interested, either. And when things got tight, I didn't want you to worry."

"I wanted to help," she said. "I'm working, making a salary, too. Besides, you were spending ranch money on all my medical procedures."

"I'm your husband. It was important to me that I take care of my wife. But I admit, with the adoption costs and the balance due on the loan to Jarrett, it was going to be hard." He moved closer. "Then Mr. Carlson called from the credit union, saying your loan came through."

She shrugged. "I knew you'd be upset, but I only did it so you wouldn't lose everything."

Trace sighed. He'd never loved Kira as much as he did in that moment. He leaned down and brushed his mouth across hers again. "You're what's precious to me, Kira." Her brown eyes were luminous. "When I came back here this morning and found you gone, I thought you'd left for good. I've never been so scared. This ranch doesn't mean anything to me without you."

"But you can't let Jarrett take your land. Please, Trace, don't be too stubborn to take the money."

He smiled. "We don't need it now, as soon as you sign the papers, EnRockies will drill on the land."

Her brown eyes widened. "Really?"

He nodded. "It's time we had a little security for our future."

"Our future?"

"Yes, yours and mine." He slipped his arms around her. "Like I was saying earlier, I came looking for you because I wanted to convince you to give me another chance. Give us another chance. I promise never to walk out on you again." His gaze locked with hers. "We'll have rough times, but we'll work on them together. When you cry, I'll hold you. When you're hurt, I'll share your pain." He cupped her face in his hands. "We'll deal with the joys and disappointments together."

"Oh, Trace."

"I love you, Kira. Never forget that."

"I love you, too, but, children—"

"I told you before, Kira, kids would be a bonus. I married you to share my life." He sighed. "I guess I'm just going to have to prove it to you."

His mouth captured hers in a kiss he hoped would convince her just how he felt about her.

Kira was weakening, but Trace always had that power over her. His hands moved over her body; soon she ached with need. She needed him now as never before. She wrapped her arms around his neck and deepened the kiss. He groaned and yanked her top from her jeans and ran his hand over her stomach.

He broke off the kiss and whispered, "Tell me I haven't lost you, Kira. That you'll give us another chance."

"Oh, yes, Trace."

He lifted her in his arms as her mouth came down on his. He carried her to the bed, set her down and finished undressing her as his mouth worked over hers, teasing her lips with his tongue. His fingers released the clasp on her bra and let her breasts spill out.

Kira arched her back as his hands cupped her, then his mouth captured the sensitive nipple. She gasped at the pleasure, but his tenderness caught her by surprise.

Trace raised his head. "Did I hurt you?"

She blinked. "Sorry, they're just a little sensitive."

He froze. "How sensitive?"

Kira knew what he was asking. She covered his hand and brought it back to her breasts. "Just a little."

"Damn. The test." He started to get up, but Kira wouldn't let go of him.

"Don't, Trace. Don't spoil this." Love and desire for this special man consumed her. "Stay and make love to me."

His brown hair was mussed, his beautiful gray eyes searched hers. He finally nodded and leaned down. "I promise you, Kira, someday we'll have a baby. It might take a little longer, but it'll happen. And together we'll raise our family. Here. At our home."

She suddenly felt pretty lucky. That's what she'd been looking for all her life. "That's all I need, Trace. Like you said, everything else is a bonus."

EPILOGUE

IT WAS late afternoon as Kira stood on the porch and watched volunteers set up the tables and portable barbecues for tomorrow's senior roundup. Although she'd taken off work the past year, she wasn't about to disappoint this year's class by canceling their party at the McKane Ranch. So tomorrow there would be about fifty kids and hopefully a lot of parents here.

Michelle had taken over the job of organizer, and she'd even roped Jarrett into helping out. The two seemed to be getting pretty close. So had the two brothers. Jarrett was even going on the roundup with Trace tomorrow.

She shifted little Nathan on her hip. The seven-month-old was getting big. She smiled at the cute little boy. It was hard to believe he'd grown so fast. He was thriving around his extended family.

"Here, I can take him for you."

She turned to see Cal coming up the steps. "I thought you were helping with setup for tomorrow."

Nathan reached out for his uncle Cal. "What can I say, I'm organized." He raised the boy high in his arms, causing him to giggle. "Besides, I promised Jody I'd bring Nathan to the house."

Kira was proud of Jody. She was working and going to college, plus raising her son. "She's supposed to be studying for finals."

"I know, but she wants to give him a bath and spend some time with him before he goes to bed."

Kira looked toward the foreman's cottage. The outside had been painted cream with burgundy shutters, and bright flowers lined the porch. Inside was nearly perfect, too. Cal had made sure of that. He'd taken both Jody and little Nathan under his care, playing uncle to the boy. It had been good for both of them.

"I'm worried that Jody isn't getting enough sleep."

"I'm getting plenty of sleep."

They turned as Jody joined them. She'd filled out since the birth of her son. The pretty girl was more sure of herself these days. Why shouldn't she be with all she'd accomplished this past year?

She was immediately drawn to her son. "How's my big boy?"

Nathan grinned showing off his two tiny teeth. She took him from Cal. After a series of kisses, she cuddled him close to her, and said, "I guess I needed a Nathan fix."

Kira's chest tightened. She understood the feeling. There was nothing like holding your child close.

"Then I guess...you can have a break," Kira said.

The girl started down the steps, then paused. "Have I told you lately how much I love you all, you, Cal and Trace? I wouldn't be able to bathe my baby every night if you all hadn't been there for me."

Okay, that made the tears fall as they thought back to the roundup a year ago. "And you're thanking us by paying it forward." After Jody graduated, she was going into social work to help troubled teens.

"I'm a long way off before I can do that."

Cal spoke up. "But the good thing is you're working toward it. And making us all proud."

Jody swallowed hard but didn't speak. Kira saw the emotions play across the girl's face. All her life Jody hadn't had many people behind her. Now she had a lot.

Kira waved to Nathan as mother and son left to go home. Their home for as long as they needed it.

Suddenly Kira's attention was drawn to the corral and to a lone rider. Her stomach got a funny feeling as she watched Trace sit atop Thunder. Her cowboy, husband and lover. Man of her dreams. All of the above.

When Trace spotted her, he tipped his hat and climbed down off the horse. He handed his reins to one of the two ranch hands they'd hired a few months ago. The extra money from the lease helped Trace expand the operation.

He started toward the house in his usual fitted Western shirt and faded jeans covered by rust-brown chaps. She knew he'd been checking the herd that was to be rounded up and branded tomorrow.

By the time Trace climbed the back steps, she felt breathless. Nothing had changed since they'd met. He still had that effect on her.

"Howdy, ma'am," he said.

She glanced over his dusty clothes. "Looks like you've been busy."

"I do have to work occasionally. I sure could use a shower." He stepped closer. "Care to join me?"

She smiled. "I might be talked into it."

His mouth closed over hers nearly before the words were out. The kiss grew deep and thorough, pulling her against him.

Suddenly there was a sound of a cry from the monitor on the railing.

He broke off her kiss with a groan. "Sounds like someone is hungry."

She nodded. "Okay, you go shower and I'll feed our daughter."

He started for the door, but paused. "Oh, I forgot to tell you that a John Kelsey and his son are coming by later to look at the bay mare, Sadie."

She paused. Trace had gotten into breeding horses this past year. He'd bought the bay mare with the idea of breeding her.

"This could be too good to turn down. Like you." He bent to kiss her again and the baby let out another hard cry.

"You better get her."

Kira raced up the steps and into the nursery. In the crib was four-month-old Jenna. "Hey, sweetheart, are you hungry?"

Her daughter whimpered as she waved her tiny arms and legs. Kira picked her up and cradled her precious baby in her arms. She was their miracle. After a quick diaper change, Kira sat in the rocker and unbuttoned her blouse. Once the child was rooted on her breast, Kira began to rock, looking down at the infant who resembled her daddy, but had her own brown eyes.

Kira closed her eyes, recalling the day she nearly lost it all until she let Trace talk her into giving their marriage another chance. They'd promised to love one another and to face whatever happened together.

The pregnancy test had been forgotten until much later when Trace came out of the bathroom holding the colored stick in his hand. That and wearing a big grin.

It showed positive. Kira had gotten pregnant.

After all the trying and praying and testing, she'd finally gotten pregnant. Little Jenna had been conceived the night Trace had learned about her past.

It hadn't been an easy time. She was high risk from the start, and the last few months had been spent in bed, but she carried their daughter thirty-seven weeks. Born three weeks early at a little over six pounds, the baby was thriving now.

Trace stood in the doorway, amazed at the sight. He blinked, hoping he wasn't dreaming as he watched his wife feeding their child. He'd never thought this day would come.

There was never a picture so beautiful, and so humbling. Kira had gone through a lot to get here, to have this baby. It took him a long time to understand. Then the day of Jenna's birth as the doctor put her in his arms, it all became clear. He never thought he could love so completely. Both his girls.

He walked in. "Mind if I join you?"

Kira smiled as she burped their daughter. "Sure." She switched breasts and soothed Jenna with a calming hand. She turned to him. "You look and smell a lot better."

He kissed her. "Glad you approve." He placed a kiss on his daughter's head, too. "I have plans once Jenna's had her fill."

Kira raised an eyebrow. "I thought you had someone coming by."

"We have time." He brushed a kiss across her lips, leaving them both wanting more. "I'll always have time for you and our daughter. You two will always come first."

"I know. A baby reestablishes your priorities."

"She makes me realize what's important in life."

Kira lifted the baby to her shoulder, patting her gently. It wasn't long before Jenna fell asleep and Kira carried her back to the crib.

Once the nursery door closed, Trace pulled his wife into his arms and kissed her. Their lips met as he removed her already open blouse. By the time they reached their room, she was half naked.

Kira couldn't have been happier or more turned on. "This is crazy in the middle of the day."

"We have to steal the time now wherever possible," he told her. "It's nearly five o'clock." He laid her on the bed and stared down at her. His eyes were filled with need and love.

"Have I told you lately how beautiful you are?"

"Yes, but feel free to elaborate." Kira helped him undress, her hands aggressively removing his clothes. His chest was broad and muscular, his waist narrow and hips taut and lean. His desire for her was evident.

Kira drew him down on her, loving the feel of him against her, also loving the precious words he whispered as he loved her slowly and completely. She clung to him, laughing and crying at the same time when the release came to them.

Trace pulled her to his side, not releasing his hold. "I love you," he said breathlessly.

"And I love you, too."

She sighed contently. "Our life is perfect."

"Just about," he said and kissed her forehead. He sat up on the bed. "But I'm hoping it's about to be."

Kira didn't know what her husband was talking about. He'd been showering her with gifts since they'd gotten back together.

"What did you do, Trace?"

"I guess you'll just have to wait about thirty minutes. Go take a shower and relax." He stood and began to pull on his jeans. "I'll listen for Jenna."

She didn't wait to be asked twice. She went into the bathroom, showered and shampooed her hair. After she dressed, Kira came downstairs to find Trace holding their daughter in his arms. He was talking to her, and she was making those cute sounds at him.

Trace saw her and his eyes brightened as he gave her the once-over. "Oh, darlin', you look good."

She glanced down at her black jeans and bright blouse, then glanced back at him. "You're not so bad yourself, cowboy."

He grinned. "Maybe we should go back upstairs."

"I thought you had a horse buyer coming soon."

He glanced out the kitchen window. "That would be John Kelsey." He took a breath and released it, then looked back at her. "That's not exactly the truth."

She stood next to him to see a car pull up in the driveway. "What's not exactly the truth?"

"John Kelsey and his son, Jack, aren't coming to look at a horse. They coming to see you, Kira."

Her eyes narrowed. Trace opened the door and guided her out to the porch. She caught sight of a tall man about forty-five. He smiled at her, then turned to the teenage boy.

Kira's breath caught when she saw the tall boy with curly blond hair and dark eyes. Her heart began to pound. It couldn't be. Not after all this time. She'd never hoped, never dreamed.

Tears flooded her eyes. She looked at Trace. "How? Why?"

Trace reached for her with his free hand. "You deserve this, Kira. It's time you met your son. Besides, Jack wanted to meet you, too."

She took a needed breath. "Really?" She couldn't move, but looked down at the boy waiting at the base of the porch.

Kira looked back at her husband. He had given her everything she'd been looking for all her life. He'd held out his hand to prove his support, his promise to share her pain and her joy.

"I'm here, Kira. I'll always be here."

It had taken a while, but she finally believe that he truly loved her. This was her home. "I know," she whispered, then took his hand and they walked down together.

As a family.

KEEPING
HER BABY'S SECRET

BY
RAYE MORGAN

Raye Morgan has been a nursery school teacher, a travel agent, a clerk and a business editor, but her best job ever has been writing romances—and fostering romance in her own family at the same time. Current score: two boys married, two more to go. Raye has published over seventy romances, and claims to have many more waiting in the wings. She lives in Southern California, with her husband and whichever son happens to be staying at home at that moment.

This book is dedicated to the Mother Lode
and all the wonderful towns along Highway 49.

CHAPTER ONE

DIANA COLLINS woke with a start and lay very still, her heart beating hard in her chest. She stared into the dark room. She'd heard something. She was sure of it.

It was midsummer and her windows were all open. That was nice for ventilation, but not so wise for safety, even out here in the country. Silently she railed at herself. She'd known she should do something about getting bars on the windows or…

But wait. There it was again. The intruder wasn't stumbling around in her little turn-of-the-century cottage. He was still outside. He was…singing.

Slowly she lifted her head. She knew that song. She knew that voice.

"Cam," she whispered, and now a different brand of adrenaline was shooting through her veins. She smiled.

"Cam, you idiot!"

Slipping out of bed, she went to the window and looked down toward the lake. She could just make out a dark figure lounging on the pier. The moonlight glinted on a bottle he was holding as he leaned back to let out a wobbly high note.

"Oh, Cam," she said despairingly, but she was laughing. It must have been ten years since she'd last seen him. Joy flashed through her as she dashed around the room, searching for a robe to throw over her light nightgown—and to conceal, at least for the moment, her rounded belly.

Everything was going to be…well, not okay, but better. Cam was back.

Cameron Garfield Wellington Van Kirk the third was feeling no pain. There was no denying it—he'd been indulging. And since he almost never had more than a single glass of wine at dinner these days, he'd been affected more quickly and more thoroughly than he'd expected. He wondered, fleetingly, why he seemed to be bobbing in a warm, mellow glow. It was unusual, but rather nice.

"Maybe a little too nice," he muttered to himself in a Sam Spade accent, trying to look fierce and world-weary at the same time. It didn't really work. But did that matter when there was no one here to witness it anyway?

Never mind. He was going to sing again. Just one more swig from this nice bottle and he was going to sing that song about Diana.

"'I'm so young, and you're…'" he began tunefully, then stopped, frowning. "Wait a minute. I'm older than she is. This song doesn't make any sense."

An owl called from across the water, then swooped by, its wings hissing in the air.

He turned and there she was, coming down toward the pier, dressed in lacy white and looking like something ethereal, magic—from another world. He squinted, trying to see her better. He wasn't used to thinking of her as part angel, part enchantress. The Diana he'd known was a girl who had both feet firmly placed in a particularly earthy sort of reality. At least, that was the way he remembered it.

"Diana?" he whispered loudly. After all, he didn't want to wake anybody up. "Is that you?"

She came closer and he watched, fascinated, then blinked hard and shook his head. It was his old friend Diana all right but it looked like she was floating. Were her feet even touching the ground? Her cloud of blond hair shimmered around her and the gown billowed in a gust of wind and he felt a catch in his breathing. She was so beautiful. How was it that he'd managed to stay away this long?

"Cam?" she said, her voice as clear as the lake water. "Is that really you?"

He stared at her without answering. "If this is heaven," he mumbled as he watched her, enchanted and weaving dangerously right next to the water, "it's more than I deserve."

"It's Apache Lake, silly," she said as she came onto the pier and headed right for him. "Heaven is still to come."

"For you, maybe," he muttered, shaking his head as he looked her over.

She might look magical but she was all woman now—no longer the barefoot girl with the ragged cutoffs and the skimpy cropped top and a belly-button ring—

and like as not a set of bruises administered by her bully of a father. That was the Diana he'd left behind.

This new Diana was going to take some getting used to. He made no move to give her a hug or a kiss in greeting. Maybe that was because he wanted to with a sudden intensity that set up warning flares. And maybe it was because he'd had too much to drink and didn't trust himself to keep it simple.

"Some of us are still holding our options open," he added irrelevantly.

Her answering laugh was no more relevant, but it didn't matter. She was laughing from the pure joy of seeing him again. She looked up at him, still searching his face as though needing to find bits and pieces of the Cam she remembered. She noted how he was still fighting back the tendency to curl in his almost-black hair. And there were his startlingly blue eyes, crinkling with a hint of laughter. That was still the same. But there was a wary reserve that hadn't been there before. He was harder now, tougher looking. The sweetness of the boy had been sloughed away and in its place there was a cool, manly sort of strength.

For just a moment, her confidence faltered. He was large and impressive in a way she didn't recognize. Maybe he'd changed more than she was going to like. Maybe he'd become someone else, a stranger.

Oh, she hoped not, but her heart was in her throat.

"Hey," he said.

"Hey yourself," she said back softly, her dark eyes luminous in the gloom as she searched for clues in the set of his shoulders, the lines of his face. "What are you doing here?"

He frowned, trying to remember. Everything seemed to have fuzzy edges right now. He'd been on his way home—if you could call the house where his parents and grandfather lived his home. Yeah, that was it. He'd been on his way home, and then, he'd taken a detour....

Suddenly the answer was clear. He'd thought he was just stopping by to say hello to an old friend, putting off the homecoming he had waiting for him at the Van Kirk family mansion on the hill not too far from here. But now he knew there was a flaw in his thinking. There had been another motivation all along. He just hadn't realized it. He'd come to find the person he'd missed most all these years. And here she was, not quite the same, but good enough.

He looked down at her, needing nothing more than the Diana she was today. He soaked her in as though he'd been lost in the desert and dying of thirst. She promised to be something better and more satisfying than mere alcohol could ever be.

They said you can't go home again, and maybe that was true. Things could never be the way they'd been before he left. But that was okay. The way Diana had turned out, things might just be better.

"What am I doing here?" he repeated softly, still struggling with blurry thinking. "Looking for you."

"For me?" She laughed dismissively, looking over his shoulder at the moon. "I think you're looking for someone who isn't here anymore."

"You'll do," he said simply.

They stared into each other's eyes for a long moment, their memories and emotions awakening and connecting in a way their words could never quite explain.

"I thought you weren't ever coming back," she said at last, and her voice had a catch in it that made her wince. Tears of raw feeling were very near the surface and she couldn't let them show. But to see him here, standing on her pier, just as he had in those bygone days, sent her heart soaring.

She looked at him, looked at his open shirt and wide belt, his attractively tight jeans and slim hips, the way his short sleeves revealed nicely swelling biceps and she shook her head. He was so like the young man she'd known, and yet so different. The dark hair was shorter and cut more neatly, though it was mussed a bit now and a spray of it still fell over his eyes, just like always. The face was harder, creases where dimples used to be. But the gorgeous eyes were just as brilliantly blue, sparkling like star-fire in the moonlight.

For so long, she'd been afraid his last declaration to her would come true. Even after all these years, the memory of those final words had the capacity to sting deep down in her heart.

"I'm out of here, and I'm never coming back."

She'd thought her world had melted down that day. And now here he was, back after all.

"Naw," he said carelessly. "I never meant it. Not really."

She nodded. She accepted that. She'd waited for a long time for him to show up again. She'd been so sure he would, despite what he'd said. But after years, when it didn't happen, she'd finally started to lose faith.

She remembered when he'd left. She'd been an angry and confused eighteen-year-old, trapped in a broken home, grasping for a reason to thrive. For so long, he'd been her anchor to all that was good in life. And then he'd left and she'd felt adrift in a world without signs or shelter. She'd been so very all alone.

"What I can't understand is why you're still here," he said.

She lifted her chin. "Where did you think I'd be?"

He shrugged. "I don't know. San Francisco maybe. Becoming sophisticated." He half grinned. "Gettin' swanky."

"Swanky?" She laughed. "That'll be the day."

As if on cue, he began to softly sing the Buddy Holly song of the same name, still staring soulfully into her eyes.

"You're drunk," she accused him, shaking her head as though despairing of him.

He stopped short and grimaced. "No. Impossible." He stared hard, actually trying to convince her. "You can ask anyone. I don't drink."

"Cam!" She looked pointedly at the bottle in his hand.

He looked at it, too, then quickly looked away. "Hey, anyone," he called out a bit groggily across the lake, for-getting all about keeping it quiet. "Tell her. She needs to hear it from a neutral source."

She bit her lip, trying not to laugh at the picture he made. "There's no one out there," she told him simply.

"Sure there is." He turned his heavy-lidded gaze on her. "Look closely, now. Can't you see them?"

Turning to lean on the railing, she looked out across the lake to the stand of pines and cottonwoods shivering in the breeze. It was so good to be here in the night with Cam, almost as though a missing part of her was back in place, where it should be.

"See who?"

"Us." He moved closer and spoke very near her ear. "Cam and Di. The boy and girl we used to be. The ghosts are out there."

She could feel his warm breath on her skin. It made her pulse beat just a little faster and she was enjoying it, for now.

It had been so long.

She'd tried asking about him over the years, first in the village, then at the Van Kirk mansion when she'd been there in connection to her job, and the response she had was minimal. She'd told herself that it looked like he was gone for good, that he'd had some sort of rift with his family that couldn't be repaired—that he was never coming back. She'd tried to convince herself to forget about him. But his influence on her was embedded in her soul. She couldn't shake him loose, no matter what.

And at the same time, she'd always known that she could never really have him. But that was a tragic fact of life, something she'd accepted as a given.

She turned and looked at him. "I don't see anything," she told him, determined to be the realist to his crazy dreamer. "There's nobody out there."

"Sure there is." He frowned as though it was a puzzle that needed solving. "Maybe you should have some of this," he said, brandishing the bottle and looked at her hopefully. "Your vision might get better."

She shook her head, rolling her eyes as she did so. He looked at the bottle, drained it, then frowned, silently reproaching himself. She had a right to hate drinking. She'd certainly suffered enough from the stuff.

"Okay. I'll get rid of it." Easy enough for him to say. The bottle was empty now.

"Wait!" She stopped him from sending it sailing out into the water, snatching it from his hand. "Don't litter in my lake. I'll put it in the trash can."

He blinked at her but didn't protest, leaning back on the railing with his elbows and watching her with the trace of a smile on his handsome face. She tossed the bottle and turned back to him. Her heart lurched at the picture he made in the moonlight, part the man he was now, part the memory of the boy. There had been a time when she would have done anything for him. And now? Hopefully she knew better now.

Looking out across the water again, she pretended to squint and peer into the moonlight. "Wait a minute," she said, looking hard. "I think I see them now. Two crazy kids stomping around in the mud."

"That's them," he said approvingly, then looked down at her. "Or more accurately, that's us."

Us. Yes, they had spent time together on that side of the lake. How could she forget? Some of the best moments of her life had been spent there.

Cam was always fighting with his grandfather in those days. After a particularly bad argument, she would often find him down at the far side of Apache Lake, fishing for rainbow trout. She would sit and watch and he would tell her stories about the valley's history or his sister's latest exploit or…sometimes, what he wanted to do with his life. His dreams involved big things far away from gold country. Whenever he talked about them, she felt a sense of sad emptiness inside. She knew she would never be a part of that world.

He always used catch and release, and she would watch regretfully as he threw the shiny, silvery fish back in and they watched it swim away. He didn't realize that she could have used it for dinner. More often than not, the refrigerator at her house was bare and her father was off somewhere burning through the money that should have gone to food, pouring it down his throat in the form of bargain wine. But she never said a word to Cam. She was too embarrassed to let him know her dinner would be a cheap candy bar that night.

Such things were not a problem any longer. She had a nice little business that kept her comfortable, if not exactly rolling in wealth. These days she was more likely to try to cut down on calories than to need to scrounge for protein.

Times had changed. She'd traded a rough childhood for an adulthood that was a lot nicer. She'd been a damaged person then. She was okay now.

Her hands tightened on the railing and she bit down on her lower lip to keep it from trembling. Who was she trying to kid? A woman who was content with her life didn't take the steps to change things that she had recently done.

He hadn't noticed yet. She resisted the urge to pull her robe more carefully over her slightly rounded belly. He was going to have to know the truth some time and it might as well be now.

Well, maybe not now. But very soon.

"Remember the night before I left?" he was saying, his voice low and slightly hoarse. "Remember…?"

He let his voice trail off and she closed her eyes. She remembered all right. She would never forget. It was the one and only time he'd ever kissed her. It wasn't much of a kiss—not at all the kind of kiss she'd yearned for. His lips had barely touched hers. But she still considered it the best kiss she'd ever had.

She felt him touching her hair and she sighed. If she turned to look at him, would he kiss her again? She tried it, moving slowly, opening her eyes to look up into his face. For just a moment, she thought he might do it. But then a look of regret came into his eyes and he turned from her, moving restlessly.

Her heart sank, but she scolded herself at the same time. What was she thinking? A romance with Cam was not in the cards—never had been.

"So where have you been all this time?" she probed to get her mind on other things.

He shrugged. "Pretty much everywhere. Served a few years in the Navy. Worked on an oilrig in the Gulf. Spent some time as a bodyguard in Thailand. The usual stuff."

She nodded. This was definitely not the sort of thing his mother would have bragged about. If he'd been at law school on law review, spent time working as an aide to the governor, or made a pile of money on Wall Street, she would have made sure the local paper covered it in minute detail. Cam had always had a tendency to turn away from the upper class path to respect and follow his own route to…what? That had often been a bone of contention between him and his family.

But who was she to complain? It was exactly that inclination that had led him to be her protector for those early years. Their friendship had started when she was in Middle School. Her father was the town drunk and that meant she was the object of vile names and other indignities that adolescent boys seemed compelled to visit upon those weaker than themselves. Cam was a couple of years older. He saw immediately what was going on in her life and he stepped in to make it stop.

That first time had been like magic. She'd gone for a swim at the park pool. None of her friends had shown up and suddenly, she'd been surrounded by a group of boys who had begun to taunt her, circling and snapping at her like a pack of wolves. She knew she could hold her own against one boy, or even two or three, but there were too many this time and she panicked. She tried to run, which only egged them on, and just when she thought she was going to be taken down like a frightened deer, Cam appeared on the scene.

He was only a few years older than the boys, but his sense of strength and authority gave him the upper hand

and they scattered as soon as he challenged them. He picked her up, dusted her off and took her for ice cream. And that began a friendship that lasted all through her school years. He was her protector, the force behind the calm, the one who made everything okay.

Even when he'd gone away to university, he'd checked on her whenever he came home. He treated her like a big brother. The only problem was, she'd never been able to completely think of him that way.

No, from the start, she'd had a major crush on him. It hadn't been easy to hide. And the effects had lingered long after he'd skipped town and left her behind. In fact, she knew very well it was her feelings for him that had ruined every relationship she'd attempted ever since.

"So you've pretty much been bumming around the world for ten years?" she asked, frowning as she looked at him again. Whatever he'd been doing, it actually looked to be profitable. Now that she noticed, his clothing was rumpled, but top-of-the-line. And that watch he wore looked like it could be traded in for a down payment on a small house.

"Not really," he told her. "The first five years, maybe. But then I sort of fell into a pretty lucrative situation." He shrugged. "I started my own business in San Diego and I've done pretty well."

"Good for you."

He shrugged again. "I've been lucky."

She knew it was more than that. He was quick, smart, competent. Whatever that business was, he was evidently successful at it.

"And all that time, you never thought a simple phone call might have been in order?" she asked lightly. "A letter, maybe? Just some sign that you were still alive and well?"

She bit her lip again. Was she whining? Better to drop it.

He shook his head. "I figured a clean break was the best way," he said softly.

She winced. That was exactly what he'd said that night, after he'd kissed her. But she wasn't going to complain anymore. It wasn't like he owed her anything. When you came right down to it, he'd done more for her than anyone else ever had. What more could she ask for?

That was a dangerous question and she shied away from it quickly.

"So what brought you back?" she asked. "Are you back for good?" The words were out of her mouth before she could stop them and she made a face, knowing she had sounded altogether too hopeful.

He looked at her, then at the moon. "Hard to tell at this point," he muttered. Turning, he looked back toward the little house she lived in. She'd done something to it. Even in the dark, it didn't look so much like a shack anymore.

"Your old man still around?" he asked.

"He died a few years ago," she told him. "Complications from pneumonia."

Complications from being a rotten drunk was what she could have said, he thought bitterly. She was better off without him. But that being said, you didn't get to choose your relatives and he *was* her father.

"Sorry," he muttered, looking away.

"Thanks," she said shortly. "For all the grief he gave me, he did manage to hang onto this little piece of property, so it's mine now. All five acres of it."

He nodded, then smiled, happy to think of her having something like this for her own. Whenever he'd thought of her over the years, he'd pictured her here, at the lake. It was so much a part of her.

"I had a funeral for him," she went on. "At the little chapel on Main. I thought it would just be me and him." She shook her head, remembering. "Do you know, most of the town came? I couldn't believe it." She grinned. "I even had a cousin I'd never met before show up, Ben Lanker. He's an attorney in Sacramento and he wanted to go over the will for me, to see if all was okay." She laughed shortly. "I think he was hoping to find a flaw, to see if there was some way he could get his hands on this property. But I'd had everything nailed down clear and legal when I was dating a lawyer in San Francisco, so he was out of luck."

He laughed along with her, pleased to know she was taking care of herself these days. Looking at her, he couldn't imagine her being a victim in any way.

"So tell me, Cam," she said. "The truth this time. I'm still waiting to hear the answer to my question. What brings you back to your ancestral home?"

He sighed. "It's a fairly easy answer. I'm just embarrassed to tell you."

That made her laugh again. "Oh, now I *have* to hear it. Come on. The raw, unvarnished truth. Give it up." She smiled at him. "What did you come home for?"

Giving her a sheepish look, he grimaced.

"Okay. You asked for it."

She waited expectantly. He took a deep breath, as though this was really tough to admit.

"I came home to get married."

CHAPTER TWO

THE smile froze on Diana's face. She blinked a few times, but she didn't say anything. Still, it felt as though Cam had shot an arrow through her heart.

It shouldn't have. She had no right to feel that way. But rights didn't wait on feelings. She stared at him, numb.

"Married!" she finally managed to say in a voice that was almost normal. "You?"

He coughed discreetly. "Well, that's not actually technically true."

She blinked. "Cam!"

One dark eyebrow rose provocatively. "Take it as a metaphor."

"A metaphor!"

He was driving her crazy. She shook her head. It was too early in the morning for mind games.

"Will you tell me what is really going on?"

He sighed. "Let's just say my mother has plans. She thinks it's time I settled down."

"Really." Diana took a deep breath. So…was he getting married or wasn't he? She was completely confused and beginning to get annoyed. "Who's the lucky girl?"

He looked at her blearily. "What girl?"

She wanted to throw something at him and it took all her strength not to snap back through clenched teeth. "The girl your mother wants you to marry."

"Oh." He frowned as though he didn't see how this mattered. "There's no specific girl. More like a category of women." He shrugged and raked fingers through his tousled hair, adding to his slightly bewildered look. "She has a whole roster picked out. She's ready to toss them at me, one at a time, and I'm supposed to catch one of them in the end."

Diana took a deep breath. This had been the most maddening conversation she'd had in a long time. The strongest impulse she had right now was to push him into the lake. How dare he come back here this way, raising old emotions, raising old hopeless dreams, and then slapping her back down with vague news of pending nuptials? Was this a joke? Or was he just trying to torture her?

But she knew that wasn't really it. He didn't have a clue how she had always felt about him, did he? Well, despite the position it put her in, that was probably a good thing.

Holding all that in as best she could, she looked out at the moonlight on the lake. Funny. Cam had come home and within minutes she had reverted back to being the little raggedy urchin who saw him as her white knight. For years she'd clung to his protection, dreaming that one day, when she was older, he would notice that she wasn't a little girl anymore, that she'd grown into a woman.

She sighed softly. It had always been a stupid goal, and still was. He was from a different world and only visited hers when it suited him. He wasn't available, in other words. And even if he were, what she'd done to her own situation alone would rule out any hopes she might have. She should know better by now. A little toughness of her own was in order. No more shabby girl with her nose pressed to the windowpane.

She tilted her head to the side, a bemused look on her face as she worked on developing a bit of inner strength.

"Let me get this straight," she challenged. "You came back because your mother wanted you to?"

He blinked at her groggily. "Sort of," he admitted.

She shook her head, eyes flashing. "Who are you and what have you done with the real Cam Van Kirk?" she demanded.

"You don't buy it, huh?" He looked at her, trying to be earnest but too groggy to manage it well. The swath of dark hair that had fallen down over his eyes wasn't helping. He was looking more vulnerable than she'd ever imagined he could look.

"Actually," he murmured, "neither do I."

"What does that mean?"

"Come on, Di, you know how it is. You grow up. You begin to realize what is really important in life. And you do things you never thought you would."

Sure, she knew how it was. But she couldn't quite believe it. Not Cam. Not the young rebel she'd idolized for so many years.

"What happened to you, Cam?" she asked softly, searching his face.

He moved toward her, his hand reaching in to slide along her chin and cup her cheek. She pulled back, looking surprised at his touch and pushing his hand away.

And as she did so, she forgot to hold her robe closed and it fell open. Her rounded belly was obvious.

"Whoa," he said, jerking back and staring at it, then looking up at her face. He shook his head as though trying to clear it so that he could deal with this new development. "What happened to *you?*"

"It's not that big a mystery," she said quickly, pulling the robe back. "It happens a lot, in case you hadn't noticed."

He stared at her for a moment, his brow furled, and moved a bit further away, purposefully keeping his eyes averted from her midsection.

"Did you go and get married or something?" he muttered uncomfortably.

She looked away and he frowned. The downside of that possibility was suddenly clear to him. He didn't want her to be married. Given a choice, he would rather she wasn't pregnant, either. But that was clearly settled and he could have no influence on it. But the married part—no, if she were married he was going to have to leave pretty quickly and probably not come back.

Why hadn't he considered this possibility? Somehow it had seemed natural to find her here, just where he'd left her. But of course things had changed. It had been ten years, after all.

"No, Cam," she said calmly. She pulled the robe in closer and looked out at the lake. "I'm not married."

Was he supposed to feel relief at that? Probably not. It was pretty selfish of him. But he couldn't help it. Still, it left a few problems behind. There had to be a man involved in this situation. Cam blinked hard and tried to act sober.

"Who's the daddy? Anyone I know?"

She shook her head. "It doesn't matter."

He shrugged. "Your call. So I guess you're doing this on your own, huh? Are you ready for that?"

She gave him a quick, fleeting smile. "I'm fine, Cam. I can handle this."

Something stirred inside him. Was it admiration? Or regret? He was a bit too groggy to tell. But the Diana he'd left behind had seemed to need him in so many ways. This one, not so much. That was probably a good thing. Wasn't it? If only he could think clearly, he might even be able to tell.

"Well, you know, if you need any help…" he began.

She turned on him, ready to be defensively self-reliant, and that was when she saw what looked like blood. It was trickling down out of his dark hair, making a rivulet in front of his ear. She gasped, then looked more closely, detecting a lot more that had started to dry against the collar of his shirt.

"Cam! What's this?" She touched it and showed him.

"Oh, just a little blood." He pulled out a handkerchief and dabbed at it.

"Blood!"

He gave her a melancholy smile. "I had a little accident. Just a little one."

She stared. "With your car?"

He nodded. "The car wouldn't go where I tried to get it to go. I kept pulling on the wheel and saying, 'Come on, car, we've got to get to the Van Kirk mansion,' and the stupid car kept saying, 'You know you'd rather go see Diana.'" He looked at her with mock earnestness. "So we crashed." He waved toward the woods. "We smashed right into a tree."

"Cam!"

"Just a little one. But I hit my head pretty hard. Didn't you hear it?"

She stared at him, shaking her head. "Oh, Cam."

"It wasn't very far away." He frowned. "I'm surprised you didn't hear it."

"I was asleep."

"Oh." He sighed and stretched out his arms, yawning. "Sleep, huh? I used to do that."

She noticed the dark circles under his eyes. For all his handsome features, he did look tired. "Maybe you shouldn't drink when you drive," she pointed out sharply.

"I didn't." He shook his head. "The drinking came later."

"Oh."

He shrugged. "Just a bottle I found in the trunk after the crash. I brought it along to tide me over while I waited on your pier for the sun to come up." He looked forlorn. "I was planning to invite myself for breakfast."

How did he manage to look so darn lovable in this ridiculous state?

"It's still a little early for breakfast." She sighed, then reached out and took his hand. "Come on."

"Okay," he said, and started off with her. "Where are we going?"

"Where else would the prodigal son go? I'm going to take you home."

The drive up to the Van Kirk mansion was steep and winding. Diana had made it often over the last few years in her little business van. Alice Van Kirk, Cam's mother, had been one of the first people to hire her fledgling floral styling company to provide fresh arrangements for the house once a week back when she'd originally started it.

The sky had begun to lighten, but true dawn lurked at least a half hour away. Still, there was enough light to let her see the turrets and spirals of the Van Kirk mansion ahead, reaching up over the tops of the eucalyptus trees, shrouded in the wisps of morning fog. As a child, she'd thought of the house as an enchanted castle where royalty lived high above the mundane lives of the valley people, and it looked very much like that now.

"Are they expecting you today?" she asked.

When she didn't get an answer, she glanced at Cam in the passenger's seat. He was drifting off to sleep.

"Hey!" She poked at him with her elbow. "I don't think you should let yourself sleep until you see a doctor. You might have a concussion or something."

"Hmm?" he responded, looking at her through mere slits where alert eyes should be.

"Cam, don't fall asleep," she ordered.

"Okay," he said, and his eyes immediately closed all the way.

"Oh!" she said, exasperated and poking him with her elbow again. "Here we are. Which door do you want?" She grimaced. "I don't suppose you have a key, though, do you?"

He didn't answer and his body looked as relaxed as a rag doll. With a sigh, she pulled into the back entrance, using the route she was used to. The servants' entrance she supposed they probably called it. The tradesmen's gate? Whatever, it was just off the kitchen and gave handy access to the parts of the house where she brought flower arrangements once a week. She rarely ran into any of the Van Kirks when she came. She usually dealt with Rosa Munez, the housekeeper. Rosa was a conscientious employee, but she doubted the woman would be up this early.

"How am I going to get you in there?" she asked, shaking her head as she gazed at the dark house. Turning, she reached out and pushed his dark hair back off his forehead. His face was so handsome, his features so classically perfect. For just a moment, she ached, longing to find a place in his arms. But she couldn't do that. She had to be tough.

"Cam," she said firmly, shaking his shoulder. "Come on, wake up."

"Okay," he murmured, but his eyes didn't open.

This made things a bit awkward.

Slipping out of the car, she went to the door and looked at the brass handle, loath to try it. She knew it would be locked, and she assumed there was a security system on the house. Everyone was obviously still asleep. What the heck was she going to do?

Stepping back, she looked up at the windows, wondering if she could climb up and get in that way, then picturing the embarrassment as she hung from a drainpipe, nightgown billowing in the breeze, while alarm bells went off all through the house. Not a good bet.

Turning, she went back to the car and slid into the driver's seat.

"Cam, I don't know what we're going to do," she said.

He was sound asleep and didn't even bother to twitch. She sighed with resignation. She was going to have to wake up the whole house, wasn't she? Now she regretted having come without changing into day clothes. But she hadn't been sure she could keep Cam in one place if she left him to go change, and she'd thought she would just drop him at his doorway and make a run for home. She should have known nothing was ever that easy.

"Okay. If I've got to do it, I might as well get it over with," she said, leaving the car again and going back to the door. Her finger was hovering half an inch from the doorbell and she was bracing for the sound explosion she was about to unleash on the unsuspecting occupants, when the door suddenly opened and she found herself face-to-face with Cam's sister, Janey.

"Diana? What in the world are you doing here?" she demanded.

"Janey!" Diana was immediately aware of how odd she must look standing on the Van Kirk doorstep in her filmy nightgown and fluffy white robe. The shabby slippers didn't help, either.

Janey, on the other hand, looked trendy and stylish in high end jogging togs. A tall, pretty woman about a year younger than Diana, she was evidently up for an early morning run and determined to look chic about it. Diana couldn't help but have a quick catty thought wondering which of the local squirrels and chipmunks she might be trying to impress. But she pushed that aside and felt nothing but relief to have a member of the family appear at the door.

She and Cam's sister had known each other forever but had never been friends. Janey had been aware of the close ties between Diana and her brother, and she'd made it very clear in very public ways that she didn't approve. But that was years ago. When they saw each other now, they weren't exactly warm, but they were perfectly civil.

"Janey," Diana said, sighing with relief. "I've got Cam in the car. He was in an accident."

"What?"

"Not too bad," she reassured her quickly. "He seems to be basically okay, but I think a doctor ought to look him over. And…well…" She winced. "He's been drinking so…"

"You're kidding." Janey followed her to the car and then they were both fussing over her brother.

"Cam, you blockhead, wake up," Janey ordered, shaking his shoulder. "We haven't seen you in years and this is the way you arrive?"

He opened one eye. "Janey? I thought I recognized your dulcet tones."

She shook her head. "Come on. I'll help you up to your room. I'm sure Mother will want to call Dr. Timmer."

"I don't need Dr. Timmer," he grumbled, though he did begin to leverage himself out of the car. "If Diana can take care of herself, I can take care of myself." He tried to pound his own chest and missed. "We're a pair of independents, Diana and I."

Janey gave him her arm and a quizzical look. "I have no idea what you're talking about," she said crisply. "Come on. We'll let your friend get back to her...whatever."

"Diana is my best friend," he murmured, sounding almost melancholy. "My favorite person in this valley. Always has been."

Janey chose that moment to notice Diana's baby bulge. Stopping short, she gasped. "Cam! Oh, no!"

Despite his condition, he immediately recognized the way her mind was trending and he groaned. "Listen, Janey, I just got into town at about 2:00 a.m. Not even I could get a lady with child that fast."

"*Humph,*" she harrumphed, throwing Diana a look that took in everything about her pregnancy and the fact that she was running around the countryside in her nightgown, delivering a rather inebriated Cam to his old homestead. It was obvious all this looked pretty darn fishy to her.

Diana almost laughed aloud. If Janey only knew the irony involved here. "Can you handle him without me?" she asked the other woman. "I'd like to get home and try to get some sleep. I do have an appointment back here with your mother at eleven."

"Go, go," Janey said, waving a hand dismissively and turning away.

But Cam didn't turn with her. He stayed where he was, looking back at Diana. "I was just getting used to having you around again, Di," he said. "A little later, when I've had some sleep…"

"You'll be busy getting caught up on all the family news," Janey said quickly. "And learning to give up living like a drifter."

"Like a drifter?" Cam looked up as though that reminded him of something and Diana laughed.

"Watch out, or he'll break out into song on you," she warned his sister as she turned for her car. As she walked away, she heard the Cam's voice warbling, "'Here I go again…'" She grinned.

Cam was back. What did this mean? Right now, it meant she was full of sadness and happiness at the same time.

"The thrill of victory and the agony of defeat," she murmured nonsensically as she began the drive down the hill. A moment later, tears were streaming down her face and she had no idea why.

But Cam was back. Good or bad, things were going to change. She could feel it in the air.

CHAPTER THREE

CAM woke to a pounding headache and a bunch of bad memories. It didn't help to open his bleary eyes and find the view the same as it had been when he was in high school. That made him want to close the world out and go back to sleep again. Maybe he would wake up in a better place.

No such luck. He opened his eyes again a few minutes later and nothing had changed. He was still a wimp for having let himself be talked into coming back here. Still an unfit driver for having crashed his car just because of a freak tire blowout. Still an idiot for having had too much to drink and letting it show.

And still bummed at finding Diana more appealing than ever and at the same time, totally unavailable. Life wasn't exactly glowing with happy discovery for him right now.

Then there had been the humiliating way he'd returned to the green green grass of home. His mother had tried to pretend he was fine and gave him the usual hugs and kisses a mother would bestow upon a returning miscreant. But, his father barely acknowledged his return. And Janey was plotting ways to undermine him and making no bones about it. He groaned. The outlook wasn't bright.

There was one more gauntlet to brave—the most important one right now—his grandfather. There was no point in putting it off any longer.

He made the water in his shower as cold and stinging as he could stand. He needed to wash away the previous day and start over. Maybe if he could just start fresh…

But he already knew it was going to take all his will to be able to stay and do what he'd promised he would do—save the family business, and in so doing, hopefully, save the family.

Funny that it would be up to him. When he'd left ten years before, his grandfather had just disowned him and his father had refused to take his side. His mother was upset about his choice of friends, and his sister was angling to take over his position in the family. To some extent, a somewhat typical twenty-one-year-old experience. But it had all been a culmination of years of unhappiness and bad relations, and something had snapped inside him. He'd had enough. He was going and he was never coming back.

Leaving Diana behind had been the only hard part. At eighteen, she'd still been gawky, a coltlike girl whose antics made him laugh with quick affection. She thought she needed him, though he knew very well she was strong enough to handle things on her own. She was fun and interesting and she was also the only person who seemed to understand what he was talking about most of the time.

But that was then. Things were different now. Diana had proven she could make it on her own, no problem. She'd done just fine without him. And she now belonged to somebody else. She could deny it, but the facts were right there, front and center. She was pregnant. That meant there was a man in her life. Even if he was out of the picture for the moment, he was there. How could it be any other way?

And all that was just as well, actually. Without that complication, he knew he could have easily fallen in love with her. He'd known that from the moment he saw her coming down to the lake, looking like an angel. He responded to her in a way he never did with other women, a combination of past experiences and current attraction. Yes, he could fall hard. And falling in love was something he was determined never to do again.

For just a moment he thought about Gina, the woman he'd lived with for two years and had almost married. But thoughts of Gina only brought pain, so he shrugged them away.

He needed to focus on the purpose of his return. He needed to get ready to face his grandfather.

Diana parked in the same spot she'd used earlier that morning. This time there was a buzz of activity all around the compound. Workmen were putting new doors on the multiple garages and a painter was freshening up the long white fence that edged the driveway. Across the patio, two men were digging postholes for what looked to be a new barbecue center. With all this action, she could see she wasn't going to need to contemplate a break-in this time. Sighing with satisfaction, she slid out of the car and made her way to the back entrance.

She'd traded in her nightgown for a sleek pantsuit she'd picked up in Carmel a few months before. Luckily she could still fit into it. She'd chosen it out of her closet specifically to rival anything Janey might be wearing. It had a high collar and a loose jacket that hid her belly and she knew she looked pretty good in it—always a confidence booster.

The back door was propped open and she went on into the huge kitchen, where Rosa, elbow deep in flour, waved at her from across the room.

"Mrs. Van Kirk is out in the rose garden," she called. "She asked that you meet her out there to go over some new plans."

"Fine." She waved back at the cheery woman and headed into the house. She'd been here often enough lately to know her way around. This place that had seemed so special to her as a child, and then so scary when she was friends with Cam but never invited in, was now a part of her workspace.

Walking down the long hall, gleaming with Brazilian cherry hardwood, she glanced into the library, and then the parlor, to check on the large arrangements she'd brought just a few days before. Both looked pretty good.

Ever since she'd stressed to Rosa that the stems could use a trim and fresh water every few days, her master-pieces were holding up better than they had before.

The Van Kirk mansion was beautiful in a way few houses could be. The quality of the original materials and workmanship shone through. The rich past and full history just added luster. It made her happy and proud just to be here, walking its beautiful halls.

As she rounded the stairwell to head into the dining room and out the French doors, Cam surprised her by arriving down the stairs and stopping right in front of her.

"Good morning, Miss Collins," he said smoothly. "You're back."

She cocked her head to the side and looked him over, fighting hard to suppress her reaction as her heart began a frantic dance in her chest. Here he was. It was really true. She hadn't dreamed what had happened the night before. Cam was back in her life, just when she'd thought it could never be.

He looked so good. Morning sunlight was even more flattering to his handsome face than starlight had been. Dressed in khakis and a blue polo shirt that matched his eyes, he looked hard and muscular as an athlete but gentle as a lover at the same time.

The perfect man—hadn't that always been the problem? She'd never found anyone better. It made her half-angry, half-thrilled, and practically hopeless. Now that he was back, what was going to happen to her peace of mind?

One casual meeting and she was already straying into

thoughts she'd vowed to stay away from. A simple look into that silver-blue gaze and her breath was harder to find and she was thinking moonlight and satin sheets and violins on the terrace. Given half a chance, she would be sliding into his arms, raising her lips for kisses….

No! She couldn't let that happen.

Very quickly, so quickly she hoped he didn't even notice, she pulled herself up short and forced a refocus. Cam was a friend and that was all he could ever be.

So think friend, she ordered herself. Lover thoughts are not allowed.

"Yes," she agreed, putting steel in her spine. "I'm… I'm back."

His gaze swept over her. "You're looking particularly lovely today," he noted, a slight smile softening the corners of his wide mouth.

The corners of her own mouth quirked. "As opposed to what I looked like yesterday, after midnight?" she said, half teasing.

His grin was crooked. "Oh, no. After midnight you looked even better. Only…"

"Did you see a doctor last night?" she broke in quickly, eager to forestall any flirting he might have in mind. They had to keep their relationship on a certain level and she was bound and determined she would be the watchdog of that if he wouldn't be.

"I guess so." He shrugged. "I was pretty much out of it."

"Yes, you were."

Looking chagrined, he put his hand over his heart and

gazed earnestly into her eyes. "I don't drink, you know. Not really. Hardly ever."

If she wasn't careful, he was going to make her laugh, and that was almost as dangerous as making her swoon.

"So you said."

"And it's true. If I'd found a box of crackers in the trunk of the car instead of a bottle of booze, I'd have been all crumbs last night, instead of the sauced sere-nader I devolved into."

She choked and his eyes sparkled with amusement at his own joke.

"But I do want to apologize. I was rude last night. I took over your lake and ruined your sleep and generally made myself into a damned nuisance."

He meant it. He was really apologizing. She met his gaze in solemn candor. "You did."

"And I'm sorry." His blue eyes were filled with tragic regret.

She laughed softly, shaking her head. She'd missed him, missed his candor, missed his teasing and missed what often actually seemed to be his sincere sensitivity to what she was feeling. But she had to admit, that sen-sitivity could sometimes slosh over into a subtle mockery and she was afraid he might be working his way in that general direction right now.

Still, they were friends, weren't they? She was allowed to act like a friend, at least.

"I'm not," she said firmly. "I'm not a bit sorry." She smiled up into his face. "Despite everything, it is good to have you back in the neighborhood."

"'Despite everything,' you say." He looked skeptical. "Seriously?"

Her smile deepened. "Of course."

The warmth between them began to sizzle and she knew it was time to pull back. But it felt like resisting quicksand to do it. If only she could allow herself this small island of pleasure. Soon enough she would leave and hopefully wall off any further contact with Cam, except the most casual and occasional kind. Would it really ruin everything to let herself enjoy him, just for this warm spring morning?

Yes. He was looking at her mouth and it sent shivers all through her. She couldn't risk even a tiny moment or two of weakness. Determined, she pulled away.

"I drove by to look at your car this morning," she said over her shoulder as she started to walk toward the French doors that opened onto the gardens.

"How's it doing?" he asked, walking with her.

She glanced at him sideways. "You didn't tell me you'd had a tire blow out."

"Didn't I?"

"No." She stopped in the doorway, turning to face him again. "It's too bad. I sort of liked your story about fighting the wheel in order to get to my place."

He snapped his fingers. "That was exactly what I was doing when the blowout occurred."

She grinned. "Right."

Mrs. Van Kirk, wearing a wide-brimmed sun hat and carrying a basket filled with cut flowers, was out among her prized rosebushes and as she turned, she spotted the two of them and began to wave. "Yoo-hoo! My dear, I'm over here."

Diana lifted her hand to wave back and said out of the corner of her mouth, "Who's she talking to, you or me?"

He stood beside her in the doorway, looking out. "I'd say it's a toss-up."

She glanced at him. "She's your mother."

His eyes narrowed suspiciously as he looked out at where she stood, waving at them. "Sometimes I wonder," he muttered.

Diana didn't wonder. In fact, she didn't have a doubt. Cam looked so much like his mother, it was cute—or frightening, depending on how you looked at it.

"Well, I'm going to go to her," Diana said, turning to leave.

He hung back. "I'm not coming with you. I've got a command audience with my grandfather."

"Oh, no." Stopping, she looked back at him. "Is this the first you've seen him since you came back?"

He nodded, a faraway look in his eyes. "This should be interesting."

To say the least. Diana winced, remembering all those old, painful arguments with the old man when he was younger. She could see by the look on his face that he wasn't as optimistic about the coming meeting as he might pretend.

"I'm surprised you're not taking in a bodyguard," she said lightly, only half joking. "I remember those sessions you used to have with him." Her eyes widened as she recalled some especially wild fights they'd had and she shuddered. "He put you through the wringer."

Cam nodded and he didn't smile. "That he did." His gaze skimmed over her face. "You want to come with me?"

She reared back. "Not on your life. When I was suggesting a bodyguard, I was thinking more along the lines of one of those burly fellows digging posts for the new barbecue center out back."

He laughed. "I think I can handle my grandfather," he said. "I'm older now. Wiser." He cocked an eyebrow. "More agile."

Diana shook her head, suppressing a grin. "And besides," she reminded him. "From what I hear, he's often bedridden. I guess that would give you an advantage."

He laughed again. "Exactly."

Word was that his grandfather was in rapidly failing health. With Cam's father spending most of his time at spa resorts that specialized in "rest cures" and his sister reportedly caught up in playing musical husbands, that left Cam to support his mother and help make some decisions. She was beginning to realize that those circumstances were probably part of the reason he'd agreed to come back home.

"I'll come out and join you if I survive."

"Okay." She winced as she started out through the rosebushes. She shouldn't be encouraging any of this "joining" or chatting or anything else with Cam. Her goal coming in had been to have the meeting with Mrs. Van Kirk and then get out of here as quickly as possible.

It was becoming more and more clear that staying away from Cam had to be her first priority.

The older woman came toward her, smiling.

"Oh, my dear, I'm so glad to see you. Thank you so much for coming by. Come sit with me in the garden and Rosa will bring us some nice tea."

Diana smiled back and followed her to the little gazebo at the far side of the flower garden. Her relationship with Cam's mother had undergone a complete transformation in the last few years. When she was a teenager, she knew very well the woman had considered her a guttersnipe who would contaminate her son if she didn't keep a constant vigil. The one time Cam had tried to bring her into the house, Mrs. Van Kirk had practically barred the door with her own plump body.

Years later, after Cam was long gone and Diana had started her flower business, the woman had hired her periodically, acting rather suspicious at first, but warming to her little by little as the quality of her work became apparent. By now, her affection for the girl she used to scorn was amazingly obvious to everyone—and sometimes resented by Janey.

But Diana was comfortable meeting with her, and she settled into a chair across from her in the gazebo, thinking once again how similar some of her features were to Cam's. She'd been a beautiful woman and was still very attractive in a plush sort of way. Her hair was auburn where Cam's was almost black, and her look was soft rather than hard, but she had the same blue eyes and sweet smile he did.

"I want to tell you how much I appreciate you bringing my son home last night after that terrible accident," Mrs. Van Kirk began. "He was certainly out of sorts for a while, but Dr. Timmer assures us there will be no lasting injuries. He was so fortunate it happened so close to your place." Her gaze sharpened and she frowned. "How exactly did you know the accident had happened?"

"Just lucky I guess," Diana said breezily. This was not the time to go into reasons why Cam felt at home enough on her property to use it as a refuge. "I was glad to be able to help."

"Yes," she said, gazing at Diana as though seeing her with new eyes. "Well, anyway, we'll have tea." She signaled toward the kitchen, where Rosa had appeared at the door. The housekeeper waved that she understood, and Mrs. Van Kirk turned back to the subject at hand.

"Now, I want you to take a look at my new roses." She pointed out a pair of new English heirlooms. "What do you think of them?"

"Oh, they're lovely. That soft violet color is just brilliant."

She looked pleased. "Yes, I've hired a new rose expert to come in twice a week and advise me. I want to make sure I'm getting the right nutrients to my little babies. He's very expensive but I'm so pleased with his work." She looked up. "Perhaps you know him. Andre Degregor?"

Diana nodded. "Yes, he's quite good." And an internationally recognized rose expert. "Expensive" was probably putting it mildly.

"You seem to be doing a lot of work on the estate," she noted, giving the older woman an opening to get the conversation back on track.

"Yes." She settled down in her seat and gave Diana a significant smile. "And that's why I wanted to see you. I'm going to begin a major project. And I want you to take a primary role in the preparations."

"A project?" she echoed brightly. What type of project would involve a flower stylist? She was beginning to feel a faint thread of trepidation about this. "What sort of project?"

"It's something I've been thinking about for a long time." Her eyes were shining with excitement. "I'm planning a whole series of various social gatherings—teas, dinner parties, barbecues, card parties—all culminating in a major ball at the end of next month."

"Oh my," Diana said faintly.

"On top of that, we'll be hosting quite a few guests between functions. I've hired a wonderful caterer from San Francisco—for the whole month!" She laughed with delight at the thought. "And I want to hire you for the decorating. If all goes as planned, this will be quite an undertaking."

"It certainly sounds like it."

"Now, I'm going to want you to put some extra effort into your weekly arrangements and prepare to work up an entire decorating plan for the various parties."

"Really." Diana's smile felt stiff and artificial as she began to mull over the implications. She had a very bad feeling about this. Ordinarily she would be welcoming the new business, but something told her she wasn't going to like this once she got the full picture.

Rosa arrived with a tray containing a sterling silver teapot and two lovely, egg-shell thin porcelain cups with saucers, along with a plate of crisp, slender cookies. Out of the corner of her eye, Diana could see Janey making her way into the garden and she offered up a fervent prayer that the young woman would find her way out again before stopping in to see them. She had enough to deal with here without Janey's caustic comments.

"You have such a good eye for decorating, Diana. I'm really going to be counting on you to help make this very special."

"What is the theme going to be?" she asked as Rosa poured the tea.

"Well, what could be more obvious?" She waved a hand dramatically and leaned forward. "I'm planning to introduce Cam back into the society he should have been a part of all these years," she said emphatically. "That's the theme."

"The theme," Janey said, flouncing into the gazebo and flopping down into a wicker chair, "is that Mother wants to marry Cam off to the most important socialite she can find for him, and preferably the one with the most money. He's raw meat for the voracious upper crust marriage market."

Her words stung, but Diana kept smiling. After all, she'd known this was coming, hadn't she? Cam had said as much, though he'd tried to take it back. He'd come back home to get married.

"Janey!" Mrs. Van Kirk said sharply.

Her daughter shrugged. "It's true, Mother, and you know it. We need the money."

The woman's sense of decorum was being challenged by her daughter's gloomy vision of reality and she didn't like it at all.

"Janey, I will thank you to keep your acid tongue to yourself. We have no financial problems. We've always been able to live just the way we've wanted to live. We're going to be just fine."

"Dream on, Mom." Janey looked at Diana and shrugged. "She won't look out and see the tsunami coming. But you might as well know it's on its way."

The older woman pretended not to hear. "Now, I want you to think this over, Diana. I'm hoping you'll be free." She sighed happily. "Such a lot of activity! It will be just like the old days."

"What old days are those, Mother?" Janey asked, the tiniest hint of sarcasm edging her tone.

"Oh, I don't know." Her mother frowned at her. "Things were more hectic when you children were younger. We had parties. Remember all those picnics we had when you were sixteen? It's been a long time since we've had an actual event here. It's exciting, don't you think?"

Diana was torn. On the one hand, she liked Cam's mother, despite her eccentricities—or maybe because of them. On the other hand, she didn't want to be involved in roping Cam into a marriage—any marriage, good or not. The very thought was darn depressing. It would be awful to see him make a bad marriage just for his mother's sake, but it would be almost worse to see him falling in love with some beautiful young debutante.

Either way, Diana would be the loser.

But that was crazy and she knew it. Cam would marry someone. He had to. It was only natural. She only wished he would do it far away where she didn't have to know about it.

"Poor Cam is going to be sold off to the highest bidder," Janey said. "I wish him better luck in marriage than I've had. But then, I tend to marry penniless jerks, so there you go."

"Janey, please," Mrs. Van Kirk said icily. She'd had enough. "I'd like to talk to Diana alone. We need to plan."

For a moment, Diana thought Janey was going to refuse to leave, but she finally rolled her eyes and rose with a look of disdain on her face. Diana watched her go and for once, she wished she could go along.

How was she going to tell Cam's mother that she couldn't do this? She hated to disappoint her, especially when she was so excited about her project. But the situation was downright impossible. She was going to have to find the right words…somehow.

And in the meantime, she was going to have to find a way to keep Cam at a distance.

CHAPTER FOUR

FILLED with comforting tea and discomforting misgivings, Diana skirted the house as she made her way back toward her car, hoping to avoid seeing Cam.

No such luck. He came around a corner of the house and met her under the vine-covered pergola.

"Hey," he said, looking surprised.

"Hay is for horses," she said back tersely, giving him barely a glance and trying to pass him.

"Channeling our school days, are we?" He managed to fill the passageway, giving her no room to flee. "I guess the meeting didn't go so well."

She looked up at him and sighed. "Oh, it went fine. I'm just a little jumpy today." She made a show of looking at her watch. "I've really got to go. I'm late."

He didn't buy it. Folding his arms across his chest, he cocked his head to the side and regarded her narrowly. "Late for what?"

She hesitated, not ready to make something up on the fly. "None of your business," she said instead. "I just need to go."

He stepped forward, suddenly looking concerned, glancing down at her slightly protruding belly. "Are you okay? Do you need help?"

He was being too darn nice. Her eyes stung. If he kept this up, she might end up crying, and that would be a disaster. Shaking her head, she sighed again and decided she might as well tell him the truth. Lifting her chin resolutely, she forced herself to meet his gaze.

"I'm going to be perfectly honest, Cam. I…I need to keep my distance from you. With all these plans and all that's going on, I can't spend time with you. It just won't work."

He looked completely baffled. "What are you talking about?"

She took a deep breath and plunged in. "Your mother just spent an hour telling me all about the plans to find you a wife. She wants me to help." She took a deep breath, praying her voice wouldn't break. "I don't think I can be involved in that."

"Diana, it's not a problem." His laugh was short and humorless. "She can look all she wants. I'm not getting married."

She blinked up at him, not sure why he would say such a thing. "But you said last night…"

He gave her his famously crooked grin. "I think I said a lot of crazy things last night. Don't hold me to any of them."

"Cam…"

"I'll tell you one thing." He grimaced and raked his fingers through his dark hair, making it stand on end in a way she found eminently endearing. "I'm never going to drink alcohol again."

"Good. You'll live longer and be healthier." She shook her head. She wasn't really worried about that. "Why did you say you'd come back to get married if you don't mean to do it? Maybe the alcohol brought out your true feelings."

He groaned. "What are you now, a psychologist in your spare time? Forget it. This is a 'don't try this at home' situation." He shook his head, looking at her earnestly. "Diana, my mother has been trying to get me to come home and get married for years. I've resisted. I'm still resisting. But she's still trying. That's all there is to it."

She frowned suspiciously. "Okay, you're saying you didn't come home to get married?"

"Of course not."

She waved a hand in the air. "But then why is your mother planning all this?"

"She's always planning things. That's how she lives her life." He shrugged. "Let her go on planning. It'll keep her busy and out of the way."

She frowned, not sure she could accept that. "I don't know."

Reaching out, he took hold of her shoulders, fingers curling around her upper arms, and stared down into her face. "Okay, Diana, here's the honest truth. My mother can make all kinds of plans, for all kinds of parties. She can even plan a wedding if she wants to. But I'm not marrying anybody." His added emphatically, "Anybody. Ever."

Anybody…ever…

The words echoed in her head but it was hard to think straight with his warm hands holding her and his hard body so close. A breeze tumbled through the yard and a cloud of pink bougainvillea blossoms showered down around them. She looked up into his starry blue eyes and had to resist getting lost there.

"What happened to you, Cam?" She heard the words as though from far away and it took a moment to realize the voice was her own.

He hesitated, staring down into her eyes as though he didn't want to let her go. The warning signs were there. She had to pull away. And yet, it seemed almost impossible. When her body wouldn't react, she had only her voice to reach for as a defensive weapon.

"Cam, what is it? What do you have against marriage?"

Her words seemed to startle him and his head went back. He stared at her for a few seconds, then grimaced.

"Once bitten, twice shy," he muttered, releasing her and making a half turn away from where she stood, shoving his hands down into his pockets.

Watching him, shock shot through her system and she barely avoided gasping. What was he saying? Did he really mean what it seemed he meant?

"You've been married?" she said, coming down to earth with a thump.

"No," he responded, looking back at her, his eyes hard. "But I did come close. Not a pretty story, and I'm not about to tell it. Just understand I've been inoculated. I've stared into the abyss and I've learned from that. I won't need another warning."

She didn't know why she was so disturbed by what he was saying. He was a normal man, after all. No, strike that, he was an abnormally attractive man, but with a normal man's needs and desires. Of course he'd had women in his life these last ten years. Naturally he'd been in love. What could be more ordinary? Just because *she* was a nut case and couldn't forget Cam for long enough to have a relationship with another man didn't have any bearing on his experiences. Some amateur psychologist she was; she couldn't even fix her own life, much less dabble in his.

"Well, if that's true, you'd better tell your mother," she said, grasping at the remnants of their conversation to steady herself on. "It's not fair to let her give parties and invite people."

"I said we should let her make plans. I never said she could put on any parties."

She shook her head. "That doesn't make a lot of sense."

"Don't you think I know that?"

He looked so troubled, she wanted to reach out and comfort him. If only she had the right to do it. But then she remembered—even if she had that right, she would have had to stop herself. She couldn't risk doing anything that might draw them closer. She had to think of her child.

"I've got to go," she said, turning and starting toward where her car was parked.

"I'll walk you out to your car," he said, coming along with her.

She walked quickly, hoping to stay at least an arm's length from him. She just had to get away.

"Diana's Floral Creations," he said aloud, reading the sign painted in pretty calligraphy on the side of her tiny little van. "Interesting name."

She threw him a look over her shoulder. "It's pretty generic, I know. I'm creative with flowers, not with words."

"No, I meant it. I like it. It suits you."

She hesitated, wanting to get into her car and go, but at the same time, not wanting to leave him.

"What made you go into this flower business stuff?" he asked her, actually seeming interested.

She smiled. This was a subject she loved. She was on firmer footing here. "I've always been good with plants. And I needed something to do on my own. I took horticulture classes in college so I had some background in it. Then I worked in a flower shop part-time for a couple of years."

He nodded, his gaze skimming over her and his admiration for her obvious. That gave her the impetuous to go on, tell him more.

"It's really a wonderful line of work. Flowers are so special, and used for such special occasions. We use them to celebrate a birthday, or a baby being born or two people getting married—or even the life of someone who has died. They add something to the most emotional times of our lives. And that interests and excites me."

"And also just to decorate a room," he reminded her, since that was what she was doing here at his house.

"Yes," she agreed. "But usually flowers are used to represent an emotion. They're symbols of feelings people have a hard time expressing in words." She stopped, coloring a bit, not used to being so effusive about her line of work. For some reason, she'd felt the need to tell him, explain. Well, now she had. She turned to her car, ready to make her escape.

But he stopped her once again.

"I'm glad you have something you love so much," he told her. "The business I've been running is a bit more prosaic." He hesitated, then grimaced.

"Okay, Di," he said, looking down at her. "I might as well get this off my chest. Here it is. The real reason I came home, the reason behind everything I'm going to be doing for the foreseeable future."

She waited, heart beating, wondering if she really wanted to hear this. She knew instinctively that whatever it was he was about to reveal would have the effect of tying her more closely to this family—this crazy outlandish bunch of people who had once scorned her and her family. And now he was going to tell her something that would make her care about them. It didn't seem altogether fair. But then, life wasn't often fair, was it?

He turned from her, flexed his shoulders and then turned back.

"There won't be any parties. There can't be any parties. The fact is, there's no money."

Diana heard what he said, but she couldn't quite digest it. Janey had said things that had let her know money was probably a consideration, even a concern, but to say there wasn't any... That just seemed crazy.

These were the Van Kirks. They had always been the richest family in town.

"What? What are you saying?"

"I've just been talking to Grandfather, finding out how bad it is. He already outlined the situation to me over the phone a few weeks ago. That's why I came home. And now I know the rest of the story." He took a deep breath and a pained expression flashed across his face. "My family is on the verge of losing everything."

Her head came up. Despite the things his sister had said, she would never have dreamed it could come to this. "You mean bankruptcy?"

He nodded. "I came home for one reason, Di. I came home to try to save my parents from losing their home."

"Oh, Cam, no."

He went on, detailing where the problems lay and how long they had festered, but Diana was thinking about his mother and remembering how she'd seemed oblivious to the dangers as Janey had taunted her with them. She'd thought Cam's sister was exaggerating, but it seemed she was wrong.

She knew without having him explain it that the issue went back years and years. Many of those old fights Cam had with his grandfather centered around the old man's fear that Cam would end up being a drone like his father was. She'd been vaguely aware at the time that Cam's dad had tried running the family affairs and had failed miserably, mostly through his own weaknesses. The grandfather had been trying to groom Cam to be a better manager. Even though Cam hadn't stayed here to take his father's place, it seemed he'd found his way in the world and made something of himself. And now it was Cam whom the grandfather had turned to in hopes of getting the family out of this mess. She wondered if he really had the experience. She knew he had the family background for it. And with his grandfather as his mentor, surely there would be hope that he could use his younger energy to turn things around.

No wonder Cam had been called back. Someone had to rescue the family, she supposed. Why he'd decided to let them pull him back, after all he'd said when he left, was another question, one she couldn't answer.

But there was no doubt the situation was dire. Bankruptcy sounded so radical. And the Van Kirks not living in the Van Kirk mansion? Unthinkable.

Still, this couldn't be her problem. She couldn't let it be. The more Cam talked, the more she wanted to go to him, to throw herself into his arms, to tell him she would help in any way she could. But she couldn't do that. She had to get out of this situation. Her baby had to be the main focus of her life, the reason for living. She couldn't get distracted by old longings. She had to get out of here and leave temptation behind. And that meant leaving Cam behind.

"I'm sorry all this is happening," she told him, trying to be firm. "But I really can't be involved. Do you understand?" She gazed up at him earnestly.

He nodded slowly. "Sure. Of course. You have your baby to think of. You need a calm environment. Don't worry about Mother. I'll explain things to her."

A few minutes later, she was in her car and heading for home again, only this time she wasn't crying. Her face was set with determination. She was going to be strong if it killed her.

Diana was up a tree—quite literally—a black oak to be exact. It wasn't something she usually did and that was probably why she seemed to be so bad at it. It was a typical well-meaning rescue mission gone awry.

She been jolted awake early that morning by small, piercing cries from outside. When she'd wrapped herself in a blanket and stepped out to find what tiny creature was in distress, she'd been led, step by step, to the big old black oak. Looking up, she saw the cutest little black kitten staring down at her with huge golden eyes.

"Oh, no, you don't," she'd grumbled at the time, turning back toward the house. "I know very well you'll have an easier time getting down from there than I would in going up. You can do it. You just have to try." She glanced over her shoulder at the little one as she returned to the house. "And then I hope you'll go back wherever you came from."

That had been hours earlier. In the meantime she'd made herself breakfast, taken the time to do a bit of book-keeping for her business and returned some phone calls, including one from her attorney cousin Ben Lanker in Sacramento. It seemed their uncle Luke, the last survivor from the older generation, had died a week before and left a piece of property in the mountains to the two of them, jointly, as the only remaining descendants in their family. She'd received something in the mail that she hadn't understood, but Ben explained what was going on and suggested they get together and talk it over.

She was tempted to put him off. She already had the only piece of land she'd ever wanted and from what Ben said, the inheritance from Uncle Luke might turn out to be more trouble than it was worth.

But then she remembered that she'd been suspicious of her cousin in the past and she decided maybe she'd better look into the facts.

"One shouldn't look an inheritance in the mouth, I suppose," she muttered to herself.

It could just be that Ben was trying to pull a fast one. He had that slippery lawyer way about him. So she told him she would get back to him soon and find a time when they could get together and go over the situation to see what would be best.

In the meantime, the little cries had grown more pitiful with time, wearing away at her like water torture. When storm clouds began to threaten, she finally decided she had to bite the bullet and climb up or she wouldn't be able to live with herself when the worst happened. She kept picturing the exhausted kitten losing all strength and falling to its death through the gnarled branches.

"I'm coming," she said reassuringly as she hoisted herself up with a foothold on the first major branch, regretting that she didn't have any ladders tall enough to do this job. "Just hold on."

It had been a while, but she'd climbed this very tree often when she was young. The only problem was, she wasn't all that young anymore. Muscles and instincts she'd had at that age—not to mention the fearlessness—seemed to be gone. And the tree was a lot bigger. And she was pregnant. To her surprise, that threw her balance off in ways she hadn't expected. But she kept climbing, reaching for the kitten. And every time her fingers almost touched it, the silly little bugger backed away and climbed higher.

"This is not going to work," she said aloud, staring up at the infuriating cat. "I'm not going any farther. You're going to have to come to me."

Fat chance. The golden eyes just got bigger and the cries just got more pathetic.

"Oh, never mind," Diana said, turning away and giving up. And then she looked down.

Somehow, she'd come further than she'd thought. The ground looked very far away. And as she clung to a space between a branch and the trunk, she began to realize she was going to have a heck of a time getting down.

And the kitten was still crying.

"You little brat," Diana muttered to herself. "Look what you've done. You've got me up a tree. How am I going to get down?"

"Meow," the kitten chirped.

And the rain began.

"I can't believe this," she moaned as drops began to spatter all around her. "Why is everything going wrong at once?"

And that was when she heard Cam's car arrive.

"Oh, no!"

She hadn't seen him for the last two days. She'd almost begun to think he might have taken her last words to heart and might just let her be alone, not try to pull her into his life again. But here he was, so she supposed that had been a bad guess.

She sat very still and watched as he turned off the engine and slipped out of the car. He looked around at the trees and the lake, but his gaze didn't rise high enough to notice her and she kept quiet while he went to the front door and knocked. The rain was still light, but it was beginning to make rivulets down her neck.

"Diana?" he called. "You home?"

Now it was time to make a decision. What was she going to do—let him know she was stuck in a tree? Or just sit here and let him drive away again and try to figure out how she was going to get down on her own in a rainstorm?

It was a rather big decision. She felt like a fool sitting here. And yet, she was liable to break her neck if she tried to get down by herself. It was pretty obvious what her decision was going to have to be, but she put it off as long as possible. She couldn't even imagine the humiliation she was going to feel when she began to call out to him, pitiful as the little animal scrabbling around on the branch above her.

Luckily she didn't have to do that. He heard the kitten screeching and finally looked up into the tree on his own. She looked down. He looked up. He fought hard to hold back a big old grin that threatened to take over his handsome face. She tried hard not to stick her tongue out at him. They both failed.

He came over and stood right under where she was. "Good view of the valley from up there?" he asked.

"The best," she answered, her nose in the air. "I come up here all the time."

"Do you?" He bit back a short laugh. "I see you have your faithful feline companion with you. What's the kitty's name?"

"Once you name them, you own them," she warned. For some unknown reason, she was unable to keep the annoyance from her tone. "Do you need a kitten? I'm putting this one up for adoption." She tried to move a bit without losing her footing. "The only catch is, you have to climb up here and get her."

"Well, I don't need a cat," he admitted. "At least not today. But I will help you down."

"I don't need any help," she said quickly, then bit her lower lip. What was she saying?

"You can get down by yourself?" He just couldn't hold the grin back and that was infuriating.

"Of course."

He shrugged. "Okay then. I'll just leave you to your own devices." He turned as though to head for his car.

"Cam! Come back here." She shivered. She was really getting wet. "Of course I need help getting down. Why do you think I'm sitting here like a lump of coal?"

He tried to control the chuckle that was fighting its way out. "A little humility is a wonderful thing," he noted.

She glared at him, but followed his instructions and

a moment later, she took the last leap of faith and ended up in his arms. He held her for a moment, her feet just off the ground, and looked down into her wet face.

"Why is it that every time I see you I want to smile?" he asked.

She tried to glare at him. "You're probably laughing at me."

"No." He shook his head, and his eyes darkened as he looked at her lips. "That's not it."

She drew her breath in and pulled away, regaining her footing and turning toward her little house. "Let's get out of this rain," she said, and as if on cue, it began to pour. They'd barely made the porch when she remembered something.

"Oh, wait! We forgot the kitten!"

"No problem," he said, pointing just behind her.

She whirled. There it was, looking like a drowned rat and staring up at her with those big golden eyes. Despite everything, she laughed. "You little faker! I knew you could get down if you tried."

"I guess you could call this a mission accomplished," Cam said as he opened the door and they all rushed into the warmth of the little house.

"I'll get towels," she said, reaching into her tiny bathroom. "We'd better dry off kitty first. She's liable to catch pneumonia, poor little thing."

Her gaze flickered over Cam as she spoke and she couldn't help but notice the rain had plastered his shirt nicely against the spectacular muscles of his wonderful chest. Why that should give her a sinking feeling in the pit of her stomach she couldn't imagine, and she looked away quickly.

"Here," she said, handing him a towel. "You take this one."

She caught the kitten as it tried to make a dash for the underside of her couch, toweled it down and then let it go. It quickly scampered into the next room.

"I ought to put her out so she can find her way home," she said, shaking her head. "But how can I put her out in the rain?"

"I think you just got yourself a cat," Cam noted, slinging the towel around his neck after rubbing his thick hair with it. "Here. You need a little drying off yourself."

She opened her mouth to protest, but he was already applying a fluffy fresh towel to her wild hair.

"I can do it," she said, reaching for the towel.

"Hold still," he ordered, not letting it go.

She gave in, lifting her face and closing her eyes as he carefully dabbed at the raindrops on her nose. He smiled, remembering the time he'd had to clean her up in similar fashion after a messy exploding bubble gum incident. She'd had more freckles then, but otherwise she looked very much the same.

Then she opened her eyes and the memory of Diana as a young girl faded. She was anything but a young girl now. She was a warm-blooded angel just as he'd seen her the other night. As he gazed down into her dark eyes, he had the sense that his larger vision was picking up details so sharp, so clear, that he could see everything about her—the tiny curls at her hairline, the long, full sweep of her eyelashes, the translucent shimmer of her skin, the clear outline of her beautiful lips. She was a woman—a beautiful, desirable woman, a woman he had known most of his life and loved just as long—loved as a friend, but the affection was very strong just the same.

And yet this was different. This was something more. A jolt of arousal went through him and he drew back quickly, as though he'd touched a live wire. But he didn't turn away. He stood where he was, watching her as she reached for the fluffy towel and began to rub her hair with it.

He knew he'd had indications of this sort of response to her ever since he'd come back, but this time it was so strong, he couldn't pretend to himself that it was anything but exactly what it was. That presented a bit of a problem, a bit of a conflict. He considered her his best friend, but the way he was feeling today was light years beyond friendship. Did he have a right to feel this way? Or was this a big mistake?

She dropped the towel onto the couch and looked at him, a challenge in her dark eyes, as though she had a sense of what he was feeling and wanted to warn him off. He felt clumsy and that wasn't like him. He just wasn't sure…

"Why did you come here today?" she asked him.

He raised one eyebrow, startled at her question. "I wanted to see how you're doing."

"I'm doing fine." She said it crisply, as though that ought to take care of the matter, and he might as well be going.

But that only put his back up and meant he was going to be staying all the longer.

"Actually I haven't been around for the last few days," he went on, "I was down in L.A. talking to some money people, bankers I've got contacts with, trying to work out some sort of deal to stay afloat, at least for now."

The challenge faded from her gaze and a look of concern began to take its place. That reassured him. The Diana he knew was still in there somewhere.

"Any luck?" she asked.

"Marginal luck." He hesitated, then went on. "I did talk to a real estate broker about selling the house."

"Oh." Her hands went to her mouth and her eyes took on a look of tragedy. "That would flat out kill your mother."

"I know."

"You didn't…?"

"Not yet. I'm hoping to avoid it."

She sighed and nodded. "Have you told her there won't be any parties yet?"

He grimaced uncomfortably and didn't meet her gaze for a moment. "Not totally."

"Cam!"

"It's making her so happy to plan." He looked back at her ruefully. "I hate to burst the bubble on her dream."

"But she's hiring people like Andre Degregor and the caterer from San Francisco. You've got to stop her."

He knew that. He had to do something very soon. But right now all he could think about was how this new electricity he felt between the two of them was working out. Not well, he took it, from the look on her face. She was wary and guarded and wanted him to leave. He rubbed the back of his neck and frowned thoughtfully, about to ask her why. But the kitten was back, looking for attention.

"Oh, kitty, what am I going to do with you?" she said, smiling down at it. "I don't need a kitten. I'm having a baby."

His immediate sense was that she'd said that as a reminder to him, and he took it to heart. He knew she was having a baby. That very fact made the way his feelings toward her were evolving all the more problematic.

"What you do need," he said to her, "living out here on your own, is a dog. Whatever happened to Max?"

"Max?" She smiled, thinking of the golden retriever she'd grown up with. "Max died years ago. He was really a great dog, wasn't he?"

Cam nodded, remembering. There was a time when Max had been part of the whole picture, always bounding out to meet him when he came to fish or to see Diana. Realizing he was gone left an empty spot. Nothing lasted forever. Everything changed.

Moving restlessly, he turned and looked around the room.

"You know, I've never been in here before."

She looked surprised, then nodded. "No one was allowed in here while Jed was alive."

His mouth twisted as he remembered. "Your father was something of a barnyard dog around this place, wasn't he?"

"That he was."

He turned back to look at her. She hadn't invited him to sit down. She hadn't offered a drink or something to eat. She wanted him to go, didn't she? He frowned. Funny, but he didn't want to leave. Everything in him rebelled at the thought.

"I came close once," he pointed out. "I came over here full of righteous anger and tried to come in to talk to him."

She looked up, curious. "What about?"

"You. I came to tell him to stop using you for a punching bag."

She flushed and shook her head. "I'm sure he agreed immediately, once you explained to him how naughty it was to beat up on your teenage daughter," she said dryly.

"He pulled out his shotgun." Cam grinned, remembering. "I took off like a scalded cat." He glanced down at the kitten, now wrapped around Diana's ankles.

"No offense intended, kitty," he said glibly before raising his gaze to meet Diana's. Their gazes caught and held for a beat too long, and then she pulled away and turned to pick up the kitten and carry it into the kitchen where she put down a tiny dish of milk from the refrigerator.

He watched, thinking about that time he'd come looking for Jed. He'd called the older man out and told him if he hit her again, he'd take her away from here. She'd told him again and again not to do it, that it would only make things worse for her. But when he found her with bruises on her upper arms and a swollen knot below her blackened eye that day, he'd raged with anger. He'd had enough.

"You do it one more time and I'll take her with me," he'd yelled at Jed. "You won't see her again."

"Where do you think you're going to take her?" Jed had jeered back at him. "Won't nobody take her in."

"I'll take her to my house. We'll take care of her."

Jed had laughed in his face. "You can't take her to your house. Your mother would die before she'd let a little white trash girl like my daughter in on her nice clean floor. Your mother has higher standards, son. You're living in a dream world."

And that was when he'd come out with the shotgun.

Cam had gone home. He told his mother his idea. Funny thing. He'd been so sure his mother would prove Jed wrong. But the man had turned out to have a keener understanding of how things really worked than he did. His mother had been horrified at the idea. She wanted no part of his crazy scheme. Her reaction had been part of what had motivated him to leave home.

Strange how that had changed. Now Diana was one of his mother's favorite people.

She came back out of the little kitchen and looked at him questioningly, as though not really sure why he was still here. But Cam was still lost in the past, mulling over what had happened with her father in the old days.

"When exactly did your dad die?" he asked her.

She told him and he nodded. "Your dad had a grudge against the world and he set about trying to drink himself to death just to spite us all."

She looked troubled and he added, "I suppose your mother dying pretty much threw him for a loop at some point, didn't it?"

Her gaze rose to meet his again. "My mother didn't die. She left when I was six years old."

That sent a shock through him. "I thought she died."

She nodded. Turning from him, she began to collect the towels. "That was what he wanted everyone to think. But the truth was, she couldn't take it anymore and she headed out. Leaving me behind."

Cam felt a wave of sympathy. He could hear the barely concealed heartbreak in her voice. He started to reach for her, but the moment he made a move, he could see her back stiffen, so he dropped his hand back to his side.

"Have you ever heard from her?"

"No." Her chin rose. "And I don't want to."

"I would think you would want to reconnect, especially now with the baby coming."

She whirled, glaring at him. "You know what? My pregnancy is not up for discussion in any way."

"Oh. Okay."

He frowned. His first impulse was to let her set the rules. After all, she was the one who was pregnant. Pregnant women needed extra care, extra tolerance, extra understanding, from what he'd heard. But the more he thought about it, the more he realized he was bending over backward a bit too much. This was getting a little perverse, wasn't it? He turned back and faced her.

"You mean I'm supposed to ignore your baby and pretend it doesn't exist? Is that what you're asking?"

Her face was set as she went on folding the towels and she didn't answer.

Being purposefully defiant, he asked, "So how far along are you, anyway?"

"Cam!" She glared at him, pressing the stack of towels to her chest. "I will not discuss this with you."

He shook his head. "Sorry, Di, that's not going to fly any longer. I need to know what's going on with you and I need to know now."

CHAPTER FIVE

"DIANA, tell me about your baby."

She stared up at him, holding his gaze with her own for a long moment, then she turned and began to march from the room.

He caught up with her, took her by the shoulders and turned her back.

"Come on, Di," he said, carefully being as gentle as he could be, especially in his tone. "You can't run away from it. Tell me."

"Why?" She looked up but her eyes looked more lost than angry. "There's nothing to tell."

He shook his head and his hands caressed her shoulders. "You can't do this. You can't keep it all wrapped up inside you."

She looked almost tearful. "You don't know what you're talking about."

"That's just it. I'm trying. But you've got to let me in."

She shook her head, her hair flying wildly around her face.

"Come on, Diana. We're friends. Remember? We need to stand together."

She looked up, still shaking her head, but slowly. "Cam…"

"It's me, Cam. You can count on me. But you've got to trust me first."

She sighed and he smiled, coaxing her.

"What are you going to name your baby, Di? Have you picked anything out yet? Tell me. Please?"

She swallowed hard and looked away. When you came right down to it, there was no one else in the world she trusted like she trusted Cam. That was just a fact of life and she couldn't deny it.

"I'm going to call her Mia," she said softly. "My mother's name was Mia."

At any other time, Cam would have been horrified to feel his own eyes stinging, but for once, he didn't care. "Oh, Di," he said with all the affection he had at his disposal. "Oh, sweetheart." And he pulled her close against him. "That's a beautiful name."

Her arms came up, and for just a moment, she clung to him. He pressed a kiss into her hair and held her close. And then she pulled away, all stiff again, and took a step back.

"When is Mia due?" he asked, hoping to keep the connection from breaking again.

But she shook her head and looked as though she regretted what she'd already told him.

"What are your plans? How are you doing physically? Diana, what can I do to help you?"

She took another step away from him. "I'm fine," she said shortly. "Just leave it at that, Cam. I'm doing fine."

He shook his head. "Don't lock me out, Diana."

She stared at him for a long moment, then sighed and said, "Don't you see? I have to lock you out. If I don't…"

"What?" He shook his head. He didn't see at all. "What will happen if you don't?"

She swallowed hard, as though this was very difficult, but she held her shoulders high and went on quickly.

"Here's the deal, Cam. You were my savior when I was a kid. You defended me from the bullies. You made life seem worthwhile. I was going through a pretty rough time where it looked like the world was against me. And then you came."

She closed her eyes for a moment, remembering that day. "And suddenly I had a champion. It made a huge difference in my life and I thank you for it to this day. But…"

He sighed. "Oh, yes, I thought I could sense a 'but' coming."

"In some ways you ruined me."

He stared at her, shocked. "Ruined you?"

"This is how. My expectations in what a man should be, in what I wanted in a man to share my life, became unrealistic. You raised the bar so darn high, I couldn't find a man who could clear it."

He looked at her in complete bewilderment and was close to laughing, but he knew that would be the kiss of death.

"That's nuts."

"No, it's true. I'm serious." She shrugged and sighed.

"I don't know if it was the real you or my enhanced imaginary you."

He groaned. "You make me sound like an action figure."

"But that image was hard for any man to overcome." She bit her lip and then went on. "I tried. For years, I tried. But I couldn't get you out of my mind." She hesitated, wanting to leave it at that. Going any further would be getting a bit risky. But she knew there was a bit more that she had to say.

"So I finally took some affirmative steps and moved forward. I had to. And now suddenly, here you are." She shook her head and looked at him as though pleading for his understanding. "I can't let myself slide back to being that dependent little girl I was in the past. I just can't let that happen."

"I understand that," he said, though it was only partly true. "I respect you for it."

She searched his eyes. "But do you understand that I can't be around you? You distort my reality."

He hesitated, wishing he knew how best to deal with this. Bottom line, he didn't want to take himself completely out of her life. He just couldn't imagine that happening. And he still didn't really believe in all this on a certain level. "That can be fixed."

"No, it can't." She took a step back away from him, as though she'd begun to realize he didn't really understand at all. "I have a baby to think about now. She has to be my focus. Cam, I just can't be around you. I can't live my life hoping to see you smile, hoping to have a minute with you, watching as you go on with what you do. Don't you see that?"

She meant it. He could see it in her face. He rubbed his neck and frowned at her. "This is crazy."

"It only seems crazy to you because you haven't thought about it like I have. Believe me, I've lived it for years. I think I have a better grasp of what I have going on inside, in my heart and soul, than you do. I know what I'm talking about." She looked so earnest. "Please, Cam. Don't come here anymore."

Now that was just too much. "What are you talking about?"

"I need you to leave me alone."

He shook his head, still avoiding the implications of her insistence. "So you're telling me…"

"I'm telling you I need space. This is a hard time for me right now and I need space away from you while I learn what I can do, and what I need."

He felt very much at sea. On one hand, he could understand that she might have had some problems. She was raised to have problems. How could she have avoided it? But he didn't see why she was taking it all so seriously. The problems all seemed repairable to him. If he wasn't around, if they were never together, how could these things be fixed? No, her insistence that he stay away didn't seem reasonable.

There was only one explanation he could think of, one factor that might make her so adamant about keeping him out of her life, and she wasn't bringing it up at all. Turning slowly, he asked the pertinent question.

"Is the baby's father liable to show up anytime soon?" he asked.

Something changed in her face. Turning on a dime, she strode to the door and threw it open.

"Go," she said.

And there was just enough anger brewing in him by that time to do exactly what she said without another word.

It was two days later before Diana saw Cam again.

Thursday was her regular day to change the flower arrangements at the Van Kirk mansion. She usually went in the afternoon, but once she found out that Mrs. Van Kirk was going to a garden club lecture at 10:00 a.m., she slipped in early in hopes of missing her. The last thing she wanted was to have the woman try to pin her down on when she would be available to begin work on the "project."

From what Cam had told her, she assumed the project was as good as dead. Though she felt sorry for Cam's mother, that did get her off the hook as far as having to come up with an excuse as to why she couldn't participate. It just wasn't clear when Cam would finally tell his mother the truth. She was going to have to have some sort of conversation about it sooner or later, but hopefully things would be settled down before that came about.

She parked in her usual spot and saw none of the usual family cars. Good. That meant she had the house to herself—except for Rosa, of course. And then there was the grandfather.

She'd never had a conversation with the old man, though she'd seen him out in the gazebo a time or two when she'd come to change the flowers. Funny, for a man who had been such an influence on the valley, and had made such an impression on Cam's life, he was almost invisible these days. As far as she knew, he spent most of his time in his room in a far wing of the house. Even though she would be working in the house for the next hour or so, she didn't expect to run into him.

She replaced the sagging gladiolas in the library with a fresh assortment of spring flowers and moved on into the dining room where she began weeding out lack-luster roses and replacing them with a huge glass bowl holding a mix of yellow tulips and deep purple Dutch irises. At the last minute, she pulled out a few extras and a couple of bud vases and headed for the stairs. She always liked to put a small arrangement in Mrs. Van Kirk's sitting room, and while she was at it, she might as well surprise Cam with a small vase, too. Just because she didn't want to meet him face-to-face didn't mean she wasn't thinking about him.

Thinking about him—hah! She was obsessing on him and she knew it had to stop. But ignoring him when she was handing out flowers wasn't going to fix that problem.

She dropped off one vase in Mrs. Van Kirk's room, then went down the hall to where she thought Cam's room must be. The door was slightly ajar and she knocked softly, then pushed it open enough to confirm her assumption. There was a large bed and a bedside table and cabinets against one wall. Banners and sports

items from ten years before filled the other wall.
Nobody had made the bed yet and the covers were
thrown back casually.

"Naughty Cam," she murmured to herself. What was
he waiting for, maid service? He should make his own bed.

She set the small vase with one yellow tulip and one
blue iris on the stand beside the bed, then stood back to
admire it. Her gaze strayed to the bed itself, and she
noted the impression on the pillow where his head had
been, then groaned at the way it warmed her just to
think of him asleep. She really was a sucker for
romance—as long as Cam was the man in the fantasy.

A noise from the hallway turned her head and in that
same moment, the door to the attached bathroom
opened and Cam came out wearing nothing but a very
skimpy towel.

She froze, mouth open, disbelief paralyzing her. In
the split second it took to recognize him, he erased the
distance between them with one long step, grabbed her
and put a hand over her mouth. She gasped as he
pulled her tight against him and nudged the door
closed with his foot.

"Shh," he whispered against her ear. "Someone's
in the hall."

She only struggled for a second or two before she
realized that he was just trying to keep her from
speaking out loud and making it obvious to whomever
was out there that she was in here with a nearly naked
Cam. She nodded and then she sagged into his arms
and he slipped his hand from her mouth and just held

her. The voices went past the room slowly. She thought she recognized Janey's voice, but not the woman with her.

But it hardly mattered. By the time the voices faded, she was lost in a dream. She was in Cam's arms. Hadn't she always imagined it would feel this way? She looked up into Cam's face. His eyes were brimming with laughter, but as she met his gaze, the humor evaporated quickly, as though he could see what she was feeling, and his arms tightened around her.

She had to pull away, she had to stop this, but for some reason, she couldn't. Every muscle she possessed was in rebellion. She felt like she was trying to move in honey—she couldn't do it. Her body, her mind, her soul, all wanted to stay right there and be held by Cam.

His eyes darkened and a sense of something new seemed to throb between them. And then he was bending closer and she gasped just before his mouth covered hers. At that point, she gave up trying. Her own lips parted and her body seemed to melt into his. She accepted him as though she'd been waiting for this all her life.

And she had.

Cam hadn't exactly planned to do this. In fact, he'd been pretty rough on himself, swearing he wouldn't do this or anything like it in rather strong terms. All those things she'd said had been rattling around in his head for the last two days. The more he thought about it the more they didn't make any sense to him—and his own reaction to them made even less sense. He'd always known she had a bit of a crush on him, but he hadn't taken it seriously. That had been long ago—kid's stuff. Things had changed. He'd changed. That was just the point.

So had she changed, too? Were his instincts right? Had her crush turned into something stronger? And if so, what was stopping her from following her instincts and responding to these new currents between them?

The baby's father, of course. What else could it be?

On a certain level, he had to respect that. The bond between a woman and the father of her baby was sacred, even if there were problems between them. He had to stay back, out of the way, and let her deal with the things she needed to deal with.

On the other hand, where the hell was the guy? What kind of a jerk was he? How could he leave Di alone to handle all these life changes on her own? She needed support. She needed her friends around her, if nothing else. As a good friend, how could he ignore that?

But she'd asked him to stay away. Reluctantly he would do the honorable thing and keep his distance, leave her alone.

But, dammit, how could he do that if she showed up in his bedroom like this? *Game over, Diana!*

He had her in his arms and he wanted her there. He had her fresh, sweet scent in his head and the excitement of her touch on his skin and the feel of her soft, rounded body against him and he wanted to drown himself in her body. There was no going back now.

Diana was finally beginning to gather the strength to resist where this was going. It was so hard to push away the man she'd wanted close for most of her life but she knew she had to do it. She couldn't believe, after all she'd been through, after all the serious thinking she'd done on the subject and all the serious preparations she'd made to resist her feelings toward him, here she was, lost in his kiss and loving it. How could this be?

Maybe her response to the temptation that was Cam was so strong because it had been so long since a man had held her and kissed her…but no, it wasn't a man's touch she craved. It was Cam's touch. Only Cam.

She finally mustered the force to pull away from him, leaning back, still in his arms.

"Oh, Cam," she said in despair, her gaze taking in his beautiful face and loving it.

"Hush," he whispered, leaning forward to drop a kiss on her neck. "Unless you want Janey bursting in here to demand an explanation."

She sighed, shaking her head. "Admit it. This isn't working."

He kissed her collarbone. "What isn't working?"

Reaching up, she pushed hard to make him release her. "Our plan to stay away from each other."

He looked amused. "Hey, don't try to pin that plan on me. I never liked it much anyway."

Her sigh was a heartfelt sign of regret. "I thought once I told you face-to-face…"

"That didn't work, did it? Want to try something else?"

"What?"

"This." He leaned closer again and began to nibble on her ear.

She pushed him away. "No! Cam, we have to try harder."

"Hold on." He shook his head, looking down at her in disbelief. "Di, you need to decide what you really want. You order me out of your life, then show up in my bedroom. Either you've developed a split personality, or you're conflicted in some way."

"I was just delivering flowers," she said plaintively, knowing it wasn't going to fly as a serious defense.

"Ah, the old delivering flowers ploy."

"Cam, I didn't mean to start anything like this."

"Didn't you?"

"I thought you were gone."

"You were wrong."

"Obviously." She managed to get a little more space between them, her gaze lingering on his wide shoulders and the beautiful planes of his naked chest. Just looking at him made her stomach do a flip and made her knees begin to tremble. She had to get away from him quickly or she was going to be lost. She closed her eyes and pressed her lips together, then opened them again with more determination. "Now how am I going to get out of here without running into your sister?"

"I heard her go back downstairs a minute ago. You should be in the clear."

She stared at him. She hadn't heard anyone go by again. She'd been deep into kissing him, too deep to be able to process anything else. But he hadn't been, had he? That was something to keep in mind.

Turning away from him, she gathered her supplies,

her hands shaking and fingers trembling, and headed for the door. He pulled it open for her and smiled.

"Give me a minute and I'll get dressed and…"

"No." She shook her head. "I'm going, Cam. This doesn't change anything."

His eyes darkened. "The hell it doesn't," he muttered.

She shook her head again, looking out into the hall to make sure it was clear. "Goodbye," she said. Avoiding his gaze, she hurried away.

She made a quick trip through the first floor rooms, giving her arrangements a last-minute check, then turned to leave and almost ran into Janey.

"Hello." Cam's sister was dressed in a black leotard with a bright pink sweatshirt worn over it. Her hair was up in foil, being colorized. Diana quickly made the assessment that the voice she'd heard in the hallway was her hairdresser. She knew the woman came to the house on a weekly basis.

"I saw your car," Janey said. "I was wondering where you were."

"I was putting flowers in a number of rooms," Diana said, trying hard to sound innocent and casual. "And I'm running late."

Janey's green eyes flickered. "Well, how's that baby coming?" she asked.

Something in her tone put Diana on alert. "Just fine, thank you," she said, looking at Janey hard before starting for the kitchen.

To her surprise, Janey stepped forward and blocked the doorway, looking at her speculatively. "You know, there are people who have practically come out and asked me if Cam is the father."

Diana's heart lurched but she stood her ground. "How interesting. Too bad you don't know the answer, isn't it?" She felt a twinge of regret. Why didn't she just tell the woman Cam wasn't the father and put the question to bed? But hadn't Cam already tried to do that? Janey wouldn't believe her no matter what she said.

"Mother is still planning her parties," Janey said coolly, her eyes flashing. "You do understand what these parties are about, don't you?"

"I think I have a vague idea."

Janey nodded. "We need Cam to marry a rich girl. That's pretty much our only hope of getting out of our current financial difficulties."

Diana held her anger in check, but it wasn't easy. "Good luck to you," she said, and stepped forward in a way that signaled she wanted to go through the doorway.

Janey didn't move out of the way, but her eyes narrowed. "So tell me, how does that fit in with your plans, exactly?"

She glanced down at Diana's rounded belly, making it very clear what she was talking about. She was worried that Diana was going to try to snag Cam for herself. Diana's anger was truly simmering now. How dare she! Well, she could just go on wondering. No matter what she was told, she wasn't going to believe it.

"I don't have any plans, Janey," she said, meeting the other woman's gaze with her own clear vision.

Janey arched an eyebrow. "Don't you?"

"No." She arched an eyebrow in return. "In fact, the parties are going to have to go on without me. I'm going out of town for a while. So you're going to have to find someone else to try to bully." With one firm hand, she gently pushed a surprised Janey out of the doorway and made it past her. "So long."

She walked quickly through the kitchen and out to her car, swearing softly to herself as she went. That woman!

It wasn't until she was in the driver's seat and starting the engine that she remembered what she'd said to her and she half laughed.

So she was going out of town. Funny, she hadn't realized she had a trip in her future until she'd told Janey. But now that it was out in the open, she was glad she'd thought of it. It was probably her only hope to stay away from Cam. And with a little distance and a bit of perspective, she might even think of a way to fall out of love with him.

CHAPTER SIX

DIANA was back in town.

She'd been gone a little over a week. She'd left her occasional assistant, Penny, in charge of supplying arrangements to her weekly clients, and she'd spent a few days in San Francisco with her old roommates.

She'd made a run up to Sacramento as well, hoping to catch her cousin, Ben, but he was gone on business, so she missed him. They had since connected by phone and he was coming to Gold Dust today so they could meet. He had some things to show her.

She was very curious as to what he was up to. Having her uncle leave them a piece of property together was interesting but she wasn't sure if that wasn't going to be more trouble than it was worth. Hopefully Ben would clear some of this up when he arrived.

They were meeting at Dorry's Café on Main and she was on her way there now. She lucked into a good parking place in front of the library under a big old magnolia tree. It was a short walk to the café, but she needed the exercise.

She had a lot of things on her mind, but mostly, she was thinking about Cam. Had absence made the heart grow fonder? Not really. She couldn't get much fonder. But there definitely had been no "out of sight, out of mind" involved, either. Thinking about Cam sometimes seemed to be her main state of being. She was getting better and better at it. And it had to stop.

But there was something else on her mind as well—or should she say someone else? She could feel Mia move, just a flutter, like a butterfly caught in a magic net, but that tiny bit of movement made all the difference. Mia was real to her now like she hadn't been before. Mia was her baby, her child, the center of her future and that meant that Mia was all the world to her.

She was definitely showing, and proud of it. But that made for a different atmosphere as she walked down the streets of the little Sierra town she'd lived in all her life and interacted with the people. Strangely she felt almost as though someone had painted a big red A on her chest when she wasn't paying attention. Suddenly everyone was noticing that she was carrying a child, and most of the looks she was getting were not sympathetic.

Still, what she saw wasn't really old-fashioned small town disapproval. What she had to face every day was even more annoying—blatant curiosity. Everyone wanted to know who the father was. They all knew very well that she hadn't dated anyone for over a year. She had taken a few trips to San Francisco, but other than that, she was busy working with her flowers and hanging out at her lake, with nary a male in sight.

Of course, things were different now. Cam was back.

And it seemed Janey wasn't the only one with suspicions. It was amazing how many ways people could contort a simple conversation into hinting around at the question—*was the baby Cam's?*

Everyone knew that Cam had been her champion once upon a time. Now she was pregnant—and he was back. Was there a connection? It was difficult to find a way to come right out and tell them there was nothing to the rumors when they never actually put the darn thing into words she could refute. They just said something here and left a little hint there and gave her looks that spoke volumes.

She was working on a way to deal with the problem without getting too rude, but as time passed and more and more people got bolder and bolder with their probing, she was beginning to think rude might be the only way to go.

But she smiled and nodded to passersby as she made her way to Dorry's. Maybe this was just the price you had to pay for living in a small town. And bottom line— she loved it here.

Cam saw her going into Dorry's and he stopped on the street to have a two-minute argument with himself. He knew she didn't want to see him or talk to him, but the fact was, he wanted very much to see her and they had plenty of things to discuss. She'd been gone for a week and he'd missed her. That morning in his bedroom had proven one thing—she wanted him. The fact that he wanted her was a given. But no matter how she protested, she'd let the cat out of the bag, so to speak. Left to its own devices, her body would take him in a New York minute. It was just her heart and mind he had to convince.

Just thinking about that morning made him throb and he knew it was going to be very hard to stay away from her. He wanted to talk to her. Hell, he wanted to be with her. Should he leave her alone, give her a few more days of peace? Or should he get on with this?

They were friends, first and foremost. He valued her like he had valued few others in his life. And from the moment he'd seen her the other night, a new element had been added. Of course she knew that. He hadn't been very subtle about it. She attracted him in every way possible.

But he wasn't a nut case. He knew she was out of bounds right now and he respected her need to stay away from him most of the time. He didn't agree with it and he didn't like it, but he had every intention of keeping his distance—for the moment. Until he convinced her it was pointless.

But did running into her here in town count? Not at all, he decided at last. After all, this was casual and public and totally nonthreatening. So he might as well go on in and say hello.

Great. That was settled. He strode confidently toward the café and went in, waving to plump, friendly Dorry with her head of gray curls and nodding to Jim, the tall, skinny mechanic who had worked on fixing his car and was now up to his elbows in a big, juicy cheeseburger. But all the time, he was searching for a familiar looking blonde.

And there she was.

"Hey, good-lookin'," he said, sliding into the booth across from her and smiling.

She looked up and winced. It was like looking into the sun. The light from the big bay window shone all around him, giving him a halo effect. That, along with his dazzling smile, sent her reeling for a split second or two. He was too gorgeous to be real. Maybe she'd just invented him in her head.

Everything about him looked smooth and clean, from the tanned skin showed off by his open shirt, to his beautiful, long-fingered hands. For a moment, she thought she'd lost the ability to breathe. Whenever she saw him unprepared, he made her react this way. No other man had ever affected her like this. Why oh why? It just wasn't fair.

"Go away," she said hopefully, but there was no strength of will behind her words.

"No," he said calmly. "You've admitted that we are friends. Old friends. Dear friends. And friends get together now and then and shoot the breeze. That's what we're doing here."

She raised her gaze to the ceiling and said plaintively, "It would be better if you would go away."

"We're adults, Di," he said pleasantly as he reached across and took a bread stick from the basket the waitress had put on the table. "We can sit in a café and talk."

She looked worried. "Can we?"

He grinned and waved the bread stick at her. "You bet."

Diana shivered and shook her head, trying to ground

herself and get back to reality. "Some other time, maybe," she said, and as she said it she seemed to pick up confidence. "I don't have time today. I'm meeting someone."

"Oh?" He tensed and his sense of humor seemed to evaporate without a trace. Suddenly he was very guarded.

"You'll have to leave before he gets here."

So the person she was waiting for was male, was he? Cam stared across the table at her. She looked nervous. Her usual calm was not evident and her hands were fluttering as they pushed her hair back behind her ear, then reached for her glass of water, then dropped back into her lap. Was he making her nervous? Or was it the pending arrival of her visitor?

He went very still and stared at the wall. His first guess was that this was the father of her baby whom she was meeting in this public place. Had to be. In which case he wasn't leaving until he got a good look at him.

He turned his gaze back and met hers squarely. "Diana, I'm going to be up-front about this. My instincts are to throw you over my shoulder and run off to a cave for the duration."

Diana had unfortunately just taken a drink of water and she nearly spewed it across the room. "What are you talking about?" she sputtered hoarsely, still choking on the water as she leaned across the table in hopes no one else would hear this.

"I'm serious." He leaned forward, too, speaking as softly as he could, but with definite emphasis, and gazing at her intently. "I want to take care of you. I want to protect you. I want to make sure you and your baby are okay." He grabbed her hand and held it. "Everything in me is aching to do that. And I have to know." He grimaced. "Are you going to marry this guy?"

She blinked at him. "What guy?" she asked in bewilderment.

"The father of your baby. Mia's father."

"Mia's… Oh, Cam." She almost laughed, but not quite, and her fingers curled around his and then her eyes were suddenly shimmering with unshed tears. "You're crazy."

His hand tightened on hers. "That doesn't answer my question."

"Who says I have to give you an answer?" She smiled through her tears. "But I will. No, I'm not going to marry anyone. I'm like you. No wedding in my future."

He set his jaw with resolution and looked deep into her eyes. "Okay," he said. "Then I'm warning you, I'm going to do what I have to do."

"As long as you leave me with my feet on the ground," she teased him. "And no caves, okay?"

He shrugged. "Like I said, I'll do what I have to."

The waitress arriving with the salad she'd ordered saved Diana from having to respond to that. She drew back and sat up straight and looked across the table at Cam. She couldn't help but love him for his concern for her and her baby. Still, that didn't change anything.

But this was no place to have that argument. As soon as the waitress was gone again, she picked up a fork and began to pick at her food, and meanwhile, she changed the subject.

"Your mother was on my answering machine twice in the last few days. I'm going to have to call her back eventually. What am I going to say to her?"

His wide mouth twisted. "A warm hello would be nice, I suppose."

She studied his face. "Have you told her yet? Does she understand that you aren't going to be doing the parties?"

Leaning back, he sighed and looked troubled. "I have told her as firmly as I can muster. What she understands and doesn't understand is another matter."

"Meaning?"

"Meaning she is so deep in denial..." He straightened and rubbed his neck. "Well, I did try to have it out with her yesterday. I'm afraid there was a little yelling."

She put down her fork and stared at him. "You didn't yell at your mother!"

He grimaced. "Just a little bit." He definitely looked sheepish. "She drives me crazy. She just won't face reality."

"Didn't you show her some documentation? Facts and figures? Spreadsheets and accounting forms?"

He nodded. "Even an eviction notice."

"What?"

"For one of our warehouses in Sacramento."

"Oh." She sagged with relief. The picture of Mrs. Van Kirk being carted out of her home by the sheriff with an eviction notice was a nightmare scenario she didn't want to see played out in the flesh.

"But I showed it to her to try to convince her of how serious this is. Well, she got a little hysterical and ran out to go to her precious rose garden and fell right down the garden steps."

Diana's hands went to her face in horror. "No! How is she?"

Cam was looking so guilty, she couldn't help but feel sorry for him, even though she knew his mother probably deserved the pity more.

"She was pretty shaken up." He sighed with regret. "And she broke her ankle."

"What?"

He shook his head, his eyes filled with tragedy. "All my fault, of course."

"Oh, poor thing."

He gave her a halfhearted smile. "I knew you would understand."

"Not you! Your mother." But she knew he was only trying to lighten the mood with a joke, and his quick grin confirmed that.

"Don't worry. It's a hairline fracture sort of thing. The orthopedist said she'll be better in about a month and good as new by Christmas."

Diana groaned. "She's got a hard row to hoe," she said. "It's hard sitting still when you're used to being busy all the time."

"True." He looked at her speculatively. "So now we're reversing a lot of plans," he went on more seriously. "We're firing a lot of the workmen she hired and we're letting the caterer from San Francisco go. And the rose expert. And the barbecue center will have to wait for flusher times."

Diana sighed, shaking her head. "I suppose you'll be laying off the floral stylist as well, won't you?"

"Is that what you call yourself?"

She nodded.

He grinned without much humor. "Yup, she's a goner."

Diana sighed again. "Your mother's been my best account."

He gave her his finest cynical sneer. "Such are the ripples in a stagnating pond."

She laughed. "Now that's just downright silly," she told him. "The Van Kirks are not stagnating. I thought you were going to see to that."

He nodded, his eyes brimming with laughter. That was one thing he loved about her, she seemed to get his silly jokes and actually to enjoy them. Not many people could say that.

"I'm doing what I can. I still can't say we've saved the house. But I'm working at it."

"I'm sure you are." She gave him a quelling look. "Now if you would just buckle down and marry some rich gal, all would be forgiven."

"Right."

"But if you're not going to have the parties…"

He frowned uncomfortably. "Well, about the parties…"

"Yes?" she said, one eyebrow arched in surprise.

He made a face. "We're sort of compromising."

"What does that mean?"

"She was so devastated, I had to give her something. So there will just be one party. A simple party. No fancy chefs, no rose experts."

"I see."

"Mother, Janey and Rosa are going to have to do most of the work themselves." He hesitated, narrowed his eyes and gazed at her as though evaluating her mood. "But since she's flat on her back right now, we need a coordinator to take charge."

Diana's head rose. Why hadn't she seen this coming from farther away? She knew she was staring at him like a deer in the headlights. She was thinking as fast as she could to find excuses for saying no to him. She had to say no. A yes would be emotional suicide.

She could just imagine what it would be like, watching beautiful young, rich ladies from the foremost families in the foothills, dressed in skimpy summer frocks, vying for Cam's attention while she was dressed like a French maid, passing the crudités. No, thank you!

"Janey could do it," she suggested quickly.

"Sure she could," he said out of the corner of his mouth. "If we want a disaster to rival the Titanic. She'll undermine it all she can." He gave her a significant look. "There's only one person Mother would trust to handle this."

She stared back at him. "You can't be thinking what I'm thinking you're thinking."

He shrugged and looked hopeful. "Why not?"

Slowly she began to shake her head. "You couldn't pay me enough. And anyway, didn't you say you were broke?"

He nodded. "That's why I'm hoping you'll do it for free."

She laughed aloud at his raw audacity. "There is no

way I'm going to do this at all. Save your breath, Mr. Van Kirk. I refuse to have anything to do with the whole thing."

This could have gone on and on if it hadn't been for the arrival of Diana's visitor. He stopped by their booth, a tall man, handsome in a gaunt way, just starting to gray at the temples, and dressed in an expensive suit. Cam hated him on sight.

"Hello, Diana," he said, smiling coolly.

"Oh." Diana had to readjust quickly. "Hi, Ben. Uh, this is my friend Cam." She threw out a pointed glance. "He was just leaving."

Cam didn't budge. He made a show of looking at his watch. "Actually I think I've got a little more time."

"Cam!"

"And I've got a sudden yen for a piece of Dorry's apple pie. It's been ten years, but I can still remember that delicate crust she used to make."

She glared at him, and so did Ben, but Cam smiled sunnily and went on as though he hadn't noticed the bad vibes, chattering about pie and apples and good old home cookin'.

"Cam," Diana said firmly at last. "Ben and I have something personal to discuss. You've got to go."

He gazed at her intently. "Are you sure?" he said softly, searching her eyes. He wanted to make certain she really meant it, that she didn't want him to stay and act as a buffer for her.

She gave him a look that should have warned him that she was losing patience. "I'm sure. Please go."

He rose reluctantly and flashed her friend a sharp

look, just to let him know he was going to be keeping an eye on him.

"Okay," he said. "I'll be over there in the corner, eating apple pie. In case you need me."

She closed her eyes and waited for him to go. Ben looked bored. Cam went.

But he didn't go far and he kept up his survey of what was going on from a pretty good vantagepoint. They were talking earnestly, leaning so that their heads were close together over the table. It tore him up to watch them. If this was really the guy…

Their meeting didn't last very long. Ben pulled out a portfolio of papers that he showed her, but he packed most of them away again and was obviously preparing to leave. Cam felt a sense of relief. There had been nothing warm between them, none of the sort of gestures people who had an emotional bond might display. If there had ever been anything between them, he would say it was pretty much dead now. In fact, Diana looked almost hostile as Ben rose to leave. And as soon as he was out of sight, she looked up and nodded to Cam, as though to beckon to him. He was already up and moving and he went to her immediately, sliding in where the other man had been sitting.

"I need your help," she said without preamble. She had one piece of paper that he'd left behind sitting on the table in front of her. "Because I don't know how to do this."

"Do what?" he asked. "Sue the guy? Charge him with abandonment? Get some money out of him for child care?"

She was shaking her head, wearing a puzzled frown. "What are you talking about?"

He blinked. "That wasn't the father of your baby?"

She threw her head back. "Oh, Cam, for heaven's sake! Ben is my cousin. I told you about him."

"You did?" Her cousin. It figured. The body language had been all wrong for lovers, or even current enemies who were past lovers. He should have known. Feeling a little foolish, but even more relieved, he took a deep breath and calmed down. "Oh. Maybe you did."

"Never mind that," she said, staring down at the paper. "Here's the deal. Ben's a lawyer. He always seems to be looking for a weak spot to exploit." She looked up, wrinkling her nose. "You know what I mean? Our uncle Luke, my father's older brother, died last week. I met him a few times years ago and he came to my father's funeral. But to my shock, he had a little piece of land in the mountains and he left it to Ben and me."

"The two of you together?" That could be a seemingly lucky break but with a sword of Damocles hanging over it.

"Yes. I assume he thought we would sell it and share the revenue or one would buy the other out. Whatever."

"Okay. What's the problem?"

She frowned, chewing her lip. "Ben wants to buy me out. But…" She made a face, thought for a moment, then leaned closer, speaking softly. "I know this is going to sound really horrible, but I don't trust him. Everything he says seems logical enough and it sounds good and all. But, well, he tried to find a way to get a piece of my lake property when my dad died. He wasn't all that open about it, but I could tell he was snooping around here for a purpose. And now I just can't help but wonder…"

"Better safe than sorry," he agreed. "Where's the land?"

"That's just it. He seems a little vague about that. He does say it's out in the sticks, far from any amenities and there seem to be some encumbrances on it that are going to make things difficult. I did get something in the mail myself, something from my uncle's lawyer, but I couldn't make heads nor tails of it and when I tried to call him, the number didn't seem to work. Ben gave me this paper with the parcel number and coordinates, but as far as a map on how to get there, he was very unhelpful."

"Has he been out to take a look at it?"

"He says he has. He says it's pretty barren. Flatland with not even a lot of vegetation. No views. Nothing."

Cam nodded, thinking that over. "So you're a bit skeptical."

She made a face. "I hate to say it, but yes. Color me skeptical."

"And you would like to go take a look for yourself." He nodded again, assessing things. "I think that's good. You need to know a little more about where it is and what condition it's in before you make any drastic moves."

"I think so," she said. "For all I know, it's a garden paradise or a great site to build a house on." She squinted at him hopefully. "I just thought you might know what state or county agencies to go to and things like that. Or maybe you have connections in the Forest Service?"

"I know some people who might be able to help." He

looked over the paper for another moment. "Can I take this with me?"

"Of course."

"Good." He folded it and put it in his pocket, then gave her a sardonic look. "I'm going to have to pull some strings, you know. I might have to call in some favors. Use my family's influence." His smile was suddenly wicked. "And after I've done all that, going out of my way, putting my reputation on the line, going all out to do something for you…" His shrug was teasingly significant. "Well, I'm sure you're going to be more open to doing a favor for me in return."

It was obvious he was still trying to get her to manage the party for his mother—the last thing on earth she wanted to do.

"Cam!"

His wide mouth turned down at the corners for just a moment. "Just think about it. That's all I ask." He patted the paper in his pocket. "I'll get back to you on this." His smile returned to being warm and natural. "You'll trust me?"

"Of course I'll trust you." She smiled back at him. It just wasn't possible not to. "Now go away," she said.

Actually he was late for a meeting at the mayor's office, so for once he obeyed her. But first, he leaned forward, caught her hand in his and brought it to his lips, kissing her palm.

"See you later," he promised, giving her a melting look.

She shook her head, half-laughing at him as he slid out and left the café. But as she looked around the room at the glances she was getting, her face got very hot. It was obvious a lot of people had witnessed that hand kissing thing and could hardly wait to get on their cell phones to tell their friends what they'd seen.

Small towns!

CHAPTER SEVEN

IT ONLY took Cam two days to get all the information Diana needed to make a trek up to see the land. She was thrilled when he called her with the news. So now she'd fed the kitten and watered her flower garden and dressed herself in hiking clothes and was ready to go. This was totally an adventure and she was looking forward to it. She just had to wait for Cam to show up with the map of the location of where she was going.

She knew she was not acting according to plan. She'd sworn she was going to stay away from Cam—far, far away. She wasn't going to risk falling back into the patterns that had ruled her life for so long. She was a grown woman with a child on the way and she couldn't afford to act like a lovesick teenager.

She knew asking for his help put her in a weaker position in refusing to help his mother, and yet, she'd done it anyway. Somehow Cam kept weaving his way through the threads of her days, finding a reason here, an excuse there, and before she knew it, she was almost back in the fold, tangled in his life, loving him again, unable to imagine a future without him.

It had to stop. Right after he gave her the map. She had the grace to laugh out loud as she had that thought. What a ridiculous fool she was!

She heard his car and hurried out to meet him, hoping to get the map and send him on his way. He got out of the car and leaned against it, watching her come toward him with a look of pleasure on his face. She couldn't help but smile.

"Oh, Cam, don't do that."

"Don't do what? Enjoy you?"

She gave him a look. "Do you have the map?"

"Yes, I do."

She looked at him. Both hands were empty.

"Where is it?"

"In the car."

"Oh." She tried to look around him. "May I have it?"

"No."

She stared at him. "What do you mean?"

His eyes sparkled in the sun. "I'm the keeper of the map. I'll handle all navigational duties."

She put her hands on her hips and gave him a mock glare. "That'll be a little hard to do, since you'll be here and I'll be the one approaching the site," she said crisply.

"Au contraire," he countered smugly. "Since we're going in my car…"

"No way!"

"And I have the picnic prepared by Rosa this very

morning and packed away in an awesome picnic basket, with accoutrements for two."

She drew in a quick breath. "I never said you could come with me."

He gave her the patented lopsided grin that so often had young ladies swooning in the aisles. "That's right, you never did. But I'm coming anyway."

Fighting this was probably a losing battle and not worth the effort as it stood, but still, she frowned, trying to think of a way out. "Can I just see the map?"

"Sure. But I'll hold it."

She groaned at his lack of trust, but that was forgotten as he spread out the map and showed her where her property lay.

"Ohmigosh, that's really far from any main roads. I thought it would be closer to Lake Tahoe."

"It's uncharted territory. Just be glad it's not winter. Think about the Donner party."

She shuddered. "No, thanks." She frowned at him, trying to be fierce. "Now if you'll just give me the map."

He smiled and dropped a sudden, unexpected kiss on her forehead. "I go with the map. Take it or leave it."

She shook her head, but a slight smile was teasing her lips and her heart was beating just a little faster. "What a bully you are."

"Guilty as charged. Let's go."

They went.

It was a lovely drive through the foothills and then into the taller mountains. They passed through small idyllic towns on the way, and little enclaves of farm or ranch houses. Cows, horses and alpacas seemed to be grazing everywhere on the still-green grasses. They talked and laughed and pointed out the sights, and all in all, had a very good time. The final segment was a fifteen-mile ride on a dirt road and that was another story. For almost half an hour, they were bouncing so hard, conversation was impossible.

And then they arrived. Cam brought the car to a stop in a cloud of dust and they both sat there, staring out at the open area. For a moment or two, neither said a word.

Finally Diana asked pitifully, "Are you sure this is it?"

"Afraid so," he said.

She turned to gaze at him, a look of irony in her eyes. "I don't think there could be an uglier patch of land in all the Sierras, do you?"

"It's definitely an ugly little spud," he said out of the side of his mouth, shaking his head. "I don't think anyone is going to want to build here. There are no trees, no view, no nothing."

"No paved road," she pointed out, wincing as she looked back at all the rocks and gullies they were going to have to go back through. "Looks like the best thing to do would be to take Ben up on his offer and let him buy me out."

"Maybe." Cam frowned, leaning forward on the steering wheel. "Though I can't help wondering why he wants it—or whom he's going to sell it to. I can't see one redeeming element here."

She let out a sigh. "Darn. I was hoping for a bit of good luck for a change."

"Ya gotta make your own luck, sweetheart," Cam said in his best Sam Spade imitation. "That's the way the game is played."

She made a face at him and admitted, "I don't even see a place to have a picnic here. And we passed a nice park about thirty minutes ago. Shall we go back?"

The ride back wasn't any better than the ride out had been, but they found their way to the nice park and sighed with relief when they got there. The park had tables with built-in benches and they set up their feast on a nice one under an oak, in full view of the small river that ran through the area. Rosa's lunch was delicious. They ate and talked softly in the noon day sunshine. A group of children played tag a short distance away. Mothers with strollers passed, cooing to their babies.

Diana took a bite of her chicken salad sandwich as she watched the passing parade. "Funny how, once you're pregnant, you suddenly notice all the babies that pop up everywhere."

He gave her a covert look. She'd brought up her pregnancy on her own. Did this mean that the moratorium on mentioning it was lifted? Just in case, he made sure to tread softly.

"You're going to make a great mom," he noted.

She flashed him a look and for a moment, he thought he was going to get his head handed to him. But then her face softened and she almost smiled.

"What makes you say that?" she asked.

"I get a clear vibe from you that seems encouraging,"

he said. "You seem to be settling into this new role you're about to play in the world."

Now a smile was definitely tugging at the corners of her mouth. "It's funny, but it has taken me a while to fully realize what I've done, what I'm about to do. Mia seems very real to me now. I can hardly wait to hold her in my arms. I only hope I'll be a good mother to her."

"I have no doubts. I remember how you took care of your father."

"Do you?" She looked at him in surprise, then with growing appreciation. "I don't think most people remember that, or even noticed at the time." She shook her head. She'd spent too much of her young life taking care of him and getting little thanks for it. But she'd done it out of duty and a feeling of compassion for the man. And though she'd gone off to the big city as soon as she could, to leave all that behind her, she'd come back when her father needed her and no one else would have taken care of him as he lay dying. So she did it.

Funny. She'd left Gold Dust because of her father and then she'd returned for the same reason.

"He needed someone to take care of him. It was a cinch he couldn't take care of himself."

He waved a carrot stick at her. "You were taking care of him when you were too young to be taking care of anything more than whether your socks matched."

She smiled. Trust Cam to have paid attention and to have realized how difficult it was for her when she was young. How could you not fall for a guy like that?

She was quiet for a moment, then said softly, "I loved him, you know."

He looked at her and saw the clouds in her eyes. He wanted to take her in his arms, but he held off, knowing how she felt about the situation.

"Of course you did. He was your father." He shifted in his seat. "Did you ever know your mother at all?"

"Not much." She shook her head. "She took off before I was six years old and never looked back."

"That's a shame."

She tilted her head back and smoothed her hair off her face. "I'm not so sure. If she was worth knowing, she'd have made a point of letting me know her." Her laugh was short and spiked with irony. "At least my father stuck around."

They packed away the remnants of their lunch, put things into the car, and walked down to watch the river roll by. There were just enough boulders and flat rocks in the river's path to make for a pretty spectacular water show. They followed the river for a bit, then sat on a large rock and listened to the rushing sound.

"You need something like this at your place," he told her. "Your lake could use some shaking up."

"I've got a nice stream," she protested. "That's more my sort of excitement. Something manageable and contained."

He laughed, leaning back beside her and tossing a flat pebble into the river. "That's all you want out of life, is it? Something manageable?"

"What's wrong with that?"

"Not a thing." He tossed another pebble. "But back about the time I left, I thought you had plans to go to the city and become a model." He shifted so that she could lean back against his shoulder instead of the hard rock. "What happened to that?"

She hesitated, then gave in to temptation and let her body snuggle in against his. "Kid dreams," she said airily.

He turned his head, savoring the feel of her against him. A sudden breeze tossed her hair against his face and he breathed in her spicy scent. "You would've been good," he said, closing his eyes as he took in the sense of her.

"No."

"Why not?" Opening his eyes again, he was almost indignant. "You've got the bones for it. You could be a model." Reaching out, he touched her hair, then turned his hand, gathering up the strands like reins on a wonderful pony. "You…Diana, you're beautiful."

He said it as though it were the revelation of the ages. She smiled wryly, appreciating his passion but knowing it was just a bit biased.

"I'm not cut out for that sort of life," she said simply.

"Chicken."

She shook her head. "No. It's not that."

He went very still for a moment, thinking over her situation. "Maybe you should have gone for it anyway," he said softly.

She moved impatiently, turning to look at him. "You don't understand. I know more about it than you think I do. I lived in San Francisco for a couple of years after college. I did all those things you do when you live in

San Francisco. I went to parties in bay-view penthouses, danced in sleazy discos, dated young account executives and overworked law students. Climbed halfway to the stars in little cable cars. Lived on a houseboat in Sausalito for a few months. Worked at a boring job. Had my car broken into. Had my apartment robbed. Had a lot of fun but finally I'd had enough and I wanted to come home. To me cities are kind of those 'great to visit but don't make me live there' sorts of places."

He smiled, enjoying how caught up in her subject she'd become. Reaching up, he touched her cheek. "You're just a small town girl at heart."

"I guess so. I love it in Gold Dust." She threw her head back, thinking of it. "I love to wake up in the morning and see the breeze ruffling the surface of the lake. I love the wind high up in the pines and the fresh smell after a rainstorm. I love that feeling of calm as the sun sinks behind the mountaintops and changes the atmosphere into a magic twilight."

"I understand," he said. "That's part of what pulled at me to come back." He hesitated only a few beats. "That…and you."

The moment he said it, he knew it was true. Through all the turmoil, all the hell he'd gone through with Gina, Diana had always been in the back of his mind, a calm, rational presence, an angel of mercy whose care could heal his soul. He'd always pushed the memories away, thinking they were a crutch he'd held on to in order to comfort himself, like a favorite fantasy. But now he knew it was much more. What he felt for Diana might be fairly hopeless, but it was real and true and strong inside him. It was more real than any other part of his life had ever been. His gaze slid over her, searching the shadowed areas along her neckline, her collarbone, the upper swell of her breasts.

She turned toward him slowly, as though in a dream. She knew he was going to kiss her. She heard it in his voice. Her heart was thumping so loud, she wasn't sure if she could breathe. He was going to kiss her and once again, just for this moment, she was going to kiss him back.

She didn't wait, but leaned toward him, her lips already parted, and his arms came around her and she clung to him, moving in a cloud of sensual happiness. Was this real? Was that really Cam's body that felt so warm and wonderful against hers?

It was over too soon. She sighed as he pulled back, then smiled up at him.

"How can I miss you if you won't go away?" she murmured, half-laughing.

"What is that supposed to mean?" he asked, touching her cheek with his forefinger.

"It means you're always there," she said, straightening and moving away from him. "You're either in my life or in my dreams. I can't get rid of you." She said it lightly, as though teasing, but she meant every word.

He watched her through narrowed eyes, wondering why she appealed to him more than any other woman he'd ever known. Holding her felt natural, kissing her had been magic. He wanted her in his bed, in his life. But what did that signify? Right now, it was just confusing.

It was later, as they winged their way home, that he brought up the topic she'd been dreading all along.

"You haven't been over to the house for a while."

"No. I was gone and then…" She let her voice taper off because she knew there was no good excuse for her sending Penny to take care of the arrangements at the Van Kirk mansion one more time, even though she herself was back in town.

"My mother is asking that you come see her," he said, glancing at her sideways.

"Oh, no," Diana said, her eyes full of dread. "She's going to beg me to take over the party plans, isn't she?"

He nodded. "Yes."

She wrinkled her nose. "Tell her I've got the flu."

This time his look was on the scathing side. "I make it a practice never to lie to women," he said, and she wasn't sure if he was joking or not.

She smiled sadly just the same. "Only to men, huh?"

He suppressed a quick grin. "Of course. A man can handle a lie. Likely as not, he'll appreciate a well-told one. Might even appropriate it for his own use in the future, and thank you for it, besides."

"Unlike a woman," she countered teasingly.

"Women only appreciate lies about themselves, and then only if they're complimentary."

She stared at him, struck by how serious he sounded all of a sudden. "What made you so cynical about the human race?" she asked him.

For just a moment he was tempted to tell her about Gina, the only other woman he'd been close to loving over the last ten years, about how she'd nearly pulled him into an ugly trap, teaching him a lesson about feminine lying he would never forget. But at the last moment, he decided it was a story best kept to himself and he passed over it. It was all very well to use episodes from the past as lessons in guarding one's trust like a stingy uncle, but to inflict those stories on others was probably too much.

"Life does take its toll," he said lightly instead.

"Are you done?" she asked.

He glanced at her in surprise. "Done doing what?"

"Done running around the world looking for affirmation."

He gave a cough of laughter. "Is that what I've been doing? And here I thought I was looking for adventure all this time."

She shrugged, loving the way his hair curled around his ear, loving the line of his profile, loving him in every way she possibly could. She'd missed him so. She would miss him again when he left. And she was sure his leaving was inevitable. She didn't know when, but she knew he would go. And this time, she refused to let her heart break over it.

"Tell me why you went in the first place? The real reason."

"You mean, beyond the fight with my grandfather? It's pretty simple. The age-old story." He maneuvered through a traffic circle in the little city they were passing through. "I had to go to see if I could make it on my own without the Van Kirk name boosting me along. I didn't want to end up like my father. And I didn't much want to end up like my grandfather, either. I wanted to be me."

She nodded. That was pretty much what she'd expected. "And now?"

He grinned. "Now I'm thinking my grandfather isn't such a bad model after all."

"Interesting." She thought about that for a moment, then went on. "Has anyone ever told you that a lot of people thought you left because of Lulu?" she informed him, watching for his reaction.

He looked blank. "Lulu?"

"Lulu. Lulu Borden. You remember her." She hid her smile.

"Oh, sure. Tall, curvy girl. Lots of red hair. Nice smile. Kind of flirty."

"That's Lulu."

He shrugged. "What does Lulu have to do with me?"

"Well…" She gave him an arch look. "She started showing right about the time you disappeared. A lot of people figured you were the one who got her that way. And that was why you took off."

"What?" He gaped at her in horror until she reminded him to keep his eyes on the road. "If a lot of people thought that a lot of people were wrong."

She nodded happily. "I was pretty sure of that, but it's good to hear you confirm it."

He frowned, still bothered by the charge against him. "What did Lulu have to say about it?"

"She married Tommy Hunsucker, so she's not sayin' much."

"Geesh." He shook his head with a look of infinite sadness. "Maligned in my own hometown."

"Sure," she said cheerfully. "Where better to have your reputation besmirched?"

"And now they think I'm a daddy again, don't they?" he said cynically, looking at her growing tummy. "At least the town has a lot of faith in my potency."

She grinned. "Legends speak louder than facts sometimes," she admitted.

"Speaking of legends…" He hesitated, then went on bravely. "Tell me why you aren't going to marry the father of your baby."

All the humor drained from her face and she seemed to freeze. "That is not up for discussion."

He turned to look at her. "Di…"

"No. I'm not going to tell you anything." She shook her head emphatically and her tone was more than firm. "This is my baby. The father has nothing to do with it."

He winced. "That's not true."

"It is true," she insisted fiercely. "That's it." She held her hand up. "End of discussion."

He didn't press it any further, but he thought about it all the rest of the way home.

It was late afternoon before they turned onto the Gold Dust Road and came in sight of her little house by the lake.

"Getting back to the point," he said as he pulled up before her gate. "Will you go to see my mother?"

"Wow, that was a subject I thought we'd left in the dust way back there somewhere. Or at least we should have."

She thought for a moment before answering. She

wanted to give him the benefit of the doubt, an even chance, a fair hearing, and all those other tired clichés that meant he probably had a point to make and she ought to let him make it.

He moved impatiently. He obviously thought she'd taken enough time to come up with a fair decision and he was beginning to think she was dragging her feet.

"Listen, Di. I owe my mother something. I owe her quite a bit, in fact. I wasted a lot of time trying to figure out what life was about and what my place was in the general scheme of things. By the time I'd sorted it all out, I was back where I'd started. But by then, I realized family was more important than anything else. And I needed to make up for some things with mine. So that's why I came back. Unfortunately they're in more trouble than I can easily deal with. But this, at least, I can do for her. I can let her have her party. And she needs help to do it."

Diana listened to him and agreed with just about everything he said. He was a good son after all. And she knew she could help. She sighed.

"All right, Cam. I'll go to see your mother." She shook her head. "But I can't go tomorrow. I've got a doctor's appointment in the morning and I won't be back in time."

"Here in town?"

"No." She looked at him speculatively, then amplified a bit. "I decided from the first that I'd better go to a clinic down in Sacramento. I found a good doctor there. And I didn't want everyone in town knowing all about my pregnancy."

He nodded. "Probably a wise move," he said.

"So I'll plan to come by and see her Friday," she went on. "I'll talk to her." She winced. "But I'm afraid I'm only going to disappoint her."

He grunted and she couldn't tell if he was agreeing with her or dissenting.

"I still don't feel comfortable being a part of the great wife search," she told him, "especially if you plan to thwart your mother on it. If you really mean it, that you won't marry anyone, I hope you're planning to tell her the truth from the beginning."

"She knows how I feel."

"Does she?" Somehow, doubts lingered. "Cam, let's be honest. Your mother is looking for a bride for you, like it or not. It's not exactly fun for me to be a part of that."

"Why is that?" He gazed challengingly into her eyes. "Tell me what bothers you about that?"

Her lower lip came out. "You know very well what it is," she said in a low, grating voice. "It's not really fair of you to make me say it. You know exactly what it is and you know there's no cure for it."

With that, she grabbed her map and slipped out of the car, heading for her little lonely house.

Cam sat for a long time, not moving, not reaching for the ignition, just staring at the moon. And then, finally, he headed home.

CHAPTER EIGHT

DIANA dreamed about Cam, about his kiss and how lovely it was to be in his arms. And then she woke up and there he was on her doorstep.

"Doughnuts," he said, holding out a sack of them like a peace offering. "For your breakfast."

"Thank you," she said, taking the bag and closing the door right in front of him.

"Hey," he protested, and she opened the door again, pretending to scowl at him.

"Too early," she said. "You're not even supposed to see me like this."

"I'll close my eyes," he lied. "I came early because I didn't want to be too late to take you to the doctor."

She stared at him, and slowly, she opened the door wider for him to come in. Turning, she looked up at him. "I don't need anyone to take me to the doctor," she said stiffly.

"I'm not trying to horn in on your private business," he assured her. "In fact, if you want me to, I'll wait in the car. But I think you ought to have someone with you, just in case. And since the baby's father isn't around to help you, you can count on me. I'll be around in case something happens, or whatever."

You can count on me—the words echoed in her head. She knew he meant it, but she also knew he couldn't promise anything of the sort. "Cam, I really don't need help."

He stared down into her wide eyes. "Yes, you do," he said firmly. "Di, I know you can do this on your own. You're very brave and you've tried your whole life to do everything on your own. I know you don't actually, physically, need any help. You're strong. You've done it all on your own forever."

Reaching out, his hands slid into her hair, holding her face up toward him. "But everyone needs somebody. No one can chart his own course forever. I'm here now. I can help you. I can give you some support and be around in case you need a shoulder to lean on. You don't have to be alone."

To her horror, her eyes were filling with tears. She fought them back. The tears were a sign of weakness, and she couldn't afford to show that side to anyone. But as she fought for control, he was kissing her lips, moving slowly, touching gently, giving comfort and affection and a sense of protection that left her defenses crumbling on the floor. She swayed toward him like a reed in the wind. He was so wonderful. How could she resist him? A part of her wanted to do whatever he said, anytime, anywhere. And that was exactly the part she had to fight against.

He pulled back to look at her, his gaze moving slowly over her face, a slight smile on his own.

"Please, Diana," he said softly. "Let me be there for you. I'm not asking for anything else. Just let me be there."

She was really crying now. Deep sobs were coming up from all her past pain, all her loneliness, and she was helpless in his arms. He pulled her up against his chest and stroked her hair. When she could finally speak again, she pulled back and looked at him. How was she going to make him understand?

"Cam, don't you see? I can't start to depend on you. If I do that…"

"I'm not asking for a long-term commitment and I'm not offering one," he insisted, holding her loosely, looking down into her wet, sleepy face and loving it. "But I am here now. I can help you. You could use a friend. I want to be that friend. That's all."

She closed her eyes. Didn't he understand how dangerous this was for her? Didn't he see how much she loved him? She had to send him away. It was the only chance she had for strength and sanity.

She felt him move to the side and heard paper rustling and she slowly opened her eyes and then her mouth to tell him to go, but before she got a word out, he popped a piece of doughnut inside it.

"Let's eat," he said cheerfully, and his comical look made her laugh through her tears. She chewed on the delicious confection and laughed at his antics and somehow her resolutions got forgotten for the time being.

But she knew this wasn't the end of the matter. She

might let her guard down for now, but very soon, she would have to erect it again. She knew that from experience. So she would let him come with her to her doctor's appointment and she would be with him for another day. And she would love doing it. But it couldn't last and she couldn't let herself be lulled into thinking that.

"If I were one to sing old Elvis songs," Diana muttered to herself the next afternoon. "I'd be singing that 'caught in a trap' song right now."

She was going to help Cam's mother. She'd always known, deep down, that she would end up doing it. The mystery was why she'd tried to fight it for so long. A lot of needless Sturm und Drang, she supposed. She was a pushover in the end.

"You're completely spineless, aren't you?" she accused herself in the hallway mirror. "Shame on you!"

Mrs. Van Kirk had looked so pathetic lying back on her chaise lounge overlooking her rose garden, and she'd been so complimentary about Diana's talents on all scores—and when you came right down to it, Diana liked her a lot. She felt sorry for her, wanted to help her have her silly parties, wanted to make her happy. So in the end, she agreed to take over all the planning for the event. She was to be totally in charge of it all.

So now she was enlisted to help find Cam a bride—what fun.

There was still the problem of how she would be paid. She'd assumed Cam was serious when he'd teased her about doing it for free, but he assured her she would be paid for her work—someday.

"How's this?" he said. "You'll have the first option on our future earnings."

"What earnings?" She knew he was working hard on setting things to rights, and she supposed there was income from the Van Kirk ranch to throw into the mix, plus some of his funds borrowed from his own business. But it all seemed like slim pickings so far.

He gave her a grand shrug. "We may just go in the black someday."

She rolled her eyes. "Great. I'll be looking forward to it."

"Seriously, Di," he said, catching hold of her shoulders to keep her from running off. "I'm going to make sure you get compensated. Just as soon as I've saved this house and have a little spare cash to take care of things like that."

She looked up at him and barely kept herself from swooning. He looked so handsome, his blue eyes clear and earnest, rimmed with dark lashes that made them look huge, his dark hair falling over his forehead in a particularly enticing way. She could feel his affection for her shining through it all. He was hers—in a way—for the next few days, at any rate. Then, if his mother's plans came to fruition, he would be some other woman's. And Diana would be left with nothing but memories.

"Forget it," she said, shaking her head, pushing away her dour thoughts. "I'm doing this for your mother. And that's it."

Of course, it turned out to be even more work than she'd thought it would be. There was so much to do. The event itself was to be called a Midsummer Garden Party to welcome Cam back to the foothills and from what they'd heard, it was already stirring interest all over the valley and environs far and wide.

"Everyone from the Five Families will be attending," Mrs. Van Kirk told her matter-of-factly.

Diana knew who the Five Families were and it made her cringe a little. The Van Kirks were one of those five, though they might be clinging to that distinction by their fingernails at the moment, hanging by the thread of their past reputation. They were all descendants of five Kentucky miners who'd come here together in the nineteenth century as forty-niners, discovered gold in these hills, settled the land and established the town of Gold Dust. They were the aristocracy of the area now, the movers and shakers of local affairs all through the valley, the main landowners and definitely the richest people around.

It was only natural that Cam's mother wanted him to marry one of the young women from that group. Why not? Not only did they have the money, they had the background to rule the area. And Cam was a natural leader as far as that went. So here she was, working hard to help him take his rightful place—at the top of the social ladder and right beside some simpering debutante.

Well, maybe she wouldn't be simpering. In all fairness, the women from the Five Families spent a lot of time doing charity activities and working on cleaning up the environment. But still, they were eligible to marry Cam and she wasn't. So a little resentment didn't seem so out of line, did it?

But she had to shove that aside and concentrate on the work at hand. Establishing a theme came first. They needed something that would allow them to make cheap, easy party dishes instead of the gourmet selections that had been the choice when the fancy chef was being engaged.

She gathered Cam and Janey together and the four of them brainstormed and what they finally came up with was a Hawaiian theme.

"Hawaiian?" Janey wailed. "That's so retro."

"Exactly the point," Diana said. "That way we don't have to spend money on fancy decor items. We can use flowers from both your gardens and my fields. We'll string leis as party favors and have flowers to clip in the hair of ladies who want that. We'll have rose petals floating in the pool."

"But the food," Janey moaned.

"Don't worry, it'll be fine—very colorful and much cheaper. Things like bowls of cut up fruit will serve two purposes—decorating as well as eating. And as for the more substantial items, I have a friend, Mahi Liama, who runs a Polynesian restaurant in Sacramento. I'm sure he'd do a lot of the food for us. Maybe some pit roasted pork and chicken long-rice and poi. The rest will be mostly finger food that we're going to be fixing ahead and freezing and popping in the ovens at the last minute."

Janey groaned. "What a drag. I like it when we hire the work out a lot better."

Diana gave her a pasted on smile. "It'll be great. Just you wait and see."

The invitations came next. They couldn't afford to have any printed up, so Diana scavenged up some lovely notepaper she found in the bottom drawer of a beautiful carved desk in the den and put Mrs. Van Kirk to work doing them by hand. That was something she could do sitting down and it turned out she had gorgeous penmanship.

"The trick is to make it look like we are taking advantage of your handwriting skills and creating something unique without letting on that it's an economy measure," she told the older woman.

"Shall I add a little Hawaiian looking flower, like this?" Mrs. Van Kirk suggested, proving to have drawing talent as well.

"Perfect," Diana said, pleased as punch. "These will be so special, people will save them as keepsakes."

Buoyed by all the praise, Mrs. Van Kirk got busy and had a dozen done by noon on the first day.

Diana conferred with Cam about the seating arrangements. It turned out that he had rummaged in the storage sheds and found at least twenty round tables and a huge group of wooden folding chair to go with them, supplies obviously used for parties years ago. They needed cleaning up and some repair, and probably a coat of spray paint, but it seemed doable and he was already on the job.

There was a large patio suitable for dancing. With a few potted plants arranged along the outer perimeter and a few trellises and arbors set up, it could look stunning.

Diana was beginning to take heart. It looked like things were falling into place pretty easily. The whole family was involved, including a few cousins who stopped by occasionally, and despite the whining from some quarters, she generally thought that a good thing.

She was especially glad to find a way to get Janey to help out. Once she remembered that Cam's sister had been quite a musician in her younger days, she knew exactly how she could use her talents.

"Here's what you do," she told her. "I've called the high school. They have a small jazz combo, a pianist and a couple of different choral groups. I think one's a cappella. Hopefully they can do some low-key Hawaiian tunes. Their music director says they need the experience in playing in front of audiences, so I think we could get them really cheap and they could trade off, one group playing during the opening cocktails, another during the meal, another for the dancing, etc. You go talk to them and see what you can arrange. You'll be in charge of picking out the music. It's all yours."

"You know what?" Janey said, actually interested for once. "Adam, the man I've been dating, has a teenage son who does that Djaying thing at dance clubs to make a little extra money. Maybe he would help out."

"That would be great." She made a face as she had a thought. "Just make sure you have right of approval on everything he's going to play first. We don't want any of the raunchy stuff some of the kids like these days."

"Indeed," Janey said, drawing herself up. "Wouldn't fit the Van Kirk image."

Diana grinned at her. "You got it."

And for the first time in memory, Janey smiled back.

They had been working on party plans for three days when Diana got a present she wasn't expecting—and wasn't too sure she wanted. She was out in the garden cutting back a rosebush in order to encourage a few blooms that looked about to break out, when she noticed a strange sound coming from the toolshed. It sounded as though an animal had been locked in by mistake.

Rising with a sigh, she went to the door and opened it. Inside she found a small caramel-colored ball of fluffy fur. The puppy looked up at her and wriggled happily.

"Well, who are you, you little cutie?" she said.

Kneeling down beside him, she pulled out the tag tied around his neck. "Hi," the tag said. "I'm Billy and I belong to Diana and Mia Collins, only they don't know it yet."

"What?"

She rose, staring down at the dog as Cam came into the shed.

"What do you think?" he asked, a smile in his voice if not on his face.

She whirled to meet him.

"*You* did this," she said accusingly.

He put a hand over his heart. "Guilty as charged." He wiggled his eyebrows at her. "A friend of mine had a whole litter of these cute little guys. I picked out the best one for you."

She frowned, feeling frazzled. "Cam, I can't take care of a puppy."

"Sure you can. I'll help you."

She sputtered, outraged that he would take it upon himself to do this to her. He looked at her earnestly.

"Di, calm down," he said. "You know very well you need a dog. This little fellow is going to grow up to be a good watchdog. He'll be there to protect you and the baby when…well, when I can't."

She understood the theory behind the gift. She just wasn't sure she appreciated the motives.

"Cam," she said stubbornly, "if I decided I needed a dog, I could get one for myself. And right now, I don't need a dog."

He didn't budge an inch, either. "You need the protection. Living alone like you do, out there in the sticks, it's too dangerous." He gave her a trace of his lopsided grin. "You never know what sort of madman might show up drunk on your pier in the middle of the night."

She turned away. So that was it. The dog was supposed to take his place. Was he just trying to ease his guilt over the fact that he was not going to be there for her when she needed him in the very near future? She could never have him, but she could have his dog. How thoughtful of him. She was tempted to turn on her heel and leave him here with his bogus little animal.

But she looked down and saw a pair of huge brown eyes staring up at her, a little tail wagging hopefully, a tongue lolling, and she fell in puppy love.

"What am I going to do with you?" she asked the pup.

Billy barked. It was a cute bark. An endearing bark. And it cemented the future for Billy. He was going home with her. There was no doubt about that. Still, there were problems and concerns attached to this gift.

She frowned, biting her lip and thinking over the logistics of the situation. "But I'm over here all day. I can't just leave him alone at the lake, not at this age."

"I agree," Cam said. "That's why I rigged up a dog run alongside the shed. You can have him here with you in the daytime. He'll go home with you at night."

Cam had thought of everything. She looked at him, loving him and resenting him at the same time. Slowly she shook her head. "I don't know what my little black kitten is going to think of this," she said.

"They're both young. They should be able to adjust to each other quickly."

She looked up at Cam. A few weeks before she hadn't had anything. Now she had a baby and she had a kitten and she had a dog. The only thing she still lacked was a man of her own. But you couldn't have everything, could you?

She shook her head, looking at him, loving him. He shrugged, his arms wide, all innocence. And she laughed softly, then walked over and gave him a hug.

"Thank you," she whispered, eyes shining.

He dropped a kiss on her lips, a soft kiss, barely a gesture of affection, and turned to leave before she could say any more.

* * *

It was at the beginning of her second week of work on the party that Diana came face-to-face with Cam's grandfather for the first time. She'd been working hard on all aspects of the preparations and she'd gone into the house to get out of the sun and found herself in the cool library with its tall ceilings and glass-fronted bookcases. It felt so good, she lowered herself into a huge leather chair and leaned back, closing her eyes.

At times like this she was getting used to communing silently with baby Mia, giving her words of encouragement, teaching her about what life was going to be like once she emerged from her protected cave and came into the real world. She knew the baby couldn't really hear her thoughts, but she also knew that something was communicated through an emotional connection that was getting stronger every day. Hopefully it was the love.

The minutes stretched and she fell asleep, her hands on her rounded belly. The next thing she knew, there was an elderly man standing over her, peering down as if to figure out who she was and just exactly why she was sleeping in his chair.

"Oh!" she cried, and she jumped up as smoothly as she could with the extra weight she was carrying. "I'm sorry, I…"

"Sit down, sit down." He waved his cane at her sternly. "Just sit down there and let me look at you, girl."

She glanced toward the exit, wishing she could take it, but reluctantly, she sank back down into the chair and tried to smile. She knew right away who this was, and if she hadn't known, she would have guessed. She could see hints lurking behind the age-ravaged face of a man who had once looked a lot like Cam, blue eyes and all.

"So you're Jed Collins's daughter, are you?" he growled. "You sure do look like your mom. She was one of the prettiest gals in the valley in those days."

"Th…thank you," she said, still unsettled by this chance encounter. "I think."

He nodded. "She ran off when you were a little one, didn't she? Ever find out what happened to her?"

Diana bristled a bit at the sense that he seemed to think he had a right to delve into her family matters at will. But she reminded herself that he probably thought of himself as a sort of elder statesman of the community, and she held back her resentment, shaking her head. "No, sir. Never did."

"You ought to get Cam to look for her. He could find her. That boy can do just about anything."

"I don't want to find her."

He stared at her for a moment and then gave a short shout of laughter.

"You're as tough as she was, aren't you? Good. Your dad was weak and he couldn't hold on to her. But who'd have thought she was tough enough to go off and leave her baby girl behind like she did? I'm telling you, nobody expected that one."

His casual assumptions outraged her. Who did he think he was to make these judgments on her family members? And yet, he was bringing up issues no one ever dared talk about in front of her. So in a way, it was sort of refreshing to get things out in the open. She'd never really had a chance to give her thoughts on the situation before, with everyone tiptoeing around it. Now was her chance, and she took it.

"You call that being tough?" she challenged, trying to ignore the lump that was rising in her throat. "For a woman to leave her six-year-old daughter behind in the care of a man who had no ability to handle it?" Her eyes flashed with anger, and that was reassuring. She would rather have anger than tears. "I call it being selfish and cruel."

He reared back and considered what she had to say as though he wasn't used to people disagreeing with his proclamations.

"Well, you would I suppose. But you don't know why she did it, do you? You're judging results, not motives."

She drew in a sharp breath. "You're darn right I'm judging results. I'm living the results."

He chuckled. "You've got fire in you, I'll say that," he said gruffly. "I know that grandson of mine has always had a special place in his heart for you." He frowned, looking at her. "But we all have to make sacrifices."

"Do we?"

"Damn right we do." He waved his cane at her again. "He promised me years ago he would marry one of the gals from the Five Families. I had everything set up and ready to go when he lit out on me. Left that poor little girl in the lurch."

He stamped his cane on the ground and suddenly he looked exhausted, leaning on it.

"Now he's going to have to make up for it." He shook

his shaggy head. "He's a good boy. I knew he'd come through in the end. Not like his worthless father."

Diana stared at him. This was all news to her. "Cam was set to marry someone when he left ten years ago?" she asked softly, heart sinking. That would explain a lot. And make things murkier in other ways.

"Darn right he was. Little Missy Sinclair. Now he'll finally get the job done."

Cam appeared in the doorway before the old man could go on with his ramblings.

"Here you are," he said to his grandfather. "I didn't know you'd come all the way downstairs." He threw Diana a glance as he came up and took the old man's arm. "Come on. I'll help you back to your room."

"I'm okay, I'm okay," the older man grumbled. "I've just been talking to the Collins girl here. Pretty little thing, isn't she? Just like her mama."

"That she is," Cam agreed with a grin her way. "And the more you get to know her, the more you're going to like her."

"Well, I don't know about that," he muttered as his grandson led him away. "We'll see, I suppose."

Diana sat where she was as they disappeared down the hallway. She would wait. She knew Cam would come back down to talk to her. And she had some things she wanted to talk about—like secret engagements and leaving people in the lurch.

She looked up as he walked back into the room.

"Sorry about that," he told her with a quick smile. "He usually doesn't come downstairs these days. I hope

he didn't say anything…well, anything to upset you."
His gaze was bright as he looked at her and she had the
distinct impression he was afraid exactly that had
happened. And in a way, he was right.

"He did say something that surprised me," she told
him, wishing her tone didn't sound quite so bitter, but
not knowing how to soften it right now. "I didn't know
you were supposed to marry someone just before you
ran off to join the circus ten years ago."

He sat down on the arm of her large leather chair and
shook his head as he looked down at her. If her use of
that phrase for his leaving didn't show him that she still
harbored a grievance from those days, her tone would
have given him a clue.

"Di, come on. I didn't run off to join the circus."

"Well, you might as well have." She bit her lip, realizing she was revealing a reservoir of long pent-up anger
against him for doing what he'd done and leaving her
behind. Just like her mother had. Funny, but she'd never
connected those two events until today, when Cam's
grandfather had forced the issue.

"There were a lot of reasons behind my leaving at the
time," he told her, taking her hand up and holding it in his.

This was all old news as far as he was concerned.
He'd thought she understood all this. Of course, he had
to admit, he'd never told her about the arranged
marriage that never happened—mostly because he'd
always known he wouldn't go through with it. And so
had the so-called "bride." It had never been a major
issue in his thinking—except to avoid it.

"Mostly I needed to get out from under the suffocating influence of my grandfather. And part of what he was trying to force on me was a marriage to a girl I had no interest in marrying. But that was just part of it."

She nodded, digesting that. "Who was she?"

He hesitated, thinking. "Tell you the truth, I forget her name."

"Missy Sinclair?"

He looked at her penetratingly. "If you knew it, why did you ask?"

She shrugged. The turmoil inside her was making her nauseous. "Did you ask her to marry you at the time?"

"No." He began to play with her fingers as he talked. "It wasn't like that. Me marrying Missy was cooked up between my grandfather and Missy's grandfather about the time she was born. I had nothing to do with it and never actually agreed to it. Never."

Diana took in a deep breath, trying to stabilize her emotions. "Where is she now? Is she still waiting?"

"Are you kidding?" He laughed and went on, mockingly. "Selfish girl. She couldn't wait ten years. She went ahead and married some guy she actually loved. Strange, huh?"

She finally looked up and searched his blue eyes. "You didn't love her? Not even a little bit?"

He pressed her fingers to his lips and kissed them, holding her gaze with his own the whole time. "No, Diana, I didn't love her and she didn't love me. It was our grandfathers who loved the idea of us getting married. We both rebelled against it. The whole thing was dead on arrival from the beginning. The only one who even remembers the agreement is my grandfather. Forget about it. It meant nothing then and means nothing now."

She closed her eyes. She really had no right questioning him about this. What did she think she was doing? He had a right to get engaged to anyone he wanted. She had no hold on him, even though the things he did could hurt her more deeply than anything anyone else alive could do.

If only she had followed through on her original intention to stay away from Cam. Now it was too late. She was heading for heartbreak on a crazy train and there was no way to get off without crashing.

CHAPTER NINE

BABY MIA was moving all the time now. Diana was bursting with joy at the feeling. The tiny butterfly wing flapping sensations had grown into full-fledged kicks. She would feel Mia begin to move and she would bite her lip and her eyes would sparkle and she would think, "There you go, little girl! Stretch those little legs. You'll be running in no time."

It was hard feeling like she couldn't tell the people around her what was happening. One afternoon, she couldn't contain it any longer. Mia was kicking so hard, it was making her laugh. She sidled up to Cam, who was overseeing some workers who were building a trellis and whispered to him.

"Give me your hand."

He looked at her, surprised. He'd just come back from a meeting with some bankers, so he was in a business suit and sunglasses and looking particularly suave and sensational. But he did what she asked, and she placed his hand right on the pertinent part of her tummy.

He stood very still for a moment, then turned to her with wonder in his eyes.

"Oh my God. Is that…?"

"Yes." Her smile was all encompassing. "Isn't it funny?"

He stared at her, his blue eyes luminous. "It's like a miracle."

She nodded, filled with joy. He took her hand and pulled her behind the gazebo where they could have a bit of privacy.

"How amazing to feel a new life inside you," he said, flattening his hand on her stomach again with more hope than success. "Di, it's wonderful."

"I can't tell you how transporting it is," she agreed. "It's really true. I'm like a different person."

His smile grew and took in all of her. "No," he said, cupping her cheek with the palm of his hand. "You're the same person. You just have new parts of you blossoming."

She nodded happily. Impulsively she reached up and kissed him, then turned quickly and retreated, back to work. But his reaction had warmed her to the core. She loved her baby and having him appreciate that, even a little bit, was super. Just knowing she had her baby with her was enough to flood her with happiness. All the worries and cares of the day fell away as she concentrated on the baby she was bringing to the world.

She had some qualms about raising Mia alone, without a father figure to balance her life. She'd gone through a lot of soul searching before she'd taken the plunge into single motherhood. Was it fair to the child?

Would she be able to handle it? She knew she was taking a risk and that it would be very hard, but she also knew she would do what was best for her baby, no matter what. And once she'd taken the step, she hadn't looked back for one minute.

She'd begun to buy baby clothes and to plan what she was going to do with the second bedroom in her house, the one she was converting into a nursery.

"I'll paint it for you," Cam had offered. "You shouldn't be breathing in those paint fumes while you're carrying Mia."

She'd taken him up on that offer and they had spent a wonderful Saturday trading off work and playing with Billy and the kitten. While Cam painted the room pink, Diana made chocolate chip cookies and worked on a pet bed she was constructing for the puppy.

Afterward, they took fishing poles out to the far side of the lake and caught a few trout, just like they had in the old days, catch and release. Diana made a salad for their evening meal and afterward, Cam found her old guitar and sat on the couch, playing some old forgotten standards and singing along while she watched.

A perfect day—the sort of day she would want for her baby to grow up with, surrounded by happiness and love. If only she could find a way to have more of them.

She walked him out to his car as he was leaving. The crickets were chirping and the frogs were croaking. He kissed her lightly. She knew she shouldn't allow it, but it was so comforting, so sweet. She leaned against him and he held her loosely.

"What would your father say if he could see you now?" he wondered.

She thought for a moment. "If he could see me now, he'd be out here with a shotgun, warning you to go home," she said with a laugh.

"You're probably right," he said. "Maybe it's just as well he's gone."

"I do actually miss him sometimes," she said pensively. "And I know I'm going to wish he could see Mia once she's born."

"Better he's not here to make her life miserable, too," Cam said cynically.

She sighed, knowing he was right but wishing he wasn't. If only she could have had a normal father. But then, what was normal anyway?

"He apologized to me toward the end, you know," she told him.

"Did he?"

She nodded. "He told me a lot of things I hadn't known before, things that explained a lot, things about his own insecurities and how he regretted having treated my mother badly. It's taken me some time to assimilate that information and assign the bits and pieces their proper importance in my life. Just having him do that, filling in some gaps, put things into a whole new perspective for me."

"No matter what his excuses, it can't justify what he did to you," Cam said darkly. Anger burned in him when he remembered how those bruises had covered her arms at times.

"No, I know that. I want to forgive him, but it's hard. It's only been very recently that I've even been able to start trying to understand him…and my mother…and what they did."

He held her more closely. "You deserved better parents."

She sighed. "I'm trying to get beyond blaming them. In a way, they only did what they were capable of doing."

He didn't believe that, but he kept his dissent to himself. If she needed to forgive them to make her life easier, so be it. He had no problem with that. He only knew that *he* didn't forgive what they'd done to her and there was a part of him that would be working to make it up to her for the rest of his life.

Billy began to yip for attention back in the house. They laughed.

"I guess I'd better get going," he said.

He looked at her from under lowered lids, looked at her mouth, then let his gaze slide down to where her breasts pushed up against the opening of her shirt. His blood began to quicken, and then his pure male reaction began to stir, and he knew it was time to go.

She nodded, but she didn't turn away.

He wanted to kiss her. He wanted to do more than that and he knew it was folly to stay any longer. Steeling himself, he let her go and turned for the car. Reaching out, he opened the door, but before he dropped inside, he looked back. And that was his fatal error.

One look at her standing there, her hair blowing around her face, her lips barely parted, her eyes full of something smoky, and he was a goner. In two quick steps he erased the space between them, and before she could protest, he was kissing her, hard and hot.

She didn't push at him the way he thought she would. Instead her arms wrapped around his neck and she pressed her body to his. He kissed her again and this time the kiss deepened.

She drank him in as though he held the secret of life, and for her, in many ways, he did. His mouth moved on hers, his tongue seeking heat and depth, and she accepted him, at first gladly, then hungrily, and finally with nothing but pure sensual greed.

This was what he'd been waiting for, aching for, dying for. All the doubts about who she might really want in her life dried up and blew away. He had her in his arms and that was where she belonged. He was going to stake a claim now, and if any other man wanted to challenge it, he'd better bring weapons.

Diana gasped, writhing in his embrace and wondering where this passion had come from. It had her in its grip, lighting a fire inside that she'd never known before. Every part of her felt like butter, melting to his touch. She knew this was crazy, this was playing with fire, but she couldn't stop it now. She wanted more and she wanted it with a fever that consumed her.

Billy barked again, and just like that, the magic evaporated, leaving them both breathing hard and shocked at what they had just been through.

"Oh my," Diana said, her eyes wide with wonder as she stared at him.

"Wow," he agreed, holding her face with two hands, looking down into her eyes as though he'd found something precious there.

"You…you'd better go," she said, stepping back away from him and shaking her head as though that would ward off temptation.

He nodded. "Okay," he said reluctantly, his voice husky with the remnants of desire still smoldering. He didn't dare touch her again, but he blew her a kiss, and then he was in his car and gone.

Diana watched him until his taillights disappeared around the far bend. Then she bit her lip and wondered why she seemed to be into torturing herself.

"The more greedy you get," she told herself, "The more you're going to miss him when he's gone."

But she had to admit, right now, she didn't really care. Right now she had gathered another memory to live with. And she would surely hold it dear.

The work was going well and the party was only a couple of days away. Janey had thrown herself into picking the musicians and the music, auditioning all sorts of groups as well as the high school kids. Every spare moment was filled with food preparation, mostly of the finger food variety—lumpia, teriyaki chicken wings, pineapple meatballs, tempura shrimp, wontons and everything else they could think of. Rosa set out the ingredients and Diana and Janey began to cut and mix. Rosa manned the ovens. Janey cleaned the trays. And once each batch was cooked, it was filed away in one of the massive freezers the estate maintained.

Meanwhile Mrs. Van Kirk was busy going through the RSVP returns and setting up place cards for the tables.

"The Five Families are coming en masse," she announced to everyone, happily running through her cards. "The eligible young woman count is at eleven and rising fast. Once they find out Cameron is up for matrimonial grabs, they sign up without delay. He's quite popular among them, you know."

Diana didn't have to be told. She already knew and she was sick at heart about it. She knew this was the last gasp as far as her relationship with Cam went. His family wanted him to marry a rich lady and that was what he was going to have to do. He might not know it yet, but she did.

He felt guilty for leaving his family in the lurch ten years before. He was ready and ripe for the picking as far as expiating that guilt and doing what would make his family happy and solvent went. He was going to have to marry someone. He just hadn't faced it in a calm and rational way.

Her mind was made up. She was going to endure this party to the best she could and then she was going to head home and stay away from the Van Kirks for the rest of her life. Every one of them. She would have Penny come and do the weekly flower arrangements and she herself would have no further contact with these people. That was the only way to preserve her happiness and her sanity. It wasn't going to be easy, but she would keep her allegiance to her baby uppermost in her mind and she would fight through the pain. It had to be.

Cam sat in his car staring at the Van Kirk mansion. He'd been in Sacramento doing some research and he had some news for Diana, who was inside, working on party preparations. He wasn't sure how she was going to take it. He wasn't sure how he took it himself.

His grandfather had mentioned the fact that Di's mother left her at a young age and that no one knew exactly why she might have done such a thing. Was she running off with another man? Had she reached the end of her rope dealing with her drunk of a husband? But if that was the case, why did she leave her child behind? In this day and age, the answers to such questions were a lot easier to find than they had been in the old days before computers and public access to so much government information.

At first Cam had resisted looking into the matter. After all, if Di wanted to know these things, she could have instituted a search herself, years ago. To go ahead on his own was to intrude where he had no right to. And yet, once his grandfather had brought it up, the mystery had nagged at him until he'd had to find out for himself.

His dilemma now was whether or not to tell Diana that he'd done it. And whether or not to tell her what he'd found as a result. What made him think that she actually wanted to know?

But it had to be done. Swearing softly, he got out of the car and started into the house, ready to go looking for Diana. The time of reckoning was at hand.

"Hi," she said, looking harried. "Listen, I need to talk to you. Ben has been calling me."

He reacted quickly to that, turning his head to stare at her. "What for?"

"He wants me to commit to selling out my portion of the inherited land." She appealed to him, a worried look in her large dark eyes. "What do you think? Should I do it?"

He hesitated. He hadn't been able to find out anything that would make him counsel that she turn Ben down, but something about this whole deal didn't seem right to him.

"Maybe you ought to wait," he said.

Diana seemed impatient. "Wait for what? We saw the land. It's not worth much. And I could use the money." She patted her rounded tummy. "I've got a baby coming, you know."

"I know." He smiled at her obvious joy every time she thought of or mentioned her baby. "I've tried to find out if there is any reason he would be so hot to have it, but so far, I haven't found a whisper of anything that would lead in that direction."

He'd come looking for her to tell her what he'd found about her mother, but as he gazed at her now, he thought twice and decided to hold off. She had too many things on her mind as it was. This business about her mother would just add to her worries and she didn't need that. He thought for a moment, then shrugged.

"Oh, what the hell. Go ahead and sell to him. Why not?"

"Okay. I'll give him a call and tell him to write up

his proposal. He said he would send me a check once it was signed." She looked up at him, eyebrows raised in question. "Maybe you could use the money to help with…?"

"Forget it," he said, but he grinned at her. "The amount we need is way beyond what you'll be getting. But thanks for the thought. I appreciate it."

She nodded. "Okay then." She noted a worried look in his eyes and she frowned. "Cam, how's the search for funding going? Have you had any luck yet?"

He shook his head briefly and gave her a fleeting smile. "No. With the economy the way it is, no one wants to take a chance."

She hated to see defeat in his face. "What about your business in San Diego? Have you thought about…" She almost gulped before she dared say the word. "Selling it?"

"Don't you think I've tried that?" He ran a hand through his hair, regretting that his response had been a bit harsh. "Of course I've thought about it. I've even put it on the auction block. So far there have been no takers."

"Oh." She was beginning to realize that this was really not looking good. It just might be that the Van Kirks were going to lose their family home and all the land they'd held for over a hundred years.

Funny how that sent a shiver of dread through her. What did she care, after all? These were people who had scorned her and her family all her life, until very recently. While she and her father had scrimped and clawed their way to a bare bones existence, the Van Kirks had lived a wealthy life of ease and comfort.

Or so it had seemed from afar. Once she got to know them better, she realized they had their own problems, their own demons to deal with. With wealth, your priorities changed, but the obstacles were very much the same. Life was no bed of roses no matter what side of the fence you lived on.

"You mean that darned old Freddy Mercury knew what he was talking about?" Cam said when she tried to explain to him how her thinking was running.

"Only if the Van Kirks end up as champions," she retorted, giving him a snooty look. "No time for losers, after all."

He put his forefinger under her chin and lifted it, looking down into her face. "We're going to come out of this okay, Diana," he said firmly. "I promise. Somehow, someway, I'm going to save the family farm."

She couldn't help but believe him. He had always been her champion, after all.

It was two days later that Cam came to her in a hurry just as she arrived at the estate. She'd barely risen from her car when he came rushing up.

"Diana, I need your help," he said without preamble. "Please. Find Janey and get her to take my mother downtown."

"What for?" The request was a little surprising, as Mrs. Van Kirk hadn't set foot off the grounds since her accident.

"Find some excuse. We've got to get her out of here. We've got appraisers and bank people coming to take a look at the house. It'll kill her if she sees that. She'll put two and two together and get…zero."

"Why are they coming?" Diana asked, not too good at putting two and two together herself.

"Why do you think? They want to take measurements and do evaluations." He gave her a dark look as he turned away. "Let's just say the vultures are circling."

That was an ominous thing to say and she shuddered every time she thought of it. But she did find Janey and prompted her to convince her mother to go into town for a bit of window-shopping. The real thing was off the budget for the foreseeable future. She watched as they drove off in Janey's little sports car, Mrs. Van Kirk complaining about the tight fit all the way. Just as they disappeared down the driveway, a limousine drove up and disgorged a group of businessmen who reminded her of a scrum of ravenous sharks.

Cam went out to meet them and began to take them on a tour of the grounds, talking very fast all the while. She wondered just what line of fantasy he was trying to spin. Whatever it was, they seemed to be listening attentively.

It wasn't until he brought them into the house that she began to realize something was wrong. She heard shouting and as she ran toward the front of the house where the noise was coming from, she began to realize it was Cam's grandfather who was causing a ruckus.

Old-fashioned cuss words were flying as she burst into the library where Cam was trying to quiet the older man. The bankers and appraisers were shell-shocked, gathering against the far wall of the room like a school of frightened fish.

"Get out of my house," Cam's grandfather was yelling. "I won't have you bloodsuckers here. I'd rather die than give in to you thieves. Where's my shotgun?"

"Get them out of here," Cam told her as she skidded to a stop before him, pointing to the group of visitors. "I'm going to lock him in here."

She shooed the men away, then turned back. "I'll stay here with him," she heard herself say, then gaped in horror at her own suggestion. The last thing in the world she wanted to do was stay here with this raving madman, but at the same time, she couldn't see locking him in here all alone. He was too old and too honored a member of this family to be treated like that.

"Really?" Cam looked at the end of his rope. "Great. Thanks, Di. I'll make it up to you, somehow."

He took off after the others, locking the door behind him, and Diana turned to look at the grandfather.

He'd finally stopped yelling and he sagged down onto the couch, his face turning an ashen shade of gray. She quickly got a glass of water from the cooler in the corner and handed it to him. He took a long drink and seemed to revive somewhat. He turned to look at her and frowned.

"They want to take my house away," he told her shakily. "I can't let them do that."

"Cam is going to try to fix it," she said, wishing she had more faith in the fact that a fix was possible. "I think these men are just here to gather some data."

He didn't answer and for a moment, she thought he'd

forgotten she was there. Then he turned, gazing at her from under bushy eyebrows.

"Let me tell you a story, girl. A story about family and friendship and history."

She glanced toward the door. Surely Cam would be coming back to rescue her soon. "Well, if it's only a short one."

"Sit down."

He did have a way with words—a strong and scary way. She sat down.

"I'm sure you know all about the Five Families, how our ancestors all worked together to establish a decent community for our loved ones here. Those bonds were still strong back when I was young. Through the years, they've frayed a bit. But two of us remained true friends, me and Jasper Sinclair. Some called our friendship historic. We were the only remaining descendants in our generation of a group of close friends who had struck out together for the California gold fields in the mid-nineteenth century, men who found their fortunes, and founded a pair of towns rimming the Gold Dust Valley."

He shook his head, his foggy gaze obviously turned backward on ancient scenes.

"Me and Jasper, we were raised to feel it our duty to maintain area pride in that culture and history. The other families sort of dissolved for one reason or another. Oh, they're still around, but their kids don't really have the pride the way they should. The Van Kirks and the Sinclairs, though, we've still got that Gold Rush story running in the blood in our veins."

Diana nodded. She knew a lot of this already, and she knew that it was a Sinclair girl that Cam had been expected to marry ten years ago.

"Jasper's gone now, but he had a passel of grand-daughters. I always said, if Cam can't decide on one of those pretty girls, he just ain't the man I think he is. You see, I promised Jasper I would see to it that we kept the old ways alive. Traditions matter. That's what keeps a culture intact, keeps the home fires burning, so to speak."

Diana took a deep breath and made a stab at giving her own opinion on the subject. "You know, in this day and age, it's pretty hard to force that sort of arranged marriage on young people. It just doesn't fit with the way we live now."

He fixed her with a gimlet eye. "Some of those arranged marriages turn out better than the ones people fall into by themselves," he said gruffly. "Look at your own parents. They married for love. That didn't turn out so well, did it?"

Diana had just about had it with his casual interest in giving out his view of her family affairs.

"Mr. Van Kirk," she began stiffly.

But he didn't wait to hear what she had to say.

"Did you know that your dad and my son, Cam's father, were good friends back before the two of you were born? Drinking buddies, in fact."

That stopped her in her tracks. "No," she said softly. "No, I didn't know that."

He nodded solemnly. "I used to blame him. Your dad, I mean. But now I realize they were both weak, both with addictive problems. Funny, isn't it?"

"Tragic is more like it," she said, but the words were under her breath and he didn't hear them.

He glared at her. "Anyway, I just hope you understand that Cam has got to marry one of them girls. There's no other way. It's either that, or we are over as a family." He shrugged as though dismissing her. "Sorry, but that's the way it is."

Cam returned before he could go on and she rose gratefully, leaving him to take his grandfather back up to his room. She felt numb. She knew what the old man had been trying to say to her. He needn't have bothered. She knew Cam would never marry her. As far as he was concerned, she was pregnant with another man's child. Besides, he didn't want to marry anyone. Didn't the old man know that?

But if all that was true, why was she crying again?

Cam sat in the darkened library staring out at the moon and wondering how things had gotten so crazy. He held a crystal glass filled with golden liquid of a certain potent variety and imbibed from time to time. But mostly, he was lost in thought.

It was the night before the party. Everyone had worked long into the evening, and would be back first thing in the morning to finish preparations before the guests began to arrive. Cam felt tired down to his bones, but he knew it was more emotional than physical.

Tomorrow the grounds would be filled with party-goers. A lot of beautiful young women from eligible families would be showing off their pretty summer dresses. Most of them were just coming to have fun, to see friends, to be at a party. But he knew there were certain expectations, mostly from his own family, that he would choose one of them to court. Preferably one of the richest ones, preferably from one of the Five Families. Hopes were high that he would do something matrimonial to save his own family from being kicked out of their ancestral home.

That wasn't going to happen. Much as he wanted to do something to save his family from ruin, he couldn't marry someone he didn't love. And he couldn't stop loving someone he couldn't marry.

He groaned, stretching back in the leather chair and closing his eyes. He should never have let his mother have her way with this party. He should never have let any of them get their hopes up this way.

Janey had actually brought the subject up earlier that day.

"Look," she'd said, waving a paring knife his way as she took a break from fashioning vegetable decorations. "It's only obvious you're crazy for Diana. You don't want to marry any of those women who are coming. I'm not sure you even want to be here with us."

She waved the knife so dramatically, he'd actually stepped back to be sure he was out of range.

"Why don't you just grab Diana and go? Take off for parts unknown. Leave us behind. We'll sink or swim without you."

He shook his head. "I can't do that."

"Why not?"

"Because it turns out, though I tried for ten years to forget it, blood is thicker than water. I'm a part of this family and I do care what happens to it."

Janey looked at him as though he were demented. "You can't just go off and be happy with the girl you love?"

"No."

Janey looked at him for a long moment, then said, "More fool you," but her eyes were moist and she turned and gave him the first hug he'd had from her since they were children.

A part of what complicated things, of course, was that, even if he wanted to go off with Diana, he wasn't sure she would want to go off with him. He knew she had a lot of affection for him, knew that she'd missed him and resented that he had gone off and left her behind suddenly the way he had—and for so darn long.

But why wouldn't she tell him who Mia's father was? He didn't know anything about the man who had fathered her baby. There was only one reason he could think of for that. She must still love him, still hope to get him to return and take up his duties as her child's father. What else could it be? And if that was still her dream, how could he get in the way?

He wished he understood women better. Somehow their thought processes were such a mystery. Just when he thought he'd figured one of them out, he found she was off in outer space somewhere, running on completely different assumptions than he was.

Gina for instance, the woman he'd lived with for a substantial length of time two years before. He'd thought they had the perfect adult relationship—companionship and sex without strings. She was the one who had suggested it and he'd been glad to accept her conditions. Then, suddenly, she wanted to get married. That was a shocker. He very quickly realized he didn't love her and didn't want to spend his life with her. When he explained that to her, she left in a huff.

A few months later, she was back, claiming to be pregnant with his child. He'd felt trapped, threatened, but he wanted to do the right thing. They planned a wedding, but he was in torture the whole time, resenting her, resenting the coming child, and hating himself for feeling that way.

Out of the blue, she died in a car accident. He was even more miserable, sad for her and the baby, tortured with the way he'd acted. He wished he'd been kinder to her.

Then, when the medical reports came in, he found out that the baby wasn't his after all. The confusion that left him in lasted for months. He couldn't even think about dating again. He didn't trust any woman he met. He'd actually begun to wonder if he would ever feel comfortable with a woman again.

Then he'd come home and there was Diana. It didn't take long to realize he was probably in love with her and always had been. The fact that it was crazy and doomed didn't bother him. He was used to life not turning out the way he'd hoped it would.

A sound in the doorway made him open his eyes and sit up straighter. There was Diana, walking slowly into the room and finally spotting him as her eyes adjusted to the gloom.

"I thought you'd gone home," he said.

"I did, but I forgot to put some of the leis we strung together in cool storage. I didn't want to leave them out overnight."

He nodded. "Will you join me in a drink?" he offered.

"No, thanks." But she came close and perched on the arm of the overstuffed leather chair where he was sitting. "I've got to get on home. I just stopped in for a minute."

"I was just sitting here thinking about you. About us."

She sighed. "Cam, there is no 'us.'"

"I've noticed that, Diana. Tell me why that is."

She looked down at him, startled by his tone. "There's a party happening tomorrow that is supposed to result in you choosing a rich bride to save the family," she said crisply. "That pretty much takes care of any 'us' there might have been."

He shook his head and took a sip of his drink. "I'm not buying it, Di. There's a wall between us and I'm just beginning to realize you put it there."

"That's crazy. I didn't invent this commitment you have to your family. It's enshrined in your Van Kirk legacy. It's like a shield carved into your front door. You gotta do what you gotta do."

"No, I don't."

"Yes, you do. You know very well it's what called you back here. You are part of something you can't shake free of. Duty, responsibility, whatever you want to call it. It's part of you and you're going to do what they expect."

He stared at her in the darkness. Was she right? Was he really going to do this thing they wanted of him?

He loved his grandfather with a fierce devotion, but he'd always resented him and his manipulating ways with almost as much passion. The senior Van Kirk had constantly tried to guide his life, but in the past, he'd resisted, sometimes violently. That was what the whole mad dash to shake off the dust of this gold country town in the hills had been all about. So he'd gone off to get out from under his family's rules and make his fortune. And here he was, coming back into his family's sphere and acting like that had all been a huge mistake. Was he really ready to follow his grandfather's wishes this time?

No. The whole idea was insane.

"Diana, I've told you a thousand times, I'm not marrying anyone."

"Really?" She clutched at the hem of her blouse and twisted it nervously. "Well, I think you ought to revisit that statement."

He frowned up at her. "What are you talking about?"

"You made a promise a long time ago, from what your grandfather tells me. And now that your family needs you to put yourself on the line, I think you ought to fulfill that promise." She knew she was beginning to sound a little shrill, but she couldn't help it. Her emotions were very near the surface and she was having a hard time holding them back.

"You need to have a nice little Five Families baby with one of those super rich girls and save the house, save the legacy, save it all. It's your destiny. It's what you were raised to do."

He stared at her, aghast. "You've really drunk the Kool-Aid, haven't you?"

"I've listened to your grandfather, if that's what you mean. And I've realized you're going to hate yourself if you don't do what you've been raised to think is your duty. You can't fight it."

He swore softly, shaking his head, disbelief shuddering through him.

"Just like I was raised to be pretty much the opposite," she went on, her voice sure but a bit shaky. "That's what my father always used to tell me. 'You're just a white trash girl. Don't get no fancy ideas, running around with a Van Kirk boy. That bunch will never accept you.' That's what he used to say. I didn't believe him then, but now I see the wisdom in accepting the truth."

"Truth." He said the word scornfully. "That's not truth. That's someone's fantasy dressed up as faux reality. You've fallen down the rabbit hole, Di. Stop listening to the Mad Hatter."

She almost laughed. "Your grandfather?"

He nodded. "Despite everything, I love that old man." He shrugged. "And you're right, up to a point. I made certain promises. I've got certain responsibilities."

Reaching up, he caught hold of her and flipped her down into his lap, catching her by surprise and eliciting a shriek as she landed in his arms. "But one thing I won't do is marry a woman I don't love," he said. "And you can take that to the bank."

"Cam…" She tried to pull away but he was having none of it.

His body was hard, strong, inescapable and she knew right away she couldn't stop him. But she didn't really want to and when his mouth came down on hers, it felt so hot, she gasped. His ardor shocked her, but in a good way, and very quickly her own passion rose to meet it. The pressure of his mouth on hers was pure intoxication. She sank into the kiss like a swimmer in a warm, inviting whirlpool, and very soon she was spinning round and round, trying to get her head above water often enough to catch her breath, but strongly tempted to stay below where his smooth strength made her giddy with desire.

He'd wanted to do this for so long, his need was an urgent throb that pushed him to kiss her harder, deeper, and to take every part of her in his hands. He plunged beneath her clothes, craving the feel of her soft flesh, sliding his hands down the length of her, sailing on the sensation like an eagle on a burst of wind. In this moment, she was his and he had to take her or die trying.

The top buttons of her blouse were open and his hot mouth was on her breast, finding the nipple, his lips tugging, his tongue stroking, teasing senses cued to resonate to his will. She was writhing in his arms, begging for more with tiny whimpers, touching him as eagerly as he was touching her.

"More," was the only word that penetrated her heat. "More, please, more!"

All thoughts of duty and responsibility were forgotten.

Thought itself was banished. Feeling was king, and she felt an arousal so intense it scared her. She was his for the taking, his forever. Right and wrong had nothing to do with it. He was all she'd ever wanted. The rest was up to him.

And he pulled back.

She stared up at him, panting, almost begging to have him back against her, and he looked down at her dispassionately, all discipline and control.

"You see, Diana?" he said. "There *is* an 'us,' whether you want there to be or not. You can't deny it. And I can't marry anyone else when I want you more than I've ever wanted any other woman."

He set her back on the wide arm of the chair and rose while she pulled her clothes together.

"I'll see you in the morning," he said, and walked away.

Diana sat where she was, shaken to the core and still trembling like a leaf. She was putty in his hands. He could do anything he wanted with her and her body would respond in kind. She was helpless. Helplessly in love.

CHAPTER TEN

PARTY time!

The scene was being set for a wonderful party. Cam had recruited some old high school friends to come help him and they had strung lights everywhere throughout the yard. They had reactivated a man-made watercourse that had been built years before to run all through the gardens, and now water babbled happily, recreating the look of a mountain stream. Cam had even found a way to put lights just beneath the surface at random intervals, so the whole thing sparkled as though it was under perpetual sunlight.

Guests began to arrive at midafternoon. The sense of excitement was contagious and the air was filled with the scent of flowers and the sound of music. Diana knew very few of the people who arrived. Some were cousins of Cam's who had come by to help a time or two in the past few days. But most of the Five Families children went to private schools, so she hadn't had much occasion to cross paths with many of them, and some of the ones she did know didn't seem to recognize her.

One lucky result of the theme was that no one had even suggested she wear a French maid's costume while mixing with the guests as she had feared at the first. The Hawaiian decor meant that she could wear a beautiful long island dress and put flowers in her hair and look just as good as most of the visitors did.

"I can pretend, can't I?" she muttered to herself as she wove her way in and out of the crowd. Still, she was the one holding the tray with the wineglasses, though, wasn't she? That pretty much gave the game away.

"Oh my dear, you look wonderful!" Mrs. Van Kirk approved, nodding as she looked her over. "I love the garland of flowers you've put in your hair. You look like a fairy princess."

Mr. Van Kirk, Cam's father, was home on a rare visit, looking half soused, but pleasant. He nodded agreement with his wife but didn't say much, except, "Hey, I knew your dad. He was one of my best friends. God, I really miss those days."

And she didn't linger to hear his stories.

Everyone praised the wonderful stream and the lights and the music and once the cocktail hour began to blend into dinnertime, the food was center stage. Diana was so busy making sure there was enough and the access was ample that she hardly had time to notice anything else, but she did see Cam once in a while, and every time her wandering gaze found him, he was surrounded by women.

"I'm sure he's having the time of his life," Janey said, and for once she sounded amused rather than resentful. She had her latest date, Adam, with her. A rather short man, he seemed to follow her dutifully everywhere she went, looking thoroughly smitten, and she seemed to enjoy it.

While she was filling the punch bowl with a fresh supply of green sherbet punch doused with rum and meant to take the place of daiquiris, Janey came up and elbowed her.

"Look at there, by the waterfall. Those three are the prime candidates."

She lifted her head to look at the three beautiful young women. "What do you mean?" she asked, though she was very much afraid she already knew.

"We need Cam to pick one of them to marry. They are the richest ones."

"And the most beautiful, too," she said, feeling just a bit wistful.

"Well, the one on the right, Julie Ransom, is only semibeautiful," Janey opined. "But she's got a wonderful personality."

"Oh, great. Better and better."

"What do you care? He's got to pick one of them."

"I know."

"Tina Justice, the redhead, is said to be a bit on the easy side, but nice. And Grace Sinclair, the one in the middle, is the younger sister of Missy, the one Cam was supposed to marry years ago. She's considered just about the most beautiful woman in the valley. Wouldn't you agree?"

"Oh, yes," she said, heart sinking as she looked at the woman who was wearing a turquoise sari and standing out in the crowd. "She's got that luminous quality."

"Yes. And I think Cam likes her pretty well. So let's work on getting the two of them together. Agreed?" Janey gave her an assessing look, as though wondering how she was going to react to that, but Diana didn't give her the satisfaction of letting on.

"You get busy on that," she said lightly. "I've got some crudités to crunch."

In some ways it was nice that Janey now considered her a coconspirator rather than an enemy, but this sort of scheming put her in a very awkward position. She didn't need it. She was going to keep her distance from actual matchmaking no matter what.

Just a few more hours, she told herself, and then you'll be free. You'll never have to look at this family again. But whether you can forget them—ah, there's the rub.

It was only a short time later that she found herself listening to the three prime candidates as they chatted about Cam, ignoring her completely. She was in the kitchen, taking cheese sticks out of the oven, when they came in to wash a spill out of the redheaded girl's dress at the sink.

"They say his mother is pushing hard to get him to pick a bride tonight," she was saying.

"Tonight?" Grace repeated, looking out the window to see if she could spot him.

"Yes! Have you danced with him yet?"

"Twice." Grace sighed, throwing her head back. "He is super dreamy. I just wanted to melt in his arms. If I can get him again, I'm going to find a way to maneuver him out into the trees so we can have a little make-out time. There's nothing like stirring up the old libido and then doing the old tease for arousing a man's interest in getting engaged. And if his mother is pushing…"

"I haven't had a go at him yet," Julie said with a pout. "You all just back off until I've had my turn."

The redhead frowned thoughtfully. "You know, they also say he's got a pregnant girlfriend in the valley."

Grace nodded. "Could you put up with that?"

Julie tossed her head. "I think I could hold my own against a little piece of valley fluff."

They all laughed and began to adjust their makeup at the kitchen mirror.

Diana looked at them with distaste. She wasn't sure if they'd seen her or not. Somehow she thought it wouldn't have mattered anyway. Thinking her a servant, they would likely have looked right through her. Nice girls.

She gathered some fruit on a platter, preparing to go out with it, but just for fun, she stopped by where they were primping.

"Would any of you ladies like some grapes?" she offered, pointing them out. "They're very sweet. Not a sour one in the bunch."

All three pairs of eyes stared at her, startled.

"No, thanks," one murmured, but it was obvious they didn't know what to make of her. She smiled and carried the tray out into the party area. But her heart was thumping and her adrenaline was up. Nice girls indeed!

The dancing seemed to go on forever. Diana managed to avoid Cam, although she saw him looking for her a time or two. She was not going to dance with him. After tonight, she was going to be a stranger. No sense in prolonging the agony.

Finally the night was drawing to a close. Adam's DJ son had taken over center stage and was announcing themes for dances. It was a cute gimmick and was keeping a lot of people on the dance floor who probably would have been on their way home by now if not for the encouragement from the DJ.

Diana was tired. She wanted to go home and put her feet up.

"The last dance," the DJ was saying on the loudspeaker. "And this one is special. Our host, Cameron Van Kirk, will pick out his chosen partner and then we will all drink a toast to the couple. Mr. Van Kirk. Will you please choose your partner?"

It was like a car crash, she couldn't look away. Which one of the beautiful young women who had come here to look him over and to be looked over would he pick? She peered out between two onlookers and there was Cam. He was searching the scene, scanning the entire assembly, and then he stepped down and began to walk into the crowd.

Suddenly she knew what he was doing. There was no doubt in her mind. He was looking for her.

Her heart began to bang against her chest like a big bass drum and she couldn't breathe. How did she know this? What made her so sure? She wasn't certain about that, but she did know as sure as she knew her own name that he was headed her way.

She turned, looking around frantically. Where could

she hide? He couldn't possibly do this—could he? It would be an insult to all those beautiful, wealthy women for him to pick the pregnant party planner as his special partner. She squeezed her way between a line of people and hurried toward the side exit. And ran right into Cam.

"There you are," he said, taking her hands before she could stop him. "Come with me. I can't do this alone."

"Can't do what alone?" she said robotically, still looking for a chance to escape. But with all eyes on her, she really couldn't push his hands away and she found herself walking with him to the middle of the dance floor.

"Please welcome Mr. Cameron Van Kirk," the DJ said, "and Miss Diana Collins. Give them a hand, ladies and gentlemen.'

The music began and Cam's arms came around her. She closed her eyes and swayed to the music, a hollow feeling in the pit of her stomach.

"You can't be surprised," he said very near her ear. "You know you're my choice. You always have been."

She pulled back so she could look into his face. "I know you think you made a great joke out of this, but…"

"Joke? Are you kidding?" He held her closer. "Diana, face it. I love you."

She closed her eyes again and willed this to be over. She knew he thought he loved her. And maybe he really did. But it was impossible. He couldn't do this.

The music ended and the applause was polite and the toast was pleasant. But people were somewhat puzzled. You could see it in their faces, hear it in their voices. This wasn't one of the girls he was supposed to pick.

Still, people gathered around for congratulations. And while Cam was involved in that, Diane slipped away. She headed for her car. She knew she was being a rat and leaving all the cleanup to others, but she couldn't help it. She had to get away. If she hadn't been here to confuse things, Cam would have been free to choose one of the rich girls. The only remedy she could think of was to clear the field and give him space to do what he needed to do. She had to get out of here.

She raced home, packed a bag in three minutes and called her assistant, Penny, and asked her to come house-sit, kitten-sit and dog-sit. That was a lot of sitting, but Penny was up for it. In no time at all she was on her way to San Francisco. It was going to be a long night.

Cam didn't know she was gone until the next morning when he got an e-mail from her. It was short and scary.

Cam, please go on with your life without me. I'm going to be gone for a week or two so that you can get used to it. When I come back, I don't want to see you. Please. Don't bother to reply, I won't be reading my e-mail. A clean break is the best way. Di.

He went straight to her house just in case and found Penny there.

"She said she had to go to San Francisco," Penny said when he demanded to know where Diana had gone. "I'm not sure where. She'll probably call me tonight to see how the animals are. Do you want me to give her a message?"

He shook his head. "I can't wait until tonight. You really can't give me any better clue than that?"

"Well… She did say something about staying where she stayed when she got pregnant with Mia. I think she wanted to revisit the base of her decision or something. She was muttering and I couldn't really catch her meaning."

His heart turned to stone in his chest. She was going to see Mia's father. He was sure of it. He should leave her alone. Maybe she could work something out with him. That would be best for Diana, best for Mia. Wouldn't it?

Everything in him rebelled at that thought. No! That was crazy. The man was obviously not right for either one of them—and anyway, he wasn't going to give up the woman that he loved without a fight. He was going to find her if he had to go door to door through the whole city.

But first he had to have a last meeting with his grandfather.

He took the stairs two at a time and raced down to the old man's wing of the house, entering his room with a preemptory knock.

"May I talk to you for a moment?"

The old man raised his shaggy head. "I was expecting you," he said simply.

Cam went in and began to pace.

"Grandfather, I've come to tell you that I've failed. I thought I had a line on some financing that might work out, but today I've been told that is no longer an option." He stopped and looked at his aged relative.

"Everything I've tried to set up has fallen through. I've come to the end of my bag of tricks. I don't know where to go from here." Taking a deep breath, he said the fatal words he'd hoped he would never have to say. "I'm afraid we're going to lose the house."

His grandfather frowned. "What about one of the Five Family girls? I saw some that looked interested last night. Don't tell me you're going to turn them down again."

Cam took a deep breath and let it out. "I think you know I can't do what you want, Grandfather. I can't do that to any of those girls. I can't do that to myself."

"Or to the Collins girl," his grandfather said angrily. "Isn't that the real problem?"

He hesitated, swore and turned on his heel toward the door.

"Hold it," the old man called. "Stop right there."

He turned back, eyes narrowed. "Grandfather…"

"You shut up," the older man cried, pointing at him. "I've got something to say."

Cam stood still, his jaw rigid, and his grandfather calmed himself down.

"Now, I know I've been a stickler for staying with the Five Families. Me and the old men of those families— we've always wanted to keep the old times alive by keeping our community together and close-knit. We figured it would be good to get the younger ones to marry in the group and keep us strong. Crazy, probably." Shaking his head, he shrugged. "Time moves on. You can't force these things on people. I know, I've tried to do it often enough."

Cam stood still, scowling.

"What I'm trying to say," the old man went on, "is that I understand. You love the Collins girl, don't you? Even if she's having someone else's baby. Even if it means we'll lose the house. You don't care. You just want her."

"I know that's how it looks to you," Cam said. "And I'm sorry. I've done everything I can to save the house, including putting my own business up for sale. But I can't do what can't be done."

"I know. I know." He sighed heavily. "Oh, hell, go marry your girl. Start over. We'll be okay. We'll get a little place in the hills and live simply. We've gone through hard times before. We can do it again."

Cam felt as though a weight had been lifted from his shoulders. "Grandfather…"

"Just go get her." He waved his gnarled hand. "Go."

Cam stepped forward, kissed the old man on the cheek and turned for the door. He was going to do what he had to do anyway, but having his grandfather's blessing made it so much easier.

Hopping into his car, he turned toward the city by the bay. Just as he was leaving, Penny called on his cell.

"I'm only telling you this because I know she's crazy about you," she told him. "She just called and gave me the number where she's staying. It's a landline. Maybe you can use it to find the address."

Of course he could. And he would.

His research led him to an unassuming row house at the top of a hill. Wearing snug jeans and a big leather jacket, he rang the bell, not knowing whether he would find her with a friend or with the man who'd fathered her baby. When a nice looking young woman answered the door, he was relieved, and it didn't take much fast talking to get past her and into the sitting room where Diana was curled up on the couch, her eyes red-rimmed, her hair a mass of yellow curls around her face.

"I'll leave you two alone," Di's friend said, but he hardly noticed. All he could see was Diana and the wary, tortured look in her dark eyes.

"I love you," he told her, loud and clear. "Di, I want to marry you."

She shook her head. "You can't," she said, her voice trembling. Tears were threatening. From the looks of it, she'd been doing a lot of that already.

He stared at her for a long moment, then looked around the room. "So where is he?" he asked shortly.

She blinked. "Where is who?"

"Mia's father." He looked at her. "Isn't that who you came to find? I want to meet this jerk."

She shook her head. "Why do you call him a jerk?" she asked. "What do you have against him?"

"He went off and left you, didn't he? He's never there when you need him the most."

She closed her eyes and swayed. "Oh, Cam."

He stood right in front of her.

"Diana, there are some things we need to get settled. The most important is whether Mia's father is going to be a part of your life or not. Is he going to be involved in raising her? I don't think you've told me the full truth about the situation yet." He shook his head, his frustration plain in his face. "I want to know who he is. I want to know where he lives. I want to know…if you love him. I want to know what place he is going to have in your life in the future. This is very important."

She raised her face to him. "Why?"

"Because I love you. Don't you get that? And, dammit all, I love Mia, even though she hasn't been born yet. I want to take care of you. I want to be with you. But I have to know…"

She began to laugh. He frowned, because her laughter didn't sound right. Was she getting hysterical? But no. Sobering, she rose from the couch.

"Come here," she said, leading him to a table at the end of the room. "I'll show you Mia's father."

She took out a loose-leaf binder and opened it to a page that displayed a filled-in form. He stepped closer. At the top of the page was the heading, a simple three digit number. Down the page he saw a list of attributes, including height, weight, hair color, personality traits, talents. As he read down the list, his frown grew deeper. It could have been someone listing items about him. Every detail was just like his.

"What is this?" he asked her.

"That is Mia's father," she said, holding her chin high with effort.

He shook his head. "It sounds like me."

She tried to smile. "You got it."

His bewilderment grew. "No, I don't get it."

She took a deep breath. "Cam, Mia's father was a

donor at an assisted reproduction clinic. I don't know him. I never met him. I only picked him out of a book of donors."

"What? That's crazy."

"Yes." She put a hand to her chest. "This is how crazy I am. I went to three different clinics and pored over charts of donors trying to find someone almost exactly like you. I couldn't have you so I tried to come as close as possible to recreating what we might have had together."

He could hardly believe what he was hearing. It sounded like a science fiction story to him. He shook his head as though to clear it. "Diana, I can't believe this."

Tears glittered in her eyes. "Do you hate me? I knew it was nuts. I felt like a criminal doing it. And…I sort of feel as though I was doing it to close that door, stop the yearning. I knew if I was going to do this, it would put a barrier between us that couldn't be overcome. But it didn't seem to matter, because there was less and less hope of ever seeing you again anyway." She took a deep breath and shook her head. "But I just had to go on with my life and stop waiting for you."

"So you got pregnant." He frowned, trying to assimilate this information. "Artificial insemination?"

"Yes."

"And then I came back."

She nodded. "How could I know you were ever going to come back? Cam, it had been ten years. Your family acted like you were dead. I had no way of knowing."

"Oh, Diana." Reaching out, he enfolded her in his

arms and began to laugh. "So you're telling me you're actually carrying my baby. Or a reasonable facsimile thereof. There is no other man involved. Just an anonymous donor."

"That's it."

He laughed again, then kissed her and looked down into her pretty face. "Let's get married."

"Wait, Cam…"

"I mean it, Di. We've already got our baby. All we need is a wedding ring."

"But what about your family?"

Quickly he told her about his conversation with his grandfather. "He basically gave me permission to marry you. Not that I was waiting on that. But it does make it less stressful."

She searched his eyes. "Are you sure?"

"I'm sure." He dropped another kiss on her lips. "Say 'yes'."

She smiled up at him. "Yes."

He whooped and danced her around the room. "I love you so much," he told her. "Last night when I made you dance with me, you looked so beautiful, I could hardly stand it."

"It was a nice party. Even if it didn't get you a wealthy bride."

"C'est la vie," he said, and reached down to pick up some papers that had fallen out of his jacket pocket when he'd danced her around the room.

"What are those?" she asked, her sharp eyes catching sight of her own name on one of them.

He hesitated, then nodded for her to sit down at the table. "I got this information a few days ago but I was holding off on telling you," he said. "You see, I did some research on what happened to your mother."

She went very still. "What?"

"And here's what I found." He spread some papers out in front of her and took another out of an envelope. "She died in a cancer clinic in Sacramento. The date makes it right around the time you were six years old."

Diana stared at the papers. "So what does that mean?"

"It's my guess, from all the records I could find and what I could piece together, that your mother got a diagnosis of stomach cancer and she went away to a cancer clinic where she could concentrate on fighting the disease."

"So she didn't run off with another man? She didn't just decide she hated us and couldn't stay with us anymore?" Suddenly Diana eyes were filled with tears again. "Oh, Cam, I don't know what to think. How do you know this? Why didn't my father ever tell me?"

"My guess is that she thought she would get well and come back and be taking care of you again. She thought she had a chance, but luck wasn't with her. She left because she couldn't take care of you and deal with your father while she was going through that."

Diana's brows knit together. "Do you think my father knew?"

"Who knows what he knew or didn't know. From what I hear, he was in pretty bad shape with the drinking around that time. She might have told him and he might have been too out of it to know what she was talking about."

"Or he might have been that way *because* of what she told him."

"True. I don't suppose we'll ever know the truth." He frowned. "So she had no living family, no one to leave you with?"

"Except my grandmother on my father's side. She was still alive. I spent a lot of time at her house in those days. But she died when I was ten."

"And she never said anything to you about your mother's absence?"

She shook her head. "Not that I remember. I was only six years old, you know. Maybe she told me something that I didn't understand at the time. Maybe she just avoided the issue. People of her generation tend to do that."

"True."

Diana drew in a shuddering breath. "It's going to take some time to understand this," she said. "To really take it all in. It's a relief to know she didn't just run off, but it's so sad at the same time, and I feel like it's sort of unreal right now. Like it's about somebody else."

He was frowning, looking at an envelope in the pile of papers he'd given her. "Wait a minute," he said. "What's this?"

He pulled it out. "Oh, I didn't know this had come. I requested some information from a friend about that land you inherited. The envelope must have been stuck in with this other stuff. I didn't see this before."

He slit it open and began to read. Without looking up, he grabbed her arm. "Diana, you didn't sign that contract with your cousin yet, did you?"

"Yes, I did," she said. "I just mailed it today."

He looked up, his eyes wide. "You've got to get it back. Where did you mail it?" He jumped up from his seat. "Quick! Where is it?"

"I put it outside for the mailman this morning. I doubt it will still be there." She had to call after Cam because he was already running to the front of the house. "What's the matter?"

The mailman was at the next house when Cam snatched the envelope from the box attached to the front of the house where she'd put it. He sucked in a deep breath and leaned against the building. "Wow," he said. "Just wow."

Turning slowly, he made his way back into the house where Diana was waiting.

"What's going on?" she said.

He waved the envelope at her. "My friend in Sacramento came through with some inside info. That piece of land? A major hotel chain is planning a huge resort there. That land will be worth twenty times what your cousin offered you for it. Whatever you do, hold on to that land."

"Wow." Diana said it, too. "Does this mean…I'm rich?"

"Pretty much."

A huge smile began to break over her face. "Then I guess you ended up with a rich girl after all, didn't you?"

He grinned and kissed her. "See? That was my plan from the first," he said. "I just had to wait until you were rich enough to help me save the farm."

"Will this do it? Seriously?"

He shrugged. "Hard to tell. But just having it means there are lenders who will give us extensions they wouldn't give us before. It'll certainly help."

"Good." Her bubbling laughter was infectious. "This is too much. I feel like I'm in the middle of an overload situation. Turn off the bubble machine."

"This is just the beginning," he told her, sweeping her up into his arms again. "You ain't seen nothing yet."

And he gave her a hard, deep kiss to seal the deal.

EPILOGUE

MORNING crept in on little dog feet but it was a cold black nose that woke Diana from her sleep. Then two doggy feet hit the mattress beside her head and she sighed. Those feet weren't really so little anymore.

"You monster," she said affectionately, and Billy panted happily, knowing love when he saw it. "Billy's here," she told Cam.

He turned and groaned, then rose from the bed.

"Come on you mangy mutt," he grumbled. "I'll let you out."

She watched him walk naked from the room, his beautiful body shining in the morning light, wondering how she had managed to be so lucky. All her dreams had come true. Did she really deserve this happiness? He was back in a moment and this time he closed the door with a decisive snap, then turned and reached for her before he'd even hit the bed. Making love was sweet and slow in the morning, warm affection building to hot urgency, then fading to the most intense love imaginable as the sensations melted away.

"That one's going to be our next baby," he said, letting his fingertips trail over her generous breasts.

"You think?"

"I know. I could tell."

"How?

"Magic."

Mia's happy morning voice penetrated the closed door. She was singing to herself.

"She's awake."

"She's awake."

"You stay right here," he said. "I'll get her and bring her in bed with us."

She went up on one elbow as he rose from the bed. "Are you going to tell her?"

"Tell her what?"

She smiled lazily. "That she has a brother coming down the pike?"

He gave her his lopsided grin. "How do you know it's a boy?"

"I can feel it."

He frowned skeptically. "How?"

She smiled as though the world was paradise and she its ruler. "Magic."

He laughed and went to get their child. He agreed. Life was good. And Diana was magic.